A ... ew
ma...

"Th... un.
Cos... ...women and the men who batter them is chilling. This book demonstrates why Matt Costello is becoming a major name in crime fiction."
—Ed Gorman, *Mystery Scene*

"AN AUTHOR TO WATCH." —*Rave Reviews*

Matthew J. Costello reveals the dark and dangerous passions that hide within us all—jealousy, obsession, rage. And his powerful insights have earned him the praise of critics and peers alike . . .

HOMECOMING

"GRIPPING, COMPELLING, IT KEEPS READERS IN A THOROUGHLY SATISFYING STATE OF ANXIETY."
—Dean Koontz,
bestselling author of *Mr. Murder*

"DEEP-DOWN TERROR, THIS IS THE REAL THING . . . THE SUSPENSE IS ALMOST UNBEARABLE."
—F. Paul Wilson,
bestselling author of *Nightworld*

"AN INCREDIBLE BOOK. IT TAKES YOU INTO DARK AND DANGEROUS PLACES. THIS IS POWERFUL STUFF."
—Rick Hautala,
bestselling author of *Dark Silence*

"HE GIVES HIS STORY A TRAGIC TWIST."
—*Publishers Weekly*

"COSTELLO'S STRONGEST BOOK YET . . . A POWERFUL NOVEL."
—Ed Gorman,
editor, *Mystery Scene*

Also by Matthew J. Costello

**BENEATH STILL WATERS
MIDSUMMER
WURM
DARKBORN
HOMECOMING**

SEE HOW SHE RUNS

MATTHEW J. COSTELLO

[signature]

B
BERKLEY BOOKS, NEW YORK

If you purchased this book without a cover, you should be aware that this book is stolen property. It was reported as "unsold and destroyed" to the publisher, and neither the author nor the publisher has received any payment for this "stripped book."

SEE HOW SHE RUNS

A Berkley Book / published by arrangement with
the author

PRINTING HISTORY
Berkley edition / February 1994

All rights reserved.
Copyright © 1994 by Matthew J. Costello.
This book may not be reproduced in whole or in part,
by mimeograph or any other means, without permission.
For information address: The Berkley Publishing Group,
200 Madison Avenue, New York, New York 10016.

ISBN: 0-425-14096-2

BERKLEY®
Berkley Books are published by The Berkley Publishing Group,
200 Madison Avenue, New York, New York 10016.
BERKLEY and the "B" design
are trademarks belonging Berkley Publishing Corporation.

PRINTED IN THE UNITED STATES OF AMERICA

10 9 8 7 6 5 4 3 2 1

SEE HOW SHE RUNS

PART ONE

TWO WOMEN

1

Emma was asleep, so easy for her, curled up in the backseat.

Kate Cowell took a breath, her hands locked on the steering wheel. She was exhausted. Her eyes stung from fatigue. Strands of her straight blond hair, dirty, seemed glued to her head.

I just want to stop, to rest. That's not so much, she thought. That's all I want.

She looked up to the rearview mirror. Emma's head rested against the door frame, lost to the world, the rude headlights of cars and trucks . . . the little girl was so tired.

It's good she fell asleep.

I only wish I could stop, Kate thought. I'm not strong enough for this. Not—

She looked at the dashboard clock: 4:30, and already it was dark. The colorful neon of the gas stations and the liquor stores, the garish blur of the fast-food restaurants, all glared in the sudden blackness.

Let this be over, she thought. When she was a little girl, she'd close her eyes—before going to the dentist, or when the noises started from downstairs, waking her—

Let it be tomorrow. Let me, magically, be past this time. So that it's all over and everything is okay.

"I'm kinda hungry, Mom," Brian said.

Her son, her big boy, sat beside her. "You're in the shotgun seat," she joked with him, trying to keep this thing light, trying to make it fun, an *adventure*. But Brian easily read her expression. She knew that. Brian was a smart boy and he knew that this wasn't going to be fun.

Not fun . . . because it's dangerous, it's illegal. Brian knew that. He was her big boy. . . .

But—and this was so important—he knew why she was doing it.

"I know, Bri. I'm hungry too. I just—" Kate checked the mirror, losing the dark reflection of Emma in the blinding headlights now hugging tight to the rear of her car. More light bounced off the side mirror right into her eyes. So tired, so achy . . .

"I need to find someplace to stay. First that, honey, and then we can get some food."

The lessons, the schoolgirl lessons she had to memorize and repeat, came to her lips. How to not get caught. How to keep going . . .

Never stop during the day.

Drive until it gets dark, and then find a motel.

Don't go to any motel chains, nothing with computers. Go someplace small. Don't worry about whether it's clean. That's not important. Pay in cash. You'll have cash. Use it for the room, for your food, and—listen—especially for your gas.

Don't use the plastic, your new credit cards. Keep them . . . for your new home.

The words, the warnings were burned into her mind. Kate repeated the drill until she knew—without thinking—how to handle every situation.

I know it, she thought. But can I do it?

The stoplight ahead turned red. Kate slowed, and anxiously checked the rearview mirror. The car was still crawling up her back. God, I don't need an accident, Kate thought. I don't need to test my new driver's license, the new registration, all the other new pieces of paper.

New pieces of paper with new names. And we have to start using the new names . . . we have to practice.

Then the blistering headlights of the car disappeared from her mirror. The car was *that* close behind her. Kate looked around, wishing she could escape. Raise her hands up and just fly away from here, *fly away* . . .

Like when she was a little girl in Schuyler, New York, and she'd open the windows at night, the terrible noise coming from downstairs. She'd hold her arms out, feeling the frigid winter cold, wanting to be pulled up and away, far away. . . .

Knowing, feeling that there could be no escape.

Coils of smoky car exhaust gave an eerie, otherworldly look to the road, lined with chain stores and bars and—

"Oh, Mom! There's a Burger King. Please, c'mon . . . can't we—"

"No," Kate snapped, her voice sharp. It was something that she did a lot lately. Snapping at Brian. Sometimes she raised her hand as if to hit him. He questioned everything, always questioning. It made this too hard.

She told him, "I'm doing this for you. You see that, don't you?" He had nodded, looking confused, guilty.

This was screwing him up, Kate knew. When this is over, he'll need help, he'll need someone to repair the damage.

And so will I. I know that now.

I just have to get through this. Somehow pass from today to tomorrow, and then the next day, without feeling anything. Always running toward the day after . . .

The light turned green, but Kate—lost, dreaming—noticed it too late. The car behind her honked loudly, rudely.

Kate quickly slid her foot to the accelerator pedal, gunning the engine awkwardly. Her car jumped forward, lurched, and Emma stirred.

"Umm . . . we're there? We there yet?" Emma said, sounding so sleepy with her little girl's voice.

Brian answered. "No. And *Mom* won't stop for food. She doesn't care *how* hungry we are."

Emma picked up the theme. "Mommy, I want some dinner. Look, it's dark out. It's late. It's *time* for dinner."

Kate shook her head. She scanned both sides of the highway. No, it's not time to eat, not by the rules of this game. We have to find someplace to stay.

She had passed a number of chain motels. Days Inn . . . a Marriott . . . Nice, safe-looking places. Not what I'm looking for, she thought. Not at all.

"I *said* when we get someplace to stay. Now, Brian—be quiet."

Brian groaned—Kate felt that anger again. She looked over at him. He shook his head and put his foot on the dash in protest.

Kate turned back to the windshield, seeing all the red lights and the Ohio license plates. I must stick out, she thought. My car . . . with New Jersey plates. I'll stick out wherever we go.

Then she saw a place. A small motel directly ahead, no big lights, no cheery familiar logo, a real dive.

The motel was on the right, so she had to change lanes. But there was no opening, no way to get over—the Friday traffic was too thick. Everyone wants to start their weekend, have all the fun they worked so hard for.

A dark eighteen-wheeler lurked next to her, with giant tires, tall enough so that it could easily swallow her car whole. Kate flipped on her turn indicator. She craned her head around, thinking that if she could make eye contact with the driver behind the truck, if he'd see her—

But that driver, a black shape in the shadows, hugged as close to the back of the truck as possible, as if he *wanted* to cut her off. And Kate was sure that the driver right behind her was growing more angry, more pissed off at her.

Maybe he'd bump her, just to show her. A little nudge, saying "Get going. . . ."

"C'mon," she said. Psychic communication. "Let me in. Come on, let me get over—"

"Mommy—" Emma said.

"*C'mon*. . . . Don't be a bastard."

She slowed more, nearly stopped. More horns honked. Now the truck and the car glided past her. Another car behind them hurried, as if it wanted to join the fight to keep Kate out of the lane, to keep her from the motel.

The entrance was close, only yards away.

"No—" she started to say.

She hit the gas pedal and her mousy-brown Toyota leaped into the right lane. Kate heard the squeal of brakes—from both lanes. But she was in the right lane.

Winning is everything, she thought.

She went another few yards and hit the accelerator again, swooping into the driveway of the motel. Horns beeped at her like angry geese.

"Great driving, Mom," Brian said. Kate waited. . . . "*Not!*"

"Are we staying *here*?" Emma said.

Yes, here, Kate thought. She pulled beside the office of the Gateway Motel. A purple neon vacancy sign flickered nervously while the red "Office" arrow pointed down to a door that looked like it led to another shabby motel room.

No question, the Gateway Motel was not the finest lodging in Youngstown, Ohio.

Probably wasn't the worst either. *Probably* . . .

"Yes," she said. "We're staying here."

The motel clerk was from central casting.

Not that he was a Norman Bates look-alike, rooting around in his bag of nuts while contemplating cutting up the next female guest. No, the clerk was your basic, bloated loser of indeterminate age.

SEE HOW SHE RUNS

His eyes widened when he looked up at Kate. He's having difficulty hiding his interest, his surprise, his pleasure, Kate thought. His normal clientele must fall somewhere lower on the evolutionary ladder.

She wanted to back out. Turn around and leave this dump.

"I'd like a room," she said.

The man's expression fell into a stupid, unbelievable grin—as if asking, "Here . . . you want to stay *here*?"

"Jus' yourself?" the man said. His leer grew even more repellent. "Yes, for me and my kids. They"—she went on in explanation—"are too tired to go another mile. It's only for a night."

The man opened his mouth and made a fish face. *Oh, I understand.* Couldn't go any farther, so we stopped at this fleabag motel, where the neon lights sputter and the sheets are changed once a week, whether they need it or not.

"Forty-four-ninety-five a night."

Amazing price, she thought. So . . . exact. Forty-four . . . ninety-five. Did the owner work that out with a calculator, to get an exact price? Is that what—

There was a noise from outside, and Kate turned to look at her car. She hadn't been watching the kids. Now—like a tight cord whipping her back—she turned around, expecting to see a police car there, an Ohio state trooper leaning into an open car window.

"Say, where are you kids from?" he'd ask, talking to Brian and Emma, asking them questions.

Brian would be okay. Brian knew what to do. But Emma . . . It would be hard for her to lie.

But there was no one by the car.

The clerk cleared his throat, waiting for his money.

Kate dug in her purse and pulled out five, no—she counted the slick bills again—*six* tens. She quickly stuffed one bill back in her purse. She felt the man's eyes on her wallet. There was a lot of cash there, and even more money hidden in her bag. A lot of cash—but would it be enough?

The clerk slapped down a key.

Number 24. The gold number on the plastic tag was nearly worn away.

"It's around the back," he said. "Nice and quiet. Away from the highway noise."

Kate nodded. *As if that's what I want.* She'd rather have something right in front, close to the greasy smell of fast-food french fries blowing from across the highway and gasoline hitting the icy ground. Close to cars and people.

"Around the back?" she said, nodding, deciding against asking for a change.

Don't call attention to yourself.

Another rule. Drilled, memorized.

Kate took the key.

"Oh, miss—" the clerk called as she got to the door.

She turned. "Your change." He grinned. The clerk held out a five-dollar bill and a nickel. Kate nodded and walked back to the man. She took the bill, and he brushed his hand against her.

I'm imagining that, she thought, like I've imagined so many things these days.

The lawyers accused me of imagining things. The judge, a gray-haired woman, looked at me as if I was making things up. It happens all the time. In court, people will say *anything*. The judge didn't even believe Brian.

Imagining things. Like the voices from downstairs when she was a kid, the sounds of yelling, the slaps, the moans. Just imagining things, that's all. Had to be imagining it, because no one ever said anything, no one ever explained. . . .

Kate left the smelly office, filled with the stale stench of cigarettes.

It was January 2. A new year. And the wind was cold and wet.

Brian played with the TV controls.

"It only gets three dumb channels, Mom. God, and look at the junky picture."

"Mommy," Emma said, "the bathroom's yucky. I saw a bug run into a hole. I don't like this place."

Kate sat on the bed, a dangerous thing to do, she knew. If she sat on the bed, she might lie down. And if she lay down, she might close her eyes. She was so horribly tired . . . but the kids were hungry.

She took Emma's hands in hers. Her little girl was having so much trouble understanding this. It was too much to ask. The small hands felt cold.

"It's only for one night, Em. One night, and tomorrow we can stay someplace nicer."

Emma pulled her hands away. "I don't want to go in the car anymore. I don't like it. I want to—"

SEE HOW SHE RUNS

She's going to say it. Kate knew that there was nothing she could do about it. Emma was going to say *it*. . . .

"I—I want to go home."

"God!" Brian groaned. "No HBO." He turned around from the TV. "This place is a dump."

Kate tried again.

"Emmie—we're going to a new home. You know that. And it will be someplace nice. I promise. You'll like it."

Imagining things . . . the way Kate's mother sat at the breakfast table, a dark blue splotch on her face. Looking at Kate, staring at Kate until Kate felt—this—*this* is happening because of me. . . .

Emma shook her head. "No I won't. I *won't* like it."

Then Brian came and stood beside his sister.

He put a hand on his sister's shoulder. "Yes, you will, Em. Mom showed us pictures of where we're going. Don't you remember? It will be great."

Kate looked up to Brian. That's it, she thought. Way to go, Bri. Good work. Just keep telling her. Brian was her big boy. He understood what was happening—what might happen.

Emma looked up at Brian. Sometimes they fought terribly, hurting each other. But now Brian squeezed Emma's shoulder and put a hand on her head, brushing her fine, dirty-blond hair.

Emma tried to say something, to hold on to her dream of going home, back to her own bed, to her dolls left behind, and to her friends—forgetting all the bad things.

But Brian rushed on. "Now Mom's going to take us for dinner, right?"

Kate nodded. Only then did she become aware that she had been crying—tiny drops falling from each eye as she fought to keep her feelings in control. Kate nodded. "Right. Let's get cleaned up—and out we go."

"I want a Kids' Meal, okay?" Brian said. Such things had long ago ceased being important to him. He was nine. He didn't need a small toy with his hamburger.

But it got Emma to smile excitedly. "Me, too, Mom. Me too! I want one too!"

Kate stood up, secretly wiping at her eyes, removing the evidence. No one would know. . . .

"Sure, sweetheart. Whatever you want." Kate went and got her coat. "You can have whatever you want," she lied.

2

Highway 70 out of Denver had been quickly cleared of snow. What was left of last night's storm—the great, still-white piles of plowed snow—lined the highway. Now only small crystalline dust devils danced in the road.

As if they're lost, Mari Comas thought.

Lost, searching for the mountains of snow plowed so efficiently by Colorado's crackerjack highway department.

But I'll be getting off soon, Mari knew. Then who knows what I might find. A shitload of snow had been dumped last night.

Ahead, she saw low gray clouds merging with blackish-gray mountains. It was an ominous sight, as if there was plenty more snow to come. Though she had the Taurus's heat on full blast, she still felt chilled. Her fingers, her feet, the tip of her nose—all felt the cold.

Maybe, she thought, I should have put this visit off. It was Friday. Heading near four, and a lot of people were thinking about a drink or ten after work.

But there was no reason for Mari to rush. Jake was at his best friend's for the weekend—a sleepover—and Mari would be alone.

There was a brief flicker of self-pity. *Poor me* . . .

She thought of the woman she was on her way to see.

Mari had called twice today—once at lunch, listening to the phone ring and ring. Then again at two o'clock, and still there was no answer.

Maybe there's something wrong with the lines. Phone lines go down, systems fail—especially when you get into the foothills of the Rockies in bad weather. And Coldwater Springs was close to the real mountains, close to the mountain blizzards and the mountain cold.

No skiers hunted out Coldwater Springs. The tourists searching for Native American artifacts, or geodes, or fossils, were distant memories of summer—along with their money.

SEE HOW SHE RUNS

Mari knew all about places like Coldwater Springs.

It was just like the town she grew up in. Coldwater Springs was a hard place filled with hard people. The men wore desperate, failed looks in their eyes, while the women—always complaining—were weathered, old before their time.

The exit ramp appeared quickly, sneaking up on her, interrupting her thoughts. Mari looked ahead to see what the roads off the highway looked like. A layer of slick-looking snow covered the road, dotted with shiny icy hummocks, speed bumps that would eat her Jeep's traction.

Mari slowed and wondered why she had come. She didn't have to.

But that part was easy.

A year ago Mari had been asked to work for a new project out of St. Paul's Hospital. It was a federally funded project for early intervention in cases of child and spousal abuse. There were workshops and counselors, and there would be people like Mari, caseworkers to help the families . . . to stop bad things from happening.

A normal report of abuse—whether against a child or a wife—might bring some Child Welfare action four, five months down the road. And sometimes that action simply consisted of a letter or a phone call.

How are things . . . any better?

Too often the action was way too little, way too late.

This new program would be different. Mari got to help people. She had found homes—not shelters, but real *homes*—for women and children who were trapped. It was good work, important work.

Mari knew that. And she needed it so badly.

Her station wagon slipped to the left. One tire whined while it lost traction. Mari turned into the skid, and then quickly pulled out, moving slowly over the crunchy snow.

She went down a curving road that led to the hollow—a steep valley that was the sleeping tourist trap of Coldwater Springs.

Most of the motels had signs up—CLOSED FOR THE SEASON—but one motel was open with a lone snow-covered car parked out front, probably the manager's car. A flickering sign giddily offered FREE HBO.

The gas stations were deserted, the self-serve pumps patiently waiting for spring.

The snowy road zigged left and then right. The depression was steep and the twisting road led to Main Street. Here, a row of shops that might have looked rustic and frontierlike under the warm sun and clear blue sky of summer simply looked silly. This wasn't Central City, with its jewel box of an opera house.

She drove down Main Street.

Ahead, she saw the small Museum of the Old West, next to it the Mountain Man Restaurant. Both establishments looked closed. Icke's Tavern—neon lights advertising beer ablaze in the window—looked filled. Winters were long here. You did what you had to do. . . .

Mari's station wagon slid again, and she quickly came to attention. The road she was looking for was close, a narrow street crossing Main and running up to the foothills.

The sky turned grayer, darker. Damn, she thought. It will be night by the time I get there. Pitch-black and cold, and there's got to be a better way to spend my Friday evening.

Some of her friends wanted her to date.

Sometimes friends can be stupid.

The town's one traffic light stopped her right next to the Coldwater Springs Trading Post. Cheap western and Native American bric-a-brac filled the window. A hand-lettered sign offered HOT COFFEE AND NEWSPAPERS.

The stoplight took forever, as if the wait might urge someone to stop and sample the wonders of Coldwater Springs.

When the light finally changed, Mari turned left and the tourist shops quickly vanished. She passed a service station, a place with pickups parked to one side and brooding, banged-up hulks, a dozen or more, stretching off into snowy fields that probably drew a stray elk or hungry bighorn sheep from time to time.

He works there, Mari knew. The husband. Alex Russ. One sick puppy. She had met him once. And she had tried to talk with him many times after that. But that one time she spoke with him had scared her.

She hadn't been scared only for his wife, Elaine . . . and for the two kids. Alex Russ could seem like a normal, good-looking guy, muscular, with a nice smile. Then—as if a gear kicked in, his face would change. As if everything had somehow been *spoiled*.

Mari asked him about slapping his wife, the bruises, trying to help . . . his eyes changed quickly. She knew something bad had gone off inside Alex Russ's head.

Click.

SEE HOW SHE RUNS

He had no record.
But she didn't think that was because he hadn't done anything....
Mari had had to take a breath, standing in the kitchen. *Click* ... she heard his gears locking into place. She took a breath, and then quietly she asked him about hitting his five-year-old, hitting Tom, smacking him for no reason, lost in his crazy anger.

Mari watched the light in Russ's blue eyes fade even more. His eyes turned cold and dark, like the mountains, like the clouds— and God, she was so scared. Alex Russ was more than an ignorant man with a temper. There was something very wrong here....

Alex Russ scares me, Mari thought.
So Mari started making plans to move the woman out, to get the family the hell out of the house. Elaine, the wife, didn't understand. She blamed herself. So typical. It's the money, the debt, the pressure. Mari shook her head. No. It's something else and you have to leave....

Then, a few days ago, something bad happened. Though it must have happened before, Russ had somehow covered it up with Elaine's help. A family secret, covered up ...

Russ had knocked his boy out and then couldn't rouse him. He wouldn't let Elaine bring the boy to the hospital near Golden. No, that might have triggered alarms. That hospital knew the Russ family.

Instead they brought Tom to a small clinic. Russ told the young doctor that the boy fell off the deck while playing. Damn, always climbing up on the railing of the deck. *I warned him.* ...

But the doctor was suspicious enough to put the child's name in his computer, and "Tom Russ" was found in the data base. The new Child Welfare laws had done some good. The police came then and they talked to Russ. He might have been arrested ... he should have been arrested, but he wasn't.

Cases like this were hard. There were agencies to deal with them. The local cops didn't want to break up families. There were real crimes.

They had their litany of excuses. Mari had heard them before. In her own apartment, talking to Rob. There were real crimes, her husband said. People getting shot up, heavy drug deals. Real crimes and people got shot. Sometimes even cops got shot.

But this time, at least they had notified Mari.
Mari had been working to get Elaine into a home, not an overcrowded shelter, where even more abuse could happen, but a real

home. But now she couldn't wait anymore. She wanted Elaine and her children out. Now. Tonight. Where Russ couldn't find them.

And—if I have to—I'll stay with them, Mari thought. Even though Alex Russ scares me, God, I'll stay with them.

The snow grew deeper as the town's plows lost interest in carving a neat path up the small roads to the mountainous nowhere, well away from Main Street.

Mari's station wagon struggled to climb up the slippery slope of the hill. A yellow sign with a black squiggle on it announced that curves were ahead. The sign was riddled with bullet holes. Things get boring and the locals take their fun any way they can.

She neared the crest of one small hill. In her rearview mirror she saw the town behind her. The lights were on and the depressing town was now an oasis compared with the barren landscape ahead.

Soon there'd be a turnoff—a dirt driveway lined with deep ruts cut by a pickup going back and forth over the same place, carving out a big hump in the dirt.

A bit of light flickered in the mirror.

She looked up and checked her mirror. But she saw nothing, thinking: How stupid. There's no one else out here. Thinking: I didn't used to be scared. Not when Rob was with me.

She chewed her lip.

Rob isn't with me. When will I accept that?

Sometimes even cops got shot....

Mari slowed and carefully turned into the driveway. The new snow had filled in the deep ruts and the bottom of her car wasn't scraping the center bulge.

"Okay," she said. "I made it. We're okay, ladies and gentlemen." She talked to herself. It made the loneliness, the mountains and darkness less forlorn.

"*We're okay.*"

She saw the Russ house ahead. There were lights on. Good, she thought. I didn't make this trip for nothing.

The house was a small dirt-brown wood house with a ramshackle addition built on. Two old cars sat on cinder blocks to the left. Mari had watched Elaine's kids play on them. The new deck, a pointless improvement, was in the back.

"Okay . . . the lights are on . . . she's home."

Mari guessed that Alex Russ was still working at the service station, Bob O's Tow and Service. Doing an oil change, fiddling inexpertly with someone's transmission.

Getting Russ to stay away from his own home involved the courts—and that could take forever. Moving Elaine out was the best way....

Russ had been warned by the cops. He said that he'd be on his best behavior. He said that he had a temper....

But that wasn't it at all.

There were many reasons people abused children. There were ignorant people who couldn't cope, who just couldn't handle a baby's crying when it didn't stop. So they'd plunge their screaming little baby into a big pot of boiling water, or snip at his toes with a scissors—*snip, snip*—or punch the baby's stomach.

That will teach you.

There were the emotionally stunted men and women who put their own needs first, who saw their "bad" children as hurting their own life, their own pleasure.

There were mentally deficient people, the mildly retarded. There were disciplinarians. All of these Mari could understand, could deal with—no matter how horrible the things they did.

But there was one type of abuser that terrified her. Someone who could be fine for months, even years, and then simply *snap*, in a violent explosion, due to a deep imbalance, an illness, that got worse with time, building.

Call them psychotics. Or—after they started hurting people—psychopaths.

Alex Russ belonged to that club. Alex Russ got angry, he got frustrated. He only wanted things to work out, that's all. But when they didn't, he hurt people. Though he had no record, Mari was certain of that.

Mari shivered.

She stopped the station wagon by the front door of the house. A stone slab served as the single step to a doorway. The screen door—*gotta keep those giant mountain flies out!*—was still up. Mari checked the windows for movement inside the house... Elaine Russ in the kitchen, fixing dinner, nervously waiting for her husband to come home.

A grim parody of weekend. Mari imagined the terror Elaine felt, living on the edge, waiting for the next explosion.

But no shadow crossed in front of the kitchen window.

Mari turned to the living-room window, a tiny room barely large enough to hold a beat-up sofa and the twenty five-inch TV set. Again there was no movement.

But lights were on... everywhere.

Mari got out of the car, and the heat was quickly snatched away by a clammy cold that surrounded her. Might be more snow on the way, she guessed. The dark clouds looked closer and it *felt* like snow. If you lived here long enough—you could smell when snow was coming.

She shut the car door and the solid thud was loud, an alarm to whoever was in the house.

Mari walked to the step. She had left her gloves on the dash and her fingers quickly felt the cold. She walked up the stone step and pressed the buzzer.

She heard a faint, pathetic sound. As she waited the wind blew at her face. Mari licked her lips. She pressed the buzzer again. When nothing happened, she raised her hand and knocked on the door.

"Elaine," she said. "Elaine. It's Mari Comas. Elaine . . ."

Her voice sounded thin out here, lost in so much openness. She knocked again, the red paint flaking off the splintery door. Her cold hand made a dry sound. A twisted clump of brush rolled past her car. It stopped there a moment—hesitated—and then rolled a few more feet until snared by a wheel rim of one of the wrecks perched on cinder blocks.

"I guess," Mari said quietly, "no one's home."

She backed away from the door.

No one's home. That's the story here, boys and girls. Elaine Russ has gone, taking the kids. But where? The girl had no relatives, no one she could stay with—or want to. She had no friends.

That was always the way it was. The women were isolated. All they had were their children and a husband. They became passive—complicit in the crime, playing their role.

Mari backed up a bit more. The lights from the windows glowed more brightly in the growing darkness.

Time to get the hell out of here, she thought.

She backed off the step. She started to turn to her car.

And she stopped.

No, if Elaine had gone someplace, she would have left a message. Mari was her only friend. Elaine Russ trusted her, she knew that Mari was working to help her, help her kids. She wouldn't simply disappear.

Unless something happened.

Mari clenched her fists, trying to coax some warmth into her fingers.

She wouldn't disappear. . . .

SEE HOW SHE RUNS

Mari walked back to the door. She knocked one more time. Then she tried the doorknob. It didn't move, but Mari expected that. Of course it wouldn't move. She pushed against the door.

This is illegal, she thought. I'm not a police officer. I can't barge in here.

There was a backdoor, Mari knew, up on the deck. That might be open. Sure, but she'd have to climb up to the deck—there were no stairs. And somebody might see.

Still—the front door was locked. It was worth a try. If nothing else, she could leave a message. Elaine Russ had her home phone number. But maybe she had lost it.

Mari walked on the crunchy snow, so deep here it reached the top of her boots. It was easily a foot of snow and she saw animal tracks. Birds' footprints and the dark, eyelike hollows made by bighorn sheep.

She turned a corner and saw the deck.

Now, behind the house, the town could no longer be seen. Mari felt truly alone. The deck—small, useless, overlooking a barren field and giant chunks of granite and sagebrush—didn't have a stairway to the ground. The bottom of the wood deck was waist-high.

Mari reached up and grabbed two slats of the deck.

The wood slats shook a bit in her hands. They might break off when I pull on them, she thought. Alex Russ was no carpenter. They might send me flying back into the snow.

Go home, girl, a voice whispered. *Go home, order in a pizza from Domino's, have a glass of cold white wine, maybe two, watch some TV.*

Go—

She tightened her grip on the wood slats and pulled herself up. Her arms felt weak and her weight seemed too much.

"Oh, God," she said. "I'm so out of shape it's pathetic."

Never time to do anything anymore, to run, to take some jazzy aerobics class. No time . . . no interest—

But she lodged a foot on the one-inch edge of the deck floor that protruded past the slats. She pulled with her arms while the toe of one boot dug into the space between the slats.

Mari was off the ground and she reached around to grab at the other top of the slats.

"C'mon," she whispered. "C'mon."

With her hissed words of encouragement, she pulled herself up miraculously—and then quickly swung her legs over.

She stood there, huffing, making clouds of vapor bloom in front of her mouth. There was a light from the door—the back of the kitchen was there. A snow-covered barbecue looked like an alien object, its shape, its purpose hidden by the untouched snow.

Standing there, looking at it, she thought about the footprints she saw outside.

Birds, sheep, mule deer.

But—where were the kids' footprints? The waffle shapes made by their boots as they tasted the snow, rolling in it, enjoying cold fluffy snow the way only kids can?

Where were those prints?

There were some big footprints leading from the front door to where the car might have been. But all around the house—there was nothing.

Nothing.

She walked to the backdoor. She turned the doorknob and it was locked. But the lock looked easy to open. She thought: I only have to get something in there, something to press against the curved bolt, to push it back. Something like a credit card . . .

Mari dug out her wallet from her coat pocket and removed a much-abused and over-the-limit charge card.

I don't care if it breaks, she thought. It's useless anyway.

The card fit into the space between the door and the frame perfectly. Almost too easily the door popped open.

Before Mari could notice anything else, she heard a sound. An engine, a car, a truck engine . . . out there, passing by the house.

Mari looked at the open door, wondering whether she should pull it quickly shut.

For a moment, though, she simply stood there and waited, listening. . . .

3

"Brian, go get some napkins."

"I don't *need* a napkin," he said. Kate looked around the Burger King at a sea of strange faces, the men looking at her. It was crush time, people lining up to have it *their way,* and all the precious tables were occupied, with no maître d' controlling the flow.

"Bri—please. I don't want to leave Emma sitting here alone."

"I'll watch her," the boy said between chews. "No problem."

"I don't need *watching*," Emma said. Already she had dollops of secret sauce trailing down her chin, landing on her dress. Emma was about as dainty as a lion.

I'm being stupid, Kate thought. What's the problem with getting up and walking to the service islands with napkins, straws, foil packets of ketchup and mustard.

What could happen?

But she didn't want the kids out of her sight—or hearing. She was especially concerned about Emma. Emma could—often did—say anything.

"Okay. I'll be right back. Watch her, Bri." Kate got up, thinking: The smallest thing turns into an adventure.

Brian nodded. "Mom, could you get us some shakes? I'd like chocolate—"

"And I want strawberry!"

Kate shook her head. "Look at the line. I'm not getting back on line for that. We'll just eat and then—"

She left the sentence unfinished. Eat—and what? Run back to the sleazy motel? Let the kids watch their shows, the sitcoms ABC labeled TGIF? Sit there, and think, and doubt . . .

And wonder if this is all wrong.

Is this a bad thing that I'm doing? We never talked about anything like this in Sunday school. No, there it was all so easy. You don't steal, you don't lie, and later—in youth group—you don't kiss with your mouth open, you don't heavy pet, and you sure don't—

She looked around. Across the room a man in a white Harley-Davidson shirt, sitting with his own family—drab-looking wife, scruffy kids—was watching her.

Kate shook her head at her kids. "No milk shakes."

She weaved through the close-packed tables to the front of the Burger King, to the napkin holders.

It took her only a few seconds to get there.

When she turned around, jerking out handfuls of napkins packed tight into the holder, she saw someone talking to Brian.

It was a tall black teenager. He had his baseball hat on backward. *I'm going backward. I can go in two directions at once, just look at my cap.* The kid's floppy, oversized jacket was open and he held a tray.

Kate hurried back to the table.

"Can I help you?" she said, realizing that she must sound like a clerk in a department store's lingerie department. May I help you, sir? Anything in particular you're looking for?

"Yo—I was looking for a spare seat. I saw your table, y'know."

There was a fourth chair, unoccupied. The kid stood there, his tray loaded with two big Whoppers.

"Er, sure," Kate said. "There's an extra chair."

The kid nodded. "Hey, thanks."

He sat down, joining her family.

Don't call attention to yourself. Rule number one. Blend in, become part of the scenery. Am I blending in? Kate thought. Is this blending in?

She passed some napkins to Emma, who grabbed a bunch and inexpertly dabbed at her cheeks. Brian shook his head. "God, she's a pig."

Through the napkins and a mouth full of semichewed bits of burger and bun, Emma responded. "I am *not* a pig. You're—you're—"

"Emma, Brian . . . come on. Stop—"

"You're a big do-do head."

"Oh, not that! God, call me anything but that!"

Their dinner guest was grinning, hunched over his Whopper, shaking his head.

"Stop it," Kate said. "Stop it now," controlling her voice.

"Mom, don't you see the way she eats? It's like going to the zoo. God!"

SEE HOW SHE RUNS

They throw God's name around like a ball. I'd never have done it, Kate knew. No, if I had done it—

"Finish up, Em. Finish—"

Kate happened to look up. Two Ohio state troopers walked in slowly. They both had their hats on—so straight. They looked at the people, scanning the tables.

They're just here for some free coffee, Kate thought. That's all. Can't let myself turn to ice every time I see a cop. They'll pick that up. Sure, police can pick up things like that, they can read guilt from a mile away.

She felt flushed. The air in the restaurant, filled with the smell of hot grease and smoke, became unbreathable.

"We've got to go," Kate said. But as soon as she said it, she saw the black kid look up. He had noticed the police come in. His eyes went to them right away, hunched over his Whopper. She knew that he saw them . . . noticed them.

He looked at her. His dark eyes, eyes with secrets, looked back at her. And she knew . . . that *he* knew.

He knows that I'm hiding something.

"Come on," she whispered to her kids. "It's time to go."

She turned around—away from the kid watching her, chewing on his burger, hunched over, hiding under his black cap.

No, Kate thought. We can't leave now. That would look weird, now, wouldn't it? Two troopers come in, and I get up and leave. Wouldn't that look weird? Maybe they'd watch me, they'd see me get into a car with Jersey license plates.

All the way from New Jersey to Ohio. What on earth for? Maybe they'll want to talk to us.

"Oh, come on," she whispered, flustered. The kids were clearing up their papers, rolling shriveled brown fries, wrappings, and unused ketchup packets into an unsightly ball.

Brian ran to a refuse container—with big yellow THANK YOU on a swinging lid. He ran back. "Okay, Mom, let's go," he said.

Kate stood up, trying not to look at the troopers. Paranoia—that's what this is. *Paranoia.* I was warned about that. It's your worst enemy. Paranoia.

I'm not paranoid.

Ha-ha. No, I just have a healthy fear of everyone.

Kate reached down and helped Emma with her parka. The purple down coat looked electric under the brilliant fluorescent lights . . . calling attention to the little girl. Brian put his parka on, but, as usual, he left it unzipped.

Kate took Emma's hand and started to pull her away.

"Yo—lady."

Oh, thought Kate, we forgot to say good-bye to our guest. Anything's possible, yes, anything's possible when your head is spinning.

"Yes," she said distractedly, not able to resist a peek at the troopers, now up at the counter. One of the troopers took a sack from one of the workers. The other trooper looked out at the very full restaurant.

He looked at Kate standing there, standing on an ice floe in a sea of tables and people.

"Yes?" she said.

"Your little girl—hey, she forgot this." The kid held up a plastic rabbit. A creature from cartoons, the prize that went with Emma's meal. Kate reached out and took it, snatched it almost. Then she added, "Thank you. Thanks a lot."

The kid grinned again, a knowing grin, partners in crime. "Yeah, word-up." He stuck a hand up and made an arcane sign. Kate smiled back. She turned and started away with Emma.

Feeling those eyes behind her.

Watching us leave.

It's so hard, Kate thought . . . so hard to even walk normally. So hard when you have to think about every step, worrying that every step might betray you.

She pulled Emma along, out of the restaurant. She pushed open a door. The cold air felt sweet in her lungs, even if it made the sweat on her brow turn icy. . . .

Kate quickly got in the car and took her children back to the motel, ignoring their pleas for ice cream. There was work to do, information to be reviewed, studied, memorized.

It was terrible to do this to them, she thought.

The rush hour was over and now the highway wasn't crowded. Even the slimy Gateway Motel seemed like a safe haven.

4

Mari stood there, her hand frozen to the doorknob, listening to this *sound*.

God! It's Alex Russ coming home, she thought. And there's no graceful way out of this. He'll see my car, catch me clambering off the back of his porch. And Alex Russ will lose his temper. With no one around . . .

He'd have every right. Damn, I'm trespassing. I'm breaking into his house.

Mari stood there, and waited, listening. . . .

She felt like a child. A kid, caught doing something silly. It was so cold out here, the wind whipping off the hills, the snow, the smell, the feel of snow in the air.

The sound!

The engine—it was a *truck* engine, Mari was sure now—was moving away, chugging up the hill, up the twisting road to nowhere. Some drunken cowboy heading home with a big dent in his paycheck from hours squatting on a bar stool, drinking and buying useless scratch-off lottery cards.

Mari listened to the engine sound fade away into the distance. She thought that she should turn around and leave. *Go back home, girl,* a voice urged. *Go the hell home.* . . .

Instead she pushed open the backdoor. The warmth reached her fingers and she stuck her head in. "Elaine? Elaine—it's Mari Comas."

Maybe she was giving the kids a bath. The two kids looked like they had infrequent encounters with soap and water. Elaine Russ had other priorities.

"Elaine?"

Mari stepped into the kitchen. She had expected to smell food, tonight's dinner bubbling away, or the stale smell of last night's meal, already festering in the garbage can.

She took a sniff. There was a smell.

It wasn't food.

Mari moved through the kitchen, and it felt dreamlike. It was like a dream you might have, she thought. A deserted house, sitting in the darkness and the cold. An empty house. Only, in the dream, the nightmare, it would turn out not to be so empty. . . .

She walked past the kitchen to the narrow hallway and on to the stairs leading to the bedrooms on the second floor.

There were three small bedrooms, all close together, where Elaine could hear every cough of her kids as they picked up all the childhood colds and fevers and flus, while her husband ordered her to keep them quiet.

Keep them the fuck quiet!

That's what Elaine told her he said. He didn't want noise.

Near the stairs, Mari checked the living room. Toys and clothes were scattered on the floor. A big Magnavox TV—the most expensive thing in the house—sat staring wide-eyed at the tattered sofa, the empty sofa.

She's gone, Mari thought. Elaine Russ had been hurt enough and she left with the kids.

No. Mari shook her head. Where could she go? Elaine Russ had no one—*no place*—to run to. Where the hell could she have gone?

The heat was on in the house. Mari smelled the hot, forced air. A dry heat, sucking all the moisture out of the wood, out of the skin. A heat you could smell. But there was still that other smell. . . .

Mari looked at the stairs.

As she looked she realized that there was one possibility that she had pushed away. Another possibility . . . What was the word?

Come on, Mari. You know the word. From clinical psych. Sure, you do. It's called repression. We repress things that we don't want to deal with. Especially—especially when they hit a bit too damn close—

She took one step. She grabbed the handrail.

Close to home.

Another step, moving up the stairs now, ever more dreamlike. There's always stairs in dreams. Seems like you're always climbing up or climbing down in dreams. Some bullshit about the part of your consciousness that you're dealing with.

Mari only had one nightmare lately, the same nightmare, the same movie always playing. A replay of that night, over and over again. The phone call. And Dan's voice, Dan, Rob's partner, speaking quietly—she could barely hear him—slowly, until Mari realized, Hey, he's crying. Big lunkhead Dan is crying. Why the hell—

Another step, and another, and again—the smell ever stronger, growing almost sharp. There was no light on up here.

I'll have to find a light switch, she thought. See if I can find something that tells me what happened to Elaine and her children. Where they might—

"Elaine?" Mari called out. Just to hear the sound, any sound amid so much stillness.

There was a door to her right, partly open, with darkness behind it. Mari's hand felt the wall, searching for a light switch, finding nothing.

There will be a light inside the open door, she knew. If I get a light on, it will be a lot easier. She moved to the doorway. She reached in and felt for a light switch.

"Damn," she said. "There's got to be a—"

Her hand went up and down, and she stepped into the room a bit more.

What am I repressing now? she wondered. What am I keeping away because if I admit it, if I allow—

Her fingers brushed against the switch. She threw the switch quickly. Urgently.

A light bulb in the ceiling flashed on.

Kate closed the Berenstain Bear book that she was reading to Emma. She had hardly been aware of the story—*Too Much Birthday*. The little bear, the boy bear, had gorged himself on cake and presents and festivities. He learned that you can have too much of a good thing.

We won't have that problem, Kate thought. Will we?

She turned to Brian, who was watching TV. Some actress has said something funny about breasts. *Breasts,* on regular TV. It's not right what the kids see . . . If we were home, Kate thought, I would have shut the TV off.

But we're not at home.

"Bri, shut that off, please. I want—"

"Oh, Mom, come on. I want to see the end."

He fought her on everything, and for now she didn't do much about it. Later there'd be work to do. It would be hard. Kate had spoken to other women who had run and disappeared. They all told her that the children would need help, to repair the damage, to get them whole again.

"Bri—Emma has to go to sleep. Besides, I need to talk to you."

Brian shook his head in disgust and then pushed the button silencing the TV. "Thanks, Mom. Thanks a lot."

She kept looking at him. "Come here, Bri. Come sit with us."

Brian stormed over and sat on the bed.

Sometimes, Kate thought, I feel as if they could slip away. Like the life I thought I had, the safety, the feeling of being protected, cared for, melting away, like snow, like cotton candy . . .

Kate took a breath. She felt Emma watching her, total concentration on her face. Which is exactly what I need, Kate thought. Exactly. "Tomorrow we get another early start, guys. I want to get near St. Louis, if I can hold out."

"Is that where our new home is?" Emma asked.

Kate shook her head. "No." She brushed Emma's hair. "But it's closer, a lot closer. Another day, maybe two after that, and we'll be there. *I promise.* We'll be at our new home."

Brian was on the other bed, still sullen over his missed show. Kate looked at him, making eye contact. "I want to go over a few of the rules . . . again." Brian groaned. "I know you understand them. But just to make sure. So . . ." Make it a game. Nice and light. A game, all in fun. "Who can tell me what rule number one is?"

Emma smiled, enjoying the game. "Don't talk to anybody."

Kate smiled. "Right. Even if I'm there, don't talk to *anyone.* You might let something slip." She checked Brian again. "Got that, Brian?"

He nodded "Duh. I've only heard it a million times, Mom."

"And rule two?"

"Never go off alone."

He can snatch them back, they had said. That happens a lot. And these paid snatchers aren't very nice. . . . Don't let your kids out of sight.

"Good girl," Kate said. "And rule number three?"

Emma grinned. "I'm Emma Martin." She smiled broadly, displaying a mouthful of baby teeth. "That's my name."

Kate turned to Brian. "And I'm—duh—Brian Martin. I've *always* been Brian Martin."

Kate nodded. It was her worst nightmare, either one of the kids letting slip their real name, Cowell. They kept their first names— it was too hard for kids to pick up a new name, too easy to slip

SEE HOW SHE RUNS

up. But the last name—they didn't use that as often.

There were other rules, but those were the big three.

Kate's own rules could fill pages, page after page of small things that couldn't—shouldn't—be done. *I have to remember them all*, she thought. As she often did, she said a little prayer, begging God to help her, to protect them.

She leaned down and kissed Emma's cheek. Her little girl scrunched a fluffy white rabbit close. Half her luggage had been filled with softies that simply couldn't be left behind.

Kate shut the bedside light off. Another lamp, by the front door, was left on. "Night-night, Emmie."

"'Night, Mom." The girl turned away from the light, toward the wall.

"Mom," Brian whispered.

Kate turned to him, feeling bad that she snapped at him. "You can watch a bit more TV, Bri. Keep it low. And then you go to bed too."

Brian turned to the TV and huddled close, the volume just barely audible.

Kate sat there looking at Emma, then Brian, and the drab room, while listening to the sound of the road outside, and all the cars roaring into the cold night.

The light flickered on, and suddenly the small bedroom, the curved shapes of shadows, clothes, blankets, a jumble of toys on the floor, was visible.

Mari's hand froze on the light switch. She heard herself breathing. Strange to be breathing so loudly, she thought. As if the air was thick, unbreathable . . .

It filled her nostrils. The smell was so much stronger now. When she finally looked at the curled lump on the bed, the sleeping child, Elaine's not-quite-two-year-old boy who always seemed to have a runny nose, she *knew*—

Oh, God, she thought. Oh, sweet God.

No.

She reached out for the blanket covering the boy, keeping him warm during the cold and windy night in this drafty house. She grabbed at the satiny fringe and pulled it back, slowly, so slowly. . . .

Don't want to wake him up.

She felt something tugging on the thin blue blanket . . . as if it was stuck. Mari saw her hand shaking. But she kept pulling the blanket back, tugging a bit now, until she saw the boy's head, Bobby's head. Bobby, an all-American boy's name. *Little Bobby* . . .

There was a hole in the forehead.

A hole that I could stick my finger into.

Dried streams of blood flowed away from it.

"No," Mari said.

She thought: I have to get to a phone. Have to get the police here, and—

Bobby's eyes were open, staring into the distance, looking at a wall, looking into forever. Looking for Mommy.

Mari let the blanket fall. It didn't cover his head.

She backed out of the room, gagging. Then, her heart racing gulping the air, she quickly spun around.

The hall was dark. It felt as if the walls could close in on her, squeezing her.

Like a dream house, she thought. A nightmare. And all I have do now is get out.

She stepped into the hall. The stairs were just there, *so close.* . . .

I should get to a phone, she thought. Before I do anything else—yes, that's what I should do.

But there were two more bedrooms. The older boy, Tom, had his room ahead, opposite the bathroom. Mari stood there, stock still, then turned and walked down the hall.

She passed the bathroom, and without knowing why, she threw on the bathroom light.

Then, another few steps, to Tom's room.

She walked in, and her hand slowly moved on the wall, not too eager to find the light.

Then it was on and, a horrible surprise party, she saw Tom, his body sprawled across his bed, dressed in a Broncos T-shirt. The orange shirt was matted with a dark purplish stain.

He might have been getting out of his bed when he was shot . . . just like Bobby. In the head . . .

Mari brought her fist to her mouth and she bit down hard, moaning into her fist, needing some other sensation.

Like that call in the night. Dan's voice heaving until Mari said "What, what, Dan? What's wrong?" . . . until the cold chill settled on her. Animal-like, it came into her dark bedroom.

"Rob," Dan said, struggling to do this right, wanting to tell her before it was on the news.

SEE HOW SHE RUNS

How many times did she say, No? No. No. *No.* Over and over, moaning, howling, all of them doing no good at all.

Like now...

The boy's hand stretched down to the floor, brushing it. Mari backed out.

The nightmare continued.

Go out in the hall, she told herself. Go *downstairs*. Just turn, and go downstairs. You don't have to look in the last bedroom. You don't have to see.

Because you've seen enough.

But she walked—so slowly—to the bedroom of Alex and Elaine Russ. Each step made a small creaking noise on the wood floor. She remembered that she had left the light on in Tom's room. I should have shut it off, she thought. That's what I should have done.

She stopped at the door to the large bedroom. Again she searched for the light switch.

But she could see it already. She could see the ugly twisted shape on the bed. Black, rumpled shadows twisted, turning on themselves, a great confused pile. Mari could see it already.

"Please. God...no..."

Mari found the switch and the overhead light—colored by a magenta Oriental shade—came on.

She saw Elaine Russ.

Elaine Russ had heard something. Mari could see that. Maybe one shot. She woke up in the middle of the night, frozen with terror—wondering: What was that? Did I hear something or—ha-ha—was it just a dream?

While her smallest boy was already dead.

Then there was another shot. *Bang.*

Maybe Tom yelled, and Elaine was already getting out of bed, maybe stupidly looking for her slippers. Maybe she had drunk a few glasses of cheap wine, and she was moving slowly, confused, wanting to get back to sleep.

But he was there. Alex Russ wouldn't race now—now that the boys were dead. He could take his time. The gears moved now, all in one direction. He would finish what he started....

Mari took a step closer to the bed.

Elaine Russ was curled up beside her bed, kneeling on the floor while her head and an outstretched arm lay on the bed.

There were two gigantic craters at the back of the woman's head.

No more pain, Mari thought. Elaine Russ won't be beaten again . . . won't see her kids beaten.

There were other holes. One in her midsection, another higher, a shot in her arm—maybe while she was flailing, trying to protect herself.

Elaine Russ knelt in a pool of her own blood.

I knew I'd find this.

And fuck . . . here it is.

Mari backed away, stepping on something.

Fuck . . .

She looked down. There was a sneaker, a worn dirty sneaker. One of the kids' sneakers . . . somehow it ended up here. Mari thought of her own son, Jake . . . such a slob, always leaving things all around.

Such a slob . . .

Like his dad.

She gasped. Trying to suck in air, but tasting death, tasting the strange flavor in the air. She moved out to the hall, sobbing, falling against a wall. Mari let her head bang against the wall. I really helped her, she thought. Christ, I really helped that poor woman.

Did her a lot of fucking good . . .

Now, didn't I?

She made another thud.

And then—she froze.

As the bang was answered by a noise from below.

5

Mari stopped. She held her breath. I imagined the noise, she told herself.

But there it was, again. A thud, a banging noise. She became a statue in the hall.

How long ago had this happened? It could have been hours ago . . . or days ago. And—and—

Alex Russ could be here.

Mari didn't move. It was still, and she only heard the wind outside scraping at the scrubby brush. She listened for the sound again. The wind gusted.

There was another thud.

Mari moved to the stairs, and then down, slowly.

Just the wind, she told herself. Blowing something, slamming something against the house.

She reached the bottom of the stairs, leaving the family sleeping upstairs. The kitchen light was on. She heard another bang, this time coming right from the kitchen.

She turned and watched the screen door slap against the door frame.

There's more snow coming, strong cold winds. She walked into the kitchen. She almost expected him to be there, Alex Russ, standing with a cup of coffee, smiling as if nothing happened, a good-looking man. Dark blue eyes, dark hair, and a great smile.

A psychotic. A psychopath. A man who killed his family. Taking care of business . . .

Hey, social-worker lady. How're you doing? Want a bullet in your head?

Mari saw the phone. It was right there, an old black rotary phone hanging on the wall. But she kept moving. I'll call from somewhere else, I'll call from the bar in town or the service station (no, *not* the service station).

Away from here. Surrounded by people.

She walked out the door, into the wind, feeling as if she was again abandoning Elaine Russ and her children.

Kate lay in the darkness, trying to sleep. She heard the two kids—so close by that she could reach out and touch them. She heard their reassuring rhythmic breathing.

Not so easy for me, she thought. Sleep may be a thing of the past.

She reached out and turned the lamp on. The tawdry motel room lit up depressed her. This all seemed like such a bad idea now.

But it will get better, she told herself. This is the low point—and it *will* get better. It has to get better.

Another little prayer. Please, God.

Though Kate thought that God was always with her, all along, when she left Schuyler, when she came to New York. God was there, every step of the way. But then he wasn't.

Kate pushed her a hair off her face. The straight blond hair was clean now.

She looked over at her children. Sleeping the sleep of the innocents. She looked at Brian. Nearly ten, and trying so hard to grow up fast.

To protect himself, she thought. That's why he's growing up so fast.

Kate reached out to the small table by the bed. She picked up a book covered with a delftlike pattern of white-and-blue flowers. It was a cute diary, a book of blank pages to write pretty poetry, to pretend that you were a writer. That had been her idea once, to work in publishing, and then write.

But now there was nothing cute in this book. It was her journal, and nearly half the blank pages were filled. A day-by-day account of everything that had happened.

How the dream ended, her life, her family.

How she decided to run from David, to save her children.

The whole story was in there.

An ongoing story, she thought.

Ongoing . . .

She clicked the top of the cheap ballpoint pen. She opened to the where a satiny ribbon held her place. There was no entry for January 2. Not yet anyway.

She put the date on the top of a clean white page.

It never ends, she wrote. Then, as if the point couldn't be made strong enough: *It never goes away . . . never.*

She felt the thickness of the pages already written, the events recorded.

And she thought of how it all began.

6

The night Kate was going to tell David that she wanted a divorce—that she had, in fact, already seen a lawyer—he had picked a quiet French restaurant in Harley-on-Hudson.

It was right by the river, with just a dozen tables, a quiet intimate place. She had asked to have dinner out.

It would be a good place, Kate thought. David won't make a scene there. He'll keep his voice down. He'll calm down before we get home.

David was coming right from the train, right from his family's brokerage firm on Wall Street. Each night he came back, and each night it felt worse. She took a breath. She sipped her wine, a glass of the house white. Too tart.

She had met David at her publisher's party. She was a young editorial assistant, working too hard but glad to be in New York, happy to be around writers and editors.

It was her dream.

She had noticed David before he even walked over to her. Tall, with dark hair. He had been watching her.

"You look lost," he had said.

She smiled. It was her first big book party in the elegant St. Regis Hotel.

"I guess I am," she said. David Cowell came closer.

"Then let me be your guide. Over there we have champagne, and—there—against the wall—there's food."

Kate grinned. "I'm not hungry."

"Then I guess the decision is made."

He took her arm and led her to the table filled with champagne glasses.

She had been lost. And David found her, guided her. Later she didn't question the assumption that they'd marry. She didn't question him when he said that they'd move out of New York, to Ardsley, a wealthy suburb, to live right near the country club.

No question about that, no, a good place to raise children.

She'd know nobody there.

The dreams of publishing, of writing, of New York were gone. This is my real life, Kate had thought. This is what I really want. . . .

The kids filled her life, as did David's business friends—though they didn't entertain much. More and more of the responsibility of the big investment firm fell on David's shoulders. He spent a lot of time at work, and then more time as the booming eighties gave way to crashing nineties. There were problems, tight money, investigations. David didn't explain much to Kate.

He said he was stressed out.

That's how he explained the problems. The fights, the outbursts, his yelling. Always getting worse, until Kate felt like a little girl again, standing by her open window, feeling the cold, wishing she would be pulled up, away. . . .

Kate had nodded, wanting to believe that it would end, trying to believe that they could be happy. Praying, of course, talking to the God that now was her only friend.

Make it work, she begged. Make my marriage work.

Over and over until she knew that it was useless. Whatever love she had for David was long gone. Maybe she married too young. But now—with the kids—it was all so bad.

She sipped her wine. *So bad* . . .

The door to the restaurant opened.

David came into the restaurant, handing his coat to the gray-haired woman in the front, who said, so sweetly, *"Bonsoir, monsieur."*

David nodded at Kate. *You're there. I see you.* Not any warmth. She merely had a place to fill.

She had dressed as though it was only another dinner date. Just the two of them. A nice dress, makeup, a touch of perfume. A dinner out. But she felt sick, thinking: It's going to be so hard.

David came to the table, leaned down, and kissed her on the cheek, a dry kiss. She smiled at him.

"Goddamn trains are late again." He sat down and looked up. He cursed around Kate, though he knew that it bothered her. But that didn't matter, her feelings didn't matter. "Damn Hudson Line gets worse every day." He studied her. "You okay? You look sick. Kids okay?"

SEE HOW SHE RUNS

She shook her head. "No. I had a busy day. There was a party at Emma's nursery school."

"Tough duty," David said, flipping open the menu. Then, already soured, under his breath, "Too fucking tough."

Already it started. Say the wrong thing, step on the land mine. *Boom* . . . like starting an avalanche, the rocks falling, trapping her.

"How—how was work?"

David's menu stayed in place. He demanded complete attention, from her, from the waiter. Kate had read about men and women and divorce . . . the problems couples had. For some men it was all about control. David wanted to control everything, and she was just another appliance. . . .

The waiter, a gaunt man with a twittering French accent, appeared. The menu slid down.

"I'd like to order wine." David looked at Kate. "You'd like more?"

It wasn't a real question.

She nodded and then—remembering her lawyer's advice to keep it friendly—added a smile.

"The eighty-four fumé." David rattled the name off the way most people would order a Big Mac. There was plenty of money. That was no problem. Plenty of money. It was all the other things that were missing.

The waiter vanished. David smiled, and the storm had passed. "You asked about my day?"

She nodded.

"Don't ask. The damn Securities Exchange assholes are still nosing around." He took a breath. "How are the kids?" The question was rote, perfunctory.

"Great. Brian's going to be in a play, *Jack and the*—"

But David's eyes had already drifted back to the menu. "What looks good? What do you want?"

The chill. That's what I can't take, Kate thought. I don't mind being alone in the big house most of the day. But to be alone even when I'm with him—

And his temper. I'm not crazy, she had thought. It's getting worse, all the time, isn't it? I'm not imagining that, am I?

She had idly touched her cheek. The first time he slapped her, she didn't know what to say.

Then, one day, he hit Brian for touching the VCR. Smacked the boy on the face. Kate tried to talk to David about it, but she could feel the pressure building. It felt dangerous, he had all this anger.

He cursed at her. "Christ, I have fucking problems with the brokerage and there's all this shit at home? All this shit with you, and he"—pointing a finger, then a fist at Brian, not yet six— "he's so damned undisciplined."

I'm only unleashing more anger, she thought.

She had thought that when Emma came, a new baby, a little girl, it might change things. A little girl to make them more of a family. But it didn't.

I was stupid to have thought that. But I love her. My little girl. And I'm glad I had her. No matter what.

David looked up. "So what do you want, Kate? What sounds good for dinner? After your *hard* day, you must be really hungry."

She smiled at his sarcasm.

She was going to tell him that it was just going to be a separation. For a while, that's all. She needed time. They both did. Only a separation.

Though Kate knew that it was going to be a divorce.

She picked the swordfish. She didn't like fish. But she'd feel less guilty when she didn't eat it. . . .

David scratched at his left temple.

"I told my father that we have to offer more services. That's the name of the goddamn game in brokerages. Full service."

He looked at Kate's plate. Only a few dents marred the creamy-white slab of swordfish.

"You haven't eaten."

She shook her head. She felt the inevitability of a train roaring down the tracks, roaring, coming closer.

"I'm not hungry. I don't—"

David shrugged. "More wine?" he said, reaching for the bottle sitting in its silver bucket. She looked at the crisp white tablecloth. When they first dated, David had taken her skiing, and he was so good on the slopes, moving so effortlessly while she plodded behind him.

"No, I—"

I have to tell you something.

Those were the words. Be direct, clear, her lawyer, a young woman named Laurie Neale, had said. Let him know that you've made the decision. Let him know that this is serious.

SEE HOW SHE RUNS

David took a drink of wine from his glass. His tongue snaked out and touched his lips. It was an odd movement, as if he felt something there. His hand came up, scratching at his temple.

Kate took a breath.

"David, I have something—"

But he wasn't looking at her. He was looking over her shoulder, looking off into a corner. Kate looked around to see if David could be searching for the waiter. Maybe he wanted another bottle of wine, or the dessert menu.

"I've made a decision—" Her voice was small. The little girl, at the window. *I've made a decision...*

Still, David didn't look at her. His hand fell from his head. It landed on the table with a thud that rattled the silverware.

"And—and—"

The train coming... almost there. The roar of the wheels in Kate's ears. The shower of sparks flying from the rolling thunder. *I've made a decision.*

Suddenly David threw his head back as if it had a will of its own. His head jerked back and then forward, whipping, comical, and he banged both fists on the table.

Kate screamed. "David... David!"

She watched him start to stand up... trying to stand up. But he collapsed back into his seat. His eyes rolled into his head, and there was only white visible, something from a monster movie. Only *white*.

David coughed, hacking at the air. Then he slid to the floor, convulsing, writhing....

Kate screamed.

She yelled—as the waiter, and the maître d', and even the lady who took their coats, all hurried over. Kate went to David, knelt beside him, and tried to hold his body still. He was shivering, his tongue rolling out.

"Call someone!" she yelled. Screaming in the quiet restaurant. "Please! Call someone!"

Someone had already called for help. It was only minutes before the stillness of the small restaurant was shattered by police and ambulance sirens... and the spinning bubble lights sent eerie red spears cutting into the dining room.

And Kate thought, holding David tightly: *I never got to tell him....*

7

Someone said to her, a voice from somewhere, "What about your children?"

Kate—sitting in the blue pastel waiting room, listening to Arsenio, waiting for the doctors—looked up at the person. It was as a nurse. A middle-aged black woman in white.

"What about your *children*?" the woman repeated. This nurse is as old as my mother, Kate thought. I should tell her. Tell this mother.

"You have someone with them?"

Kate nodded then—remembering her manners—and said, "Yes. The sitter can stay. She'll stay until we can come home."

From the expression on the woman's face, Kate realized that she had just said something silly. *When we can come home, when we can come home.* What's so silly about that?

Because . . .

Maybe there is no we.

She felt the sick guilt. They don't know, she thought, that I was just about to tell David good-bye. Now—the night nurses, the young doctor that breezed by before—they all look so concerned. The nurse had patted her hand. Kate nodded, feeling deceitful.

The TV audience laughed. They thought that it was pretty funny too. Pretty damn funny . . .

Then Kate was alone.

Mary Williams, a middle-aged grandmother, was baby-sitting, and she could stay the night. Especially at ten dollars an hour. No problem there. Mary's baby-sitting money was sometimes more than her husband brought home from the Shopwell where he cut meat.

Time passed. Arsenio was gone, someone changed the channel, and David Letterman came on. A dog sang. *Imagine that.* "Home on the Range." The nurse came by again and asked her if

SEE HOW SHE RUNS

she needed anything, some coffee, *anything*. Always polite, Kate shook her head. I'm fine. I don't want to be a problem. The nurse lowered the TV's volume. It was late.

Kate felt tired and achy.

She could only imagine what was going on past the double doors.

Once—during the night—she let herself think maybe he won't come out. Maybe it will end this way.

It was a bad thought. God wouldn't like that thought. She had to wipe at her eyes, clearing away tears, tears for herself. She went to the rest room and saw herself in the mirror. Her skin looked blotchy and gray, her eyes sunken.

She thought: This is the beginning of something, not the end.

When she came out of the rest room, the doctor was there. Not David's regular doctor. He was away skiing somewhere . . . Aspen . . . somewhere.

This doctor walked Kate back to the waiting room and guided her to a plastic seat. He sat next to her. The doctor was young, close to Kate's age. He fidgeted with a pad, writing things down. A prescription for David, that's what it was.

If he takes two of these he'll never have the problem again.

Kate cleared her throat as if she had to say something. Can I still get divorced? Is that still—

The doctor looked up.

"Mrs. Cowell, your husband has suffered a hemorrhagic stroke."

Kate nodded.

But that didn't make sense. Old people got strokes.

"A subarachnoid vessel near the cerebellum became clogged. It's a type of aneurysm. In seconds, the vessel exploded and blood leaked out, pressing against the surface of the brain." The doctor took a breath. "Damaging it, Mrs. Cowell."

"Something in his head . . . exploded?"

"The vessel became blocked. It happens—we can't predict it."

Kate nodded. This was worse than a cold. Maybe—maybe even worse than a heart attack. The doctor's last words hung there. *Damaging it . . .*

"Did you see any early warning signs? Was your husband acting distracted, clumsy. Was his speech clear? Did he complain of a headache?"

Kate shook her head. "No. He came directly from work. We were having dinner. He may have had trouble there."

The doctor nodded. Kate looked at his name tag. Rosenthal. We don't know any Dr. Rosenthal, Kate thought. I hope he's good. I hope he knows what he's doing. I hope—

"Sometimes, if you see signs, it helps us assess what was going on just before the stroke. I gave your husband a CAT scan and—"

Kate kept nodding as if she knew what these things were.

"And X rays, of course. There are more tests we'll have to do, but we pretty much know what area of the brain has been damaged."

That word again. *Damaged* . . .

"The hemorrhaging has stopped, and in a way, he's lucky, Mrs. Cowell. It could have been much worse. Your husband has a good shot at nearly full recovery. It's hard to tell now but—"

The nurse came over to the doctor and touched his shoulder. She handed him a clipboard with something on it. "Okay," he said, looking at it. "Right . . ."

"I have to go. But I'll be back." Dr. Rosenthal stood up. "Would you like a cot, a room to rest in?"

Kate shook her head. "No, I don't think I could rest."

"It may be a long night."

Kate nodded.

The doctor turned, but then said, "I'll come back and tell you what else we learn."

Kate thought of Emma . . . she still woke up in the middle of the night. Emma would do that tonight. Mary Williams would go in to her. And that might scare Emma.

She needed her mommy. And her dad. David would toss her around and Em loved that. Kate had been planning on taking the little girl away from her father. Now . . . everything had changed.

Kate took a breath, smelling the hospital.

She went back to watching the TV.

She fell asleep, and she dreamed that she was strapped to a molded plastic chair, like the one she was sitting in, sleeping in. She couldn't move, no matter how much her muscles ached, no matter how much pain she felt.

When she tried to scream, a gag suddenly appeared, covering her mouth.

I can't scream.

Someone touched her.

And she woke up.

SEE HOW SHE RUNS

• • •

"Wh—" Kate said, blinking, trying to force her eyes open.

Dr. Rosenthal looked tired. The waiting room was still empty, but Kate heard sounds. The voices of nurses, the squeak of food carts being wheeled down the halls. In a moment she understood. It was morning.

"I let you sleep," the doctor said. Kate nodded. "But we've got a clearer picture now." He held up a clipboard and there was a sketch of something round and squat. It took a second to register that it was a brain.

"The initial tests are done . . . and I wanted to show you this. Right here—this is where your husband's brain has been damaged. It's the right side. He's what we call a right hemiplegic, and that means that the right side of his brain has been damaged." Kate kept looking at the sketch and the area circled by the doctor's pen. Nodding.

Yes . . .

"That means we can expect temporary loss of speech. Some paralysis, perhaps in one arm and one leg. There will be weakness, double vision, other minor things. But the damage could have been worse."

"Could have been worse," Kate repeated. "How?"

Dr. Rosenthal looked right at her. "Some people die, Mrs. Cowell. Some people never recover. As it is, your husband has an excellent possibility of a nearly full recovery. He will need a tremendous amount of rehabilitation, but we know how to do *that* here. A team of people will work with him. And—of course"—he patted her hand—"you will be part of that team."

Another nod. Of course. "There can be a full recovery?"

"*Nearly* full. It's still impossible to say how much damage has occurred." The doctor took a breath. "I do have a question."

Kate waited.

"Did your husband have a substance-abuse problem, alcohol, drugs?"

Kate slowly shook her head. The question was so unsuspected. David drank, but never to the point of drunkenness. "No," she said.

The doctor's face looked confused. Kate wondered, What is he getting at here? What did they find?

Rosenthal took a breath. "Would you like to see him?"

Kate looked up from the clipboard, the sketch, to the doctor. That's the correct answer, she thought. *Of course, I do.*

Rosenthal took her hand and led her out of the small waiting room, through the double doors, and down the long corridor, where it felt like everyone—the nurses, the people with the breakfast trays, laughing, talking—were looking at her.

She stopped at the door where a plaque said INTENSIVE CARE UNIT. The doctor had to guide her gently by holding her shoulder. She walked into the room slowly, studying the large room, the other beds, the equipment, the nurses' station. She avoided looking ahead, at David's bed.

But the doctor urged her forward and Kate walked closer to the bed. It reminded her of the time she saw her grandmother for the last time. The old woman's eyes were shut tight, sealed with dried mucus. With every breath she took, a terrible rattle filled the room of the nursing home, like an engine breaking down, ready to sputter to a dead stop.

She looked at David. All his power seemed gone.

But David, though his eyes were shut, breathed easily. An IV hung over him, the clear liquid dripping into a tube, and then trailing down to his arm. Is that his paralyzed arm? Kate wondered.

Other tubes snaked under the sheets. Kate thought she knew what they were to. Tubes to take away his urine.

He looked immobile, frozen.

She went to his bedside. His head looked puffy and distorted. There was a blackish blotch near his forehead partially covered by a bandage. Was it a bruise of some kind or just some dye the doctors marked his head with?

X marks the spot.

David's right hand lay motionless. Kate touched it—out of curiosity, out of tenderness—she didn't know.

Later, she would realize that she'd been suffering from shock and exhaustion.

"Will—will he wake up?" Kate said.

"He's heavily medicated. While we monitor his condition, we'll try to keep him sleeping and quiet. Sometimes there are aftershocks. In a day or two he should be able to awaken. We'll know the full extent of the hemorrhage."

"And he'll see me, hear me?"

"Yes," Dr. Rosenthal said. But his voice sounded tentative, Kate thought, holding back information. Like when she asked David, "Where will we live?" as she dreamed of a New York

SEE HOW SHE RUNS

apartment, of art galleries, and Broadway shows. "Don't worry," David said. "I'll take care of everything."

"But—he may not know who you are. He may not understand your words. They won't mean anything. It will come back—most of it will come back. But, as I said, it will take time. Time, and *lots* of work."

The doctor pulled a chair close to the bed. "Here, sit. You can stay as long as you like. Then go home. Get some rest. We'll talk more later."

Kate turned to him. He's leaving, she thought. And I'm supposed to stay here.

"If you need anything, let the nurses know," he said.

"Thank you," Kate said.

Then he was gone. She looked back at David, sleeping so quietly. She looked down at her hand covering his.

I have to stay now, she thought. That's it, isn't it? I have to stay. There's no way out now. It's a duty, an obligation.

She felt as if she had to cry—but there was nothing there. I'm all dried up, she thought.

She pulled her hand away, down to her lap.

She spoke to him.

"David, I'm here. Everything's fine. You're okay." She took a breath, a deep, resigned breath. "We're all fine."

David awakened the next night. His parents were there. His father, playing big shot, talked about this expert and that. "Only the best," he said. He talked about flying his son to Houston.

"Best damn stroke recovery center in the country," his father said. "That's where David should be."

Kate didn't say anything. They didn't ask her opinion.

A neurologist, a family friend, disagreed. He politely told David's father that his best chance for recovery was here, "surrounded by his family, his loved ones."

David's father nodded.

So then, it was decided.

David opened his eyes. He looked around the room, at his parents, at Kate, at the doctors and nurses. He winced, as if the small movement gave him pain. He opened his mouth.

"Maybe he'd like a drink," a nurse said. She took a cup with a straw and brought it close to David's lips. But he quickly shut his mouth as if he had no understanding what the cup and the straw could possibly have to do with him.

"We're all here, David," his father said, so loud, as if he was running one of his board meetings.

Kate felt David looking at her. She looked back. His eyes were filmy, occasionally fluttering. That's probably the medication, she thought.

"Hello, David," she said. She patted his hand. It don't respond. "We're all here for you."

He opened his mouth as if he was going to say something.

"I think—" Dr. Rosenthal started to say.

But David's voice interrupted. He made a sound, a primitive sound that chilled Kate. It was the sound a grown-up baby might make, someone terribly mentally disabled, someone who never learned to talk.

"Heg . . . yah . . . uh, uh—erg, erg . . ."

David's voice rose, growing more exited as if he was frustrated, or scared by the sounds it was making.

David's mother came to him and patted his brow.

"That's okay, honey," she said. "That's all right. Don't talk. Don't worry."

"Erg . . . erg . . . er!"

The voice rose, crazy, terrifying. Dr. Rosenthal smoothly stepped close and stuck a needle in David's arm. In seconds, the eyelids lowered and there was a hushed quiet in the hospital room.

David's father spoke again, chairman of the board. "Now— Doctor—can you tell us everything we need to know?" He looked from Rosenthal to the neurologist, who let Rosenthal answer.

Kate watched. Don't worry.

She watched . . . while the sounds of her husband's unintelligible mumblings still rang in her ears.

That night Kate tried to tell the children about Daddy. Emma had just turned three. She was so little. . . .

Kate explained that Daddy was sick, but he'd get better. Sure, and soon she could go see him. We should all pray for him, Kate said.

Brian sat perfectly still, his face dark and confused.

Emma said, "I want my daddy."

Kate nodded. I was going to take you away from him. Though you love your daddy, I was going to take you away from him.

Later, when Emma was asleep, she told Brian more. There were no tears from Brian. He had felt it, the chill when David came home. He had seen his father hit her. He had been hit. That

SEE HOW SHE RUNS

turned the switch . . . for Kate . . . for Brian.

Brian was afraid of his father.

David yelled at him. He called him a "stupid boy, you stupid boy!" and Kate watched Brian shrink back, frightened by the words, terrified and hurt by his father.

Brian would have understood about the divorce.

But now she had this to explain to him. She sat him down at the kitchen table, the wonderfully big and bright kitchen filled with shining appliances and a butcher-block table that was larger than the dining-room table that she grew up with.

The kitchen dwarfed them.

She took Brian's hand, his two hands, and held them tightly in hers. As if to say, "We're together in this." She told him enough so that he'd understand. Something happened to his dad's head. He'll be in the hospital for a while. When he comes back, he'll be different. Dad will have to learn some things all over again.

"And we'll have to help him," she said to Brian.

"But why did it happen?" Brian asked.

Kate shook her head. "I don't know. I wish I could tell you, Bri. But sometimes—bad things just happen."

She almost added—

And there's nothing we can do about them. Nothing at all.

Instead she brushed her son's hair with her hand and said, "Come on. Let me put you to bed."

That night Kate found the old diary, a book of blank pages. I can talk to these blank pages, she thought. I need someone to talk to.

She started writing. . . .

8

Suzy Tyler was a regular. She often came to the Spur, a bar perched halfway up the mountain road leading south. Though she wasn't young anymore, she kept her hair blond, her lips red, and sometimes she'd get lucky.

Out on the street, in daylight, she might look a little drawn, her hair a little frizzy. Under the harsh lights of the diner where she waitressed, she'd look her thirty-five years. Easily.

But perched on a bar stool, the cracked plastic digging into her panty hose, she could look good.

The bartender had once nailed Suzy. In the back room, after closing. Quick and dirty. But he was married, and that one taste was enough. She never pressed him again. Suzy knew the rules.

What she looked for was a new face, someone different. Denver was a good fifty miles away, down nasty twisting roads. She occasionally drove there and hit bars where the drinks were too expensive. But it was here that she was comfortable. She was the queen of this place.

She could look at men having a drink with their wives, watch the smoke come out of the wives' ears when their husbands looked at her legs, her ass. That was fun.

Tonight she was on her third Wallbanger and nothing was happening. No one was hitting on her. A football game was on. Suzy didn't watch football, didn't follow the Broncos, couldn't care less. She liked looking at the players' butts, hard-looking things. That was okay, but the game—who could understand it? She drained her drink.

Some nights Suzy left early, bringing home a vague dissatisfied feeling. Nights like that, she'd think about moving off the mountain, getting into the city.

But Suzy Tyler was a realist. She knew what she'd be in the city, what her chances would be of finding someone. Here, she was a local attraction.

She drained her drink. The song on the jukebox was loud, thumping. The music didn't fit the football game at all.

> *I've got nowhere to run,*
> *And I've got nowhere to hide.*
> *'Cause you see . . . I'm a long way from home . . .*

The bartender came over. "Another?" he said. Suzy nodded.

A few couples were dancing, doing a gawky two-step to the rock and roll. Somebody at the other end of the bar cursed. Maybe Denver was losing the football game. The guy let out a big "sheee-it."

"On the house," Bill said, tapping the bar filled with carvings. Suzy smiled. She licked her lips, teasing him. She brought the sweet drink up to her mouth.

SEE HOW SHE RUNS

There didn't seem to be anything happening in the Spur tonight. Another song started, and Suzy nodded in time with it, mouthing the words.

The bartender watched her, smiled at her. She was looking good tonight. He cleaned a glass slowly.

Suzy felt like she had to pee. She put down her drink and slid off the stool. A piece of torn plastic gouged into one stockinged leg. "Shit," she said. "Damn." She slid off the stool, trying not to do any more damage.

She hit the floor, tottering on her heels, wobbily for a minute. Pissed off . . .

She felt a hand grab her arm, steadying her. A voice, low, cutting through the blare of the song, asked, "Are you okay, miss?"

Suzy turned around to see what the cold wind had blown in through the front door of the Spur.

Mari called the number again. And again she got the answering machine. Jenette Prior, Assistant DA for Domestic Violence, had given Mari her home phone number. But what the hell good was it?

Mari had left three messages, and there had been no callback. She listened again as the announcement message kicked in— "Hello, I'm not available right—" and then she hung up.

Prior had her home phone number hooked up to a machine that she never checked. Absolutely useless . . .

"Mom," her son Jake said, "can I stay up and watch—"

Mari cut him off, shaking her head. "No. No, I want you to get ready for bed."

"Please, just—"

Mari waved him away, and Jake retreated, groaning about how unfair she was. Sometimes, when he got really mad he'd throw his father in her face.

Dad let me stay up. . . .
Dad let me do this. . . .

But that destroyed Mari so easily. She'd freeze. She'd feel her face lose all its color. Jake saw that. And he'd quickly say, "Hey, I'm sorry, Mom. I didn't mean—"

But she'd turn away, defeated.

Now she hovered near the kitchen phone, feeling cut off. Elaine Russ and her children were now in the hands of the police. Alex Russ was a suspect, no more than that. The story made a big splash in the evening news. TRAGEDY IN COLDWATER SPRINGS.

There were shots of the ramshackle house stuck on a barren plain at the foot of the mountains. It didn't look so ominous in the daytime. Try it at night, Mari thought, try visiting it when it's pitch-black out and there isn't anyone around for miles.

The TV news reporters spoke to some of the Coldwater locals.

"They were a nice family," Alex Russ's nearly toothless boss said. "Real nice . . . Don't know how somepin' like this could happen."

I do, Mari thought. I do, asshole. . . .

Then there was another shock. The news showed a photo of Alex Russ, a goofy high-school photograph, back when he played football for Medford. A photograph with a kid's face.

But when Mari had seen him two weeks ago, Russ had the beginnings of a beard. Russ was a man, not some kid with zits. The photograph was useless.

His car was gone, a beat-up gray Chevy Camero that Russ probably kept running through constant attention.

That might be easy to find . . . if Russ hadn't changed the plates on it. It would be easy for him to pick up some plates. There's always plates lying around the service station. Big Bob O, the station owner, gosh, Mari bet he didn't have a *darned clue* how many plates he had lying around.

So where could Alex Russ go, with only this stupid high-school picture to haunt him?

Anywhere . . .

A reporter compared the Russ killings to the story of John List.

John List had lived with his wife and three children in a nice section of New Jersey in 1971. They were the Brady Bunch, the kids wearing bell-bottoms and "moddish" bangs. Happy wife and straight-shooter Dad.

List and his family were devout Christians, fervent believers in the power of Jesus and prayer. Except prayer didn't do anything to help his family when Dad lost one job after another and plunged deeper and deeper into debt.

Until God told him that it was *best* that John List end his family's suffering. So he killed them in their sleep with a cheap handgun.

SEE HOW SHE RUNS

Then he disappeared . . . for a long time, until his photo, aged with the help of a computer, was broadcast on *Unsolved Mysteries*.

Eighteen years after he had killed his family, he was found, right here in Denver, with a new family, kids, a pillar of his community, a regular churchgoer.

Of course . . .

For eighteen years he had disappeared. It wasn't hard. Even today it wasn't hard to disappear.

The phone rang. Mari's heart did a funny flip. She reached for the handset, cutting of the annoying ring.

"Good night, Mom," Jake said, still sullen.

I failed Elaine Russ, Mari thought. She's dead because I didn't see how much danger she was in. God, I let her stay there. There were other choices, there were shelters. I should have done something—

I know that. And there's only one way to make it up to the dead woman, to her children.

She said, "Hello."

Expecting Jenette Prior to be there, with the news. They got Russ. *He'll be arraigned Monday, and you can come. You can be there. . . .*

"Good evening, Mrs. Marianna Comas?" Funny, when she heard someone call her Mrs., it was as if Rob were still here, as if they still had a life.

She didn't know the voice. Who could be calling now? *I'm not Mrs.*, she wanted to say. *I'm not Mrs.*—

"This is the *Denver Record* calling. How are you tonight?" The voice didn't wait for an answer. "We're having a special get-acquainted offer, and you can have delivery of the paper, right to your door, every morning for—"

She hung up.

Mari turned around. Jake was gone. I forget him too much, she thought. I gotta stop doing that. She walked down to his bedrooom, his dark room, where he waited for a good-night kiss.

Everything felt safe. Kate had found a small motel outside of St. Louis, a mom-and-pop operation that looked as if it might be run by a real mom and pop. Except they asked a lot of questions.

Traveling alone?
Nice kids . . . where are you folks headed?

You kids going to miss some school?

Kate had to smile and keep answering. After they checked in, she didn't want to take Brian and Emma out for food.

I don't want to sit someplace, she thought, and have people looking at us.

Instead she suggested that they pick up some heros, or subs or grinders, or hoagies, or whatever they call them in Missouri.

Everybody had their own special name for the stupid things, she thought. You can tell that you're in a different state when the name of a sandwich changes.

Brian begged to go somewhere, to get away from the motel room, from the car. Kate shook her head. I don't want to do that, she thought. But Brian laid out the guilt, the hours in the car, how they were stuck in a small room.

Kate nodded. Brian was right.

She remembered seeing a mall a mile back. Ozark Hills Mall. It had a big K Mart, a Sears, and a strip of stores between them with indoor parking.

Please, they begged.

It seemed like an innocent enough thing to do. We could eat there, Kate thought. That's what we could do. Let the kids walk around. They need a break.

I need a break.

So after everyone hit the bathroom and splashed water on their faces, they got back in the car and Kate backtracked to the mall.

The indoor lot was three levels high, with parking meters in front of every space. Kate looked down at the scattering of coins on the dash. Enough for an hour or so, she thought.

That's all we'll need.

She pulled into an empty space, fed the meter, and took her kids to explore the wonders of the Ozark Hills Mall.

The man's hand rested on Suzy's shoulder and she spun around to check who was touching her. She'd make a snap decision, evaluating the guy, deciding whether he had any possibilities, if maybe she didn't have to go home alone tonight. . . .

Suzy turned around and saw him. He was tall, with a light beard, a nice smile, and blue eyes. She smiled back. The music stopped while customers at the tables rooted around in their pockets for coins.

The man said, "Looked like you were going to fall."

SEE HOW SHE RUNS

He looked Suzy up and down. She smiled. He was judging her, wondering whether he wanted to spend some time with her. Her fingertips brushed the back of his hand.

His blue eyes sparkled in the swirl of lights inside the bar.

"Thanks for the rescue," she said. She didn't want him to go away. So she looked right at him, the invitation direct.

His hand slid away from her shoulder. But Suzy's hand followed, squeezing his in appreciation. She was experienced at this. Many nights at the Spur, with truck drivers and cowboys, gave her experience. The man's eyes squinted, and the color seemed to fade. He looked around, his coat on, as if he were checking the place for anyone he might know.

He acted as if he was about to leave, as if it had been a mistake coming in here.

"I was just going to freshen up," Suzy said. "Maybe you'd join me for a drink?"

The man's eyes, checking the room, stopped darting back and forth and came back to look at Suzy. He smiled at her.

The cloud passed. He wasn't going to leave now.

"Sure," he said. "Why not?"

Suzy smiled back, and then turned and walked back to the smelly bathrooms of the Spur.

Both the kids were sticky from giant cinnamon buns. The sweet smell of the hot buns filled the food-service area, stronger even than the smell of greasy fries and cardboard pizza.

Brian had checked out new CDs at Music Express, picking up the new Hammer. Brian had a CD player at home. It was something he had left behind.

That was another promise Kate had made. "I'll get you another one," she had said. "Soon as we're settled."

Emma was leaning into Kate, only steps away from asking to be picked up.

The mall crowd had thinned. They must close them early out here, Kate thought. Midwest blue laws? Get the mall closed so people will go home and get a good night's rest for church on Sunday.

I want to take the kids to church tomorrow, she thought. That's important. I can find a little church somewhere.

The parking lot was nearly empty when she led the kids out of the mall. It was only—what? Eight o'clock. Seemed early to be closing, she thought.

"Mom," Brian said. "Hey, Mom, there's something on the windshield."

Kate was still looking around the deserted parking lot, feeling nervous. But this isn't Manhattan, she knew. Got to remember that. Got to learn to relax a bit. It's not dangerous here.

She looked at her car. Brian ran ahead to the windshield. Funny, Kate thought, it looked just like—

"God, Mom, it's a *ticket*."

"Wha—"

"Duh. It's a *ticket*. Look." Brian handed the ticket to her.

"Mommy, I'm tired," Emma said. "Pick me up."

Kate pulled Emma close, hoping that would quiet and comfort the girl.

But: "*Mommy—*"

Kate took the piece of paper from Brian. It can't be a ticket, she thought. That wasn't possible. But Kate looked at the meter, the red flag, and she realized that they had spent more than an hour in the mall.

She looked at the ticket. It had her license-plate number on it. No, not mine, Kate thought. It was a plate number from New Jersey. Now it was in some computer. And who knew what the computer would say. . . .

Kate looked up.

"Mommy! Let's go!" Kate patted Emma's head. There was a sign over the spaces. ALL OVERTIME TICKETS MUST BE PAID AT THE PARKING OFFICE, MAIN LEVEL.

Right, thought Kate. That's what I have to do. Pay the overtime. It's not a real ticket. Maybe it won't go into the computer. Maybe I can stop that from happening.

She turned to the car and had another thought. Maybe when I pay, they'll check on this car, the plates, the phony registration, my phony license. I'll be there with the security guards, with their guns.

She stopped herself. She took a breath. *No*. No one's out looking for us. We're not missed yet. My answering machine is taking messages. The mail is not piling up in the mailbox. No one even knows we're gone.

But the paranoia—that's what this is, she thought—was here, holding her, teasing her. A hundred questions that she should have asked before suddenly appeared.

I never wondered about the license, the registration. Where did they come from? How phony are they?

SEE HOW SHE RUNS

Kate unlocked the car doors.

"Great work, Mom," Brian said. "You got us nailed for parking."

"In you go," Kate said to Emma. The little girl crawled into the backseat and curled up, too tired from running, needing her own bed.

"Good move, Mom, real—"

Softly, almost a whisper, Kate got in and said to Brian, "Shut up. Just be quiet, Brian."

Never say shut up, she used to tell him. No one says shut up. But he kept yammering at her while she tried to think about what to do, what in the world she should do.

Just leave. That's what. Drive out and let the stupid parking violation bureau in—

Missouri . . . Let it go into the damn state's computer.

She started the car. No. That would mark my trail. It would be a dumb thing to do . . . a stupid thing.

"We shouldn't have stayed in there so long," Kate said.

She backed up. Brian was quiet now, shocked by her barking at him, upset, maybe even a little scared. "I should have come back to the meter with more change. We don't need *this*," she said.

She heard Emma breathing heavily in the backseat.

"What are you going to do?" Brian asked.

She brought the car around one curve, heading down to the bottom level, the main level. She saw a small gray cinderblock building jutting out from one wall of the main mall structure. The sign said PARKING VIOLATION OFFICE.

There was a door with a glass window, and there were men inside, and tables, machines. One man, a uniformed security guard, turned and looked at her.

Kate glanced down at her hand. She realized that she had the ticket clutched tightly, nearly crumpled.

"Got to stop," she whispered, more to herself then her son. "I've got to stop."

So she did.

9

The man asked her to dance, and Suzy, even after three drinks, moved smoothly on the floor, shaking her butt, laughing, enjoying this new guy, this new good-looking guy who had come into the Spur.

After a few dances she had beads of sweat on her brow and her feet hurt from trying to prance around in heels.

But it felt good to be laughing, enjoying herself. Then there was a slow ballad, Waylon Jennings singing about "Midnight." The guy pulled her close, so close she smelled his sweat. His arms held her tight and she pressed against him.

Tighter and tighter he held her. When Suzy pressed against him, encouraging him, he gently pressed a knee into her.

She pulled back. Grinning at him. "You wouldn't be trying to turn me on now, would you?"

He laughed back. "Could be." Again he dug his knee into her, only this time she didn't find it so cute. It seemed insistent, so she pulled away.

"You haven't even told me your name," she said.

The man looked away, at the door, at the bar. Considering the question.

"What's the matter?" she said. "Hiding something?"

He looked back at her, his eyes glowing. Anyone looking at the couple, now standing still on the rough wood floor, would think that they were having an argument.

"My name's Tom." He said it flatly.

She smiled. "Okay, Tom. Nice to meet you."

Another cloud passed, and Suzy smiled. Lots of guys walked into the Spur. Some of them were married, looking for a night's excitement. If that's what this was, it would be okay with her. It wouldn't be the first time.

"I'm Suzy Tyler . . . and I'm *very* glad to meet you."

SEE HOW SHE RUNS   55

She came close, whispering to him.
Opportunities like this weren't meant to slip away....

Kate walked into the parking-lot office, interrupting the conversation, cutting off the laughter of the two men inside.

Sometimes, when she was little and came downstairs, her parents would stop talking, putting their discussion, their argument on hold. Kate had learned not to interrupt, to stay in her room, listening to the yelling, wondering what it was all about.

One of the men wore a brown uniform with an emblem of some kind, while the other wore a white shirt and a tie, loosened, the collar open to air out his chubby neck.

"Miss?" the man with the white shirt said.

"My car—I stayed too long. I mean, the meter—"

She looked up to the uniformed guard. He had short dark hair and a small black mustache. His two hands were wrapped around a coffee cup, warming them.

She felt him studying her.

"Let's see your ticket, miss."

Kate nodded. "Sure." She passed the man in the white shirt her parking ticket. The guard still kept watching her. She smiled. My heart's going crazy, she thought. Her mouth felt rubbery.

"And your license and registration."

Kate looked back to the man at the desk. He was hitting keys on a computer keyboard. "I—I thought I could just pay the overtime. I—"

The man smiled. "Why certainly you can, ma'am. But this is still a parking ticket. It's been logged in and we have to note that it's been paid. And who paid it."

Kate nodded. I should have kept on going, she thought. I should have just left. What were the odds that they could find me from that ticket. Now—this isn't good.

She dug in her purse, looking for her wallet.

I could, she thought, tell them that I left my license in my car. *Just wait. I'll go get it. Won't be a minute.*

No. That's stupid. Do that, and what—pull out of here like I just robbed the bank? That would be great.

The security guard walked closer to the desk and the computer monitor. He put his coffee cup down.

"Here it is," Kate said, hoping there was no tremor in her voice, nothing to give away her horrible tension.

She handed her phony license and the registration to the man in the white shirt. He took them and started hitting keys, slowly, hunting and pecking for each letter of her name, each digit of her license. One long, labored keystroke after another.

The security guard looked at the screen, then up at Kate. "Are your kids okay out there?" he said, nodding his head in the direction of the window. "You can bring 'em in here if you want."

Kate turned and saw Brian sitting in the front passenger seat, watching. He looked terrified. Great, Kate thought. That's just great.

She turned back and smiled. "Yes, they're okay . . . they're tired. My little girl's asleep in the back."

"Damn," the man at the keyboard said, staring at his screen. "I don't get this—"

The security guard also looked down at the screen.

This is unreal, thought Kate. I can't stand this. How long will this go on?

"What is it, Walter?" the security guard said.

Walter looked at Kate's documents and then leaned close to his screen. "I put in this number here—and—for some reason—"

Kate looked back at her car, at Brian watching. She chewed her lip and then forced herself to stop. That's a suspicious thing to do. Can't do that . . . Can't act suspicious.

"So what's wrong with it, Walt?"

Kate stood there, listening to the hum of the fluorescent lights, frozen, trapped.

Suzy and her new friend, the man who said he was Tom, were back on the bar stools. Tom held up her empty glass and tilted it back and forth. "Another?" he said.

She laughed and put a hand down and touched his thigh. That was part of her repertoire, keep the guy interested, keep the train moving along.

"I dunno," she said.

Tom responded by reaching down and touching her thigh, high, and then slipping his hand up higher, pushing up her tight skirt.

"Then," he said, "I guess that we're done here."

Suzy licked her lips. He gave her another squeeze and pulled his hand away. They both knew it was time to move along.

"So," he said. "Had enough dancing . . . had enough Wallbangers?" Suzy laughed.

SEE HOW SHE RUNS

She thought he was funny, cute. Though anyone looking at the man would think, What is he so worked up about? Why are his eyes on fire?

She nodded. "I guess that I am done."

He smiled. "Then—why don't we go outside, get some air, take a ride."

"Sure," she said lightly.

A new storm had been predicted, more snow, though they had plenty in the mountains, more than enough. But that storm wasn't due for hours.

They could take a ride.

The man slipped off his bar stool. He put down a few dollars on the bar—nothing for a tip—and then held out a hand for Suzy. She was even more wobbly now, the drinks taking their toll. She leaned on Tom.

He pulled her coat off the rack near the door and led her out into the cold.

Mari came into the kitchen. She cleared the sink of a few glasses and a plate dotted with Jake's cookie crumbs. She took a rag and wiped the kitchen table.

Shit, Prior's not going to call, Mari guessed. Damn Jenette Prior and the detectives on the case won't see any reason to tell me what's going on. I'm just a social worker.

Hey, my responsibilities are over. And boy—what a good job I did.

She opened the refrigerator. There was a bit of wine hiding at the bottom of a bottle of cabernet sauvignon . . . barely a glass.

She dug the bottle out and poured the wine into a glass sitting in the dish drain. She took a sip. It tasted bitter, acidic, grainy. She sat down again.

The phone rang, horribly loud, and Mari snatched the handset off the cradle before it could ring again.

"Mari, Jenette Prior returning your call."

"Oh, thanks, Jenette." Be nice, Mari reminded herself. You may not like the bitch, but she has information that you want. "I was hoping you could tell me—"

"Mari, I can't tell you *anything*. I'm sorry—but even if we had something—which we don't—I can't go giving out information. I'm afraid you'll have to get your news the same—oh, could you hold a second. I have another call."

Mari heard a click and then Prior was gone. Prior was good at her job, good at prosecuting abusers and rapists. "Nailing their asses to the floor," was how the assistant DA described it.

But Prior doesn't think much of what I do, Mari knew. The court was the place to get the creeps away from families, away from the kids and women they liked to hurt.

Put them in jail. Maybe she's right, Mari thought. Look at all the good I did. She took another sip of the wine.

"Okay, I'm back."

"It's just this, Jenette. If you've got Alex Russ, I'd like to—"

"That I *can* tell you. Alex Russ is gone. He's gone. We've alerted the neighboring states. And I've been trying to get a handle on the car he's driving, the license plates. His boss has been absolutely useless."

Good, thought Mari. She's talking. Just don't push too hard and maybe she'll keep talking.

"That photo you have, Jenette. It's no good. Alex Russ doesn't look like that."

Prior took a breath, as if she had heard this before, as if she was irritated. "I know. I *know*, but that's all we have. There were no photos in his house. Elaine Russ didn't have any living relatives to speak of, no big photo albums. We have some artists working on it."

"I could help. I saw him a few weeks ago and—"

"Great. Good enough." The conversation was over. Quick as that. "I'll tell the detectives. Hey, look, Mari—it's been a bitch of a day—"

So hard. Tough as nails. Prior was one of the boys.

"I gotta go."

"Thanks," Mari said. Be nice. Keep those lines of communication open. "Thanks for calling back."

"We'll talk," Prior said. And then she was gone.

Mari held the lifeless handset. She drained the glass of wine. There's nothing left for me to do except go to sleep, she thought.

Try to avoid football tomorrow. Rob used to like football. Sunday and the NFL.

Now I can't stand it.

Try not to think about Elaine Russ.

Try not to wonder: Where the hell has Alex Russ gone?

And is he going to get away?

SEE HOW SHE RUNS

* * *

"You see—the problem here is your number, your registration's just not going in."

The two men were hunched over the screen.

Kate let her hands slip from the counter. Oh, what is happening here? Please, God, she thought . . .

She backed up a step.

What am I going to do? Tell them to keep my license. I don't need it. You keep it. I'm going to get out of your nice state now and—

"Miss, I'm sorry. But your license number here—state of—"

There was great hollow cavity in Kate's chest. There was no air in the room. The buzz of the lights seemed to enter her head, cooking her brain. She heard the sizzle.

"Oh, hell—oops, ma'am, I'm sorry. I'm real sorry. I didn't see this. It says New Jersey, plain as day. Right there. And I put in the code for New York. Ain't that strange?"

The security guard looked up, smiling, grinning at Kate. Everything was okay, now everything was fine.

"You're getting old, Walt. That's the problem." The guard patted Walt on the back. Walt hit some more keys and then the printer started rattling, off to the side.

"That will be—er—one dollar and twenty-five cents, ma'am." Kate handed the man two dollars. "And I'm sorry for the little delay. Y'know, it was easier when we just told people how much they owed." He chuckled as if he had said something funny.

Kate smiled. Yes, that's funny. Anything . . .

The man handed Kate back her change, license and registration, and she turned and started for the door.

"Oh, ma'am. Wait." Kate stopped. "Wait. You forgot your receipt." Walt ripped something from the printer. He handed it to her.

Kate took it, saying thank you, and her voice sounded to her as if it came from a place far away, so thin and faint.

A place without air.

Suzy Tyler expected this fellow to have a nice car. But she stopped when she saw a battered heap, ugly gray under painted blotches and rusty holes that stood out even in the faint light of the roadside parking lot.

Tom went straight to the driver's door. Suzy thought he might open her door. She liked it when men acted like gentlemen. But it wasn't a priority.

The man just got in and waited. Suzy hesitated only a second and then got into the car, too, sliding into the big, icy seat. She had felt warm and excited in the bar. Now she felt her mood changing.

"I'm cold," she said, slipping into the tattered passenger seat. Her own car, a new red Corolla, was much nicer. The cold air had taken all the fun out of this for her.

The man looked at her.

He nodded as if he could tell that maybe Suzy would rather go home. Then he started his car. It slowly chugged to life while he kept hammering the gas pedal. Finally the engine roared and he sat back.

"I'm cold," she said again.

He turned to her. "I heard you. The heat takes a minute. Just hang on." She didn't want to be here now. He knew that. After getting him going, she didn't want to be here.

She couldn't tell, back at the bar, that his wires were pulled tight in this man. She had no way of knowing that now. He could feel them tighten some more and—for a moment—he was back at the house, doing what he had to do, the smell of gunpowder filling the rooms, the strange, slippery look of blood.

Suzy looked back at the Spur through the frosty windshield. She thought about getting out. Popping open the door and walking away. Music was still playing inside and the bartender would make her another nice drink.

"I think—"

"Listen," the man said, turning to her. "Listen. Have you ever been down south, to New Mexico?" The question seemed to come from nowhere.

Suzy nodded. A trickle of heat started sneaking out of the blower by her feet. She looked at the bar.

"You have anything to drink here?" she said. Some guys kept flasks in the glove compartment. Warm things up, get her over the hump.

The man didn't answer her. Instead he smiled again. "Have you ever gone there?"

She looked at him. With the heat on, an odor filled the car, stale, mildewy. A rotten smell.

"Yeah, sure. I went there on vacation. With a girlfriend. There was lots of pottery. Indians. Mexican food . . . if you like that—"

SEE HOW SHE RUNS

"Where'd you go?"

"Santa Fe. It was so damned expensive. Lots of tourists. Y'know, I'd like another drink. What do you say we—"

"There were a lot of people there?"

"Hey, why are you so interested in my vacation?"

He reached out and grabbed her arm, a tight, firm grip. But then his hand loosened and slid down to cover hers.

"I'm just . . . curious."

The smell in the car got worse. Suzy felt sick. She was ready to leave. Her hand fell to her lap, and his hand followed, rubbing her knuckles, massaging her hand, pressing down.

It was right over her crotch.

"Yes . . . sure, there's lots of tourists, skiing, festivals, expensive spas, I couldn't do—"

He pressed harder, and she slipped her hand away. But his hand stayed in her lap. She looked at it, the hand sitting there.

"Look, Tom, I—"

His hand moved. It crawled down and pushed under her skirt, like a small animal. It was an awkward move, nothing sweet and sensual about it. Suzy's body tensed.

Then he reached up and pressed his hand against her crotch. His other hand reached for a breast, pushing aside her jacket. Latching on. Suzy shook her head.

"No . . . I think I want to go home. I'm too—"

Tom leaned over. He covered her mouth with his, cutting off her words. She mumbled through his mouth. *No.* But she couldn't get the word out.

He popped her blouse open, the buttons flying off. His other hand pulled at her black panty hose, yanking them down.

"N-no," she said when his mouth slid off for a moment. But he was strong, ripping her panties down now, tugging a breast free from her bra.

She had said no. But she knew that no matter, he was going to do this anyway. She knew she was being raped.

He yanked her panties down. He moaned, speaking to her. Suzy tried to close her legs, but then he was on her. He pulled down his zipper, and it sounded so loud and clear. He moaned again.

Then his hand was free, and he grabbed her face.

She looked at him, at his eyes looking right at her. His hand squeezed her cheek, pinching her. She made a painful yelp.

That might not be all, she knew then. Rape might not be the only thing that could happen.

His mouth covered hers again, and his teeth mashed against her lips. He chewed at her lower lip, chewing, lightly, then harder. She cried now, a small child, a puppy, caught.

When she cried loudest, he moved on top of her. He entered her. She was dry, and the pain made her want to double up—if she could only move.

"Please, please," she said, when he pulled his mouth off her. Begging. It was the only thing she could do.

He shook his head. He bucked into her, back and forth. His eyes were filmy, lost. As if he was thinking about something else, remembering something else. He looked as if he wasn't even here.

He took a nipple and tweaked it, just a bit, then more, twisting it around, corkscrewing it while she yelped, her voice going higher and higher.

Her eyes were squinted—nearly shut—but Suzy saw that the car windows were all fogged up. If anyone looked over, they wouldn't see anything. And her yelping would sound like someone having a good time.

He twisted her nipple a bit more, and her yelp degenerated into crying.

Her head banged against the glass.

It lasted forever.

It lasted only minutes.

He stopped bucking. She had her eyes shut tight, squeezed tight. She tasted something on her lips, something warm and salty. Her body throbbed from the abuse.

He slid off her.

"Get out," he said.

She couldn't move.

"Get the *fuck* out," he said again. She felt him reach over her and open the door. The cold rushed in.

"Move," he said.

Suzy made sure that her shoes were on. She pulled her jacket across her chest. She got out and the car slammed behind her.

The car, the creepy gray car, chugged away, up the mountain road.

It was snowing. She felt the snow then, icy white flakes that landed on her face while she stood there, sobbing.

Kate carried Emma to the motel room. She stood by the door while Brian fiddled with the key.

"C'mon, Brian. She's heavy."

"I'm trying, Mom. I can't—"

After a few more turns the door popped open. Kate carried Emma inside and put her on the bed. The girl's eyes briefly fluttered open and then shut. Kate rolled the bedclothes around her.

She can sleep in her clothes, Kate thought.

Brian turned on the TV.

"No," Kate said. Brian turned to her and made a face as if he was about to argue. But he stopped. He can see my fear, she thought. Even he can see my crazy terror. Brian shut off the TV. He got into bed beside Emma, stealing back a bit of the covers.

"Good night, Mom."

Kate nodded. "Good night, sweetie," she said. Kate sat there, on the bed. It will get better, she thought. It has to get better. It isn't always going to be like this. This is the bad part. It will get better.

The bad parts always end. If you wait long enough.

She felt a tear run down her cheek. Funny . . .

I didn't know I was crying. Didn't even know it.

It will get better. . . .

I believed that once before, though. Didn't I? I believed that the bad part was over, and that things were going to get better.

I was wrong on both accounts.

Wrong-o . . .

The bad part hadn't yet begun. And things got much worse. . . .

10

When David came home, he was like a disoriented houseguest. An odd, distracted overnight visitor passing through on his way to nowhere.

He entered the house, this place that he said Kate would love.

"Ardsley is a good town," he had said. "Very good schools, the club—right *there*." She didn't question it. David was in charge. Later she wondered if he knew how lonely she would be, how hard it would be to meet people. There were just the kids, and David, growing darker every week.

He entered the house, slowly, holding on to her arm, needing her now. He peered around at the familiar environment, reaching out to touch things with his good hand.

(That's what everyone called it . . . his *good* hand. The left hand still had a tremor, it was still weak. It would be months before he could grab things with it, grab them and hold tight.)

The children had seen him, of course. They had visited David in the hospital. They had heard Dad say his fist words—"pido" meaning pillow, as in "fix my pillow." That made Emma laugh. And "foo" for food. Brian didn't laugh. He smirked at his father speaking baby talk.

Kate had chewed her lip, glaring at Brian. The boy kept his distance.

Emma, though, had seemed to like this new man, her daddy suddenly turned into a baby. She'd get on the bed and ask him questions about his bandage, taste his hospital food.

By the time David left the hospital and went to the Northern Westchester Stroke Center—a recovery center—he was talking in simple sentences. He couldn't get around without a walker. And he'd still suddenly fall asleep—he was on a lot of medication.

His head would fall to his chest, and Kate would be left there, sitting beside him, in the shadows made by the late-afternoon sun, wondering:

What do I do now?

Please, God . . . What can I do now?

She knew that there was only one answer. *You stay.* You do what you have to do. This happened, and you can't run away.

Kate, at night, alone, cried in her bed, muffling the sounds against her pillow, such a familiar comfort. Like a little girl. Still, the little girl trapped in a bad place.

The morning David came home, she cried while pulling the brush through her hair. Telling herself, ordering herself to *do* what had to be done.

Emma was excited. Brian was in his room, reading a book.

He said: "He's spooky, Mom. I *know* he's Dad—but he's so *weird.*"

Kate nodded.

Now David was here, wandering through the rooms, a ghost, a stranger. And when Kate spoke, her voice sounded as if it was coming from a million miles away. . . .

SEE HOW SHE RUNS

• • •

"Can I help you upstairs to rest?"

David nodded, but he kept moving into the kitchen. He used a cane now. In a few weeks, with more work, he wouldn't need that. He's doing great work, his therapist said. He might actually be able to walk normally . . . with just the slightest falter to his step.

David stopped in front of the refrigerator. He reached out and touched the door. He fingered the magnets, some with photographs—Kate and the children at the zoo, a family hike only months before the accident.

(That's what everyone called it, the *accident*, as if David had been hit by a truck, rear-ended, smashed through the windshield.)

He touched one magnet, and it slipped off the refrigerator door and clattered to the floor.

"Oh," he said. "It f-fell. I—"

He looked around. It was still hard for him to communicate. It took time to get out his ideas. The words were heavy bricks he had to pick up, move into place, one at a time—

Kate hurried to pick up the magnet. "Don't worry," she said lightly. "It's—"

He reached down and pushed her away. With his good hand, he pushed her head, just a bit—and in her crouch, off balance—she fell back. She rolled back, smashing against the wall.

"*I* get it," he said. "I—" Searching, for a more precise phrase. "I *can* get it."

Kate landed on her bottom. She looked up and Brian was at the door, looking at his father, then at her, on the floor. Kate flushed.

"I—I can *get* it," he said.

She nodded as David bent over and picked up the round magnet. He held it with his good hand. She watched him turn and look at Brian. He held the magnet in his hand.

She expected him to smile. *Look, I did it*. But his face was angry.

That was the first time that Kate had the thought: Nothing's changed. He's the same person I was going to divorce. Had to divorce. Because I didn't know him. But it was only a short time before she started to think: No, that's not quite true.

Not the same. He's different, and now it's worse.

• • •

Money wasn't a problem.

Kate found herself part of an extensive team of people devoted to David's recovery. David's mother and father spared no expense.

There was the physical therapist, a burly, squat Italian man in a sweat outfit who laughed and cajoled David into exercising every muscle. The den was filled with exercise equipment, and soon Kate grew used to the sound of David working out, making the weights rattle and clatter as he pulled and pushed on bars.

A speech therapist attacked his language difficulties. She was young, younger even than Kate, a pretty brunette who told her, "He's so funny! Your husband's *very* funny."

Yes, Kate thought. Then you take him. You sit and have dinner with him while he asks his slow-witted questions, while I cut his roast beef, while he watches and checks if I make a mess of it, ready to yell at me.

You take him.

The neurologist called once a week, collecting a sizable check from David's family. A nurse visited daily, a brusque black woman who didn't have a smile in her repertoire of facial expressions.

Kate was part of the team. Everything they did, she was supposed to do at other times. Read to him. Talk—all the time—keep talking, keep the flow of language speeding toward him. Encourage him to walk. Get him out of the house.

Be positive, talk of the future.

One night Brian ran upstairs, away from her. He wanted to plan his birthday celebration and Kate was distracted. He ran up the stairs, yelling, kicking at the door, saying, "You don't have any time for me, Mom. It's always *Dad*. His stupid exercises. It's always *him*."

Kate tried to explain. It's what I have to do. She couldn't tell Brian that she felt guilty. She couldn't tell him that it's hard to take care of someone you don't love, someone you should love. It's hard when everyone else seems to care and you don't, when—

I just wanted out, and now I'm here.

Trapped. Forever . . .

She found Brian and sat with him, talking. We're together in this, she thought. You . . . me . . . and Emma.

At night it was the worst.

The neurologist had mentioned it, smiling, nearly smirking. Kate had asked about sex. She needed to know. What if something

SEE HOW SHE RUNS

happened . . . while they were making love.

"You know," the doctor said, "sometimes recovering stroke victims have a *tremendous* increase in their sex drive. We're not totally sure where *that* comes from." More laughter. Isn't that funny? He talks and eats like a baby, yet he's horny all the time.

Now, ain't that a laugh riot?

"Probably something to do with the inhibition center in the brain. We see it especially in hemiplegics." The doctor looked up. A brilliant neurologist, one of the country's best. Enjoying her embarrassment. "You may find yourself, er, busier than normal."

Kate nodded.

Nothing happened the first few nights. Probably because Kate fell asleep, turning away from David. He sat up, watching TV. The TV was always on, as if it had just been invented. Game shows. Soap operas. Stupid sitcoms, all the day and on into the night, when celebrities Kate didn't know came and sat on Arsenio's couch and talked about their careers, their glittering careers.

The third night David shut the bedroom TV off.

Kate tensed.

He turned to her. She felt the bed shift. She heard the rustle of blankets. He touched her breast with his good hand, a clumsy caress. He whispered in her ear. Maybe it was supposed to sound cute. He said, "Hello." Like a little kid. *Hello . . . Are you there?*

He squeezed her breast roughly. The hand, his arm was strong— all those weights banging up and down.

Tentatively he brought his other hand around and brushed her side awkwardly.

No, Kate thought. I've got to work through this. It's natural, they told her. Natural to have some problems, some difficult feelings. That's normal.

It's okay not to get turned on.

She chewed her lip. Then he pressed against her back, rubbing his erection against her. He squashed one of her breasts against her body.

Got to get through this.

She turned to him. She reached down and grabbed him, stroking him. She heard his breathing quicken. For a moment she thought of trying to hurry and finish him this way. The idea, the thought of him sliding on top of her . . . no, she'd have to get on top of him. That was clear.

I'm dry, she thought. *Can't do this—*

She leaned close. "I have to put something in," she said, her hand moving on, up and down, hoping it would end. But then she slid out of bed, into the dreamlike glow made by the blue bathroom light. She had some lubricant there, and her diaphragm, sitting in cornstarch, waiting.

It's been a while, she thought.

She went back to him. And she made love to him, doing what she had to, part of the team, helping bring David back to the world of the living.

David hit Kate for the first time only one week after he had come home.

Emma was at her nursery school and Brian was on a class trip to the Museum of Natural History. The physical therapist had left, calling good-bye to her, signaling Kate that she was on again. *Back on duty.*

Kate got up from the kitchen table and walked into the living room. David was planted in front of the big Sony TV watching a game show, sitting zombielike in front of the tube.

He didn't look up at her. She had a feeling . . . as if he were mad at her for something she did, as if he were holding a grudge. Pouting, sitting on the couch. She stood to the side.

"David—don't you think you should do some exercises. Maybe we could do some reading—"

Pat the bunny. Go, dog, go. Dog. Big dog. Little dogs . . . filled with the simple words he was beginning to recognize.

She took a step toward the TV and shut it off.

"Turn it on," he said, an order.

Kate walked closer to him. "C'mon, David, let's do something, and—"

It was completely unexpected. His hand, the good hand, flew up and slapped at her face. It landed squarely, with a loud noise.

She opened her mouth, ready to yell, but he beat her to it.

"T-turn on the TV," he said. Then louder, his voice bellowing, so loud Kate felt herself shrinking back from him: "Turn on the f-fucking TV!"

Sometimes they curse, they said. *Curses, foul language . . . just kind of comes out. It happens. . . .*

She backed away. She walked to the TV. There was a remote somewhere, always getting lost. Or maybe he had it, she thought. Maybe he just wanted her to do this.

SEE HOW SHE RUNS

She pressed the power button. The TV flashed to life, and there was applause, and music. A model was fondling a red car, its curves outclassed by her sleek, shimmering shape.

Kate's face stung. She was sure there was a red mark there. She backed out of the room and didn't go to a mirror.

I don't want to see.

With every step away, she thought: Nothing's changed.

She went back to the kitchen.

The next time he hit her, Brian saw it.

Emma was still sitting out in the living room, dawdling, her dolls scattered around the floor. Kate was in the dining room cutting David's chicken.

He started shaking his head. She looked at him, waiting for him to say something. But his eyes glared and his face turned red. He opened his mouth as if he was going to say something.

"What's wrong, Dad?" Brian said. Kate felt the horrible fear that ran through Brian. This isn't fair, she thought. "What's—"

David looked down at his plate.

He shook his head. "That's n-not cutting. That's not—"

From nowhere, his hand came up—his *other hand*—flew up and pushed the plate of food off the table onto the floor.

"You're p-p-pulling it part. Damn . . . you—"

The words failed him. And now, suckered in, Kate was still there, bent over the table, the plate, now gone, now invisible, and she felt his hand slam at her, so strong, stronger every day. This time it sent her reeling back, falling against the refrigerator.

Brian stood up. "Don't!" the boy yelled. "Don't hurt Mom!"

Kate leaned into the refrigerator.

"Don't hit Mom!"

Kate heard the sound of Emma running into the kitchen. She quickly straightened herself. She felt her face. Touched the mark.

Just like her mother used to . . .

It will bruise this time, she knew. It was more than a slap.

Emma ran into the kitchen. Kate looked over at Brian, then to David. Her husband was looking at the boy, his mouth open. Looking at the boy, and Kate saw the anger in his face.

No. You can hit me, she thought. That's okay. That's . . . all right.

"Brian," Kate said quietly. Have to keep calm. Everything's okay. No problem here. "Brian, go upstairs."

The boy shook his head. "No, Mom. He might hit you again."

"*Brian—do as I say*. Go to your room."

Emma stood at the entrance. "Daddy dropped his plate? How did Daddy—"

Brian started moving, cagily moving past David, whose eyes followed him. He left, and Emma came to David and tugged at his sleeve.

"Daddy, what happened to your food? Did you drop it."

David turned to Emma. Kate watched him turn and she saw the color leave his face. He nodded.

"Yes." He raised his hand up in the air. "It fell." He looked up at Kate. "But Mommy's going to c-clean it. She's—"

Looking at Kate, right at her.

"She's going to fix me a new plate."

Kate nodded. She went to the cupboard, grabbing a clean plate, then clean utensils from a drawer, thinking.

Of course I will.

This is nothing. The doctors told me this would happen. It's nothing. It's what has to happen, this anger, the flashes of temper. It's all normal.

"Adjustments," the neurologist told her, "will have to be made."

11

Kate had gone out shopping. At least that's what she told David.

I'm going shopping. Emmie needs some clothes, and I'll get some school things for Brian.

But it had been only to get out of the house, to breathe the air, to walk through the mall and not feel this incredible pressure, the sound of David moving through the house, the steady *clang-clang* of the weights, the TV babbling, crazy, a constant companion.

Brian wanted to come, but Kate felt guilty leaving David alone. Besides, she reasoned, Brian had a project to do for school, a

SEE HOW SHE RUNS

report on Utah. Every kid got a state, and Brian got Utah. The whole family knew so much about Utah now. All about Brigham Young and the city he built in the desert.

It was nearly dark when Kate brought Emma home, loaded down with clothes that she barely remembered buying.

She pulled into the driveway. There should have been lights on all over the house. But there was only one light in the kitchen, and another upstairs. Kate killed the engine.

Her hands held the steering wheel tightly.

"What is it, Mommy? What's wrong?"

Kate shook her head. "Nothing, sweetheart." Kate got out and opened the rear door to get at Emma's child seat. Nearly three, Emmie still faced another year of being strapped in.

Safe and snug.

Kate took Emma's hand and led her to the house.

There's something wrong, she thought. There's something wrong here.

She started to hurry, pulling Emma along.

Or maybe there's nothing. Just my imagination . . .

The young minister at the stone Episcopal church—he was not much older than she was—had said, "Don't let your imagination run away. Things will be hard, but don't imagine them to be worse than they are."

He smiled. There was no solace in talking with him. Everyone felt sorry for David.

She went up the steps, pulling Emma to the door, turning the knob. The house felt cold, as if the heat had been turned off.

She stopped at the doorway.

"David . . . Brian?"

A strange memory floated through her head. Staying up late one night when she was a girl, curled up with a bag of Jiffy Pop popcorn watching the movie *In Cold Blood*, watching that family in Kansas die.

You never know.

She could get so scared. . . . There had been a prison breakout a few years back. Three convicts got out and hid in the woods surrounding Ardsley until they decided to take over a house. They kept a family prisoner, torturing them, beating them.

The wife and a daughter had been raped.

Eventually the convicts left the house and were caught. And somehow—the family had to go on.

Another few steps into the dark living room. "Brian. Brian, where are you?" Kate turned on a light.

"It's cold, Mommy. Where's Daddy? Where's—"

Out of nowhere there was a clang. It made Kate jump. Then another. *Clang . . . clang.* David was upstairs, at his weights, and—

Kate started up the stairs, slowly, grabbing the handrail. Emma started to follow, but Kate quickly turned to her. "No. No, Emmie. Stay down here."

"But—"

"Stay *here*."

Then back up, her every step accompanied by the rhythmic clatter of the weight machine.

"David," she said, and she went into the room filled with his apparatus, the best his family's money could buy, over five thousand dollars' worth of Nautilus equipment.

David was wearing only shorts. Kate saw the glistening wet sheen on his torso. He was pulling on a metal bar with his good arm, yanking it up and down. She saw beads of sweat on his brow.

His eyes were on fire.

He looked at her and—without a thought—she stepped back.

She opened her mouth. I have to ask, she thought. I must—but then she heard the sound, the muffled sound of crying coming from Brian's room. . . .

He was in the closet.

Kate opened the door, and Brian was squatting in the closet, on the floor, curled up.

"Brian—what is this? What's wrong?"

But I know that. Don't I? thought Kate. I know what's wrong—

Brian looked up, his tears picking up the light, his eyes sunken, watery. "He hit me, Mom. He *hit* me, slapped me. He said I was *stupid*. Just because—"

The boy started crying again. Kate crouched low to him.

"Oh, God, Brian, baby, sweetheart. I'm sorry, I—"

The clanging had stopped. She didn't notice that. But now she heard the steps behind her, and the telltale creak of the floorboards.

And David's voice.

"He didn't p-put my weights back. It was a mess in there."

SEE HOW SHE RUNS

Kate turned back to David. She nodded. Brian sometimes went into the exercise room and played with the weights, futilely straining to make his boy muscles grow, impatient for age and hormones to turn him into a man.

She turned back to Brian and saw a mark on his face. A puffy area. She whispered, "He hit you, Brian? Daddy hit your face?"

The boy nodded. "And he kicked me, Mom. *He kicked me!*"

There's a corner here, Kate thought.

I've reached a corner, a turning point. This time, *this* event marks the place, a beginning . . . and an end.

She turned to David. But he had already walked back to the exercise room. Emmie played downstairs, her singsong voice traveling up, so clear, so sweet, so free of worry. Kate reached in and put her arms around Brian and then she slowly pulled him out of the closet.

It was only a matter of time after that.

The end occurred after Emma's birthday party. It wasn't really a kid's birthday. It was all of David's family, his parents, aunts and uncles, most of them connected to the Cowell family's brokerage business.

Kate had nobody. Not here, not at the party. There was just her father now, still in Schuyler, New York, a dull-eyed man who smiled when he saw her and then slipped into sleep. The man who used to rule their house, who made Kate look at the stars and wish to fly away.

Kate was alone.

All day she was waiting on these people, fetching things for them. Another drink, more hors d'oeuvres? They all admired how well David was doing, what a *fine* job he'd done getting himself back together.

"Why," his father said loudly, "it won't be long before Dave is back at the brokerage. You and the kids must be real proud, eh, Kate?" he said. "Real proud."

She nodded, her hands filled with half-empty glasses.

Kate found herself looking at these people, at David's father, his mother, wondering. They sent their boy to Whitside, a top Manhattan prep school. Then David went to Columbia, living at home while he got his business degree, then his law degree. He had everything.

She caught David looking at her, and she only saw—along with the smile he wore—his anger.

I'm doing something wrong. And when everyone's gone—

Emma got pretty dresses for gifts, and a beautiful doll—Samantha, dressed in a late-Victorian gown of crimson. She sat on David's lap—and Kate felt this urge to go over and gently pry her off. No, honey. Don't sit there. . . .

Emma squealed as each expensive new present was opened.

Expensive . . . Kate thought about the money, so much money. It was something she had to think about. Because—because, she thought, if I've reached that turning point, I will need money. There may be groups, organizations to help women. Sure, there must be.

It will all work out.

Someone tapped her shoulder.

It was David's mother. Her gray hair was sleek, shining. At sixty, she was still an imposing figure, painfully thin and clear-eyed.

Kate felt something. Just talking to the woman, something familiar—

"Katherine," she said, always preferring a bit of formality between them. The women's face was serious, set—but she made a smile and said, "The party is wonderful, dear. And little Emma—you and David must be *very* proud, she's absolutely—"

David was tickling Emma, making her squeal as she opened each new box, each new toy, making her squeals even louder. Brian stood off to the side, watching.

Their eyes met. Kate looked at Brian. . . .

Familiar, this feeling. As if suddenly it was—

"But, Katherine, I'm concerned about David." The voice was commanding, harsh now. "Is he happy? Does David have everything he needs? Dr. Neuwirt says he's made remarkable progress. But—please don't take this the wrong way—how are things between the two of you?"

The chill . . . And then Kate understood. How it must have been for David, having everything, having nothing. Now carrying on the family tradition . . .

Kate looked away from Brian, to Emma and her dad.

She opened her mouth. "Oh—we're fine. I mean, it's been hard. He still fights about doing his exercises, writing . . . and reading, and he won't—"

Still colder, and the clear-eyed woman nodded, probing deeper. "Yes, but between the two of *you*? I'd like to know that everything is good for my son."

SEE HOW SHE RUNS

For her son . . . Not the family, not the children. Certainly not me.

Kate chewed her lip. I need someone to talk to. Not the young minister, with his beard and his glib answers. How come I have no friends? What happened to all my friends? What happened to my life?

But she realized: I left them behind and entered David's world. There were only his business acquaintances and the wives of his business acquaintances, and their children.

"What is it, Katherine?"

Kate felt her eyes going filmy. God, she thought. Not here. The living room filled with noise, a terrible swirl of noise.

Kate took a breath. "It's just that—well, you see—" She lowered her voice. "The doctors told me that there would be this problem with his temper. They said that happens. They warned me, and—"

When she turned back to David, he was looking right at her, staring, not smiling anymore, not tickling Emma but holding her tight.

Kate shook her head.

"Go on," the woman said. An order, like David speaking, commanding Kate to speak.

Kate shook her head. "I'm *afraid*. I mean, he's hit me. And now—"

Kate chewed her lip. Someone said something to David, and he turned away, freeing Kate from his stare. She whispered: "And now the children. He—he—"

David's mother grabbed Kate's arm. She squeezed it.

"Katherine, you listen to me. You listen—"

When Kate looked at the woman, she saw the fierceness there. This had been a mistake, Kate knew. A big mistake.

"My David has been through a *terrible* thing and—he's coming along just fine."

The woman looked over at her son. Of course, Kate thought, *her son*. What could I have been thinking to talk with her, to say anything to her? I must be . . . crazy.

The woman turned back to Kate. "He'll continue to do fine if he has your support—" A squeeze on her arm. "You should have only *one* thought, for you, or your family. And that is to make sure David gets completely well."

Kate nodded, everything growing filmier. She nodded, just wanting this woman, this crone, this clear-eyed vulture lady to

let her go. It was a all mistake. *I shouldn't have said anything.*
She turned to Emma.
I was worried about my kids.
With a nod, signaling her agreement, the woman released Kate's arm.
"Mommy, Mommy, did you see the doll I got. It's 'mantha."
So cute, the way little kids say things. So cute. *'Mantha...*
"Come see! Daddy has it—"
Emma tugged on Kate, pulling her away, to the doll, to David, who waited for her....

Then the horror was there. In her house, something from a nightmare—but so real.
Kate had stayed in the kitchen, cleaning until there was nothing left to clean. She knew David waited for her. He was angry. It didn't go away. He didn't forget.
In her fear, her desperation, she thought: Maybe I could do something to turn him on. Distract him . . . put on something sexy. He was always grabbing at her, always horny. I could do that, she thought.
She ran a sponge along the countertop. She heard David standing behind her, breathing.
"What are you d-doing?" he said. He spoke more clearly every week now. He could even pick up things with his other hand.
"Still cleaning," she said lightly. "It was a big party."
He took a step into the kitchen, mimicking her. *"Still cleaning."* A sick parody of a complaining housewife. Kate felt old, older than any of his wrinkled aunts, older than his mother. She had to tell herself, I'm only—what?
Twenty-nine.
"Just *cleaning*," he said again. Another step. Kate tensed.
"I don't mind," she said, smiling.
He tilted his head. "You didn't like the party?"
"No, it was fine, it was—"
Another step, and she was cornered. "You don't like my f-family." His eyes flashed at his stammer, angry at himself.
She made herself smile, to laugh even. What an absurd thought. "I like them fine, David. I'm just tired and . . . I think we should . . ."
He stood next to her. "I saw you. I saw *that* face. You didn't like the party." His eyes went wide. Instinctively Kate looked down to his hand.

SEE HOW SHE RUNS

His good hand.

It was clenched.

"David," she said quietly, her eyes meeting his. Then she looked down again. It was moving. "David, don't—"

Hit me, she was going to say. *Don't hit me.* But she had to raise her arms quickly to ward off the blow. And David's powerful fist smashed into the side of her head.

She yelped, yes—she thought—as if she had backed into an open drawer. *So* clumsy of me. What a klutz, I really should be careful.

"Don't hit me!" she said, but in a low voice. Because she didn't want to yell, to scream. To awaken the children. I don't want them to see this.

While she was protecting her head his fist rammed into her midsection. She couldn't breathe. She doubled up. The sponge bounced from her hand to the floor. She saw sparks jumping on the linoleum. She tried to suck air back into her lungs.

She was on her knees.

Her fingers splayed on the linoleum. She thought that David was going to kick her. But instead he walked away, walking nearly normally now.

Such a good recovery.

She spit at the floor. There was something salty in her mouth, some phlegm. She spit at the floor and saw the filmy dollop of red.

That night she slept on the couch. She woke to Brian touching her cheek. He was crying.

"I—I fell," she lied. In his eyes, in her son's eyes she knew that she couldn't postpone it any longer. Something had to be done. No matter what people say, she thought. No matter how guilty I might feel. I have to save my kids... myself.

She thought that she had time to make plans, to see people. Kate thought she could plan. She slept on the couch again the next night, and the next. Emma was confused but accepted her explanation.

I don't want to wake Daddy.

She thought she had time.

I can stay away from him. And Brian can stay away. There will be time. I can think about what to do. I can get help. There are people, groups that can help.

That was her idea.
When she thought that she had time.

But one night she woke up in the odd, shadowy stillness of the living room. She had heard a sound. She thought: A prowler. Someone's outside, or *no*—the stupid cat is clawing at the backdoor.

She lay on the cold couch, two scratchy blankets pulled tight.

Her eyes were open wide as if that would help her hear. She listened for the sound again. She waited, but the only noise was her breathing, and—inside her head—the thumping of her pulse. Her fingers were cold, clutching the rough blankets tight, and—

No, there *is* a noise! She heard something upstairs. Was it someone talking? Was Brian up? Sometimes he had nightmares.

Lately he had nightmares. It was new. Since his father came home.

What a bad wife, they'd say. How could you think of leaving the man, after such a heroic battle to get back his life. They didn't live with the nightmares. What a bad wife . . .

Another noise upstairs. Suddenly Kate realized that she was downstairs . . . and her children were upstairs.

She slipped out of the protective warmth of the blankets. A car moved down the block and a milky light filled the living room and then quickly disappeared.

She started up the stairs, hurrying, her feet feeling the thick pile of the carpet.

Brian's room was first, and she saw him curled up, his quilt a tangled mess, wrapping him safe and secure in a snug cocoon.

Then she moved past the master bedroom. She glanced in, just to check on David. The bed looked flat, a flat sea marred by the irregular bulges of the sheet and the electric blanket.

He's up, she thought, getting a drink, wandering around. She almost turned then and went back downstairs.

I don't need him screaming at me, raising his fist—

But there was this noise. The bathroom light was off. And the noise was ahead, in the small bedroom, Emma's bedroom.

Kate shook her head. She whispered, "No." She flew down there, ran to the girl's room.

Maybe Emma awoke. Maybe the girl called out, and—I wasn't there. So David went in. She likes him. He's like a big doll with her. She wants to please him.

SEE HOW SHE RUNS

She entered the room. David sat on the edge of the bed. And Emma—was all curled up, sound asleep.

David had his hand on her. She's asleep, Kate thought. Then why is—David hadn't heard her, didn't know Kate was standing there.

She heard the sound.

David's arm moved up and down.

In the darkness, she saw him move, saw him masturbating—

That's what he's doing. Right there, sitting next to Emma. Sitting next to my sweet Emma . . .

Oh, God, oh, sweet God, no—

She screamed.

"Get out!" she yelled. "You—get out of here!"

She jumped on his back. Emma, such a deep sleeper, made a groaning noise. "Get—the hell—out! Get out—"

Kate pounded his back with her fists, over and over. Pounded them. "You get away!"

She shrieked. He slapped back at her, and she fell to the ground.

By the time Brian ran into the room, David had left. Emma rubbed her eyes and said, "What is it, Mommy? What's wrong?"

Brian stood by the doorway.

Now Kate knew.

She had been wrong.

There was no time for planning.

PART TWO

ACROSS THE DIVIDE

12

Jesse Sawyer grabbed the handset of the portable two-way radio and clicked it on, checking that the batteries worked. He charged them every night, but still this checking was something he did. So when Annie asked him, always worrying, "Is your radio charged?" he could answer yes.

Annie was still asleep, buried under a heavy quilt in the bedroom at the back of the small house, protected by the dark and the blanket.

When she got up, she'd turn on the radio and wait for him to check in. And they'd talk while she drank his coffee.

Jesse pulled on his Gore-Tex parka. It had three different layers, two with plastic zippers and a final layer that buttoned. It was the warmest coat he'd ever owned, and today he'd need it.

More snow had fallen last night. He'd have to make his way to the Mountain Pass Road, and then climb up, past the timberline to the west side of Mt. Truchas. Then, having checked the road, he'd be free to come back home and sit by his radio, monitoring anyone who might be lost in the mountains, anyone who might get in trouble and have a two-way radio.

That was the extent of his responsibility. This part of the Sangre de Christo Mountains, a broad strip that wandered down toward Santa Fe and Pecos, was the section of the National Forest where he was the assigned forest ranger.

The Rio Grande Valley cut the range in half, and this rugged spur of the Rockies was his baby.

He'd check the road to make sure that no one got stranded, some stupid tourist looking for the ultimate cross-country experience, sliding ass end off the road into a snowbank, trapped while the temperature dropped way below zero and the wind found every tiny crack in a car's frame.

There were other things that concerned Jesse.

He took a sip of his coffee, scalding hot, the way he liked it.

In a minute he'd dump what remained into a plastic cup with a special bottom that fit into a holder inside his Land Rover.

He hoped he wouldn't be gone too long.

He looked around in the early-morning darkness for his gloves, also Gore-Tex, wondrously warm no matter how cold it got.

He walked into the dark bedroom. He once left without kissing Annie good-bye. And—somehow—she remembered, confronting him when he came back, telling him not to ever do that again.

"I want my good-bye kiss," she said sleepily.

He smiled. She raised an arm to him and then, from the other side, her stunted half arm that ended in a rounded nub. She pulled him tight.

He wondered if a kiss from him would still mean so much to Annie if they had a kid. It wasn't something they talked about anymore.

He bent down and kissed her. She stirred.

"More snow?"

"Yes. Only a few inches. Just a dusting."

She opened one eye. "Be careful."

He rubbed her cheek with a gloved hand and then started out of the room.

"And turn on the radio."

As he passed by the two-way radio he turned on the master switch and there was an oddly soothing hiss of white noise filling the house with the warmth of an electronic fireplace.

Jesse grabbed his coffee and walked out the front door.

Alex Russ decided to stop driving.

The damned snow swirled in front of his windshield, a dry snow that bounced off the glass and swirled in front of his car.

"Shit," he said. He wanted to keep moving.

But Russ pulled to the side of the road. Already he had gotten lost somewhere near a town called Monte Vista. A wrong turn, and he was looking at a black wall of mountain ahead.

There's no way south. Not here, he had figured. I need a goddamn road map, that's what I need. I'll have to find a gas station and get a map.

He was making plans, thinking. That was good. . . .

The man at the gas station had asked, "Where are you heading? Maybe I can help."

Russ almost told the old fart to mind his own business. Who the hell did he think he was? But that wouldn't be good.

SEE HOW SHE RUNS

I'm starting to think now.

No more screwing around. This is new. From now on *I think*. Because if I don't start thinking, then they're going to find me.

"Got a girl waiting for me." Russ grinned.

"What town?"

Russ had smiled. Simple question. Got to answer it, he thought. But I wish I had another name of a town, wish I had the damned map. . . .

Russ kept smiling.

"Down near Santa Fe."

Shit, he thought. Now, what does that mean? Near Santa Fe? *Near Santa fucking Fe.*

The old man's face had wrinkled up at that. "You're not going to try to get to New Mexico . . . not tonight?"

There's something wrong with that? Russ thought. What is this, am I screwing up again, not thinking? *What the hell's wrong?*

Russ smiled, and the man smiled back. "Don't know—my girlfriend's waiting." Russ kept grinning. "Y'know."

The man nodded. "Well, I understand that, son. Sure I do. Best be careful. There's a mountain storm coming. You'll run into some snow if you hit the highlands. Here—"

The old fart got off his chair and went over to a rack of maps, old maps, bent from years of people pawing through them. The man pulled one out.

"Now, there's a couple of routes you could take. A couple, but here—let's see if we can get you through the valley and keep as low as possible. It's a bad time of year, son, to be on the mountain roads . . . bad."

Russ had hunched over, watching the man's bony finger outlining a possible route. But he didn't worry about snow. That was the least of his worries.

And now—damn—he was stopped by it.

He guessed he had crossed the border, but with all the snow flying around, he hadn't been able to see shit. I'm in fucking New Mexico, he thought, Then where the hell's the sun? Sunny New Mexico . . .

But at least I'm thinking now. Not like last night, screwing that girl. That was stupid. Don't know what's wrong with me. I'm trying to put things back together, and that wasn't smart.

Everything's going to be okay now, though, because I'm thinking.

He sat there, watching his fuel level creep down. Can't sit here for long, he thought.

He heard a sound. Distant, muffled by the sealed windows and doors of his car, and by the snow. Russ turned around. His back windshield was completely covered.

But he heard something, a steady thumping noise. He opened the door, and there, on the road, just behind him, was a truck with a plow and bubble light swirling round on top.

The dry snow flew into Russ's face.

The truck slowed and then stopped.

Jesse kept the Land Rover in a small unheated garage a few yards from the house. Behind the garage was an antenna that stretched higher than the nearby blue spruces.

Tracks dotted the new snow outside, bighorn, elk, and—

Jesse stopped. He saw the other tracks a bit farther from the house, the oversized cattracks of the cougar.

Every day the cat edges a bit closer, he thought. Winter was tough, the game moved down, and the cougars followed. The range was getting smaller. Condos crawled up well into the valley, and ski lodges filled the mountains.

Thousands of acres of brush, the tall reedy grass favored by the browsing animals, had disappeared. The seasonal die-offs were bigger.

The cougars got braver.

Jesse walked over to the cougar tracks. He knelt down and touched one. Then he quickly looked up. The sky was turning light with the sun hidden behind the still-gray morning clouds.

But—he told himself—there's no reason the cat couldn't be around.

No, sir. None at all.

Jesse's rifle, a Winchester his father had passed on to him, was in the truck.

He looked around. But there were only the tracks, as if they had appeared by magic. Only tracks, no animals. Jesse stood up and spoke to himself. "Nobody here but us forest rangers." He started back to the garage.

Last month a jogger was running a tough loop around a hill down near Galisteo. He was warming up for the Iron Man Competition—running a hundred-mile marathon, climbing hills, trekking through the desert, through mountain trails.

And the poor bastard must have stumbled into the path of a cougar.

Later everyone wondered what the hell the cougar was doing down near the town? The jogger could have seen the K mart out on Route 25 even as the cat pulled him down. That part was probably fast, a good swipe from the tremendous paw, and *wham*.

The jogger would have been quickly pinned to the ground.

The cougar should have moved on then. Bored, the cougar should have moved on. But food was getting tight, there were too many people, too many houses creeping up the mountains. There were too many people coming to the Southwest.

It was making the animals weird.

The cougar ripped the man apart. The next day a kid found the jogger with his midsection opened up, a human piñata. There were bite marks and gashes on his throat. Part of him was gone.

The cougar had eaten some of him.

The newspaper didn't publish any photos. How thoughtful . . . but they said that the victim's eyes were open. Wide open.

Yup . . . Had to be a bad experience, thought Jesse.

He looked around, spooking himself by thinking about it. It's bad enough that we have the snow up here, and the wind, and the ice on the roads. Now we have to worry about crazy cougars.

He shook his head and opened the garage. The door groaned noisily as it rolled up. He climbed into his Rover and started the engine. It coughed as if it had no intention of starting. But Jesse kept it well tuned, with fresh plugs and a strong battery. On the third try the Land Rover kicked into action.

He sat there, waiting for the engine to warm up, waiting for some heat to drift up from the vents.

"Need some help, fellow?"

Russ looked up through the flurry—the snow *was* lessening. It hadn't lasted long at all.

He shook his head at the guy sitting behind the wheel of the plow. "No. I just stopped. Couldn't see anything."

The man in the big plow nodded. He shook his head. "I got some asshole who likes his damn driveway plowed *first thing*." The man looked up. "The snow ain't hardly over, and hell, he wants a damn plow." He shrugged. "You best be careful ahead, though. The road goes down pretty steep. It gets nasty on some of those curves. Test your brakes and take it slow."

Russ nodded. Everyone was so free with their advice. Everyone always had so much fucking advice to give. . . .

"Hey," Russ said. "Tell me. Am I in New Mexico yet?"

The man grinned. "For the past fifteen miles you have been, pal. Don't you know where you're going?"

Know where I'm going . . . know where the fuck I'm going?

It was like being back in goddamn school. You got to do this, Alex. Got to work at this or you'll screw your fucking life up. Got to get it right.

Everyone knows so damn much.

"Oh, sure. Hey, thanks for the warning."

"You take care." The man in the truck grinned, nodded, and pulled away from Russ. Russ rolled up his window and watched him move down the road.

The flurry lessened until only a few stray flakes seemed to be falling, and then—so quickly, as if by magic—the sky was clear.

Russ put on his wipers, letting them struggle to throw the snow off the front windshield. He walked around to the rear of the car to push the snow off the back windshield with his elbow.

Watch the road. It get's nasty. Some bad curves ahead.

Everyone with the fucking advice . . .

Russ pushed at the snow.

Everyone always knows so damn much.

The back windshield was clear. He looked around. He had a thought.

It's quiet up here. Not many people. Quiet and dark and protected by all that black rock, rising high, well into the clouds.

I got to remember this. I may need a place like this. I've got to remember it. . . .

Jesse passed the timberline. His Rover had chains on all four tires, but still—when it hit spots where a thaw spread water across the road—the four-wheel-drive vehicle swiveled on the highway.

Every time that happened, Jesse's breath caught. There was no way to plan for it, no way to tell that under the snow ahead there was a fine sheen of glasslike ice ready to—*whoops!*—send the Rover sliding, to tease it close the edge.

He was on a section of Mountain Pass Road that probably hadn't seen anyone on it for the past day or two.

Still, there was no telling when someone might wander up from Santa Fe or Terrero, and then continue upward. There were plenty of warning signs posted, big signs that told any foolish explorers exactly what awaited them.

SEE HOW SHE RUNS

WARNING: THIS MOUNTAIN ROAD IS SUBJECT TO SUDDEN AND VIOLENT SNOW SQUALLS. ICY CONDITIONS AND SUDDEN CHANGES IN THE WEATHER ARE COMMON. PROCEED WITH EXTREME CAUTION.

There was something missing from the sign.

His Rover jiggled again, the chains surprised by another icy patch.

Cougars. No warning about cougars . . . He never saw a cougar on the road. The cats seemed to know that they were no match for cars and trucks.

Jesse took a curve, slowing down to crawl—10 mph. The grade was much steeper here. Up ahead, he saw the spot he wanted to check. He took the sharp curve and saw great brown shapes standing in the road. He was moving so slowly that he was able to stop easily.

Elk—three of them—all looked up at the same time. They didn't move. Jesse could see the outline of their ribs . . . they must be hungry. Not much fat on them.

They stood there, a big male with antlers that stretched two feet in each direction, a female, and another younger male.

Jesse waited. The big male shook his head, probably a signal of some kind, and then the trio galloped to the left, into the snowy brush, all of it probably picked clean. Winter was bad for these animals, and each week got worse and worse. . . .

After they were gone, Jesse pulled the Rover ahead. A gust of wind sent a spray of crystalline snow across his windshield. He slowed, threw the wipers on, and then, leaning forward, he saw what he was looking for.

He put the Rover into neutral and pulled on the brake. He picked up the two-way radio.

He pressed down the transmit button. "'Morning, Annie. Are you up yet? Over."

He took his finger off the button. After a few moments the radio crackled to life.

"Hi, Jess. I was going to get some more wood. Over."

Jesse thought about the footprints outside the house. "Don't worry about that," he said. "I'll be back soon. Over."

"I don't mind—over."

"Let me do it. Okay? Over." There was silence. He didn't want to tell her his stupid fears. There was no answer. He pressed down on the radio button again. "I'm sorry I snapped. I'd rather do it."

"Right," she said. Her voice changed, and something was gone. "Over."

"I'm looking at the Old Man's Nose," he said. "If you hear a gunshot and a rumble, don't worry. Over."

"Okay." Then: "Be careful. Over."

"Sure . . . See you soon. Over."

He got out of the Rover and slipped the radio into his back pocket. It was the deal he had with Annie. Where he went, the radio went. If ever there was an accident, he could reach back there, dig out the two-way radio, and call for help. And if he didn't answer her, she'd know something was wrong.

He slammed the Rover's door and walked to the side of the road, away from the cliff.

A thousand yards ahead and up from the road was a piece of rock called Old Man's Nose. With the new white snow dripping off it, the formation indeed looked like an old man's face, with a head full of snowy-white hair and this jagged, ugly nose.

During the summer yuppie climbers day-tripped up from Santa Fe with the best synthetic lines, pitons, hammers, and boots, and climbed the Nose.

Every day in summer there'd be a couple of climbers on the Nose.

Jesse walked a bit closer to it.

But now it was quiet, surrounded by snow. One large pile of snow was building at the top of the Nose. It was mostly formed by the regular snowfalls, but helped by the strange shape of the rock, there was now a large overhang. The Nose was dripping. . . . And that overhang would build and build—until eventually it fell onto the road.

Effectively closing it.

The warning signs said *nothing* about avalanches.

Jesse had to watch for avalanches. They could build in the gaps made by the folded layers of rock or along the jagged edge of faults that crisscrossed the Sangre de Christo range. They'd build, and when they started falling, they'd move at a hundred miles an hour, smashing trees and closing roads.

Jesse had several spots he watched.

It was time for this one to come down.

He walked back to the Rover and took his Winchester down from the gun rack. He dug in the pocket of his parka and put in a bullet. It might take a few shots. He wondered if he was getting too anxious to get the snowballs down, to stop the avalanches.

I worry too damn much, he thought.

SEE HOW SHE RUNS

He raised the gun and took aim at the top of the Nose, a mound of snow and ice, getting larger and larger.

Just my luck it will fall when some asshole comes cruising along.

He took aim on a spot at the center of snowy outcrop. He took a breath, held it, and fired.

The noise was loud, echoing off the slope, and Jesse lowered the gun. Nothing happened. It was as if he hadn't fired at all.

Could be it's so frozen that it isn't going anywhere. Not without something more explosive.

Jesse fitted another shell into his rifle. He raised it, took aim a bit lower. The snow looked ready to go. This should do it, he thought.

He fired.

Again he quickly lowered his rifle. Nothing happened. It was quiet. A fine spray of snow flew at his face. He was about to turn away when he heard a sound, a lazy cracking sound, as if a giant tree trunk was snapping in two. He watched the mass of snow and ice move, in slow motion, breaking away from the Old Man's Nose.

It fell in one great chunk, tumbling to the rocks, breaking up into smaller pieces, dissipating before it reached the road. A few icy chunks rolled onto the road and sat there. Small enough for Jesse to move by hand.

Another few weeks and they would have made a nasty avalanche.

Jesse lowered his gun. His face—the only part of his body uncovered—stung from the wind and the cold. He turned and walked back to the Rover, thinking about the warmth of his small house, and of a second cup of coffee.

13

Kate looked at the mirror and smiled.

I'm somewhere in the middle of Kansas, somewhere in the middle of a great flat plain leading to the mountains. The town was called . . . Medford. The sign as she drove in said, WELCOME TO MEDFORD, KS. THE TOWN WITH A FRIENDLY SMILE!

Emma knocked on the bathroom door.

"Are we going now, Mom?"

Kate shook her head. Not quite yet. "In a bit, pumpkin." Kate brought her hand up to her hair, fingering the long blond strands. She loved to comb her hair, pulling at her long tresses, counting, thinking.

"Brian found a big Indian outside, Mommy. I can *see* him."

"We'll see lots of Indians, Emma." Kate corrected herself. "Lots of Native Americans."

But she didn't hear Emmie at the door anymore. The girl was probably standing by the motel window, looking out at the wooden Indian across the street. Kate had seen it last night when they drove up to the motel. The giant wooden Indian, stone-faced, looked right at the motel.

Probably the big tourist attraction in Medford, she thought. The town with a friendly smile and a giant wooden Indian.

We're headed to cowboyland, Kate thought. Pickup trucks and ten-gallon hats. Urban cowboys and—

Mountains. The mountains were ahead. After I cross those, Kate thought, I'll feel safe. The mountains will be a wall cutting us off from everything.

She looked down at the narrow counter above the sink. She saw the long, sharp shears. Brand-new shears she had bought, shiny, new, and sharp so that they'd cut easily. She picked them up.

She made them click a few times, like a real barber, she thought. *Snip, snip*—now this won't hurt a bit. . . .

SEE HOW SHE RUNS

Kate grabbed a handful of her long hair, and with only a pause to take a breath, she snipped it off. There, she thought. I'm lopsided. Now I have to continue, I *have* to finish this.

She reached over and—more awkwardly—cut an equal amount of hair from the other side. She looked in the mirror. I look horrible, she thought. She glanced down and saw her hair on the floor.

I'll have to clean that up, she thought. Make sure that there are no traces.

So the cleaning lady doesn't go running to the manager. Look . . . look! Holding the clumps of hair.

Kate let the just-cut clump fall to the cracked linoleum floor.

She cut some more of her hair, first one side, then the other, trying inexpertly to keep the sides in balance, wondering how much she should take off to create a different look, and finally cutting too much, just to get her head to look symmetrical.

When she was done, she had short hair, a boylike blond cap on the top of her head. She laughed. Then, still laughing, she started crying.

Mari Comas caught up to Dr. North during his rounds on the pediatrics ward. "Dr. North—I called your office. They said you were here."

North was in his sixties, Mari guessed, maybe older. He had a ruddy face and snow-white hair, but he didn't look as if he was anywhere near considering retirement.

"I thought you'd come by," North said quietly. He walked to a bed. A young girl was sitting up reading a book, *The Bobbsey Twins and the Lost Wreck.* Mari glanced at the girl.

He expected me, she thought. Here I was trying to figure out how to explain this to him, to make him understand. And, hell, he *expected* me to come, waiting, prepared.

Normally Dr. North was friendly. Now he simply nodded to Mari before moving to the girl.

"Good morning, Miss Alice. And how are the twins faring today?"

The girl smiled. Her face was pale and Mari wondered what her problem was.

"I've nearly finished, and they—"

North had his stethoscope on the girl's chest. "It's cold. I'm sorry. Someday," he said, smiling, "they'll make them so they're nice and warm. Now let me listen just a second."

The girl smiled at the doctor, reassured. Mari stayed near the back, feeling like an intruder. She looked around the large ward, at the nurses bustling about. A child cried at one end while other children—obviously feeling their oats—were laughing, talking to each other.

"Sounds good, Alice." North looked up and put a hand on the young girl's brow. Was it to check for fever, Mari wondered, or an ancient act of protection, a near-mystical act of healing?

I don't belong here.

These are people who do good. These are people who help.

While what I do is fuck up. Today Elaine Russ and her children will be buried because I didn't help them in time.

She thought—again—of the smells, the sound of the house. The coppery smell of blood, so overpowering. Far more powerful than any help Mari could bring. Blood had the final word. . . .

"I think," North said, "you know, I think that I have a box in my attic—yes, a box filled with old Bobbsey Twins books. Not the new ones, but the real classics. My little girl ran through them." He smiled. "When *she* was little."

Mari knew that North's little girl was now a pediatrician.

"I'll check in my attic and bring you a bunch."

The girl smiled. North patted her leg and moved away.

When they were well away from the girl's bed, Mari asked, "What's wrong with her? She looks fine."

North turned and looked at Mari. "Some kind of intermittent kidney failure. Don't know what it is. Not yet, at any rate. This afternoon we'll put some tracer fluid into her and see what it tells us." He smiled, a resigned smile. "If we find out the problem, maybe we'll be able to help her."

He kept his eyes on Mari.

"I wanted to see you," Mari said, feeling uncomfortable under his stare.

Dr. James North had spearheaded the Abuse Intervention Project that was run out of St. Paul's. It was he who had approached Mari to leave Social Services' Domestic Violence Department.

It was a chance, he told her, to work in a direct way with the abused and—North was quick to point out—the abusers.

"Abuse is *everyone's* problem," he had said.

The neighbor across the street, the people around the block, relatives, friends. Abuse wears many faces. And it's not simply a case of calling the police. Sometimes a helping hand, an offer to watch a child, to let someone simply get away, is enough to stem the tide.

North had recruited her.

"Damn," Mari said. "I wear my heart on my sleeve," she said. "I guess you heard that."

North wanted her for the project, and Mari had finally said yes.

She was here now to tell him that she was quitting.

"You heard what happened... to Elaine Russ?"

North nodded, still looking at her, waiting, daring her.

"I should have done something. I should have known. It's my—"

The doctor reached out and grabbed Mari's arm. His grip was strong. There was no frailty here at all.

"Don't," he said. "Don't *ever* blame yourself for what happened. You did everything that you could. There's nothing more that anyone can expect."

She turned away. Another child, a little toddler, was crying. The little boy said a word over and over, plaintive, irresistible. "Mommy... Mommy..."

Mari turned back to North. He still held her as if to let her go would free her to run away from the ward, out of the hospital.

"I saw them," she said, begging for his understanding. "I walked in there—and—I must have known. The smell, I could smell—"

North nodded.

"Then—then, oh, God, the kids didn't have a chance, no chance at life. And I don't think I can face that again. Can't you see? Can't you—"

North came close, and he put an arm around her. He held her, supported her. He walked her out of the ward, past windows that overlooked West Colfax Avenue, the library, and the financial district where life went on.

Because people don't see...

"I want to show you someone," North said. "And I want you to remember what I said when you first started working for the project. We can't save everyone. We can't help *everyone*. You knew the numbers, you knew that one out of every two children who are returned to abusive homes dies. You knew that."

Mari nodded. North led her into the IC pediatrics unit. She shook her head, but North held her close.

"That's the size of the problem, Mari. Sometimes we don't know the truth. A parent brings a child to a hospital claiming that he fell down the stairs, he's *always* falling down the stairs, they say. Now—the child can't move because his neck is broken."

North took a breath.

"What you saw was far worse. But you can't let it push you away, Mari."

They stopped at a hospital crib.

There was an infant in the bed. He had tubes running into his nose, and more tubes snaking under his blue blanket. The top of the blanket had fluffy lambs gamboling, prancing in the air.

"What happened to him?"

Mari saw a small blotch on one cheek, a small bruise on the baby's otherwise clear white skin. His eyes were shut. He breathed through his nose and made gurgling sounds through the tubes.

"He was brought here two nights ago, the mother brought him. She said he was crying, and—all of a sudden—he closed his eyes. He wouldn't wake up, she said. Wouldn't wake up . . ."

Mari watched as North leaned forward and grabbed the satiny fringe of one of the blankets.

Now she wanted to say, *Don't pull it back. Please don't pull that back.*

"You know—before our project—a report of abuse might bring action three, maybe four months down the road. Oh, the investigation would officially 'begin' within seventy-two hours. But nothing would really happen for a *very* long time. And that 'action' might be a phone call, a letter—"

He pulled the blanket back, and now, on the tiny baby's body, Mari saw the black-and-blue islands, one great patch merging with another, stretching down across the little chest.

She wanted to reach and touch the baby's mottled skin.

"His name is Jeffrey. He has a brain contusion. He fell, his mother said at first. But then she told us about her husband. She told us how he couldn't stand the baby's crying. Jeffrey's had major damage to his internal organs. His pancreas has been perforated. He has a fractured rib. Which is amazing—the bones are so flexible when they're this young. . . . He must have been hit *very* hard."

Mari turned away. She brought her fist to her mouth. She knew about things like this. It was the reason she joined North, joined his project. To stop this, it was so important.

SEE HOW SHE RUNS

"Jeffrey was colicky—and this is what his parents did to him. This is what they did to a seven-week-old baby."

Mari shook her head. *Go away,* she wanted to say. *Please go away.*

She whispered, the sound almost lost in the quiet hum of the monitors and machines in the intensive-care unit:

"Will he live?"

Mari risked looking back. She saw North gently cover the baby, tucking him in.

"There's an operation scheduled this afternoon. We're not optimistic. Jeffrey had his seven weeks of life. Some people might say he's better off. . . ."

North guided Mari away.

It was so hard to breathe. It was far harder to breathe here than back at the Russ house.

Away from the crib, North turned Mari to face him. "That's why you joined us, Mari. I don't think that you can walk away from it."

She nodded, knowing that he was right.

"Take some time off. Then call me later."

She nodded. She almost said thank you. Thank you for doing this to me, thank you for making me see that there are some things that you can't leave.

She squeezed his arm. He seemed like an old man, an old doctor now.

But if I can't leave, then I can't leave *any* of it.

For the first time since Friday, Mari knew that there was something she could do. . . .

Kate opened the door. Emmie was still kneeling on the cheap chair, looking out the motel-room window. Brian sat before the television, his constant companion on their journey.

The cartoons follow us everywhere, the Ninja Turtles, the wisecracking rabbits. They're traveling with us too.

Kate cleared her throat. "All done," she said.

Emmie turned around and Brian looked up from the TV, glancing at her, then doing a double take.

"Mom. God, Mom—you look like—"

But Kate moved from Brian's openmouthed stare to Emmie, kneeling on the chair. Emma's face looked so unsure, so serious. Like the time one of her dolls got covered with mud . . . she had left it outside, in the rain. Kate had washed the doll, and all the silky blond doll hair kinked up into something monstrous.

Emma had accepted the doll. It was hers. Even if it looked funny, she loved it.

Kate took some steps toward Emma. The little girl didn't move. "So what do you think?"

Emma didn't say anything.

Brian spoke. "Mom. I'm sorry. But you look *real* gross."

Kate, still watching Emma, ignored Brian. *This isn't fair to her,* she thought. *None of this is. . . .*

"Em . . ."

"Why did you do it?" Emma asked, though Kate had explained all about it. A new life, a new look, new names. She tried hard to explain it all to Emma . . . failing every time.

Kate made herself smile. "Well, I think it's great. No long shampoos, it's great for swimming, and I'm even going to change the color." She wrinkled her nose, as if she was just playing beauty parlor, as if Mom was just playing dress-up. "Maybe I'll tint it a nice auburn."

"But you're a blonde," Brian sputtered.

He understood. Kate didn't have to worry about him. Brian understood why this was important.

She moved closer to Emma. "You know, we'll look like twins, Emmie." Even closer, reaching out, touching Emma's fine short hair with just a hint of a curly wave.

More like David's hair, she thought.

"We can even get some matching clothes."

Emma's face brightened. She loved her dolls, and she loved clothes, all the cute outfits that they made for three-year-olds.

"Really?"

"Sure. Maybe nice matching jumpsuits. Or I know! We'll be in the West, so we'll get a cowgirl set, matching boots, cowgirl skirts, and—"

And how will I pay for that? Kate wondered. Funds were limited. Even the credit card she had been given was to be used only for emergencies, and the bill immediately paid. Things would be tight.

But for now she could just enjoy Emma's smile. The girl stood up on the cheap motel chair. She stood and she could just reach up and touch her mother's head.

Emma's hand ran through the hair. "It feels nice . . . and soft," she said.

"It looks weird," Brian said.

Kate reached out and hugged Emma. "I'm glad you like it." She pulled Emma close. "I'm so glad, honey." She hugged her tight.

"Mommy . . . when do we get to our new home?" Emma asked.

Still squeezing, Kate whispered in her ear: "Tomorrow, sweetheart. Tomorrow we'll get to our new home. You'll start a new nursery school. And everything will be"—Emma hugged her back, hard—" . . . fine."

14

Jesse saw Annie in the kitchen, standing beside the propane-gas stove. He walked into the entranceway and hung up his parka on a wooden hook.

"Hey, babe," he said. "It's getting real nasty and cold out there."

Annie turned, and Jesse could see that she was down, feeling blue. Some mornings Annie got up, and a cloud passed in the night and stuck there. Jesse wondered whether this life, living on the mountains, was too much for her.

Sometimes—especially in summer—Annie could be gone for hours, climbing the trails, picking up clumps of mountain violets and tiny white asters, bringing them back to their small dark house.

Other days—especially after winter locked in—weren't as good. There was no hiking, no flowers. Days could get bad.

She looked up at Jesse. "I was going to have a nice cup of tea." She shook her head. "But we're all out."

Jesse continued into the kitchen. "I can hustle down to the store later—"

Annie waved the suggestion away. This time, using her stunted arm, the arm that ended in a rounded stub at her elbow. There were times Annie got mad and she gestured, using that arm as if she wanted to feel more anger, more pain.

"No," she said, her voice steely, resolved. "There are a lot of things we need. I'll go down into Santa Fe."

"Fine, I'll drive you."

Annie put the pot back. "No. I'd just like to go . . . myself." She tried to smile. "I—"

He nodded.

Knowing what was coming.

"I need to get away a bit, Jesse. Do some shopping. Maybe visit Terry." Terry was an old school friend, married with kids. It was always worse when Annie came back from visiting Terry, back from seeing all that she wasn't ever going to have.

Jesse tried to keep it light, knowing the spiral Annie was headed into. "Okay. Maybe I could meet you for dinner later." He smiled broadly. "We could have a night on the town."

Annie walked toward him, squinting, shaking her head. "I—I just want to go pick some things up, Jesse. No big deal. We can eat when I come back—"

She moved past him, into their small bedroom. The mountain house, provided by the Department of Agriculture, was so small, and it seemed even smaller in winter. At times Jesse stood here and thought: I'm going to lose her. If I stay here, she's going to go away.

He reached out and stopped Annie. He turned her to face him. He spoke softly.

"Okay. I got the message, Annie. But do you really want to go see Terry, do you—"

She pulled away, not saying anything, drifting into their bedroom. He thought of the first time he saw her. How he had stared at her, and how she caught him. . . .

Jesse's cousin Steve, fresh out of college, had been getting married at the Santa Fe Plaza Hotel, right off the Plaza of the Governors. The food was chic Mexican and the band played everything from sleepy Southwestern ballads to Beatles tunes.

It made Jesse feel old, as if marriage couldn't have anything to do with him.

He saw Annie standing by a punch bowl. She must be a friend of the bride, he thought. He looked at her, seeing her reddish-brown hair, so rich and shiny, her green-blue eyes that sparkled from across the room. Eventually his eyes trailed down.

He saw her right arm. And—at that moment—Annie turned and caught him looking. Of course, she could feel it. . . . She must have lived a life of people looking, staring at her arm. She was so pretty, so beautiful—but then there was always this surprise,

SEE HOW SHE RUNS

the half arm, the rounded nub to catch people's gaze.

Every time Annie had to take a breath and pretend not to notice.

Jesse could see the whole thing, her life, the pain, in an instant. When he looked up, he saw Annie looking back at him, hurt, disgusted.

She quickly turned away. For a moment he was frozen there. I'm such an idiot, he thought, such a clod. . . .

He had only a second to make his decision. He started walking to her even as she retreated with her punch glass, retreating from the hurt, the casual stare that had turned her into a sideshow curiosity.

He caught up to her.

He touched her shoulder.

"Hi," he said, not knowing whether he was driven by embarrassment or by her beauty.

She turned back to him, cold and hurt. "Yes?"

"Er, you're not from Steve's side, are you?"

She shook her head. "I went to college with Sharon."

Jesse had nodded, not knowing what to do. In a second she'd turn and hurry away, carrying away the hurt, trying to hide it.

"I hadn't seen you before and—"

She started to turn. The band had been on a break. But then it came back and a song started, a country-and-western song, a slow ballad. People started dancing.

She was nearly gone, looking for an escape.

"Would you like to dance?"

She stopped. She fixed him with those brilliant eyes. Did she wonder, Is this to make up for the cheap glance? Is that what this is?

"I don't know . . . I just got a drink—"

Jesse smiled. "It'll wait," he said. He took her glass from her and found a place on an empty table.

She smiled back.

That was how it started. With him being simply another person hurting her.

"Take the Rover," he said. "I won't be going out again. I may hike down to the Eastern Stand." The Eastern Stand was a thick forest that, over his protest, had been partially opened to the logging interests. Already Jesse had caught signs of the loggers going beyond their charter, widening the ugly patch of logged wood. They didn't give a damn. Neither did Washington....

"I don't like the Rover," Annie said. Changing gears was awkward for her. But Jesse knew that there were icy patches all down Mountain Pass Road. And the traction of the Rover would be necessary.

"It's bad, babe. Trust me. Take the Rover, and take it easy."

She pulled her parka off the hook. Jesse heard keys jingling in her pocket. "You sound like my father," she said.

She was almost gone, out the door, trying to run away again, from the house, from winter, from feelings he could only guess at. He kept asking her to marry him. But marriage, to Annie, meant children.

She wasn't ready to risk that. Not now, maybe never.

She was almost gone.

He went to her. He stopped her, grabbing her shoulders. He turned her around.

Shy, like a child fighting to hold on to a pout, she turned to him, eyes down. "I'm like your father, eh?" Jesse said. He raised his hands to her cheek. He held her face. "I don't think so." He leaned forward and kissed her.

Stubbornly her lips remained sealed. He pulled back, smiling, and he thought he saw a quiver at the corners of her mouth, a crack in the facade.

He kissed her again, and now her lips came apart a bit, kissing him back. He held her close, kissing her as her mouth opened wide and he tasted her lips, the brush of her tongue.

She pulled away and laughed.

"I don't think your father ever kissed you like that." He looked down, at the bulge in his jeans. "Now look what you've done."

She laughed again, a full-throated, hearty laugh. She was back, back from the gray world. She reached down and stroked the outline of his erection and squeezed.

"Maybe . . . before you go—" Jesse said.

Annie grabbed the doorknob. "*That* will keep," she said.

She opened the door. The wind sent a fine spray of snow swirling in front of the open door.

Annie trudged over to the garage and the Land Rover.

"Be careful!" he said.

He stood there, watching until she turned the four-wheel-drive vehicle around and drove down the driveway to Mountain Pass Road.

• • •

SEE HOW SHE RUNS

Las Vegas was fifty miles away? Las Vegas?
Shit, the sign said that Las Vegas was fifty miles away!
But that was impossible.

Russ had pulled his car off to the shoulder. Now he looked down at his map, folded to show a square revealing Colorado and New Mexico cut in half by the mountains.

But no, there it was. *Las fucking Vegas*. Right there, in the middle of nowhere. Russ scratched his head. That's got to be wrong. Must be some other kind of Las Vegas. Maybe there's *two* Las Vegases. The gambling one and this shithole.

The road was empty. The last shit town he passed was called Springer. But at least Russ knew that he was in New Mexico. There were all these New Mexico road signs. He wanted to keep on going.

At the left bottom corner of his map he had made a circle around Santa Fe.

He said the name: "Santa Fe." What happened, back there... that's over, he thought. I'm going to Santa Fe and I'm going to start a new life. That was bad back there. No job, no fucking job, and no way to get money...

He had told Elaine, he told her. Christ, stop spending so much goddamn money. But there are always things to buy for the kids. She always had something that she just *had* to spend money on. A winter coat for Tom, new shoes for the baby.

But there was no fucking money! Didn't she know that?

Elaine made it so that there was only one way out, only one way to wipe the slate clean. Hell, I spared them a lot of pain. They would have turned into welfare kids, homeless kids on the streets. And Denver gets cold... so damn cold.

He took a breath now. The car's heater wasn't doing much.
For a moment—
Sitting there in the car
He remembered....

He remembered coming back to the house, late at night. The gun had been in his coat pocket. But he hadn't made the decision. Not yet. It was just an idea he had, a fantasy. Like the dancing girls in the Denver strip joints who sit at your table and tell you how funny you are, and how cute, while you feed dollar bills into their panties.

That wasn't real. It was fantasy.
The gun in his pocket wasn't real either.

It was just an *idea*.

He stood in the kitchen, in the dark, for a long time. Thinking about it.

He walked around the dark room. At first—he thought—I could say someone came and did this. Someone came to rob us. I wasn't there. Shit, and look what they did! Christ, look at what they did!

He had shaken his head. What could anyone possibly want to steal? What did we have that was worth a fucking thing?

He knew Elaine had spoken to that woman. Russ had seen that woman, the bitch had been in his kitchen, watching him open his beer.

Russ remembered her....

When she came, I sat down. It was my fucking house. Still my fucking house. And I had to look at this woman, this social worker. She put some pamphlets on the table. "Seven Warning Signs of the Abuser"... and one with an 800 phone number. Abuse hot line.

He had stared at her. *Who the fuck's house do you think this is?* It's mine. Until the goddamn bank takes it away. And you can get your social-working ass out of here.

That day the bank had called. Three times. They were moving ahead with the foreclosure. Yessir, Mr. Russ. We're moving ahead. A lousy $33,000 mortgage for this shithouse and they were going to shut me down.

It's all yours now, he thought....

He took a breath, and he was back looking out his windshield, at the empty highway. Russ rubbed his chin, his beard. He was tired. I need some sleep, he thought. Got to clear my head. I'm thinking too much.

He pulled out the keys and opened up the car door. He felt the cold, still air.

He walked around to the back of the gray car. He opened the trunk. There were a half-dozen license plates there, all left behind by guys who sold their cars to Big Bob O's or dropped them off for work and disappeared. The plates should have been turned in. That was the law.

But—and this was important—you can get away with breaking the law. It can be done.

There were two New Mexico plates. He picked the one that looked the newest, the finish still shiny, the plate not too bent.

He had a screwdriver and some other tools sitting in the trunk.

SEE HOW SHE RUNS 105

He knelt down and removed the Colorado plates. I'll have to do something about the registration sticker, he thought. Put something on the dash . . . make it hard to see.

You can get away with things, he knew.

I've always gotten away with things. Wasn't high school one long party, getting out of shit? And maybe I could have ducked out on Elaine, even after she was months into her pregnancy. But he thought—how crazy—that he had really wanted a family. Never had family . . .

The license plate fell off and rattled to the ground. His hands were aching from the cold. Got to get some gloves, he thought. My fucking hands are killing me.

He put the New Mexico plate on, hurrying, losing a screw as it fell to the ground and bounced under the car.

He pressed himself flat to the ground and looked for the screw. He had to stretch and reach well under the car. Then he took his time, feeling his cramped fingers losing control, barely able to hold the screw.

He inserted it into the hole and fitted the bolt behind it.

It had been a hard decision, he thought. How long had he stood in the dark kitchen? Once, he thought that he might just leave, just walk out the door.

But no. Then they'd always be after him for money, for support. That social worker would look for him, hunt him. It would never end.

No. Not unless *I* finish it. Oh, then they might still look for me.

But I'm good at getting lost. Eventually they'd just be dead people. Dead people don't need money.

That thought made the most sense to him. You take care of your own problems. It was the best way.

It would be all over. . . .

He gave the screwdriver one last twist and the plate was tight. Russ stood up and hurried back to the car. He got in before he realized that—*shit!*—he had left the keys in the goddamn trunk lock. Now that wasn't good, forgetting things. Can't be screwing up like that, missing things, forgetting shit.

I'm going have to be real careful.

He hurried back to get the keys and then scooted into the car. It was much warmer inside.

Las Vegas was ahead.

Well, he thought, I think I'm going to cruise right by Las Vegas, just keep on going.

Because if I bust my ass, I can be in Santa Fe by this afternoon. Ready to begin again. If the fuckers don't find me, I can begin again. . . .

15

The waitress stood there, asking—yet again—"Would you like a menu?"

Mari shook her head. Then, realizing that the waitress resented that her booth was going to waste when it could be producing revenue, Mari looked up and said, "I'll have more coffee, and an English muffin."

The waitress nodded, shaking her head, unimpressed. "And your friend?"

"He'll be along." She looked out the window. "Soon."

The waitress disappeared. The Pay Dirt Coffee Shoppe was down from radio station KAMA, only a block away from Cherry Creek Road. The lunch crowd had obviously disappeared, and whatever goodwill the waitresses started the day with had already been spent.

Dan told Mari that he'd meet her. And Mari knew what a risk that could be. Dan had been there that night, had seen it all happen—though he never talked about it with Mari.

She kept the newspaper story for days, it was so sick—her last contact with Rob.

Rob and Dan had been checking on an informant. They didn't know that the informant was having a visitor, some dealer who was looking to stash his wares.

The informant reluctantly let Rob and Dan in. They talked, and they were almost out the door when someone—probably Rob, Mari thought. *Probably Rob,* damn him. He was like Columbo, spotting things at the last minute. *Oh, just one more thing* . . .

Rob saw some plastic baggies, a scale in the kitchen, and he knew there was someone else there. And with the same instinct, the dealer knew that he had been uncovered. Like a lizard under a rock, he scurried out of the bedroom. He held a machine gun. Rob and Dan pulled out their guns.

Rob was in the front. Mari wasn't surprised. Though she guessed Dan felt bad about it.

There was firing. The dealer was cut down, collapsing into a cheap coffee table. Dan was wounded in the shoulder.

And when it was all over, Rob lay on the floor. One side of his head looked fine. But there couldn't be an open coffin at the wake because there was this horrible hole where the right side of his face used to be.

Mari had to be strong for Jake.

The boy looked so funny dressed in his suit. So funny . . .

Mari still had nightmares about it. She'd relive that moment when they came back to their apartment alone, and Jake sat at the kitchen table, his tie pulled loose, heaving, sobbing so loudly while Mari tried to hold him, to tell him to please stop, until all she could do was join him. She'd dream about the two of them crying there, in the kitchen, forever. . . .

Dan came by. He took Jake places. Dan tried to fill the gap. And, as time went by, Mari suspected Dan would like to do more.

But that was impossible.

No, she'd never be with another cop.

Now she wanted his help and he agreed to meet her.

She saw a black Chrysler pull alongside the coffee shop. The antenna sticking up at the back was a dead giveaway that it was a detective's car.

She watched Dan get out. His tie was open, and after getting out, he stretched. On the phone he had told Mari that he had been up most of the night. She watched him walk into the restaurant, looking so tired.

Mari took a deep breath.

This will be okay, she told herself.

She could picture Rob walking beside him. *Gotta let go,* she told herself. Just let go. . . .

Dan walked into the coffee shop. The owner, a little Greek man who played maître d', came up and fawned. Mari watched Dan indulge the proprietor with a tired smile. He looked around and then spotted her. He smiled and Mari waved back.

He walked down to the booth and sat down. The waitress

appeared instantly, testimony to the powers of the badge.

"Hot coffee?" she asked brightly, all signs of her former fatigue now replaced with an unseemly attentiveness.

"Yeah. Thanks. And bring us"—Dan looked at Mari—"a couple of burgers?"

Mari shook he head. "I'll have some soup. What soup do you—"

"Minestrone. Beef and vegetable. Potato leek."

Seamlessly the waitress shifted gears, projecting her wondrous ennui straight at Mari.

"Minestrone."

The waitress disappeared. And then Mari was alone with Dan.

"How's Jake doing?" They had gone to a Broncos game together a few weeks back. Dan was being real good to Jake. . . .

"Good." As good as any boy can when he loses his father.

Dan was a good five years older than Rob. He had been like a big brother to Rob. And now he's like a big brother to us, Mari thought.

He looked at her. "And how about you? How are you doing, Mari?"

He's going to ask me out. Dinner or something. It was time, all of her friends said it. Time to get out again, see what the world was like.

"I'm fine," Mari said.

And Dan smiled at her lie.

The car's AM radio made some crazy static. Every time the music hit a low fucking note, the speaker started buzzing.

Russ banged the dash-mounted speaker with his hand.

"C'mon, damn it."

It was a song he liked. By the Stones. Ladies and gentlemen, the Rolling Stones. He took Elaine to see that movie, that *Steel Wheels* movie from their last tour. The Stones could kick ass. They looked like shit—all wrinkled, old men—but man, they could still rock.

Of course, that was before the kids came, and the house, and then all those bills, all that money going the fuck *out*—until there was no money.

And the fucking pressure kept on building.

He tried to think of solutions.

There were houses filled with some old bag's jewelry in a box, and fat wallets lying on end tables. I could do that and maybe make my problems go away for a while.

SEE HOW SHE RUNS

But every time he kept coming back to this thought:

They'd still be there. Elaine, the kids. Still there, sucking money out of me that I don't have. It was all a terrible fucking mistake. And mistakes had to be corrected.

Russ banged the speaker.

Jagger was wailing that it was a *gas*.

Russ pushed down on the accelerator. The car looked like a piece of shit, but it had a nicely tuned engine. Should know, did it myself, Russ thought. She has a real V-8, with new plugs and a rebuilt carburetor.

And it wouldn't be long now. He just passed a town called Rivera, and a sign said that Santa Fe was only fifty miles away.

You can correct your fucking mistakes.

"It's a gas, gas, gas," Russ sang out, loud, off-key.

Then something bloomed in the rearview mirror. It was like magic. Russ was alone on the highway, and then something was *there*. A black-and-gold car. No, not a car. It had a light on it.

Russ eased up on the pedal.

It's a cop. But—take it easy. He might only be out on patrol, Russ thought. Take it the fuck easy....

His eyes immediately went to the dash, to his Colorado registration. I should have planned better. Damn, I should have taken care of *that*.

He looked up to the rearview mirror.

And there, the cop's bubble light was on, followed by the wail of a siren. Russ banged the steering wheel.

Russ started breathing fast. He shook his head. *I'm only fifty miles away. Fifty goddamn miles away from a new life. A new fucking start.*

Again his eyes shot up to the mirror. And like a snake, slithering through the slick grass, the cop car glided close to his rear, the siren wailing, the bubble light so colorful and bright.

And Russ started to slow down.

"Why'd you stop, Mom? What's wrong?"

Kate could navigate four different ways into and out of Manhattan, dealing with gridlock and cabbies from other planets.

But here, out in the middle of nowhere—off Interstate 80 at last, stopped on the two-lane highway—she wondered whether she had missed her exit.

I'm so tired, she thought. All that driving, and not much sleep, tossing and turning, waking up every time a car tumbles into the motel lot.

You're almost there, girl, she told herself. *Almost there* . . .

"I—I don't know, Bri. We're supposed to be on Route Eighty-five. It says"—she picked up the piece of paper with the directions—"Route Eighty-five all the way into Santa Fe. But I don't know. The sign says Highway Twenty-five, and we didn't change roads."

Brian sat up. It was a cloudy day and the gray of the highway was reflected by the cool steel clouds.

I should keep my mouth shut, Kate thought. No reason to make Brian nervous. No need to let him think that we're lost.

A truck, a giant eighteen-wheel behemoth, went roaring by, shaking the car, sucking at it.

"Let me check the map." Kate put aside the directions. The route was highlighted on the map of New Mexico in pink.

There, she thought. There's Interstate 25, and it keeps going down—

Then Interstate 25 seemingly disappeared. It turned into 85. And farther—her finger kept following the route—the black marker with a white "25" reappeared.

"Okay. I think we're okay." She turned to Brian and smiled. "No problem. The road just has two names."

Brian shook his head, a little old man. "You sure, Mom?"

Kate nodded and then turned to look back at Emma. "Yes, and now we'll just sail there. Right, sweetie?"

Emma had her favorite doll on her lap. She had named the doll Patty, and Patty, perpetually grinning, wore overalls and a tiny backpack. Emma like to stick things in Patty's backpack, cookies, pretend things. . . .

Emma didn't look up.

Good, thought Kate. The worst part's almost over.

The worst is over. And she got back onto the highway.

The car started again. Emma hoped that maybe they'd stop and get a hamburger. She didn't really like hamburgers.

Patty didn't like hamburgers either.

No, Emma liked the *fries*. Covered with ketchup. Hamburgers looked ugly. But Mommy made the car move again, fast. And Emma pushed her feet against the chair, pushing herself back, trying to get comfortable. One of Mommy's big bags was next to her.

Emma started to open Patty's backpack. It was hard, the two

SEE HOW SHE RUNS

buckles were hard to open. Emma had to tug on them, pulling at the buckles.

But then the little pack was open. And inside—Emma dug around—there was little pink pony, a tiny pony with long pink hair flowing behind it.

It was *so* pretty.

There was a little brush, just for the pony. And—just inside the pack—there was a little pocket with a button, a tiny *secret* pocket.

He had said: "That's a good place. That's a good place for the secret."

Emma chewed her lip, pulling at the button. It hurt her finger to press against the button. She made a small grunting noise.

It popped open.

And inside the tiny pocket was a small piece of paper.

Emma pulled it out.

First looking up—to make sure nobody was watching 'cause, 'cause—

"It wouldn't be a secret, pumpkin," he had said. "Then it wouldn't be a special secret, now would it?"

Mommy was driving. And Emma couldn't see Brian at all. She pulled the piece of paper out.

And there were the numbers.

"You have to push all of them," Daddy had said. "And say 'collect' . . . if ever you want to talk to me."

There were . . . Emma counted them again . . . nine numbers. She almost knew them by heart.

It was fun having a secret.

I can talk to my daddy anytime that I want, she thought. Anytime at all. Because I have his secret number.

Emma smiled. It was so much fun.

And she carefully put the piece of paper back inside the small pocket inside Patty's backpack.

Dan Stein rubbed his eyes.

"I feel," he said by way of explanation, grinning, "like a zombie."

Mari nodded. "How long have you—"

Dan laughed. "I think I last slept Saturday night. I'm getting too old for this." His words, just seeing him, brought Rob back, and Mari had to look away.

The waitress appeared and put down his cup of coffee. Dan

nodded to her. He ripped open two packets of sugar and dumped them into his coffee.

"Living healthy?" Mari said.

He smiled. "Oh, is sugar bad for you?"

Mari grinned back. There was something gentle, comforting about Dan. His eyes stayed on hers for a moment, taking her full measure.

Mari looked out the window. "Dan . . . I—" She took a breath.

Dan touched the back of her hand, recalling her attention. And his hand didn't stay there. Just a touch. *Hello, I'm here.*

"Look, Mari, I was wondering. Next week Bill and Al got their kids—"

Cops and divorce and weekend fathers. Somehow we beat that, Mari thought, Rob and I had beat that. . . .

"They're going on a little ski weekend. Actually more than a weekend. It will be four days. I was wondering, y'know, if I might take Jake. It will last until Wednesday."

Mari looked at Dan. She felt Dan's tired eyes on her. She knew he was working a high-profile drug case and a nasty homicide, the story had been in the news.

A producer at KAMA had been shot in his apartment on Saturday, and drugs were involved. It was the lead story, pushing poor Elaine Russ off the tube. And Dan was one of the detectives on the case.

She watched him cup his hands around the hot coffee.

"Sure. He'll like that," she said. Though Mari knew it was just more time alone, in her apartment. *I don't like being alone.* "Jake will love it."

Dan laughed. "If I don't break my neck skiing."

"Be careful," Mari said, meaning it. There was silence for a minute, as though there was something else to say.

Then: "It's a real nice place. Lots of cops and their kids go there. We'll have a ball."

Mari nodded, postponing her request, the reason she asked Dan to meet her.

The waitress appeared with a juicy-looking hamburger for Dan and a bowl of oily-looking soup for her. The few vegetables in the minestrone looked like the flotsam and jetsam after a U-boat attack. Mari picked up the spoon while Dan tried to hide his puckered hamburger under ketchup.

"Dan, I wanted to see you, to ask your help."

SEE HOW SHE RUNS   113

He nodded, wrapping his hands around his burger and picking it up. And while he ate she told him about Elaine Russ, about finding them.

He nodded. "I heard."

Unimpressed . . . *People kill people all the time in his world.*

Mari spoke quickly, telling Dan how she had been trying to help Elaine, to get her a place to stay, somewhere away from her husband.

He shook his head, his fatigue back now. "Why didn't you get her into a shelter?"

"God . . . You know what those places are like. It's bad enough for the women, the battered wives. But the children. There's more abuse going on in those places than—"

Dan nodded. He sipped his coffee. "Right . . . one crazy bastard who did it," he said. "They got the guy's picture everyplace."

Mari shook her head. "No. They don't. That's an old picture. Alex Russ doesn't look like that. He was growing a beard. That's a high-school picture." She breathed out. "It doesn't look anything like him."

"He's gone," Dan announced. "I'd guess he's flown the coop. That's for sure."

"I know." Her hand reached out toward him. "Dan, I feel . . . I feel it was my fault."

He looked at her, and she started to feel her control slipping. *I wasn't going to do this,* she thought. *Wasn't going to let myself slip like this.*

"Hey, Mari. That's crazy. He was a sick fuck. Who could know?"

"But I should have helped her, I—"

Dan looked up at a clock above the counter-service area. His day wasn't over. He looked back to her. He probably had places he was supposed to go, people to see.

He sounded stern to her. "Look, I have to go. People are waiting for me. But you're not going to blame yourself. Do you understand?"

She nodded.

"Good. Now, what is it that you want? What did you want to ask me?"

Mari tried to smile.

And she told him.

• • •

The cop car was right on his ass. Russ toyed with the idea of gunning it. Let's see who's a better driver, dude. Let's just see....

Once Russ challenged Henry Stumpf—Hank the Stumpf, in his Mustang. Let's do that scene from that old movie, Russ said. The one where they race their cars to the edge of a cliff. And the first one to stop is chicken.

Rebel Without a Cause.

And Stump, the old Stumper, nodded, thinking, looking for a way out. Everyone thought I was crazy, but it was the Stumper who tried to back out.

"You're crazy, Russ. You're nuts."

And in front of everyone, Russ said, "And you've got no balls, Stump. No balls whatsoever."

So they did it. No cliffs, but they used the straightaway that led down from the mountains, down the ass end of Coldwater Springs. The road went straight and then curved left.

First one to stop was chicken.

And Stump stopped his pretty red Mustang yards away from the curve.

Russ grinned at the memory. Chicken, *fucking chicken*...

While I kept on going, flying off the road. Ripped up the underside of my car. But who gave a fuck. After that, he thought, everyone *knew* me....

He checked the mirror.

The cop's probably got a V-8. Yeah, definitely a V-8, and it would be no contest. And then, boy, I'd be in deep shit.

Besides, I haven't done anything yet. I was only going a little too fast on a deserted highway. No big deal, probably could talk my way out of the ticket. No big fucking deal.

Keep cool, he thought.

Russ nodded at the rearview mirror. He moved his foot from the accelerator to the brake and pressed down slowly. The cop car was right there, headlights on, bubble light swirling around. Russ slowed down.

He looked ahead for a spot to pull over.

He felt cold. His heart was thumping. He could hear it thumping away inside his head. It was a noise that started when things began to go bad. He told the school shrink about it, this thumping... and he always knew something bad would happen. No matter how hard he tried.

It felt as if he was back in the house. Making his problems go away. *Bang, bang, bang*... that had been so easy.

And—

Oh, *shit*. The gun, the goddamn gun was right under the seat. And a knife, a sleek four-inch blade that folded into a real ivory handle. The guy at the sporting-goods store said the handle was real ivory. The fat man laughed and said, "Hey, with a blade like that you don't use it for cleaning fish."

Ha-ha . . .

Russ grinned back.

Russ pulled off the road. He reached down and flapped his hand around. He felt the gun. He pushed it as far under the seat as he could. He brushed against the knife handle.

And he picked it up and quickly stuck it into his back pocket as he slowed down, slow, slower, the gravel spraying up, hitting the bottom of the car.

Slower . . . to a dead stop.

And breathing hard, he waited for the cop.

16

Suzy Tyler sat at the pull-down table inside her trailer. She stubbed a cigarette butt out in the overfilled ashtray and quickly grabbed her pack of Marlboro Lights. She tapped out a fresh cigarette. Lit it, and she continued sitting.

The small color TV was on and Oprah was featuring incest victims. Suzy watched the show and chewed her lip.

That morning Suzy had checked herself. She saw, in the hand mirror, scratches inside her vagina where the man had grabbed her with his fingers. And there were big, ugly bruises where he had held her arms tight while he pushed against her.

When she called in sick at work, she didn't tell them . . . *I was raped.* She didn't say, *I can't come into work today because I was raped last night.*

She had taken three showers and she'd probably take a few more before she tried to sleep, to put this day behind her.

She inhaled deeply.

On the TV, a young black woman was telling Oprah about her father, how he used to come into her room after her mom was asleep.

On the table there was a piece of paper with a phone number on it.

The rape hot line. She had been surprised to see that, there, in the front of the Metro Denver Phone Book, there was a special number . . . just for rape victims.

Suzy had the number, but she didn't call.

She didn't know the man's last name. She didn't even know whether Tom was his real name. She had never seen him before. She felt embarrassed, so dirty and stupid. . . .

She got up from the table and walked to the small refrigerator that hid under the narrow kitchen counter. She pressed down on a latch with her foot and the small fridge opened. She dug out a bottle of Old Milwaukee light.

Suzy unscrewed the top.

She had the number, but she easily imagined the questions, the cops that she'd have to talk to, their faces. She could see them, looking at each other.

You got into a car with this guy, this stranger. Well, what exactly did you think was going to happen?

She took a slug of her beer. Oprah cut away to a commercial. A perfect woman in a perfect house was excited about her laundry.

Suzy Tyler looked at the phone. Like she had been doing all day . . . She picked up the handset. She put down her beer and her hand hovered over the push buttons.

She pressed "8," then a "0," then another, and then—she hung up the phone. Her head tilted forward and she was sobbing. Her head rocked back and forth.

In her mind she pictured the trial, sitting on the stand, all eyes on her, while they asked her questions, questions about fucking, who, when, *how often*.

The lawyer would come close and yell at her.

Saying: "You got into the car with him, didn't you? *Didn't you?* You got into the car—and what do you suppose was going to happen?"

Suzy shook her head. And then she spoke, to her empty trailer. "I can't." Then louder, sobbing full out now. After all, who could hear. "I can't."

Oprah's audience was clapping.

SEE HOW SHE RUNS

• • •

Russ waited, forcing himself to breathe evenly, nice regular breaths, he thought. He waited until the cop was next to his car before he opened the window.

"Yes?" Russ said.

The cop wore sunglasses, though the day was gray from the pavement to the sky.

"License and registration, please."

Russ nodded. "Sure," he said, digging into his pocket. "I guess . . . I was going a bit fast back there. An open road." He smiled up at the twin raccoon eyes of the cop. "You don't feel the speed."

The cop said nothing.

Russ got out his wallet.

He had a license. That was no problem. His license was good. Except, well, if the cop checked, he might find that the name Alex Russ made the computers act up. Lots of tickets hanging on it.

But he had no registration, not for this car. That might be okay. Lots of people travel without their registration. *Er, I forgot it . . . left it at home . . . in the cookie jar.*

Yeah, this could all be okay. The cop might just give me a warning, Russ thought. Take it slower, guy. And don't hit any armadillos.

Armadillos are the fucking state mascot.

Russ pulled out his license. "Here we are, and—" He made a show of looking for the registration. "Now, where the hell is—"

Russ flipped through some credit cards, all dead Indians, a union card, also expired, a picture of his wife and kids. He lingered on that, hoping that the cop saw it.

See, I'm a family man.

"Oh, God," Russ said. "My wife uses this car a lot. She must have the registration. I'm sorry."

The cop fingered Russ's license.

Had he seen it, Russ thought? Had he spotted that there was a Colorado sticker on the windshield and New Mexico plates.

Do pigs love mud?

The cop nodded.

C'mon, Russ thought. Make this easy for both of us. Give me a lecture. *Take it slow, pal. Enjoy your visit to the Land of Enchantment.*

Instead the cop said, "I'll be right back." Russ nodded. "You just wait here, please."

A very polite cop. They must train them how to deal with the public. Everyone has to act so nice.

The cop moved away. The cop's car was only three or four car lengths behind Russ's heap. Russ took a breath—he looked in the rearview mirror.

Mari reached out and touched Dan's hand. "Dan, there's something I need you to do for me. I need to know what's happening with the Elaine Russ case." Dan looked away, taking another sip of his sweet coffee. "I want to make sure that nothing falls through the cracks."

He shook his head. "I don't know, Mari. I'm sure that the state-police detectives are working on it. I'm busy enough as it is. If I go asking questions, finding out who's handling the case, they'll want to know why the hell I need to know."

Mari smiled, trying to keep from outright begging. But I'll do that if I have to, she thought. *If I have to beg . . . I will.*

"Dan—I know cops. You always talk. You work with the state police. I'm only asking you to let me know what's happening."

Dan dug around his cheek with his tongue, thinking. He started to shake his head again. She could see that he was finding it hard to say no to her.

"Please, Dan. I screwed up. That woman—she was more of a girl—and she'd still be alive. And the kids, God—I don't know how I can—"

Dan put a hand up. "Okay. All right. I'll keep my ears open. Okay?" He smiled. He pointed a finger at her, smiling. "Now can I finish my burger?"

Mari smiled back. He was a good man. But he was a cop, and cops get killed. "I owe you one," she said.

His face looked serious for a moment. Then he laughed. "Be careful that I don't take you up on it."

The waitress came over, coffeepot in hand. Dan looked up to her and said, "Hit me again. . . ."

There were only seconds to act. In those seconds, with the damned icy wind cutting into the car through the open window, Russ knew he had to do something. He breathed in and out fast, gulping the air now.

His right hand went to the gearshift while the other popped the emergency brake.

SEE HOW SHE RUNS

He kept breathing hard, his eyes locked on the rearview mirror. The cop had nearly reached his patrol car.

Russ threw the car into reverse.

The cop had his hand on the door to his patrol car.

"C'mon, c'mon, c'mon," Russ chanted. He pushed the accelerator to the floor. The rear wheels of the car screamed. And, in the rearview mirror, Russ watched the cop turn, the door opening, the cop looking up. . . .

Russ turned the wheel slightly. His car was pointed all wrong.

Don't want to hit the patrol car, he thought. Don't want to do *that*.

The cop seemed frozen.

Then the cop backed away from his car, as if he could move away from the accident. Which was just the wrong thing to do.

Despite his freezing hands and his panting breaths, Russ grinned. *Wrong fucking move*. In the mirror the cop watched the rear end of Russ's car flying toward him.

Russ chewed his lip. Up in the mirror the cop turned to run, but Russ's car had a nicely tuned six, and it was *flying*.

Russ heard a thud, loud, much louder than he thought it was going to be. He hit the brakes.

He fumbled to put the car in drive. He pulled forward.

Suppose someone comes along? he thought. Suppose someone sees me out here, gunning back and forth, and the cop lying on the ground. Things could get complicated pretty fast.

Russ pulled up until he could see the cop lying on the ground, one hand stretching into the westbound lane of the highway as if desperate to hitch a ride.

He didn't move. Russ stayed there, watching.

He's dead, Russ thought. Sure thing, he's *dead*. I can just get on the road and head on my way . . . except—

Except—what if he isn't dead? What if he only got banged up? I thought a tire went over him. It felt like it did. But Christ, who knew?

Russ kept chewing at his lip, thinking. No more mistakes man, he thought. The screwups must stop.

"He's dead," he said to himself. He nodded. Sure, look at him. The cop's bought the farm. No quick twenty years and out for him. He just entered early retirement.

"Dead as a roadkill," Russ said.

But if he wasn't . . . if he *wasn't* dead, why, then he saw me, saw my car. They'd know . . . Alex Russ is in New Mexico, heading toward Santa Fe, right across the mountains. It would get into the computers. They've got computers.

Russ shook his head. He reached out and touched the door handle. *Got to be sure.* Then, as he popped the door, he thought, this is just as well. I can take a look and then drag him back to his car. Hide the body. Make it look as if it's only a speed trap.

He popped open the door and got out. His legs felt wobbly, as if he was walking on a trick walkways from Lakeside Park, this goofy bridge that wobbled back and forth.

The cop lay there, looking like a deer smashed by the grille of a Mack truck.

"Hey, buddy," Russ said, moving closer. "Hey—"

The cop wasn't moving at all. Dead, thought Russ, no question about that. God knows what my car smashing into him did.

"Hey, buddy, you okay?" Russ grinned. Sorry about what happened. I got a little excited and backed up into you. *Oops.*

He stood by the body. He looked down at it. The cop's hat was off his head.

Got to bend down, Russ thought. I've got to go down and feel around for a pulse, make sure there's no breathing going on here.

He started to crouch.

The police radio sputtered to life. Someone called out some numbers. Calling for this guy? Russ wondered. Shit, is somebody calling for this guy? Then he had a bad thought.

Could the cop have called in before pulling him over? Maybe he knew that the plates were no good?

Russ crouched next to the body. He looked at the back of his own car, the smoky exhaust looking mean. He saw the license plate.

I've got to get that off.

He turned back to the body. Where do I touch? he wondered. Where do I feel to get a pulse? Maybe I could just press against—

He leaned one hand against the back of the cop, pressing, thinking he'd check if he was breathing.

The cop's back didn't move.

And then it did, and quickly the cop turned. Russ saw his face, a bloody mess, broken chips of white and foamy blood. The cop brought an arm up and smashed Russ in the crotch.

Russ rolled to the side, groaning. And everything was different now. He was rolling around, groaning, moaning to the cold pavement. While the cop—

SEE HOW SHE RUNS

He turned, and saw the cop pulling himself into a crouch, rearing up like some monster that wouldn't die. Russ went wide-eyed at the sight. He was dead, *he was fucking dead*!

Russ's nuts throbbed, but he tried to crawl away from the cop.

A hand locked on Russ's ankle. Despite everything, the grip was strong. Russ looked back. With his other hand, the cop was digging out his gun, fumbling with the holster, moving slowly, awkwardly, still in pain.

I can't run, Russ thought. I can't run away from this thing.

The cop still fumbled, blood dripping from his lips, spitting at the pavement.

Russ felt the knife in his back pocket.

Wouldn't want to use this for skinnin' fish, eh?

It was a race. Russ trying to get the knife out, the cop pulling at his gun, each tug making the cop groan and spit.

The knife felt like a slippery fish in Russ's hand. The smooth ivory was too slick, too cold to hold. The knife clattered to the pavement. And Russ, moaning, nearly weeping, used both his hands to grab it, fumbling to open the knife up, locking the four-inch blade into place.

The cop had his gun out. It was pointing straight up, then down, wavering, wobbly, reacting to every twitch of the cop's body.

Russ turned.

He yelled. He growled like the lions in the zoo. Growling at the cop while he slashed at the cop's wrist. Russ's leg was released.

The gun started to focus now, coming close to pointing in Russ's direction.

Russ bellowed again, and he crawled close to the cop, both of them on their knees. He crawled on top of the cop and slid the blade across the cop's throat.

Blood shot out. The gun fell from the cop's hand and he brought his two hands up to his neck. For the first time, Russ saw the cop's eyes. They were dull now, preoccupied.

Bloody spatters landed on Russ's shirt, his pants . . . his shoes.

Russ crawled away, as if he was a kid playing a game. I got you . . . now see if you can get me. Just see. . . .

Russ crawled away. Then he tried to stand. His balls throbbed. He wondered if there was major damage. He heard a cracking sound.

He looked up. The cop had knelt and then keeled forward, arms out, onto the ground, his head hitting first. There was a loud *cracking* sound.

"Fuck you," Russ hissed. He pulled his license from the dead man's hand and started backing up to his car. "Fuck *you*."

Still watching the cop, still moving backward, Russ felt behind him and grabbed the door handle of the car.

"Fuck you," he said one last time, and then—painfully—he slid back into his car. Now—at least—he knew that the cop was dead. He drove away, muttering to himself, wincing at the pain, but muttering—

"I'm thinking now. Now I'm really thinking. . . ."

17

The sun made a brief appearance before it slipped below the blue-black mountains. And Santa Fe shimmered, so neat, like a movie set . . . the clean yellow-orange stone of the adobe-style homes, an old church with scrubby pine trees standing guard outside, a street of glittering shops with hand-carved furniture and elegant jewelry.

We're here, Kate thought. We've made it.

They passed a giant pottery outlet and Brian asked, "Mom, what's a jackalope?"

"What honey?" Kate was looking for Cerillos Road. They'd be living outside the city . . . which was just as well. Downtown Santa Fe was too orderly, too neat, she thought. We'd stick out.

"A jackalope . . . The store back there said, 'Home of the Jackalope.' It had a picture of something that looked like half rabbit and half deer. Is it real?"

"I don't know, Bri. I never heard—"

And suddenly there was Cerillos Road, just ahead. Kate took the turn and she saw a restaurant, La Cantina Real. God, I'm hungry for something more than a burger and fries, she thought. I need some greens, something not deep-fried or flame-broiled.

"Is this where we'll be living?" Emma asked.

Kate shook her head. Traffic on the road was moving slowly. They were hitting rush hour.

SEE HOW SHE RUNS

Can't imagine that Santa Fe could have a rush hour. What does everyone do here... where do they live?

"No, honey. We'll be outside the city. But it's close by."

"It's pretty here," Emma announced. Then: "I like it."

"Good, sweetie. I'm glad."

But as Kate drove down Cerillos she watched the pristine world of adobe homes and sparkling sidewalks give way to bars and a row of gas stations, until the beauty of the city seemed far away.

Kate looked at a piece of a paper she had crumpled up in her hand. She was looking for a road called Pasada. It was just off Pasada. Our new home...

For how long? Kate thought. Surely this isn't where we'll live forever? This is only a stopover. Someplace to catch our breath.

She stopped at a stoplight. On the corner there was a bar, the Dead Run Inn. A sign in the window announced that there was LIVE MUSIC! that Friday... the North County Rangers. The door to the bar opened, and a cowboy walked out, complete with boots, bowlegged gait, and a face hidden under the brim of a comically large hat.

"Wow, a cowboy," Brian said.

"Maybe," Kate said. "Or he might work at a convenience store."

The person behind Kate honked his horn and she looked up to see that the light had changed. She jerked the car forward.

I'm so tired. We're almost there, but I'm so tired....

Then, there it was... Pasada Road.

Annie Sawyer didn't shop in the boutiques around the Plaza of the Governors. They were for the tourists. All of them were too expensive. But Terry, her best friend, had the money.

Terry had brought her little girl along, and Annie had to force herself not to stare at Melanie. The girl had her father's dark eyes and hair... and she was so quiet and beautiful. In secret moments Annie fantasized what it would be like to have a little girl like that for her own. A little friend, someone to love, someone to take places, to the Fine Arts Museum, to the pueblos, shopping for pottery or turquoise jewelry, or hiking with Jesse in the mountains.

"Melanie, honey—stay close," Terry said.

Terry said she was looking for a dress. There was a big fancy party to go to. She always had parties to go to, when the summer opera season began, when the West End Playhouse opened, or the museum had a new show. Santa Fe was an arts community, and Terry got to enjoy it all.

She didn't forget Annie. She always invited Annie . . . who just made excuses.

That's not my world, Annie knew. *And I'm happy, with Jesse in the mountain, Jesse and me . . . we're happy.*

"Oh. Mommy, this would be beautiful."

Melanie came back holding a slinky black evening dress covered with sequins.

Terry reached out and grabbed Annie's arm, laughing. "Very nice—but it's not that kind of party, hon." She waited a moment until Melanie had left to return the dress. "Though I think Daddy might like it."

Annie smiled. But she felt sad, cut off from this world of her friend. *In a little while I'll go back to the mountains, as if I have to hide, as if I have to run away.*

"Which reminds me—I need to pick Jim up a new shirt or two. He'll never get down here."

Annie nodded, looking at expensive dresses, idly fingering the material.

"Now, this looks great," Terry said, and Annie turned to see what her friend had picked out.

Jake was psyched about the prospect of a long skiing weekend with Dan. Mari smiled, trying to act as if she was glad—though she never liked being alone.

"But now you have homework to get to," she said. Jake looked at her for a moment as if he could see that something was wrong here. Then he nodded and walked back to his bedroom.

Mari walked over to the TV. She wanted to catch the news, but already the overstuffed weatherman was pointing north. A big cold front was running right along the Rockies, he said. Look for a week of colder-than-average temperatures.

It already seems too damned cold.

Yessir, we're looking at a week or more of arctic air, with a chance for some precipitation heading into next week.

More snow . . . wish I liked skiing, Mari thought. Then I wouldn't hate the stuff so damn much. Her father, a full-blooded Navajo, never understood what the Anglos saw in skiing. In winter, when the snow stopped all construction, her father settled in with his TV, waiting for spring.

SEE HOW SHE RUNS

The weather report ended and then there was a movie review, a new comedy that wasn't funny. That didn't matter either. Mari didn't get to the movies much.

Mari opened the refrigerator. The dwindling bottle of Chardonnay was still there.

I'd like a glass of wine, she thought. Before I defrost something for dinner, before I zap some burritos in the microwave for Jake and me. A nice glass of wine . . .

She grabbed the bottle and pulled it out, imagining the clear, cleansing taste of the dry wine.

Then the phone rang. . . .

"*This* is it? This is where we're going to live?"

Brian leaned forward, looking out the windshield, his face filled with disbelief.

Kate nodded. *Yes, this is it.* The sky had turned rich purple at the horizon, while clouds overhead turned inky and black.

The place was disappointing. No, more than that. It looked desolate, a place for drifters. The apartment complex was a squat green building, the paint obviously chipped and peeling even in the dull light. A half-dozen apartments were on each of two floors. It looked like a converted motel.

And Kate was sure that there must be a broken ice machine somewhere. The asphalt parking lot was cracked, and the cars and Jeeps parked in the faded spaces looked old and abandoned.

This is no place for a family, she thought.

It did have one spectacular aspect. The twin ranks of apartments all faced east, with an uninterrupted view of the mountains.

"What a dump!" Brian said.

Kate turned to him. She quickly glanced back at Emma. The little girl was studying the building, her eyes wide and her lips puckered, mulling this over.

"Brian, you calm down. You haven't even seen—"

"But Mom, *look* at this place. It looks like—"

Kate reached out and grabbed his arm. She made no effort to hide her anger, trying to get through to him.

I don't want Emma upset. We have to make this easy for her.

"Ow," he said, responding to her squeeze.

She stopped, catching herself. "I'm sorry, Brian. I'm sorry—"

He rubbed his wrist in an exaggerated way, laying on guilt.

"I'm sorry. Now let's go take a look." Kate turned to Emma and smiled. "Okay, honey?"

And Emma, holding on to her doll, holding Patty tight, nodded.

Annie drifted away from Terry and her little girl. They were still looking at dresses, still playing mother and daughter, talking about parties.

Annie thought she'd look for something for Jesse, maybe a new shirt, though all he wore were regulation L. L. Bean plaids. Maybe a nice sweater, though they were trying to save money.

She looked at a pile of jaunty ski sweaters, with reindeer and giant snow crystals. Jesse would hate them, she knew. He disliked everything that had to do with skiing and tourism. To Jesse, this part of the world was a sacred preserve . . . and it was being ruined by the ski lodges, the mountain condos—while the animals, the wildlife kept getting pushed away.

She moved down the aisle.

When she heard a step behind her.

Someone was looking at her. Odd, she thought, I can always feel it when someone looks at me, standing there. For a second she thought it was Terry, watching her.

Maybe even feeling sorry for me.

Poor Annie won't have any children because she's scared, afraid that her children will turn out—

Annie turned around. There was a man there.

He was looking at her arm. Annie saw him staring, a quizzical expression on his face. She felt like walking up to him, waving it in his face.

Here, take a good look, a real good look. You know you'd be amazed at what I can do with this—absolutely amazed. Still, it's pretty strange looking, isn't it? And do you want to hear what the kids said to me in elementary school, how they wouldn't let me play jump rope?

How I learned the word freak *so very young?*

How I went to the library and read about freaks and freak shows?

Annie felt her face redden, her anger building.

The man held a pair of gloves. He had a beard. Finally his blue eyes looked up to meet hers.

He smiled. "Oh, hey—I'm sorry. God, what an idiot I am."

Annie nodded. All my life people have looked at me. And I never get used to it. She felt like saying, *Yes, you* are *an idiot. Why don't you keep your eyes in your head.*

Instead she nodded and said, "Forget it." She started to turn away.

But the man came up to her. "I was just stopping to get some gloves. It's so damn cold." He laughed. "I thought it would be warm here."

Annie kept walking. That was another thing, people felt as if they could talk to her, that it was okay to come up and start talking to her, that she had to listen.

"Yes," she said. She turned at an aisle and made her way back to where she hoped Terry was waiting.

"Santa Fe—you know, I thought it would be warm. I mean, I've never been here. It's pretty, but—God—so cold."

Annie looked up at him. He had bright blue eyes and she imagined that—with the beard gone—he'd be a good-looking guy.

Stupid, but cute.

"Yeah, it gets cold enough here," she said. She was aware of keeping her stunted arm held behind her.

She looked down and saw the man's work boots. There were stains on them. Must be a painter, Annie thought, with those stains . . .

She heard Terry.

"Oh, Annie—I think Melanie and I have found the *perfect* dress."

The man stopped. "Yeah, well. Take care," he said.

Annie nodded, the odd encounter over.

Terry came over, holding a blue-and-white dress that wasn't quite so skimpy. Annie reached out and touched the shiny material.

"Very pretty," she said. Then she looked back to see if she was still being watched. But the blue-eyed stranger was gone.

Kate knocked on the door again.

"Nobody home, Mommy?" Emma said.

Kate pulled Emma close, hugging her, rubbing her shoulders, trying to keep her warm. The sensation seemed ancient, but familiar.

She remembered sitting with her own mother in the dark, her mother holding her close, rocking her, cooing . . . everything will be fine . . . everything will be *okay*.

Her father drifted around upstairs, banging things, moving. . . .

If we simply sit and rock and stay quiet, everything will be all right.

"No," Kate said. "We're expected. I mean, sometime in the afternoon, that's what I said."

"It's more like night, Mom," Brian said, still disagreeable, unhappy at the prospect of living here.

She stood beside Number 12, the uppermost apartment on the left. She knocked once more, and then the door popped opened. Kate immediately smelled something strange. An old man with tan skin and shoulder-length black hair stood at the door.

"Oh, I'm sorry," he said. "I didn't have—"

The man's skin, nearly black, was crisscrossed with lines. His long, straight black hair hung to the sides; he would have looked almost effeminate if his face wasn't so lizardlike.

He grinned, displaying a generous amount of yellow, uneven teeth. "I didn't have *this* in." He pointed to a plastic plug sitting in his ear with a wire trailing down.

Emma leaned closer to her mother. She squeezed Kate's hand.

"Well, *come in*. It's cold tonight. The cave winds are starting. Always the coldest when the cave winds start..."

Kate walked in, and Emma and Brian hung close by, comical as if they were about to explore a haunted mansion.

The Indian's apartment was filled with smells, spicy foods, and other odors, maybe incense. The walls were filled with fierce-looking masks, and the shelves were loaded with dusty pottery.

Looking back at the man, Kate saw that he wore a string tie held with a turquoise clasp in the shape of a steer's skull.

"Mr. Morningsun?" Kate said.

Thinking, this is *too* much. This is too crazy for the kids....

The man walked over to a cheap couch and swept some newspapers off it to the floor. "Please, call me John." He grinned. "Because if you call me by my Pueblo name, you should"—he looked at Brian and winked—"call me Chief Morningsun." He reached out and brushed Emma's hair.

The little girl went stiff. "We're all going to be good friends. Now sit. We have lots to talk about."

Kate sat—and her children sat on each side of her, as close as they could.

"Now, before we start—how about some nice cinnamon tea?" John laughed again. "And don't worry, I'll feed you too. You folks will love it here."

Kate looked at Brian, then to Emma. She smiled, as if to say, *Sure we will.*

SEE HOW SHE RUNS

While she felt that this whole adventure had never seemed more wrong.

Mari picked up the phone and it was Dan. In the background, on Jake's tape player, it was Hammer time. "Jake," she called to him. "Turn it down."

"Hi, Mari. Did you tell Jake about the ski weekend."

"Yes. I'll get him so—"

"No, that's okay."

"He's very excited." She wondered: Who is Dan really calling?

"Great. That's great." There was a pause. "Mari, I was able to get something on the woman who was killed . . . something about her husband."

"Yes."

"You know that this isn't your business anymore."

No lectures, please, she thought. "I know that."

"Right. Well, the detective running the case is an old buddy. He told me some stuff, stuff that's not in the papers."

The music stopped. Mari thought that Jake might come out into the kitchen. But another rap song started.

"Alex Russ had no record. Oh, he had some traffic stuff. But he got into some trouble in high school. He was being counseled all through his last two years—when he wasn't suspended."

"What did he do?"

"*Lots*. He attacked a teacher. That didn't go to the police, but he cornered his English teacher in the john, screaming at him for flunking him. There were other violent episodes with kids. He cut a kid once, and this time cops were called."

Jake made the music louder and it was hard to hear.

"Wait a second, Dan. Hold on. Jake . . . Jake! Turn that down, will you? I'm on the phone." The volume column dropped back a notch or two. "Okay—go on."

"Don't know why kids likes that rap stuff."

"You said—"

"Yeah—well, there are medical records on Alex Russ. Turns out he spent a lot of time in the clinic as a kid. His parents were looking for some help, counseling, psychological stuff. I guess Russ gave them problems."

She thought of the dead bodies, the blood-soaked sheets. I guess they didn't get to the bottom of Russ's problem.

She thought of Elaine Russ stumbling up from her bed, realizing what was happening, the dullness of her horror, standing there in the dark, smelling the smoke, knowing that her children were dead.

That now she was qoing going to die . . .

"Mari . . . you still there?"

"Yes, sorry. I was just lost . . . thinking."

"That's all they got. Except—the school shrink gave a diagnosis. 'Suspected psychosis,' the shrink said. He recommended intense therapy."

Mari nodded to herself. "Does—does your friend have anything on where Russ went?"

"No. He's disappeared. There's one other thing, though—" Dan took a breath. "They're not optimistic."

Mari nodded. Not optimistic. Jake came bopping into the kitchen. He rubbed his stomach, signaling that he was hungry.

She smiled at her son. "Thanks, Dan. Thanks for calling." Dan didn't have to do this. And Mari could guess why he was doing it. "I've got a hungry boy to feed."

"Oh, sure. Right. Tell Jake hi," Dan said. "And I'll see him in a few days."

"Will do, and thanks."

Mari hung up the phone. She turned to Jake. "How about some burritos, big guy?"

"Sure." Jake came over and looked up at Mari. "Mom, when are you going to start dating?"

She laughed. Everyone with the same question.

"Don't you worry about that." She shook her head. She laughed again. "The last thing I need is a date. God . . ."

She was sure of that.

At least she thought that she was sure about that.

18

Kate squeezed Emma's hand to reassure her. Everything's okay, pumpkin . . . no matter how strange things seem.

"Here you are," said John Morningsun, the scraggily-looking chief. "Now this is *real* cinnamon tea, nice and fresh."

He put the tray with the four cups and a small honey pot down on his tiny coffee table.

"I've never had tea," Emma said quietly.

John winked at her. "Oh, really. Well, then today will be a *special* day for you, eh? Your first cup of tea, and you meet a real Pueblo chief."

Brian's eyes narrowed. "You're a real Indian?"

John's wrinkles suddenly pointed down, as if he was angry— but then, just as quickly, he grinned. "Listen, my Anglo friend, there is no such thing as an 'Indian' except in India." He leaned close to Brian and Kate watched Brian trying not to pull back, "And this is not India. The Pueblo, the Zuni, the Apache, the Navajo—those are just some of the people who lived in this land back when your ancestors didn't know squat about popcorn."

John laughed, and then so did Kate.

Brian relaxed. Emma took a sip of her tea. "It's good." She turned to Kate. "I *like* it, Mommy."

"Of course it's good. You visit me, and I'll make you a different tea every day. What do you say?" John looked at Kate, asking her approval. "And—I almost forgot."

He quickly got up and ran into a small room near the back, his bedroom, Kate guessed.

John came back with a small doll, with floppy ears and a stylized rabbit face.

He handed it to Emma. "This is what my people used to give their children—before Super Nintendo. But it's not only a doll. It's a special spirit that watches over children."

John looked up to Brian. "But we don't give these dolls, the kachinkas, to boys. Boys grow up to be braves. They get different playthings."

John looked at Kate. "With your permission?" He dug in his pocket and pulled out a small pocketknife. Brian took the knife and pulled out the sturdy, squat blade.

"I never let him have a knife," Kate said.

Brian turned to her. "Please, Mom? Please?"

"He's in the West," John said. "It's a different world out here."

"Please . . ."

"And I'll teach him the proper way to handle a knife, to be safe with it."

Kate nodded. The kids were both happy now, sitting in this strange apartment. That was pretty remarkable. She looked at the rug on the wall, a beautiful swirl of lines and geometric designs.

We're in a different world.

"Okay," Kate said.

"Good." John spoke to the children. "It's important that you get presents. We're all going to be great friends. Now, let me get your bags into your apartment. It's just next door. You can get some sleep."

He got up and walked to the door. He looked at Kate.

"Then your mother and I can talk. . . ."

"Thank you," Kate said. "Thank you for everything."

John nodded. The children had fallen asleep quickly, and now the Pueblo chief turned more serious. He came and stood next to Kate in the small kitchen of her new apartment. A stale smell lingered.

She wondered how old John was. It was hard to tell, looking at his sun-blackened skin. But he wasn't young.

"I know you're tired," he said. "But I think that we should talk."

She nodded. John gestured at a chair. Kate walked to the children's bedroom. She stopped, listened for moment, and then shut their bedroom door.

When she came back, John was grim-faced. She sat down, and he pulled a chair close to her and sat near her.

"I know you have been told all the things that you must not do. But I want to make sure. There will be others after you,

SEE HOW SHE RUNS

other women who need this place, and what we do here must be protected."

Kate nodded. The friendly Indian was so serious now....

"You will make no calls. Eventually there will be a time when you can contact anyone you need to contact. But for now, you will call *no one*. In two days you can take your children to the school. I have the information there, the name of the principal. You will say that the children's school records are coming. They will bother you for them, but don't let that upset you."

John rubbed his chin. And Kate wondered who was this man who acted as a protector for women who were running away.

How did that happen?

She wasn't sure she'd ever be able to ask him.

"You have money?"

"Some. A little. But I'll need a job."

"I know. There's a big restaurant on Alameda. They always need people, waitresses. I know the owner. She is a Pueblo. I've told her about you. She always needs good workers. She thinks that you're divorced. Do you have new papers, a new Social Security number?"

"Yes..." Kate started to dig out her wallet.

"No. I don't need to see them. And you have rehearsed your children? Your girl, Emma—" John looked up, concern in his narrow eyes. "She is so little."

"Yes. But she knows what to do. We've practiced." John didn't seem convinced.

"You must be careful, *all the time*. People will be looking for you. People are searching for you and your children." He took a breath. "There are people who could steal your children back."

"I wouldn't let that happen." Kate said the words flatly. It was a fact, indisputable.

"There's one other thing. You should not make any friends. Not now. It's hard, but you should be alone." He smiled. "I will have to be your friend."

It was as if John could see her weakness, the little girl, curled up in the dark....

Kate nodded. "Thank you. Thanks for everything."

John took a breath. He looked at Kate. "You are tired?"

"Yes."

He nodded. "Then I will go."

"No," Kate said. "Stay a bit. I've had no one to talk with for days now. Just the kids. Please stay."

John nodded, looking at her. And Kate saw pain in his eyes. The pain seemed worse when he looked at her, as if it reminded him of something terrible.

"We can talk," he said. "And you can tell me what brought you here."

Kate looked away. What brought me here?

That was easy . . . that was an easy moment to pinpoint. In the time line of this nightmare, leaving, running, that was an easy moment to mark.

What brought me here . . .

When it all became hopeless, when the trap seemed inescapable, when the nightmare was total in its ability to hold her and—worse—hold the children—

It was all finely focused to one point in time.

So she told John Morningsun about it.

19

The divorce wasn't hard.

As bad as it got, Kate always thought: I can deal with this.

Getting divorced had been the easy part. It was a legal process, and in New York there wasn't much David could do to stop it—even with all his family's money, the lawyers, the connections.

But even before she got the divorce, there were warning signs. Her young lawyer, Sharon Friedman, warned Kate that the custody hearing would be difficult.

At the hearing, Kate explained what David was like now . . . maybe the way he always was. The anger had been there, even before his accident. She told how she was about to tell David about the divorce in the restaurant.

The judge—a gray-haired woman who looked as if she should be home baking cookies—looked down at Kate through her bifocals. The judge sat back when Kate described David's incredible rages. And Kate felt like a schoolgirl again. So nervous, making so many mistakes . . .

SEE HOW SHE RUNS

She tried to describe how David's weights clanked through the house, as if he was training for something terrible. She told the judge that David hit her, that he hit Brian.

Kate stopped. She took a breath. It was so stuffy in the White Plains courtroom. And then she told about coming into Emma's room and finding David, sitting there. . . .

Sharon had advised against it.

"The judge won't like it. No, she'll see it as a ploy. They hear so many stories, Kate. Incredible stuff . . . Mothers, wives—they'll say anything. The judge knows that."

Kate grew indignant. "It happened! Isn't that the important thing? He was there, touching himself. He touched Emma while she slept."

Sharon shook her head. "I *know* what you're feeling. I understand your anger." Kate thinking, Sure you do. "I'm simply trying to tell you how the court will see it."

Later, sitting there, looking up at the judge, talking, fighting tears, Kate saw the judge's tired, impassive face. There was nothing there except fatigue. And sitting there, Kate knew—with a dull horror—that Sharon had been right. It had been a mistake. Her charges were only seen as another ploy.

It was noted in the record. Along with Kate's protestations.

I was in control, Kate thought. Wasn't I in control?

She spoke to God as she got up and left the stand.

I was in control, dear God. Wasn't I?

When she walked back to the desk to Sharon, her lawyer looked away—and Kate knew that it hadn't gone well.

It was her first taste of things to come.

And then there was David.

Their friends, some of them Kate thought were her friends as well, acted funny. One wife she knew said, "But how could you leave him? David needs you."

Though David was no longer pathetic—his speech was good, his movements almost normal—he was still pitied. And when Kate tried to tell a friend about David's violent episodes, insinuating that there was something more, the woman put up her hands.

"I *don't* want to hear this," she said.

Kate stared at her. And she heard doors being shut. Door were shut, friends vanished—overnight!—and then the bills started to come. Papers had to be filed, clerk's fees paid. Her lawyer—gently—brought up the question of her hourly charges, phone calls, office expenses. The meter was running.

But Kate had little access to money. She felt squeezed. She thought that she just had to hold on until the settlement.

Her lawyer gave her a warning about that. "David's money isn't really *his* money," Sharon explained. "It's tied to trust funds, the family brokerage. On paper, he doesn't have much."

David's lawyer outgunned Sharon. There was nothing Kate could do about it. Except to say, *Stop. I can't waste any more money.*

The big house was sold at a loss. The housing market, even in upscale Ardsley, was dead. There had been a fat mortgage, and closing costs, the agent's fee. Kate had to rent a small place in Harley. The schools weren't so great.

But there'd be enough money for the children, for clothes and school supplies and food. But if Kate wanted to live—if she wanted a life—she'd have to work.

I'll have to leave Emma with someone, she thought. I never wanted to do that. She's *so* young.

Then there was David.

Kate thought that the divorce ended it. That it was all over. But she quickly learned that divorce ended nothing.

David's petition for joint custody moved the judge. His speech was faltering, pathetic, as if he were playing a musical instrument.

His left hand dangled to his side, struggling to gesture ... though Kate knew he had some control over it.

He looked over to Kate.

"I l-love my wife," he said. His voice caught, and Kate looked away. "I love her. I didn't want this divorce. And—"

On cue. As if rehearsed. There were tears. David's lawyer—a friend of the family—was one of the best. He wore a charcoal-gray suit and had silver-gray hair. Kate saw that Sharon Friedman looked scattered and disheveled standing beside him.

The judge listened attentively. Kate remembered what Sharon had said.

"Listen, Kate. It's a goddamn—oh, sorry—it's an old-boy network. They *all* know each other, they all give each other work. They're in here every week—the lawyers, the judges—cutting deals, making arrangements. They see each other at the same parties, the same fund-raisers," Sharon said. "It's an old buddy club, from the clerks on up to the judges."

"So what do we do about it?" Kate asked.

Thinking, So what can Sharon do about it? And she wondered

whether she should have some other lawyer, knowing that she couldn't afford anyone else, that she couldn't start all over with a new lawyer.

She owed Sharon so much money, and another lawyer, a better, more expensive lawyer, would have to start all over.

Kate was tapped out. She needed a deal, even a bad deal. Sharon was blunt.

"You need to settle."

So she did.

She was awarded custody, but the judge gave David generous visitation rights—every other weekend, one day and night each week. Two full weeks in summer and alternate holidays.

"The court recommends that the children have the closest possible contact with the noncustodial parent," the judge said, her voice gravelly, unconcerned. "The court also counsels the custodial parent to refrain from inflammatory accusations."

Kate glared at the judge.

Later, when Kate told Brian, a terrible look crossed the boy's face. And she told him: "Don't worry. I'll be right here." She tapped the phone. "Right here. You just call."

And Kate lied to herself. Those things, the things David did—they might not happen now that we're divorced. They might not happen ever again.

The important thing is that we're free.

I can make a life for me and the kids.

But she was wrong.

The first time David showed up at her new small rented house to pick up the kids, he looked around, smirked, and said, "Nice place . . . r-real nice." He looked up to Kate, who stood by the entrance to the kitchen. "And not such a bad neighborhood."

"It's all I could afford," she said. She risked saying something further. "You saw to that."

David's eyes flared. But Emma bounced down the stairs then with a small overnight bag. She was excited. Her daddy spoiled her, with ice cream and toys.

"Your choice," David said. "Y-you wanted this."

She watched him clench his fist. She thought, Get him out of here . . . please make him leave.

David looked up the stairs. "Where's Brian?"

Kate shook her head. "I—I don't know." That made her feel

a chill, the way he said it. *Where's Brian?*

She stepped into the small living room, moving past David. He's filling out, all those weights, as if he was driven to build a new body.

"Bri," Kate said. Then, louder: "Brian, your father's waiting."

Then she heard Brian slowly thump down the stairs. He was not happy to be going. They had talked about it and Kate had explained that there was no choice.

"I've b-been waiting," David said. Kate looked to him, seeing the anger in his eyes, and she feared for Brian.

But no, she told herself. It's *okay*. There's nothing wrong. It will be fine. David will be on his best behavior.

She stood in the darkness after they were gone, trying not to cry.

Brian didn't say anything when he came home two days later.

He ran right up to his room. "Brian . . . Brian, honey, what's wrong?"

David's car pulled away, a getaway car, roaring away.

Emma seemed happy. She was hugging a new doll, a curly-headed doll with a backpack. She seemed happy, bouncy. Nothing could have gone wrong, could it?

Kate knelt down. "Emmie, Emmie, honey, what's wrong with Brian? What's wrong with your brother?"

Emma looked up, her face serious, repeating the day's lesson. "Brian was *bad*." The little girl shook her head. "He wouldn't do what Daddy said. And Daddy got mad."

Kate chewed at her lip. Brian was her big boy, her little man. He's just a kid, she told herself. He's only a little boy and—

Emma's face brightened. "But look, Mommy. Look at what Daddy bought me. Isn't she cute? I'm calling her Patty. She has a backpack, see? Patty and I can go on adventures together."

Kate stood up, letting her hand drift through the waves of Emma's hair.

Kate looked at the stairs.

I have to talk to Brian. I have to find out what happened. I have to help him, help him deal with this.

She looked at the stairs, and she felt helpless.

Then the calls started. In the middle of the night the phone rang. Kate would blink awake and reach out, knocking over the gooseneck lamp on the end table, her hand flapping at the phone.

SEE HOW SHE RUNS

She'd pick up the handset, and say hoarsely, "Hello? Hello . . ."

And a rude click would answer her.

Not every night, but enough so that now she always looked at the phone before she went to bed, looked at it and wondered whether it would ring tonight.

"It's him," Kate told Sharon in her office. "I *know* it. David is calling."

She still owed the lawyer money and it was hard to go to her for help, knowing that it only added to the bill. "David's calling me."

Sharon shook her head. "You don't *know* that. It could be anyone. An obscene caller, a heavy breather. You don't know that it's your ex-husband."

Oh, yes I do, thought Kate. But Sharon was right. She had no proof.

"Get an answering machine. Screen all your calls."

"Screen my calls? What do you—"

Sharon looked up from a desk piled with paper, briefs, yellow pads, the detritus of dozens of other cases. "Don't answer your own phone anymore. Listen to whoever comes on the machine, then—if you want—pick up."

And that was it. There was nothing else to be done. Kate got up.

He's doing things to me. And I can't stop him.

Then, one night, she saw the car.

Kate just happened to go to the living-room window, and she saw a car parked across the street, up the street a bit. She was about to turn away from the window when her hand froze on the blinds. Her hand froze, and her heart stopped.

There was someone, a black shadow, *sitting* in the car.

The car lurked just beyond the pool of yellowish light made by the street lamp.

It was hard to tell. . . .

But it looked like—no, she was *sure* of it. It was David's car. He was sitting there, outside the house, watching, waiting.

"I l-love Kate," he said in the court. "I don't want this, I want us to stay together."

Watching, waiting. For what, she thought? To see if I bring someone home, if another man comes here. Not too likely that would happen.

She sometimes fantasized about meeting a man, someone young, someone who didn't wear a suit, who smiled, who took her dancing, who held her close, and—

The car engine started up. A smoky cloud of exhaust escaped from the rear of the car and drifted toward the street lamp.

What can I do? Can I call the police? Can I do that?

She watched the car drive away.

That night the phone rang. Twice, at two, then a little after 3:00 A.M. It rang, and the new answering machine came to life.

But no one left a message.

Then Kate lay awake, digging her hands into the bed sheets, trying to breathe normally, trying so hard to get back to sleep.

20

Then, one night, David was there again—parked outside—and Kate ran to the phone, hurrying before David left.

She called the police. She spoke quickly. "My husband—my ex-husband is parked across the street, watching me."

She listened for some expression of alarm from the police. Instead, the officer said, slowly, "Okay. Somebody will get over there." No rush, no urgency.

Kate went to the window, thinking: Please hurry. While he's still here. Hurry!

It took forever, but a patrol car eventually showed up. At the same time David's car started to pull away. Kate ran out the door, yelling at the police, screaming, a crazy lady, pointing toward David's car.

"That's him! There he is!"

Later she would realize that she had sounded hysterical. Out of control. *Losing it*.

She would begin to see the trap she was falling into.

"Over there, please, he's over there." Louder, shrieking. "Hurry, he's getting away. He's right *there*."

A dark-haired officer with a mustache was out of his car. The cop looked in the direction Kate was pointing. "Take it easy, miss. I see—"

David's car was moving out of his parking spot, pulling onto the center of the street.

The cop leaned into his patrol car. The bubble light flashed to life. A bright white light at the side flashed at David's car, bathing it in brilliant light. The siren wailed.

Kate thought of the kids sleeping. Waking up, hearing the siren.

Hysterical. Out of control.

David's car stopped. The cop walked up to the driver's window. Another cop stepped out and came up to Kate.

"Why don't you go inside, miss, and wait? Wait and we'll come in after we talk to him."

Kate saw the first officer standing beside David's car, talking. Shouldn't they be pulling David out? Kate thought. Isn't that what they do?

The cop next to her touched her arm. "Go ahead, ma'am. Go inside. We'll be right in."

Kate nodded and walked back into the house, looking over her shoulder, watching the cops standing by David's car.

She saw movement at a neighbor's window, curtains being pulled aside, blinds moved, as they watched what was happening.

Kate sat on her couch and waited. And it wasn't long before the two policemen were at her door. She thought she saw an uneasy smile cross the face of the younger cop.

Why is he smiling? There's nothing funny about this.

They stood there, looking big, filling the small living room with their dark blue uniforms, their nightsticks, their guns, and a radio from which a low voice babbled incoherently.

The cop with the mustache started talking. "We, er, spoke to your ex-husband, Mrs. Cowell. He said he was just sitting out there."

They waited.

Kate looked from one to the other, waiting for the rest. "And?"

The cops looked at each other.

"He said that he wasn't doin' nothing, ma'am. He was just sitting there, he said. Did you see him do anything?"

Kate's mouth fell open. "He's *out* there, spying on me. He's watching my house."

The cop with a mustache took a breath. "But has he done anything to you?"

And Kate felt it again... the same feeling she had in court. *Can't they see what's happening to me, to my kids?*

"He's been calling. In the middle of the night, a couple times each—"

The younger cop had a pad out. "And you've reported these calls?"

Kate stopped. She shook her head. The leather cover of the pad closed, slowly. "No. I mean, I never hear anyone, I don't know whether it's him. I mean, I do know but—"

Hysterical. Out of control.

The cop with the mustache took a step closer to her.

"Look—there's nothing we can do here. You say that he's waiting outside. But the street, the sidewalk is public property, Mrs. Cowell. If your husband—"

"Ex-husband."

Then the cop sighed. "If he wants to sit out here, I'm afraid he can. There's not a damn thing we can do about it." He took another deep breath.

And Kate thought: Aren't all cops divorced? Don't they all have lousy marriages, and they drink and play with their guns and beat their wives and—

And I'm asking for their help?

"If you have a problem with your husband—"

"Ex-husband," Kate hissed, not caring how wild-eyed she seemed.

The cop nodded. "If you and your 'ex' have a disagreement, you should work it out someway. There's not a hell of a lot we can do."

Footsteps on the stairs.

Brian came down, squinting, looking at the policemen.

"Mom," he said. His voice sounded raspy, scratchy, snatched from the warmth of his sleep, his dreams. "What's wrong, Mom?"

She went to Brian. "Nothing, honey."

"Then what are they doing here? Why are policemen in the living room?"

"Nothing. Go back to bed, honey. Please go—"

Brian stood there, looking at the policemen. "Why are they here? Is there something wrong?"

"No, Brian. No, I said." Her voice turned shrill. "Now, I said go back to—"

"Mrs. Cowell, we're going to go now."

She turned to the police. Doing their job, protecting David's right to sit outside the house.

She watched them.

Not the courts. Not the police. Not my lawyer.

There's no one to protect us.

She turned back to Brian. A gust of cold air swirled past her as the door opened. Cold air, reaching into the room.

"I'll explain tomorrow, Bri. Please . . ."

Brian shook his head. He wanted to know now. And Kate thought, He's just a boy. But we're together in this.

She put an arm around him. "Tomorrow. I promise. I'll tell you tomorrow."

Brian stood still a moment. Then he nodded. Kate came next to him. She heard the car engines starting outside. The police car, then David's car.

She walked Brian upstairs.

No safety, she thought. There's no safety, there's no end. There's no sanctuary for us. And even upstairs, after putting Brian back to bed, she stood in the hallway, listening to the cars pull away.

David was gone for tonight.

But now she knew that he could be there, outside her door, anytime, night or day, in his car or standing outside, watching, waiting.

Watching. Waiting . . .

Anytime.

21

The phone calls continued. And David would be there, sometimes walking around the block as if on guard. Or—as fall turned cold—sitting in his car.

Kate was a prisoner.

Every other weekend David pulled into the driveway of the

small house and came to the door. Kate always tried to hurry the kids, to get them ready, to keep David from coming inside.

Somehow that never worked. Somehow Emma always forgot something or Brian wouldn't come quickly, and David came in and stood there, looking at Kate.

His eyes locked on her.

Once she said, "Why do you call me? Why do you keep calling me at night?"

David smiled. "B-but I haven't," he said. His grin widened. "May-maybe it's one of your boyfriends." His eyes widened, and Kate wanted to back away from him. "Why don't you call the police? Yeah, call the police." He laughed. "They'll h-help you."

Kate retreated. She knew that David's visitation rights were a license for him to terrorize her. No one ever took anything away from him, ever.

And he wasn't going to let her do this to him.

Brian started having nightmares. He'd wake up in the middle of the night, sitting up in his bed, huddled up like a terrified toddler calling for his mommy.

"What is it?" Kate would say.

Brian shook his head and sometimes he'd say nothing. He'd just shake his head, trying to shake the fuzzy images away.

Other times he'd say, "Mom, I don't want to go see him." He didn't say "Dad" or "Daddy." He'd look right at Kate, composed, a sane boy making a desperate plea. "I don't want to go. *Please*. I don't—"

And she'd sit there, holding Brian's hand while he told her the things David did, how he yelled, how he'd slap him if he didn't hurry, how once he kicked Brian while he lay on the floor reading.

Kicked at him, yelling, "Get up. What do you think you're doing—get up!"

There was no reason. David could turn angry for no reason at all. . . .

Kate squeezed his hand. "I know, honey," she whispered. "I know. But the courts . . . the courts say—"

Please, Mommy. Please.

Then Kate, holding him tight, would ask. She'd have to ask . . .

What about Emma?

How is he with Emma? He doesn't hit Emma, does he? And

SEE HOW SHE RUNS

at night, do you see anything, anything—

Brian shook his head, irritated that Kate was asking about the little girl, that he didn't count.

No. Emma was Daddy's little baby. He was always buying her things, always sitting her on his lap. He never hit *her*.

Kate dared probe, had to.

"But is there anything else. Do you see him with her and does he . . ."

Brian looked up at her, a confused expression. There was no recognition of what she was talking about.

Not this time . . .

It was a crisp winter day, blue sky, no clouds.

Kate stood at the front door watching her children with David.

Emma was already in the car, singing happily to her doll. Brian stood by Kate.

"I don't want to go."

David said. "You c-come on now."

"Go," Kate whispered, feeling terrible, a traitor. "You *have* to go, Brian."

He turned to his mother. "I don't want to go, Mom. I hate it being with him. I hate—"

Kate had her hand on Brian's shoulder, urging him to go with David, even though it tore her up. *What am I pushing him to? What the hell am I pushing my son to?*

Then David grabbed the boy's wrist. David's good hand, strong now, so strong, closed around Brian's wrist and he started dragging him down the front steps.

The boy's legs slipped and started banging noisily against the stone steps.

"David!" Kate yelled. "God—stop it. He'll go, he'll—"

But David didn't stop. He kept moving, and Brian was off his feet, deadweight, howling, crying while David held his wrist and dragged him down the driveway.

Kate stood still. She watched Brian trying to scramble to his feet, but then David would savagely jerk him forward—pulling the boy like a sack of potatoes.

Kate screamed at him. "Stop!"

And she banged the wooden door frame with her hands. She banged it, over and over until her hands throbbed from the pain.

Brian screamed for her. "Mom!" he called, gasping at the air. Kate heard the car door being shut, the engine starting.

And she stood there and watched the car back out of the driveway, Brian in the back, curled up, his face pressed close to the window, looking right at her.

Emma sat in the front, playing with her doll, oblivious to her big brother. "He's always getting in trouble," Emma would say. "He's always making Daddy mad."

Kate watched the car pass the front door. She saw David pat Emma's leg.

Kate shook her head. Now she pounded her head against the frame, whispering, "No . . . no . . ."

No.

Brian and Emma were dropped off late Sunday. And Brian came into the house with a purple blotch on one side of his face.

"Mommy, I'm tired," Emma said, breezing past Kate. Kate touched Brian's shoulder. She nodded to Emma. "Go—go upstairs, get ready for—"

She stopped Brian, turning his face, his sweet handsome face, toward her. "Brian," she said, whispering, still a traitor. "What happened?"

The boy didn't say anything. He shrugged and slipped his face away from her hand. He moved his jaw as if it was stiff, throbbing.

Emma walked up the stairs.

Brian looked up at his sister, waiting for her to disappear.

"What happened?" Kate asked.

Brian waited. Kate saw a horrible dullness in the boy's eyes. She had read how men who have lost something, through a stroke, an accident, have this anger against their sons, against their offspring, who seem so strong.

Her fingers touched the bruise. "I'm going to call the police." Kate went to the phone.

"Mom," Brian said quietly. "Mom—something happened."

Kate was dialing.

"Something happened with Emma."

Kate froze.

"Emma was in the bath, Mom. Dad gave her a bath."

Kate felt a throbbing inside her head, a pain exploding from nowhere, flashes of color before her eyes. The handset of the phone hung in her hand. What did I want this for? she thought. Why did I pick up the phone?

SEE HOW SHE RUNS

"I heard Emma squeal. I—I walked to the door. I remembered what you had said."

Kate nodded.

"The door was open, Mom. The door was *open,* and Dad was on the floor. His hand was in the tub. Emmie was squealing, Mommy. She said, 'Stop it, Daddy.' She said—"

Stop it.

Stop. It.

Oh, God. Stop . . . it.

The phone came to life. "Please hang up and try your call again. Please hang up and try your call—" Kate pressed down to disconnect. And this time she called the police, thinking it would help.

A crazy thought. Thinking that it would help.

The police came. They took Brian's statement—they said that they'd have to talk with Emma. They said they'd go see David.

In a few days Kate's lawyer Sharon Friedman reluctantly agreed to take David back to court.

"He can't see them," Kate said. "I can't let him see them alone anymore."

Sharon nodded, but she offered little encouragement. "They hear this stuff all the time, Kate. *All* the time."

"But I called the police. They saw Brian's bruise. He told them about Emma."

Sharon shook her head. "The courts hear this stuff every day, Kate." She picked up a piece of paper. "David said the boy fell while shooting baskets. And he denies the charge of touching Emma. He called it sick."

Kate nodded. "So what are you saying here? That I can't protect my own children? That he can go on hitting Brian, he can—can—" Her voice started to give way. "He can abuse Emma. Is that what you're saying?"

Kate didn't feel her voice spiraling upward . . . hysterical, out of control.

Sharon put a hand up. "Kate . . . I'm not the one you have to convince. It's the courts."

Kate shook her head. "Isn't there anything we can do?"

Sharon riffled through some papers. "I've asked the court to order a psychological evaluation of David. But there's no telling how that will come out. And—" the lawyer looked up at her— "I have to warn you. The judge will be looking at *you* too. They see a lot of funny stuff. You have to be in control, Kate. You can't lose it."

Kate heard Sharon. She heard her.

But she didn't remember.

Weeks later, sitting in the courtroom, Kate leaned over to Sharon and whispered, "What's that mean?"

The court-appointed psychologist was reading his report.

"Shhh," Sharon said.

The report was loaded with jargon . . . and Kate heard her own name.

"On both the TAT and MMP, Mr. Cowell evidences a strong will and a desire to father his children. While he is still recovering from his massive hemorrhage, his emotional control is not perfect. Occasional outbursts should be expected. Still, we find no sign that his massive trauma has rendered Mr. Cowell unfit as a parent."

"What?" Kate said audibly.

The judge glared at her.

"Watch it," Sharon whispered.

"Dr. Rosen," the judge said, the same woman Kate had faced in the past, peered through the split lenses of her bifocals. "Did you find *any* evidence of a sexual disorientation, any evidence of"— the judge looked down at the papers in front of her— "a tendency toward sexual abuse that could be directed at Mr. Cowell's children?"

Dr. Rosen shook his head. "No."

"I can't believe this," Kate said. "Didn't he talk to Emma, Brian—"

"Counselor, if you will please keep Mrs. Cowell quiet . . ." the judge said.

Kate shook her head. This was crazy.

She stood up. "No! No . . . I mean, Your Honor, this is all wrong. This is sick. I called the police. My son had a *bruise,* and he saw his father with my little girl."

Out of control, the voice spiraling, up, up.

"—saw h-him sitting on the bed, Your Honor."

The judge shook her head. "Counselor, would you *please* ask your client to—"

"And this man, this expert says that he's—"

"Kate," Sharon said, tugging at her skirt. "Kate, sit down. This isn't helping. Kate—"

SEE HOW SHE RUNS

"What—what do I need, Your Honor? Eight-by-ten glossies of the welts on my boy's body? Photographs of David fondling my little girl? Is that what I need?"

Kate turned to the court, the clerk, the empty seats—except for David's mother and father glaring at her—David and his attorney, sitting impassive. "What do you need to stop him from hur-hurting us?"

"Kate!" Sharon stood up next to her. "Sit down, please."

Kate let herself be pulled down, still shaking her head. Dr. Rosen looked uncomfortable, his orderly report stopped in midstream.

God forgive me, Kate thought. God forgive me, but I feel like I want to kill them. Kill them all.

They won't protect my children.

The judge shook her head. And then—

And then the judge laughed.

"That was quite a performance, Mrs. Cowell. But I have to tell you that your outbursts are *not* helping your case."

"Your Honor..."

It was David's lawyer, Mr. McManus, a sleek silver fox. He smiled with the judge. But his voice was liquid honey, soothing, so calm and controlled.

"Your Honor, in the light of Mrs. Cowell's display, we'd like to request a psychiatric evaluation."

Sharon sprang to her feet. Kate didn't understand what was being said. "Your Honor, I don't—"

"My client is worried that Mrs. Cowell is unfit to be the custodial parent, Your Honor, that she is, in fact, obsessed with sexual matters. And this is making the custodial home an unhealthy atmosphere for the children."

The judge was listening. Yes, this makes sense now. This makes sense. The mother is obsessed....

Kate shook her head. No, this can't be happening.

Sharon turned to her. "Don't say a *word.*"

"Further, my client would like to move that court grant a temporary order of joint custody."

—can't be happening.

The judge shook her head. "I'd like Dr. Rosen to finish his report. And then I'll set a new hearing date to consider your request. Now, Dr. Rosen..."

The psychiatrist cleared his throat, ready for his moment on stage, his moment playing in the old-boy network.

Sharon wrote on a yellow pad.

Now you've done it!

"In sum, I'd recommend that the father, Mr. Cowell, be given unrestricted visitation privileges. Further, the custodial parent has obviously coached her children—which will create a most unhealthy relationship between the father and his children—"

The judge nodded. This all makes sense.

"Therefore, we'd like to ask that if any evidence of a mental disorder in the custodial parent is found, then the children are to be placed in their father's care."

The air left the room. Kate thought that she'd throw up, keel to one side and hack at the worn, wood floor.

But it was over, all decisions postponed.

"God, now you've done it," Sharon whispered to her. "Now you've really done it."

It was wonderland. It was the Red Queen's tea party. It was off with their heads. It was everyone over the cuckoo's nest. It was bedlam.

It was insane. It was horrible.

The judge laughed. . . . Kate kept thinking. She laughed. Insane . . .

And yet—it was all too real.

22

She had a terrible thought.

What if David were to die?

It was a fantasy, soothing and wonderful. Despite the guilt, she wondered . . . would she have someone kill him? Would she do that?

She cried at how desperate and helpless she had become.

Brian begged to stay home, but Kate told him there was nothing she could do. He had to go with his father. Then, as if reading Kate's mind, Brian said, "I want to kill him."

The phone kept ringing late at night—only now David was talking to the answering machine.

SEE HOW SHE RUNS

"I don't h-hate you, Kate," he'd say. "I love you. I love you—"

She turned off the answering machine and took the phone off the hook.

Brian had another accident. He fell down the stairs. Clumsy kid. Kate called the abuse hot line. Someone there asked her, "Is there a marital dispute pending in court? Are you currently in court?"

"What does that have to do with it?" Kate said.

"It's something that we have to ask."

Kate said yes, and suddenly the voice on the other end was simply taking down information, the size of the bruise to Brian's side, just below the rib cage. The father called it an accident. And it could be, the voice said, couldn't it?

"But my son *says* that he was punched, that his father—"

It was useless. She could be accused of harassment. The more she charged David, the more hysterical, the more crazy she seemed.

"You could lose them, Kate," Sharon warned. "The court can take your kids away from you."

"I wish he was dead," Kate said. The fantasy, so absurd . . .

Sharon laughed. "Now, that would cost a lot of money. And before you do that—before you go to jail for the rest of your life, I hope you pay my bill." It was a joke. But Kate knew that Sharon was concerned about getting her money.

The clock was running, the meter ticking away, *and I have no money.*

One morning she asked Emma . . . about taking baths at Daddy's. Emma listened, spooning up her Kix, dribbling milk and the yellow puffs of the cereal to the table.

"He likes doing that," Emma said. "Sometimes he gets in, too, sometimes—"

Emma stopped.

"What?" Kate asked. Then quietly, desperately: "What, baby?"

Emma shook her head. "I can't tell you, Mommy, Daddy said it was a secret. I'm not supposed to tell anyone, not *anyone,* he said."

But Emma did, with Kate holding her hand, and rubbing at her tears with her other hand, saying, "Yes sweetie, go on. It's okay."

Listening.

Picturing Emma in the tub, and David there, taking his clothes off.

"Go on, honey." Not wanting to scare her, not until she heard it all.

About David . . .

Touching himself while Emma watched. Somehow getting off on that. Then dipping into the water, playing a game—it was just a game—touching the little girl, my sweet—

Kate moaned. Emma knew about strangers, and "bad touches," but this was Daddy. . . .

"Are you okay, Mommy? Mommy?" Kate nodded. Emma looked down at her hand. "You're hurting my hand, Mommy. You're squeezing too tight."

Kate let her go.

But she told herself that she wouldn't let go of her, of Emma or Brian, ever again.

Kate sat in Sharon Friedman's office—the day before the hearing. Today was the day she was going to ask her.

"There was this woman," Sharon said, "who shot her husband. He had been sexually abusing their son. She shot him, but it didn't kill him. Now listen to this. The woman gets put in jail. I think she eventually got a sentence of reckless endangerment. And do you know what happened to the boy?"

"No," Kate said quietly.

"The husband got custody. And that's not the craziest story. The court doesn't like to play with a parent's rights. And since a lot of women will charge their husbands with anything to screw them, the courts shrug it off."

"What about tomorrow?"

"I don't know. I think that joint custody is a possibility. You have to consider that."

"What about getting someone to be there—during David's visits? Someone to supervise."

Sharon shrugged.

"I don't know." The lawyer looked out her window. Puffy flakes of snow danced by the window. It was a week after Thanksgiving and winter seemed to be coming early.

"The judge hasn't been too helpful."

"Tell me. What do you think will happen?" Kate asked again.

Sharon turned back to her. "Bottom line? You'll get a warning about your charges. The judge doesn't believe you. Child Welfare will probably visit you, and David, to check on you. She may even give him joint custody." Sharon nodded. "I'm sorry. The system doesn't work too well."

Yes. I'm sorry. Not too well, Kate thought. The system . . . sucks.

SEE HOW SHE RUNS

Kate cleared her throat. "I want to go away."

"I'm sure you do, but—"

Kate leaned across the desk. She touched her lawyer's hand. "No. No, you don't understand. I won't allow him to hurt them anymore. I can't allow that. I want to leave with them, disappear."

Sharon shook her head. "That's illegal. I can't advise you about that."

Kate kept her hand covering Sharon's. "Sharon, there are people who help women like me, women running away from their husbands. You can help me find them. Let me talk with someone. Please, Sharon. We're going to lose tomorrow. Please. I *beg* you."

The lawyer stood up. She was young, but with her frizzy hair and pear-shaped body, she seemed in rehearsal for middle age.

"Kate, that's not a solution. You don't know what it would be like to run away."

She squeezed Sharon's hand. Tight, tighter . . . "Please. I'm out of money. I'm out of hope."

Sharon went to the window. She pushed her hand against the cold glass. Kate watched her.

I need help, people to tell me what to do. I can disappear, she thought. I can take the children and disappear.

Sharon turned back to her desk. She opened up a drawer and pulled out a book. She flipped through some pages and then picked up a pad.

She wrote something down and then ripped out the piece of paper. "Here. But you didn't get it from me. And tomorrow, in court, I want you to sit quietly no matter what the hell happens. Do you understand? God, they could put a restraining order on you if you keep losing it."

Kate nodded. "Yes. I will." She looked down at the name. Jayne Pezoric. And the number.

"She's in Atlanta," Sharon said. "And we never had this conversation."

Kate got up with the piece of paper in her hand and left the stuffy office.

The court hearing went as Sharon Friedman predicted.

David wasn't given joint custody, but he was granted unsupervised visitations. And the judge warned Kate against turning the children against their father.

Kate sat quietly. She nodded.

It was made clear that any more legal activity by Kate would be viewed as harassment, further evidence of an instability, a sexual preoccupation that would result in a change of the custodial arrangements.

Kate nodded.

She thanked the judge. Wishing that the insensitive bitch would explode, flare up, self-combust in a brilliant display.

The judge banged the gavel.

Kate owed money to a sitter . . . more money that she didn't have.

She turned and thanked Sharon.

But not for what happened in court . . .

She met Jayne Pezoric in a diner by Kennedy Airport. It was 3:00 P.M. and the woman would spend just a few hours with her.

Kate got to the Idlewild Diner early, ordered coffee . . . and waited.

Pezoric was late, bustling into the diner. She had blond hair, scattered and blown by the icy winds that swirled around the airport.

She sat down with Kate, shaking her hand. Pezoric was forty-five, maybe fifty. The waitress brought another cup of coffee. They had spoken on the phone about the details of Kate's case. Pezoric had also spoken to Kate's lawyer.

This was the planning meeting. The one and only face-to-face meeting.

"God, I'm so cold," Pezoric said. She smiled. "It's still mild in Atlanta."

She had a trace of a Southern accent. Pezoric had once been on *Donahue*. She was part of an underground that saved women, saved children. She didn't hide what she did. She had even been arrested and tried for it.

She wasn't scared of anyone.

"You'll need as much money as you can get," she said. "Borrow from any friends you can trust, credit-card accounts—"

"They're all dead," Kate said. She grinned sadly. "The cards, I mean. And I don't have a lot of friends. Mostly David's friends, and they—"

Pezoric nodded. "Whatever. Just get as much money as you can. Get some food for the trip. You don't want to be stopping too much. We'll give you a route to follow. But you'll have to find small motels, places without computers. The kids—" Pezoric shook her head. "That's the hard part, you have to rehearse them, real well. How old is . . . ?"

"Brian is nine, Emma is almost five." Kate cleared her throat. "But she's very smart."

"I hope so. Damn, one slip and your husband will find you."

"You think that he'll come looking for me?"

Pezoric sipped her coffee, holding the warmth close to her face.

"You tell me. He'll be outraged, he'll feel violated. From what you've said, he's obsessed with you. Now he'll have the legal system completely on his side." Another sip. "You'll be the outlaw, honey."

Kate chewed her lip, thinking about that.

"Are you sure that you're ready for this? You'll have to be strong. Your kids will need you to be real strong."

Kate had read about abusive parents. She read how the bruises get worse, the terror grows. She nodded.

"I'm ready."

Pezoric dug in her purse. "These are new papers for you. Social Security card, license, medical records, even some credit cards—but don't use them." She laughed. A car had been arranged. "I have the name of your contact in there. Pack very little with you, clothes, a few toys. Remember—you're leaving your old life behind."

The door to the diner opened and a cop walked in. He looked around.

Pezoric saw Kate looking at him and she turned to look over her shoulder. Then she turned back to Kate, her voice low.

"That's another thing—get a grip on your paranoia, girl." Pezoric smiled. "Otherwise you'll be crazy before you get there."

The cop took a seat at the counter and a young waitress came to him.

"Get there . . ." Kate said. "Get where?"

"Santa Fe," Pezoric said.

She might have said Disneyland. Bermuda. Mars.

"*Santa Fe,*" Kate repeated. She opened up the large envelope that Pezoric handed to her and looked at her new name, wondering, worrying about her new life.

Hoping that the old one was ready to die.

PART THREE

SANCTUARY

23

Mari went down the twisted road, down into the narrow canyon with shadows that looked like the coils of a snake, and she tried not to think about her last visit to Coldwater Springs.

It had been dark then, she thought, night. Now it's sunny. Why, the place doesn't even look the same.

Not at all.

Down, curving past a small house, a house in miniature with a tiny porch and gaunt wooden posts straining to hold up a slanted overhang laden with wet snow.

She saw faces looking at her, people walking down the canyon to the town, looking at her car with hopeful eyes. A tourist. Yes, *a tourist* is coming. There will be money spent, meals ordered, trinkets bought. Send out the word. *A tourist.*

Her father used to laugh at all the tourists buying Indian knickknacks. He'd laugh and say, "See. We're getting our revenge." Her father always laughed so easily. Until the day his wife died, a quiet, olive-skinned woman who obviously loved him so much. And then her father never laughed again.

She took a turn and saw the remarkable vista lying at the end of the street. The snowcapped edge of the Colorado Front Range came into view, a movie shot. The ticky-tacky downtown led to the incredible jagged teeth of the mountains.

Why teeth, she thought? Why do they look like teeth to me? The snow stuck to the gray mountain rock like icing. Evergreens ran up the sides like moss, then thinned out, the mountains balding as the altitude got to be too much, until she could see—all alone—the last few trees.

The car's heater poured out heat.

And yet she shivered, looking at the mountains—as if they meant something bad, as if the jagged crests, the teeth were waiting, a vision.

For no reason at all she felt scared.

Mari saw the changing stoplight ahead just in time, and she hit her brakes. "Shit," she said.

She picked up the language from her father. He cursed all day while working on the skyscrapers and he didn't see any reason to stop when he came home.

A local—a young man in blue jeans and a well-worn parka flying open despite the freezing temperatures—glared at her.

He looked at Mari's car as if daring it to move.

C'mon. Go ahead. Hit me, hit me . . . you bitch.

Mari looked at him, backdropped by the mountains. His eyes were rheumy and red, and he strode unsteadily with a wobbly sense of purpose. He's drunk, thought Mari. Just after 10:00 A.M. and he's stumbling around the town drunk, careening from one bar to the next. From the Last Frontier—there, across the street—to another bar, the Gold Rush. Mari followed the man making his way across the street.

Mari thought of Neil Young's album . . . After the Gold Rush. His whiny voice, songs of loss, of pain. Plenty of pain in this town, she thought.

What happened to tourist traps during a recession? What happened to the bait, to the people . . . ?

The light changed.

It wasn't always that way. Mari had done her homework. Coldwater Springs used to be quite the resort, offering a pure, healthy springwater. The hot springwater, unfortunately, traveled down from icy mountain caverns, arriving in the town frigid cold.

But that was no problem to the turn-of-the-century entrepreneurs. The fabled waters were heated and the Coldwater Spring spa played host to celebrities from Theodore Roosevelt to Sarah Bernhardt. Mark Twain even referred to the town—albeit with some derision—in one of his letters.

And gold had figured in the Coldwater Spring's history—briefly from 1860 to 1870. Gambling houses and bordellos proliferated on Miner Street. But the brief gold rush gave way to the mundane mining of ever-dwindling reserves of iron ore, a vein that was finally declared tapped out in 1955.

The town should have closed up then, Mari thought.

And after that, all that was left were the tourists. People looking for ersatz frontier life, a view of the mountains, the sight of bighorn sheep munching on sage, relieved to have beaten another hunting season.

The local Native American population was not organized into any formal tribal structure. They made trinkets—or, in some cases, bought them from rack jobbers who probably imported the tacky Indian dolls, belts, and tomahawks from Taiwan.

Mari came to another hill, and then another dip down, until she was at the bottom of the canyon.

A large, puffy white cloud cut off the sun. She followed the route that she took last time. It seemed like a year ago, walking through that house, smelling the blood, imagining the screaming, the cries, the gun sounding so loud where there was no one to hear.

She left Miner Street and started up.

Bob O's Tow and Service was ahead.

I don't have an appointment, thought Mari.

I can only hope that Mr. O is in. . . .

Kate stopped the car in the parking lot of St. Theresa's parochial school. Children walked into the building, some streaming from buses, others walking up from the Paseo de Perlata.

Brian got out of the car and started walking away. Kate got out.

"Brian . . . wait. We'll go in together."

The boy turned and stood there, his face locked into a scowl. He was getting difficult. There was nothing to do in their small apartment, he complained. There was no cable, there were only *two* stations. He missed his video games, he missed his friends, he wanted to go out to eat.

And he didn't want to go to this school.

"Why are we going to Catholic school?" he said. "Why can't we go to a regular school."

"What's a cat lick?" Emma asked.

Kate tried to explain it to Brian, as if that might help. Brian knew why he and Emma were going here. The principal, a nun dressed in a well-tailored Lane Bryant suit, had been understanding about the problem with transcripts. Kate had the phony medical records for the kids. The principal understood that their school records would be coming.

And no, there was no problem with the kids starting school. As long as the records were on their way.

Kate smiled. She said: "I'm sure their records will be along."

It was a lie, but Kate was getting good at that. She stuttered, spelling out the last name, this new name that she hoped the kids would remember.

"Brian M-Martin," she said. Her voice caught. Martin—it sound so phony. Did the principal's eyebrows go up a bit there? Did she have a button she could press under her desk, alerting the FBI? Are we already entering the FBI computer? Kate wondered.

Kate paid the registration fee in cash. More money gone... the money going so fast.

Kate handed the money to the principal, the envelope filled with tens and twenties.

The woman smiled. "No, Mrs. Martin. You can give this to the office secretary."

Kate pulled her hand back, the envelope feeling like blood money, payoff money, an absurd prop from a black-and-white gangster movie. The envelope hung in her hand, stuck to it.

"Yes," Kate said. And it was easy. Now the children had a school to go to... Brian to fourth grade, Emma to a kindergarten class.

Kate walked them into the modern rust-colored building. Once inside the door of the overheated building Kate smelled crayons, and food—lunch simmering in the cafeteria. Chunky paste and construction paper, the cloistered smells of an elementary school.

Brian started to pull away. "I *know* where to go," he said. "You showed me my class."

Kate nodded. He was making things so hard.

"Could I have a kiss?"

Brian stopped, thinking it over. Then he quickly leaned forward and gave Kate a peck.

She tried to bring her hands up quickly, to whisper to him: *Don't forget your name. Don't forget who you are... and don't ever forget that I did this for you. I did this—*

She got a pamphlet once from the Lost Children Foundation— a group set up to help bring parents who have abducted their children back—out of hiding.

It's always a mistake to run with the children. Always.

That's what it said. Kate read the sentence over and over. *That can't be true. You don't know what was happening to my kids, what could have happened....*

She saved the pamphlet.

Brian walked away, joining other kids streaming toward a class.

Emma squeezed Kate's hand.

"Where's my school, Mommy?"

SEE HOW SHE RUNS

Kate looked down, smiled, and then led Emma down a hall, remembering the new wing that the principal showed her. It got noisier here as little kids moved with their mommies down the hall. Kate looked at other women, many wearing big fur coats, beaver, fox, some with cowboy hats.

There was money here.

It was all unreal.

She walked down the hall. There was a cutout of Ernie on the door. And someone had cut out a word balloon that said: WELCOME!

"Here we are, sweetheart."

Emma's hand tightened on hers. The room was bright and sunny with plastic climbing toys and bookshelves, and she saw a young woman, the pretty teacher greeting the children as they came in.

"I—I'm scared, Mommy."

The teacher had short curly brown hair, clear blue eyes, and a deep tan. She must ski, thought Kate. Such a deep tan in winter.

The teacher noticed Kate and walked over.

"And you must be *Emma*," she said. The teacher looked up at Kate. "Everyone's *so* excited that you're joining us."

Kate looked at her daughter. She gave her hand a final squeeze. And then let it slip away.

As if rehearsed, the teacher took Emma's hand and led her to a table where some children were playing with large gobs of Play-Doh.

Emma looked back at Kate.

"Good-bye, honey," Kate whispered. Emma smiled, a brave smile. And before the smile faded, Kate turned away.

She couldn't stand there in the hall trying to feel normal again.

She couldn't do that.

Because she had a job interview.

Later, driving to the restaurant, Kate looked at the clean streets, the orange buildings, and thought: Where did this start?

A stoplight turned red and she slowed and stopped at an intersection.

When I married David? When I married an image, a fantasy of married life. I didn't really know him. His stroke didn't change him, not completely. It had been there, the coldness, the demands. I simply never saw it. . . .

And why was that?

Why, dear God, was that?
The answer was there. Maybe for the first time.
She took a breath. But she smelled, tasted from years ago, the dry, stale air of her home. The sounds . . . her mother crying, the yelling. Her father walking around, yelling, and her mother, later, holding her.
This is our secret, Kate. It's no one's business.
The world was never to know what happened inside the house. None of it . . .
That's where it started. I know that now, Kate thought.
She heard someone beeping a horn. She looked up, and the light was green.

Business was good at Moll Imports. Actually it was too good for owner Gary Moll. While his new-car sales were way off—the recession, to be sure—his lot was filled with BMWs, Volvos, and Mercedes-Benzes all needing oil changes, tune-ups, lubes, and the occasional major servicing.
Rare was the car that escaped Moll Imports with anything less than a $250 bill. A five-hundred-dollar tab was more common. It was expensive work keeping those kraut engines humming smoothly.
But Gary Moll had a not uncommon problem that went with such success. There was tremendous competition for mechanics among all the upscale dealer/service centers. This was Santa Fe, after all, surrounded by desert, the mountains, and Albuquerque was a good hour away.
All the import service centers claimed to provide factory-trained mechanics. But in reality they took whoever could learn to use the metric tools and get an oil pan under the right spot.
Moll Imports' turnaround time on servicing was getting longer. People *could* go elsewhere.
And, to be sure, Gary Moll didn't want that.
He couldn't put a sign in the window—MECHANIC NEEDED. The customers might wonder about the quality of the service.
So he put an ad in the classified section of the *Santa Fe Register* with his private number. And he posted ads in a few of the bars of Santa Fe, and farther away in Taos and Galisteo.
The situation at Moll Imports got worse when one of his better mechanics, who had been actually trained by Volvo, jumped ship to Wallace Pinkins Motors, a fat, squat dealer not above stealing an employee.

SEE HOW SHE RUNS

Now Gary Moll had serious problems.
And that's when someone named Tom Abbott called.

They met in a bar near the dealership. Gary Moll doubted that Tom Abbott's real name was Tom Abbott. Abbott seemed ill at ease, always looking around, checking the door. And Moll wondered what this guy's story was.

Was he an ex-con?

Maybe Abbott just got out of the state penitentiary in Albuquerque.

They had a second beer at the Busted Fence, a small country-and-western bar on Cerillos Road. And though Moll was concerned about the risk of hiring him, he was still interested in Abbott. He said he had worked on *all sorts* of foreign cars.

That's just what Moll needed to hear.

Though he didn't want Abbott fucking up someone's new 740 sedan or Mercedes coupe. That wouldn't do.

So he asked the kid some questions. Nothing too personal... car questions. "Ever work on a BMW transmission? Ever do a brake job?"

And it sounded like the kid knew cars. This Tom Abbott, whatever the hell his name was. So Moll nodded and said: "How'd you like to work for me?"

Abbott nodded, and then he grinned. He started to speak.

The kid said something. He cleared his throat. "Mr. Moll, sir..."

Moll nodded.

"I've got a problem." The boy rubbed his beard and shook his head.

"I had a wife." Tom Abbott laughed. "Still got her actually. She's after me for some money and, sir, I'm just trying to get on my feet. So, I was wondering—"

Moll knew his suspicion was confirmed. The boy was carrying some baggage with him.

"It would make it a lot easier, sir. *Lots*—if I could get paid off the books. I mean—for a while. If that's a problem—"

The door to the Busted Fence opened, and cold air whipped in. And then Tom Abbott whipped his head around like he was an attraction at an amusement park, his eyes popped open like a jack-in-the-box.

Another small flag of caution waved inside Moll's mind. *Don't let the kid get away, but let's keep a watch on things.*

Abbott grinned. "I don't want her coming after me, Mr. Moll. Not until I can get on my feet, get some money together."

Moll nodded. He handed Tom Abbott his business card.

"No, problem," he said. "No problem at all, Tom." He grinned. "You can start tomorrow."

And the next day, when Moll walked through his shop, he saw his new employee changing oil, putting on tires, simple stuff, taking the pressure off the real mechanics.

Moll stopped by the kid. Down on his knees, using the pneumatic wrench to tighten the lug nuts on a rear wheel.

"How are things going, Tom?" he asked.

For a second the kid didn't respond. Then Alex Russ remembered his new name.

He looked up and smiled. "Fine, sir. Just fine."

And Moll smiled back. . . .

Manuela Perez walked Kate through the kitchen.

She pointed to a metal strip with clips, all now empty. Manuela, short, dark-haired, and dark-eyed, was a Zuni Indian. "Like me," John Morningsun had said. "We stick together."

Manuela leaned up and pushed against a clip.

"You put your order in the clip here." She made the clip snap loudly against the metal. The large kitchen was nearly empty. Two men stood to one side cutting vegetables. It was hours until Manuela's opened for lunch.

Kate had been late. She had taken the turn at the Allplus—a convenience store with a gas station, or vice versa—but she had turned left instead of right. The divided road seem to go on for miles, giving her no opportunity to turn back.

Manuela was the owner; her recipes for basic Mexican dishes had made the restaurant a hit. She didn't mind showing Kate that she was annoyed—even though Kate had been only fifteen minutes late.

"Then you go get your drink order from the bar and pick up your food after that."

Kate looked around. "Where do I get the food?"

Manuela shook her head as if it was a stupid question. She knew nothing of Kate's history. John had told Kate that.

"She only knows that you need a job—and that she's doing me a favor."

SEE HOW SHE RUNS 167

And I need the money, Kate thought. Though I never thought that I'd be a waitress.

"Over *there*. You check the slip—and make sure it's your order."

The restaurant had a limited menu—chalupas, tostadas, fajitas. Simple but good.

John had laughed. "You'll make a lot of money in tips."

Though Kate would only get to work lunch and a few hours after that. She didn't want to leave the kids at night. Not now, not yet . . .

Kate nodded.

"There's a washroom back there, some lockers, and if you drive here, park off to the side. Don't take a space that a customer could use."

Kate smiled. "When do I start?"

Manuela's dark eyebrows went up. *"Today."*

Mr. O . . .

Is that what I should call out? Mari thought. Mr. O . . . Mr. Bob O?

The gas station with its one antiquated Texaco pump outside looked deserted.

Is it some local holiday? Mari thought. A day off for Coldwater Springs as it celebrates its slide into oblivion?

She went to the office window of the station, so smeared as to be nearly opaque. She saw a calendar in the back. A leering cowgirl in a rawhide bikini—just visible through the glass. The cowgirl was blowing the smoke from the barrel of the gun, her red lips pursed, blowing. . . .

There was a map rack, but most of the metal pockets were empty.

There was no sign that said OPEN or CLOSED.

Mari went to the door of the station, expecting it to be locked. Gone fishing. Sleeping late.

CELEBRATING COLDWATER SPRINGS DAY.

She stepped in. A bell jingled, dully, over her head.

There were two pickups, dark rusted hulks hoisted high above the bays of the service area. She listened. There was no sound.

No one working, no one puttering around trying to get the pickups on the road.

A car passed by outside, climbing, heading toward the mountains.

Toward the Russ house.

Don't want to go there again, thought Mari.

She looked into the service area. She stopped.

She listened. . . .

There was a door leading to the back. And another door to the side. The green paint on the backdoor was peeling off in great strips, like skin peeling.

She heard a noise, coming from the back.

Was Mr. O out back, playing with his car wrecks?

The walls of the service area were filled with license plates, trophies from cars that made it here and never escaped.

She heard a noise again, from the back, near the doors. And Mari—the smell of oil or automotive grease filling her nostrils—followed the sound. . . .

24

The cougar raised his head. A sudden flurry sent icy specks biting into his eyes. He blinked and turned away, stung.

Then, when the gust faded, he turned his head back and sniffed the air.

But there was nothing familiar here. Nothing at all. There were many scents, but none that told the cat that it was someplace that it had been before.

The cougar took a step on the crunchy snow. Another step, and no matter how lightly he trod, each step made a crunching noise, a warning sound so loud it disturbed him.

And every step brought pain.

The pain came from his right rear leg. There was something there that hurt him. It wasn't so bad now, but if he were to run, or leap, the cougar remembered how bad that felt.

He stopped and licked the spot. But there was nothing there to lick. The blood was crusted and dry. His tongue didn't soothe him. Something was *below,* buried in the meaty haunch of his leg.

He licked again. It did nothing.

SEE HOW SHE RUNS

There was a sound. The cougar turned and looked forward. It was a deep, rumbling sound. And down there, through the trees, where there was no snow, no brush, no trees, something was moving fast. Something large, twisting left and right, roaring, smoky puffs trailing from behind.

After it was gone, the cougar sniffed the air, and the smell stung his nostrils.

A strange smell. A new smell.

He was wandering, drifting.

Ever since . . .

He heard something when it happened. A loud cracking sound. Then there was the sharp pain—for the first time. Something bit into his leg. But when the cougar howled and spun around, talons out, there was *nothing* there, just this pain, growing, and red, the color of a kill, staining the snow.

The cougar had glanced around, looking for something to attack. A small bluish cloud hung near a stand of trees.

That's when his leg was hurt.

He had dashed away then, feeling the wound tearing, and something deep inside digging at him, running, leaving a bright red trail.

Now the wound was covered.

There was nothing to lick.

And it hurt so much to walk. To run was impossible.

The cougar was hungry. There were no scents here to help him, no familiar trails to follow, no line of hoofprints leading to a large herd of the animals with sleek brown coats and dark eyes that froze with terror when he leaped out.

He couldn't find them.

He wandered.

Moving lower, each step jabbing at his back leg. Hungry, looking for the trails that were gone. Hungrier, snorting at the air, facing into the snowy spray.

And the hunger only added to his misery.

The teacher was nice. She was pretty and she smiled a lot and she was great at reading a story, better even than Mom.

Emma liked her new teacher. And the children, though they didn't even know her, they were nice too. One girl was real nice, Lela—it was a funny name. Lela shared her Play-Doh with Emma, and asked Emma if she wanted to be friends.

"Sure," Emma said. "We can be friends."

Later, the teacher, Miss Williams, took the children outside. And Emma and her new friend, with her pretty long dark hair and deep dark eyes, got onto two metal tricycles and they pedaled side by side.

Lela asked Emma where she lived. "Maybe we could play together," she said.

Emma looked away. She wasn't sure whether that was something she was supposed to say. Emma smiled. She laughed. It was *too funny*. All these secrets and hiding. Though Mommy said it was important, it was so funny to have secrets.

"I don't know," Emma said.

Lela nodded. But she was a curious girl. And she went on asking *lots* of questions.

One ugly green door led outside. And the other, the door Mari stood beside, with cracked green paint from centuries ago, led to—

She should have called out his name again.

Mr. O . . . Mr. Bob O?

But she had felt silly calling out so many times. He obviously wasn't in. And this door—

The sound had stopped.

Just the wind, she thought. Flapping at loose roof tiles, pushing against a cracked windowpane. That's all. . . .

She pulled open the door.

And inside the darkness, she saw the gray outlines of a sink, a toilet, and someone sitting there. She quickly went to shut the door.

God, how embarrassing, she thought.

But first she caught a glimpse of the man fumbling with *something*. . . .

"Hey, what're you doing?" he said, an old man's voice, rum-soaked, scratchy, a voice to make tree stumps cringe.

He fumbled with his erect penis. With blackish hands.

Mari shut the door.

She felt her face redden to a deep flush.

Old Bob O was passing the time with a little handball. Gets pretty lonely around the service center.

He'll probably stay in there until I'm gone, she thought. I should have knocked, yelled out his name again—

She started to back away. What the hell's wrong with him? Couldn't he have locked the door?

SEE HOW SHE RUNS

Mari turned to leave the station.

I'll come back later. Maybe he'll forget what I looked like, she thought.

She walked over the black, smudgy floor, past the waiting, rusty pickups, out to the main office.

When a door banged open behind her.

"Hell, where do you think you're going?"

She turned. He was following her, still tucking in his grimy plaid shirt, an artifact from some prehistoric L. L. Bean catalog. He had a close-cropped beard and mustache, gray and wiry. He grinned at her, and there were more black spaces in his mouth than white.

She was scared.

Not too many customers likely to drift this way. Mari turned and looked back at the door to the office, to the outside.

"I'm sorry. I called out for you, but—"

The man grinned, showing more gaping holes, and the wires on his face were alive now, making him look like a porcupine man.

He came closer. His baggy pants hid any evidence of his former activity.

"Jes' takin' care of *personal* matters."

Well, thought Mari, he must have a healthy attitude to self-exploration. There must be a well-thumbed copy of *The Joy of Sex* around here.

He wiped a hand on his blue overalls. At least Mari thought they were blue. Could be they were some other color, long stained by grease and oil to an iridescent violet.

Mari thought that he might stick out his hand to be shaken.

Her stomach did a little flip-flop.

"You need a sign," she said. He looked confused by her statement. "Something on the door to indicate that it's a bathroom."

"And maybe *you* need some manners," the man said, grinning.

A pickup, new and shiny, years from falling into the clutches of Bob O's repair bays, pulled into the station.

The man looked up and saw the customer.

"I have some questions I wanted to ask you."

The man moved past her, out to the lone pump.

He kept walking.

"About Alex Russ . . ."

Bob O stopped, his hand locked on the pump.

"Fill her up," a man in a cowboy hat said. Bob O didn't look up. He licked at his mustache. The brilliant morning sun made the moisture glisten. His eyes narrowed.

"I spoke to the police. I tol' them everything."

She nodded while he unscrewed the man's gas cap.

"I know. But I'm not the police."

He looked up at her, his eyes narrowed, and she wasn't sure whether that was suspicion in his eyes . . . or fear. But he stood there.

"Do you have any idea where Alex Russ might have gone?"

And Bob O laughed.

It was *madness*. I'm going crazy, Kate thought.

At first Manuela's was empty, like a deserted Tex-Mex train station, or perhaps the indoor waiting area for a ride at Disneyland. There were windows with Indian designs back-lit by lights. Beautiful Zuni rugs hung on the wall, and the floor was an enormous checkerboard of large, red stone tiles.

Then people came, filling the place. Rosy-cheeked skiers down from their morning runs, their tights electric blue, yellow, orange, outshining the windows, the rugs.

Old men in fur coats with ruddy skin arrived with beautiful young women in tow, the women wearing fur jackets—the better to show off their deerlike legs in black tights and boots.

An actor arrived with a woman. Kate didn't know his name—she had seen him before. He played bad guys.

By 12:00 P.M. Manuela's was filled. And it stayed filled.

Kate had one of the cooks yelling at her. He was a short man, his long hair pulled back in a ponytail. His white outfit and apron were doted with green and red blotches, battle scars of guacamole and salsa.

"What is this—" he yelled.

Kate didn't know he was talking to her.

She started to hurry back to get a drink order. A liter of margaritas. Sounded good to Kate. Curl up somewhere with a liter of margaritas and a plate of nachos.

And screw the salsa.

"Hey," the voice louder. "You! New server. What is this?"

The Indian spoke loudly, clearly, with a flat tone, no inflection. She found their voices sad, as if speaking English made them sad.

Kate stopped and blew at a long stray hair that she missed clipping. "Excuse me," she said. Her own voice sounded out of place.

SEE HOW SHE RUNS

The cook waved her order slip. "I can't read this."

Kate grimaced. "Oh, sorry." She hurried and took it back from him. "Er, it's two chalupas, a tostada special."

The cook snatched it back from her. The other waiters and waitresses were drifting by, clipping their orders in place, picking up platters at the other end, everything moving smoothly, a well-oiled machine.

And I'm messing up, Kate thought.

Cut me some slack.

The cook waved the piece of paper, and another cook looked over and grinned.

"No, miss—" He leaned forward to see her name tag. "*Kate* . . . I won't remember it if you recite the order to me."

Laughter exploded from the other cooks.

"Write it so I can read it. *Please*."

More laughter, and Kate felt their enjoyment of her screwup. Make it easy on me, she thought. That's it, make it *real* easy.

Kate snatched the paper back and rewrote the order, printing it as neatly as possible. It took forever. Waiters and waitresses floated by her as Kate fell well behind.

She handed it back to the cook.

But he was gone.

"Here it is," she said. "Here's the—"

He didn't turn back to her. "Put it up there," he said, gesturing at the metal clip . . . now filled with more orders ahead of Kate's.

Her mouth fell open. She had been here and these orders just arrived.

But she shut her mouth.

She clipped the order into place, behind a half-dozen other orders. Then she turned and went outside.

And someone new was sitting at the just-cleared table.

It was a man, sitting alone. He seemed to be looking for her, waiting. Maybe he had been seated for a long time.

Kate smiled, and she hurried over to the young guy, sitting alone, watching her. . . .

25

Barron McManus was only one of many lawyers on retainer through the various Cowell enterprises. There were lawyers who oversaw acquisitions and lawyers who prepared the contracts for the everyday transactions at the Wall Street brokerage.

But Barron McManus, silver-haired and currently going through his own nasty divorce, had the responsibility for the messier matters that affected the Cowell family interests.

A number of lawsuits had, over the years, been filed against various Cowell enterprises, and Barron McManus organized the teams that successfully defused the threats.

McManus was the one lawyer who knew the personal matters of the family. He had been there when David, the family's only son, had his stroke. McManus thought it was a terrible tragedy, a stroke so young.

Now David sat with McManus—looking, if anything, physically stronger than before. He stumbled over some of his words. And his left arm still seemed to hang there.

But David Cowell looked *strong*.

Barron McManus had his papers, his notes, spread out on the table.

David and his mother sat side by side. The woman had a hand resting on David's arm. She leaned forward, listening to McManus's words.

David's father had excused himself from attending this meeting. "Take care of my boy, Barron," was all that David Cowell, Sr., had said.

It was enough.

David stirred uneasily in his seat. His fists were clenched. "T-tell us what you've found out," he said.

McManus smiled. The woman's eyes were locked on him.

"First, there have been *no* reports filed by any police department in the country. David, if your ex-wife has run—and I believe

SEE HOW SHE RUNS

that she has—she has had no contact with the authorities. And I suspect"—the lawyer slipped on his glasses—"that she has had some help."

"Who'd help someone do something like this?" the mother said.

"Oh, there are groups. There's an"—McManus looked up and smiled—"an underground of sorts. Groups to help women. And groups to help fathers."

David's fist opened—closed—opened—closed.

"So what c-can we do?" he said.

McManus put up a palm. "First, let me tell you what's already been done. There have been recent laws—the Parent Kidnapping Prevention Act, for one—and new procedures to stop just this sort of thing. Kate and your children are already in the FBI computer.

"There's also a nationwide data bank maintained by the Department of Health and Human Services. If she or your children have any contact with an official government agency, free medical care, a parking ticket, schools—the computers will pick it up."

David smiled. "Then we'll find her?"

McManus held up a hand. "Not necessarily, David. You see, if Kate did get help from an underground group, after the charges she made against you—"

"Lies, garbage, filth . . ." David's mother said.

McManus looked at the mother. He nodded, and then turned back to David. "Yes," he said. "But if she *did* get help, they could have provided new identification, driver's license, Social Security card. In that case, I'm afraid that the computers won't be much help."

"What else?" David asked. "What else can we do?"

McManus cleared his throat. "Tell me, David—do you think Kate could have gotten much money?"

He shook his head. "No. She had to pay her lawyer, and she still owes a lot."

"That reminds me. I will be talking to her lawyer. I will probably subpoena her. She may know nothing. She might claim client confidentiality."

"The bitch . . ."

"I can get around that. But with no money, though, Kate will be exposed. These underground groups—there's one that operates out of Atlanta—have limited funds. She'll try to make a new life. There are schools, things like that. We may get a lead."

David smiled. The lawyer shifted in his seat.

"But I'm afraid that even if we locate your children, David, we still have a problem. We can get a warrant, but it will be damned hard to execute across state lines. Kate could petition the local courts for protection—and perhaps get it."

David stood up. "Th-that can't happen."

His mother's hand closed on the sleeve of his jacket.

"I said that it *could* happen. I could fight it. And most states would honor the extradition order. But courts can be unpredictable. You have discredited your ex-wife here . . . but in a new state—"

McManus opened up his palms.

"David . . . There have been fathers who have stolen back their children . . . and mothers who run again, playing with the kids like football. Most of the kids end up needing extensive therapy when it's finally over. Regardless, you can't do a thing unless we find her."

A light flashed on McManus's desk. He had left word that all interruptions were to be avoided—save one.

"Excuse me," he said. He picked up his phone.

He nodded. "Yes," he said. "Yes. Good. In a few minutes, Susan." He put the handset back.

"So, y-you're saying that we can't arrest her if we can't find her?" David said.

"Exactly. I've written down some organizations that might help us. There is a support network, David. It might be good for you to hear what other noncustodial parents have gone through . . . what you can expect." McManus slid the paper to him.

He didn't know whether David could read the paper or not.

"There's the Lost Children Foundation—they have a mediation program if we can locate your ex-wife. They'll attempt to talk her into returning. They also have a network of investigators."

McManus didn't tell David that they didn't have to take the case. If they felt that there was real abuse here, they could let it pass. . . .

"And there's the Fathers Union for Equal Justice. They have helped some fathers snatch back the children. Sometimes, not often, the father can get custody after that. It's happened."

Mrs. Cowell looked at the paper and then at the lawyer. "But you don't think that these groups will help David?"

McManus took off his glasses. "They *could*. They're certainly worth talking to. But sometimes these women disappear, Mrs.

Cowell. They *vanish*. Ten, twenty years. It happens."

He felt David's eyes on him, locked on him. "If we get them back, David, the children could be yours. The court takes a dim view of kidnapping."

David's eyes narrowed. His voice was raspy. "H-how do we get them back?"

"I think that there's only one way to go with this. One way, David . . . If you'll wait a sec—"

McManus picked up the phone. He pressed a button. "Okay, Susan. Would you ask Mr. Wharton to join us." McManus hung up, and then sat back, and waited.

26

The first time Kate saw the man, he was looking at her, smiling. He had dark hair, jet-black hair, and clear blue eyes. His smile was hidden behind his beard, but his eyes clearly expressed his amusement.

She came to him, annoyed that he found her so funny. Is it *that* obvious that I'm new? she thought.

"What would you like?"

He laughed. "Maybe a menu." And despite everything, Kate grinned.

"Sorry," she said. She shook her head and then she hurried to get a menu. She handed it to the man and was about to turn away, ready to careen into the next foul-up.

"Your first day?"

Kate stopped. No secrets here. "So obvious?" she said.

The man nodded. "Don't worry. You'll get the hang of it. I just had my first day in a new job."

Now Kate nodded. There was still a crowd waiting for seats. She looked toward the big entranceway. People were crowded there. Then, in the back of the crowd, she saw a policeman wearing sunglasses and a hat. He was talking to the fat woman, the hostess who allocated the precious seats at Manuela's.

The policeman was talking to the fat woman.
Kate watched.
"Something wrong?" the man said.
Kate turned back to him, knowing that her face looked troubled. "No. Nothing. I—I'll be back for your order."
And she turned and left.

Santa Fe...

Atchison, Topeka and the *Santa Fe*... that was a train, a railroad. I've seen that, Russ thought. On the side of milelong trains leaving Denver. And then there's *Santa*... Claus. A big, fat imaginary asshole.

I thought it would be warmer here, he thought. More like Florida, or Southern California. Instead it's fucking cold.

Though it *is* pretty here, off in the desert, surrounded by mountains. Nice and isolated.

And could things have gone better? No—he answered his own question—they could not.

I have a job.

He turned and looked over his shoulder.

The cute waitress looked worried, scared. She looked back there, at the entrance—

Russ craned his head around and—

Shit. There was a cop there, a fucking cop. Right near the pretty windows with the colored lights, talking to a fat woman, glancing back here.

Russ turned back.

He felt his heart beating, and he started breathing fast again. He tried to think—is there anything that could lead them here?

No. I've been careful. I haven't screwed up.

I have to learn to relax, go with the flow. He shook his head, looking at the menu in his hands. The words meant nothing.

Just a cop, that's all... checking in. I made a good start here. Real good. A new job, a room just blocks away on... on—

He put the menu down and dug out his map of Santa Fe. It had little pictures of places in the city, the landmarks... a church, fountains, Indians with feathers.

I haven't seen any of those, he thought. No Indians with feathers. Not yet...

Canyon Road. That's where he had a room, a little street off Canyon Road. An artist colony, lots of artists, and galleries. Driving up the steep hill the first time, he saw people with

SEE HOW SHE RUNS

money, expensive cars, fur coats, and stupid cowboy hats.

Russ licked his lips. He wanted to look back again, at the cop. Got to fight that, he thought. Got to fight that temptation, that itch to turn around and *look*. That would be suspicious. That wouldn't look good. . . .

He waited. Reading the menu items. Chalupas. Tostadas, burritos, enchiladas—

He turned.

The cop was gone.

He shook his head. *Gone*. No problem. And then he had a thought: Why did the pretty waitress look so worried? What made her go bug-eyed when she saw the cop? What's her secret?

Funny, he thought. There was a connection between them. She looked so scared. . . .

He closed the menu and looked up. He waited for the brown-haired waitress to come back. So pretty—pretty and scared . . .

Emma had her doll out, sitting right on her lap while she ate her lunch. She had five tiny peanut-butter Ritz cracker sandwiches sitting in front of her.

Four for me, she thought—and one for Patty.

Her new friend Lela, who had such pretty straight black hair, was talking to some other girls, so Emma was alone.

So far she liked it here. The teacher was real nice, and the children weren't mean. Nobody made fun of her when she brought out Patty. They did that at her old nursery school. They laughed at her.

Now she was alone.

She popped a whole Ritz peanut-butter sandwich in her mouth. Her lips barely closed over the cracker. It felt funny. She thought she might laugh. But she crunched down, and the cracker slid into her mouth. She felt like a monster eating like that.

That's how monsters eat. That's how they eat buildings and cars and people—

Crunch, crunch—

Patty sat on her lap. Her blond hair was stiff. No matter how much Emma combed it, Patty's hair kept the same shape.

Emma looked at Patty. She turned the doll around. And then she undid the small straps to Patty's backpack.

Emma looked around. Kids were eating sandwiches, talking. The teacher was at her desk talking to a little boy who was crying. Another boy must have hurt him. That's what *boys* did. They hurt kids.

No one was watching Emma.

The backpack was open.

Emma dug out the piece of paper, the special piece of paper with the numbers on it. She had practiced with her daddy. She knew what to do. . . .

He said to call *anytime*. And if she called, he said, there'd be surprises. Maybe new clothes for Patty? Emma asked.

She held the piece of paper. Emma stood up and put Patty down on her chair. She'd be okay there. Emma walked to the front of the class, to the teacher.

The teacher had her hand on the crying boy's shoulder.

The teacher looked up.

Her face was serious—because the boy had been sad. She looked up.

"Yes, Emma?"

Emma made a fist, burying the piece of paper in her hand. "Miss Williams, I need to use the bathroom."

The teacher smiled. "Yes, Emma. It's right outside our door." Miss Williams stood up. "You're new. I'll take you there."

Emma shook her head. "No, my mommy showed me where it is. I can go there all by myself."

The teacher smiled back. "I bet you can. Okay, go ahead."

Emma turned and walked to the door, out of the classroom.

Mari looked around the grimy office for a clean place to sit. No such area exists here, she thought. All the flat surfaces, from the counters to Bob O's cluttered desk, were as greasy and black as the shiny stains that covered the floor.

Bob O's name was Owsley, Mari saw from a pad of receipts sitting on the cluttered desk. And now Bob Owsley sat in the only chair in the office, an orange leatherette item with a gash at the center, revealing dirty white tufts of genuine who-knew-what.

Bob O fiddled with a desk drawer, cursing at it before it opened. Mari imagined that this was pretty much how Bob O's life went—cursing at a difficult world, fuckin' this, damn that—trying to get it to cooperate with him.

She expected him to emerge with a pint bottle of something—Old Mud Eye. It was that kind of occasion.

Instead he pulled out a red-and-green foil pack—*Red Man*, it said. He peeled away a bit of the foil and hungrily chewed off a blackish piece of chewing tobacco.

Not a pretty sight.

SEE HOW SHE RUNS

For the next few moments most of what Bob O said was lost to the gooey morass.

"He seemed"—*smack, smack*—"like a good kid, like a nice"—*smack*—"clean-cut fellow. Y'know what I mean?"

Mari nodded. She was fascinated by Bob O's chewing pattern. Squirrels would turn green with envy.

"But"—it sounded like *bluhh*—"Alex Russ would go weird som'times. I paid him regular, but he was always naggin' at me for an advance. He'd get pissed when I asked him to do stuff." Bob O spit to the side. "I don't make too damn much with this little shop. Business isn't so hot." A gummy pause. "The recession, y'know. And Russ, he always wanted more money and less work."

Owsley nodded. "Then there was other stuff."

"Other stuff? Like what?"

"He was a crazy fucker . . . excuse the language."

Mari smiled. *I know he was crazy,* she felt like saying. He had trouble dealing with life and had a burning need to hurt the people around him. He hit his wife. He hit his kids. He hit the youngest little boy and left a circle of nasty blue blotches hovering right near his kidneys.

Now none of that mattered anymore. Because the dam broke. The dam broke, and Alex Russ made them all go away. All his problems went away.

He made them go away.

The air inside the office made Mari's stomach tighten.

"Crazy damn kid, weird. He worked real well at first. But then I'd ask him to do something. Get some tires off a heap I just bought, do some work on one of the engines, and he'd look at me. Shit, as if *daring* me. I tell you—when he looked at me like that it gave me the creeps."

Mari looked at the office, at the station, the repair bays. She imagined Alex Russ here, feeling trapped, some gears inside his head acting funny, slipping, the wires in his mind pulled tight, tighter—

"Took balls for me to let him go."

"You fired him?"

Bob O nodded. "The prick *hit* me. I told him, hey, go out back and stack some tire rims. They were lying in the back. I wanted them covered. Hell, they were turning to rust. It was raining."

Bob O pushed back in his chair. "That's what I told him. And he looked at me, and he looked damn mad. But I'd had enough of his shit. I pointed a finger at him and said, 'Now you get the hell back there and do what I tell you. Enough shit.' "

A car pulled into the station.

Bob O stood up. " 'Get the hell back there,' I said, and—"

He staggered close to Mari, the chew in his mouth a sludgy mixture that he worked over and over. It made smacking noises now with each chew.

"And y'know what he did, crazy Alex Russ?"

Mari shook her head.

"He threw a punch—right here." Owsley pounded his midsection. He took a step to the door. "Knocked the wind out of me. And then he says—"

Bob O pulled open the door. The cold air poured in, but it barely took away the heavy smell of grease and oil.

"Doubled me the fuck up. And he says, 'Don't *ever* talk to me like that.' Put his goddamn nose right up to me. 'Don't *ever* talk to me like that or I'll cut you a new asshole.' "

Owsley shook his head. He started out the door while Mari followed.

Owsley kept walking. Mari noticed that he had a slight limp. Or maybe all that chewing was too much for his central nervous system to handle—and still walk.

"Russ grinned and said, 'I'll cut you a new asshole, old man.' " Owsley walked to the pump, but he glanced at Mari, grinning. "And I believed he would."

A Humpty-Dumpty woman with glasses in the car said, "Fill her up, please."

The wind pressed Mari's coat tight against her. It was so cold and bleak here.

"I *knew* he'd do it. Took balls, then, to let the bastard go. But I gave him a few weeks' money. He liked *that*. He wasn't so mad—I said business sucked. But I just wanted him the hell out of here."

Owsley looked around, from his station, to the mountains, to the town below. "I still think he might come back." He licked his lips with his brown-black tongue. "I still worry."

The pump clicked off.

Bob O clumsily fiddled with the nozzle, extricating it.

And Mari felt Alex Russ here.

A nice kid.

Cut me a new asshole...

"Do you have any idea where he might have gone? Did he ever talk about going someplace, someplace he liked?"

Owsley walked to the window. He took money from the driver, who had opened the window just a crack.

"I'll tell you." Owsley dug into his pants pocket and pulled out a small crumpled wad of bills. "People thought he was a good-looking boy. Som'times he could talk nice. There was som'thing about him. But he was stupid. He didn't know much." The man shook his head, fingering out a few dollars for the woman's change.

"He didn't talk about anything... anyplace." He looked up. "For all I know, the bastard's in those mountains somewhere, freezing his ass off, thinking about other people he'd like to kill."

And Bob O finished his recitation with a powerful brown wad of spit that went flying to the side of the pump.

The door clicked shut behind Emma. She heard voices in the hall, but they were far away. It was a big school—so big, with all these corridors.

Right across the hall was the bathroom. Emma read the word: GIRLS.

Most kids my age can't read, she knew. But Emma could even read books.

She looked at the door and then—the piece of paper held tightly in her hand—she looked right.

A phone was on the wall.

It might be too high, she thought. I might not be able to reach it.

She looked behind her, through the window, at the kids eating lunch, the teacher still talking to the boy, another boy now standing close by. Then Emma turned and started for the phone.

She counted as she walked. One, two, three—as if she were marching. Her steps echoed in the hall, the sound of her feet slapping against the floor.

She wondered what she would say if someone stopped her.

Then she had the answer. *I'm calling my daddy. It's our secret. I'm going to talk with him.*

She reached the phone and looked up at it. It was high. She'd have to reach on her tiptoes. And even then... She went on her tiptoes and grabbed the thing you spoke into. She held it next to her ear. She heard a hum.

Daddy had told her how to do it. It was easy. Just dial all those numbers, with the "0" first, and then say, "Collect."

Whatever *that* meant.

She dialed.

She looked back to the room. Maybe another kid might come out, looking for her. Then she looked the other way, to where there were voices, closer now.

"This is Southwestern Bell, how will you pay for this call."

Emma said the words. Then—magically—Emma heard the sound of ringing. . . .

Kate handed the man his check. He took it, scanning Kate's math. She started to turn away.

"Er—do I pay you or—"

Kate stopped. The lunch hour was nearly over, her trial by fire almost ended. She wanted to leave here and never come back. She needed to see her kids.

"Either way . . ." she said.

The man dug out his wallet and put two tens on top of the check. "You did good," he said. "First days are bad—boy, I know that. But you'll have me coming back."

Kate smiled. The kindness was unexpected. "The food's good?" she asked.

"Oh, it's okay. It's the service that I like."

She laughed. "It will get better," she said.

The man stood up to leave. And the thought occurred to Kate that it was the first decent contact with another human that she'd had all day. . . .

It rang once, and then again, and then—

Emma heard her daddy's voice.

"Hi, Daddy, I—"

But then the operator was there, talking over Daddy's voice, because, because—it was a recording. It was his answering machine.

Daddy's voice disappeared.

"I'm sorry," the operator said. "But your father doesn't appear to be there."

His voice was gone, the message . . . the machine. . . .

"Can I . . . say something to his machine?"

There was a pause. Emma looked down at the door to the classroom. She should go back. It was too quiet out here.

"I'm sorry—but he'd have to be there, to accept charges. Why don't you try later?"

Emma nodded at the phone. She said, "Okay." And then "Thank you."

She had to stand on her tiptoes, and then even leap up a bit to hang the phone up.

Emma walked back to the class. The piece of paper was crumpled in her hand, crumpled and damp in her sweaty hand.

That's okay, she thought. I'll try again later.

27

The door to the office opened, and everyone sitting in Barron McManus's office watched Patrick Wharton walk in.

David Cowell and his mother looked up. Wharton was a tall man, broad, and he knew that he looked exactly like exactly what he was . . . an ex–FBI man. The lawyer had told him the terrible story of David Cowell. Wharton had nodded—and then, as he always did, he said a small silent prayer for the family.

Dear Lord . . . Lord Christ, protect the children of this family. Watch over them, Lord.

It was Wharton's way of focusing. This wasn't merely work. This was a holy mission.

Wharton stood, smiling. He saw the lawyer, McManus, stir in his seat.

"David, Mrs. Cowell. This is Pat Wharton. I've told him everything about your problem."

Wharton stuck out his hand, and David reached up slowly, tentatively, to shake it. *The boy's done well,* thought Wharton. *You could hardly tell he's had major damage to his brain.* The handshake was strong, firm.

He shook the woman's hand.

"You think that we ne-need a private investigator?" David said.

Wharton looked away. He would have thought that they knew of his coming, his special services. "Perhaps I should—"

But the lawyer shook the suggestion away.

"David, Pat Wharton's more than that. Pat has worked exclusively in the area of child abductions. He has valuable connections."

Wharton sat down in an empty chair to the side, filling it. His body had begun to slide, starting to thicken in the middle. His only vice was an occasional pastry.

"Mr. Cowell, I have many of my connections in the Bureau. I can get a lot of help—official and unofficial." Wharton gestured, putting his big hands out in front of him. "I work in one area, Mr. Cowell—child recovery. If the Lord wills it, if there's a way, I'll find your children."

The mother spoke, her face squeezed together. "What does that mean? Barron, what does he do?"

"He may find the children, and—if David wants—he can bring them back."

"*If* I find them," Wharton added. "Lord willing," he repeated. "I have lots of resources, but it isn't easy. And there's one thing you should be aware of. . . ."

Wharton looked over and saw David Cowell's face redden as if he was excited. He kept clenching and unclenching his fists.

The man must be destroyed, thought Wharton. Losing his children. Such a terrible thing.

Wharton cleared his throat, a nervous tick. "It can be a shock to the kids to be picked up by a stranger." He laughed. "They've been told so much about strangers. They can get scared. It can be . . . upsetting."

David stood up. Wharton saw one of the man's arms rise up as if a reflex.

"I don't care," David said.

"Of course, I make every attempt to make the process as unthreatening as possible."

The mother reached out for her son, to pull at his hand, to pull him back into his chair.

"I want them back," David said. "And I w-want her, I want that—"

"David, now *sit* down."

"—that bitch."

SEE HOW SHE RUNS

Wharton looked over at McManus. That language offended the ex–FBI man. Perhaps this was a case he should let go. The man seemed very upset.

"David, if you'll just *wait* a moment. Mr. Wharton, I'm sorry, but David is very upset."

Wharton nodded. Of course . . .

His mother reached for him. *"David . . . "*

But David was ignoring them, turning to them, talking to them, explaining it all. "She stole my kids. She stole my life. I—I was getting better, and she—oh, Christ—she took it away."

No, Wharton thought. This will never do. Taking the Lord's name . . . perhaps I'd better . . .

McManus stood up. "David. Would you please let Mr. Wharton talk? He can't help us unless he explains how he works."

David stood there, frozen, staring at McManus. He took a breath, and then sat down. McManus smiled.

"Pat, if you'll explain what we need to know . . ."

Wharton took a breath. He had seen upset families before—wives, husbands, their children gone, stolen. He nodded to the group.

"If I might make a suggestion first . . ." Everyone was watching him. "I'd feel better . . . if first—" Wharton looked around. "If first, we bowed our heads and prayed for the children. Can we all do that?"

There was moment's hesitation. But the lawyer was the first to lower his head, and then David Cowell and his mother followed.

Wharton closed his eyes. "Lord, in the hard days to follow, we ask that you watch out for this man's children and bring them back to him, Lord."

And when the praying was over, Wharton told them exactly what he'd do.

The cougar stopped moving.

Up ahead, there was movement, an animal standing alone, nibbling at the bushes, taking a few steps and then chewing again.

The cougar didn't move. The pain in his leg throbbed now, constantly throbbing. And there was something new, a terrible hunger. The cougar kept his eyes locked on the animal.

Then, as if sensing that it was being watched, the small elk raised its head. The cougar was close enough to hear the animal sniff at the air. The elk pounded at the snow. Once, and then again.

The cougar turned, looking for others to join the elk. Sometimes there were three or four together, sometimes a large one with great antlers that reached to the sky.

But the lone elk stood there a moment, its dull brown eyes looking ahead.

It sensed something wrong.

But the cougar, still not moving, knew that he hadn't been seen.

With another snort the elk lowered its head and started chewing at some brush. The cougar waited. Then, slowly, he took a step. The dry snow crunched, so noisy . . . the cougar paused after each step. Another step, taking more care to bring his paws down gently, pressing gently into the crunchy snow.

The elk drifted a few feet away, idly eating here, eating there, trying to find a few dry leaves that escaped the cold.

The cougar moved toward it, but too slowly. He could see that it was drifting away.

Each step made his leg hurt.

But he was hungry now.

The prey must not get away.

The cougar picked up speed. His steps came faster, and faster. The cougar hugged the round, and now there was a pattern to the steps, a rhythmic pattern to the sound of paws hitting snow, and then:

The elk stopped. It raised its head and sniffed the air.

The cougar sensed the animal's awareness. It was young, but it now knew that there was danger here.

The cougar started running.

The elk looked for a clear path, found one, and then bolted.

The cougar ran full out, his front paws reaching out, digging into the snow. His mouth was open, wet, eager, his breath creating a foggy bubble in front of its maw.

But when the back legs had to thrust, there was pain, and then weakness, the muscles of the leg tightening. There was more than just pain, there was something *wrong*. . . .

The cougar fell to the side and yelped.

The elk was only feet away, clumsily darting through a path, and—

The cougar sniffed the air.

There was another smell here. Not one of the animal smells.

There was a different smell, something new.

The cougar howled and hurried to its feet. He tried to run again, to make his legs work smoothly, kicking at the snow behind, grabbing at the packed snow in front.

The elk had stumbled on some rocks. Its hooves were struggling on the rocks, its run slowed now.

The cougar leaped up, howling at the animal. His claws were out. The cougar felt the hide of the animal, and he closed its claws on the skin.

But the elk shook one way and then the other, and the cougar's claws slipped off, cutting through the hide. The cougar rolled off the back of the animal, onto the snow, landing on its bad leg.

And tremendous pain made everything go white. The elk disappeared as the pain made everything brilliant white, not just the snow, or the clouds, but everything. . . .

The cougar howled again and sprang to its feet.

But the elk was well ahead now, galloping down a trail. The cougar tried to run, but his bad leg slipped on the ice, wobbly, out of control.

And by the time the cougar stood up again, the elk was long gone. . . .

Kate held Emma's hand and walked her to the car. She saw that Brian came out of the side door of the school all alone, walking by himself, while the other children were clustered together, talking.

Brian walked alone, his face grim, set. Staring ahead, looking at nothing.

When he got to the car, Kate said. "Brian, how was your—"

The boy opened up the backdoor and got in.

Emma sat in the front seat. She seemed happy. That was good, Emma liked the school, she had even made a friend, she said.

But Brian . . .

Kate got in and pulled away out of the St. Theresa's parochial school parking lot.

"Brian, what's wrong, honey? What happened?"

She looked at him in the rearview mirror. Brian looked outside, and for a minute Kate saw so much of his father in him.

I'll have to work through that, she thought.

"Bri . . ."

"Mommy, my new friend wants me to come to her birthday,"

Emma said. "Lela is going to be six and she wants *me* to come."

Kate nodded. "That's nice, honey." Her eyes went back to the mirror. Brian wouldn't look forward.

She came to Paseo de Perlata and turned right.

"I had a crummy day, too, Bri. Want to hear about it?"

He said nothing, so she let him sit quietly.

When they got back to the apartment complex, Kate saw John Morningsun standing at the railing, waiting for them.

"I only get involved, Mr. Cowell, when there has been an *illegal* abduction." Wharton gestured with his hands as he spoke. "A spouse can run, and then use the new state laws and a change in jurisdiction to keep children away from the other parent. And that's a terrible thing . . . to be deprived of seeing your own child. In a case like that, recovering the children might be the only answer."

The lawyer turned to David. "If we get them back here, I think that we'd have a good shot at joint custody, David."

The father looked calmer now. That's good, thought Wharton. He didn't know why the woman took the children. It didn't really matter . . . they always make up stories.

"My first objective will be locating your ex-wife and the children. Then I will personally carry out surveillance to determine the patterns of their new life—and how best to effect a recovery."

"I—I don't want my little girl scared."

Wharton shifted in his seat. "I can't promise you that it won't be frightening, Mr. Cowell. But, with the Lord's help, I'll do everything I can to move quickly, perhaps with an accomplice, perhaps not. I'll reassure the children that they'll soon see you. And—as I said—you parents have done a fine job of telling kids about strangers. They may fight me."

David nodded.

McManus said, "David, we can arrange the finest counseling for the children when they are returned. I will try to get you awarded temporary custody. That should be doable."

David nodded. He turned to Wharton. "How much?"

Nice and direct, thought Wharton . . . though he didn't see how money could be a problem for the Cowell family.

Wharton turned to David. "Twenty-five thousand if I'm successful, plus any expenses, electronic surveillance equipment, any as-

SEE HOW SHE RUNS 191

sistants who assist me when I carry out the actual recovery, and—"

David nodded. "And i-if you fail? If you can't find them . . ."

Wharton nodded. "Half that."

"Is this okay, David, I assumed that—" McManus said.

"That's fine." David turned back to Wharton. "Just get them back. I don't care if you, if you—"

David's mother reached out and touched her son's arm, trying to stop the next words.

"I don't care what you have to do to the bitch—"

Wharton laughed. "I'm afraid I wouldn't do anything to her, Mr. Cowell." He laughed again, but it sounded hollow.

It was time to wrap this up, thought Wharton. Get my check and start the work . . .

"One thing, Mr. Cowell. I'll have to get stuff from you—photographs, information about the kids, that sort of thing. But there's one thing—do you have any idea at all where your wife might have gone?"

There was a pause and then—eerie moment—Wharton saw a smile cross David's face. Wharton was confused. Cowell knows something? And he hasn't said anything to me?

Then David shook his head. "No. N-not ex-exactly."

His fists clenched. His left hand started shaking. David had a big grin on his face.

Wharton waited. David looked at Wharton, smiling, grinning.

Then David told them about Emma's doll, Patty, and the secret hidden in Patty's backpack.

And Wharton felt cold in the office.

Jesse got out of his Land Rover.

Just last night there had been a fresh inch of snow dumped on the mountain. It was strange damn weather. The clouds kept hanging around the mountains, drifting away, picking up moisture, and then drifting back, dumping more new snow.

It was a strange damn winter.

He headed down one of the trails used by the cross-country skiers who liked working at a hearty ten thousand feet. Lately it had been too nasty even for those brave souls.

There were no ski tracks on the snow. Still, Jesse wanted to walk the trail. There were snow buildups—small, potential avalanches hanging from nearly every crag. If the ski trail needed to be closed, he'd have to put up some markers.

He looked down, and he saw prints. Wapiti prints . . . elk. A young elk, from the size of the hooves. All alone and browsing on the dried leaves of shooting star and blue columbine.

The elk must have followed the cross-country ski path. Now Jesse followed the trail, glancing up to check the cliffs, looking for the telltale hummocks of snow and ice, building, growing, ready to fall.

A gust of wind sent a snow devil dancing in front of him, spearing his face with crystalline ice.

He blinked, then shielded his face with his bulky Gore-Tex gloves. He felt tiny shards of dry snow scratch his neck, biting at the open creases at his neck.

The mini-tornado moved on.

Jesse brought down his gloves.

The elk tracks continued, and there, just steps ahead, were other tracks marring some of the neat hoofprints. Jesse walked toward them.

At first it was hard to tell what had happened, what other animal had come along. He kept walking, over the tracks now, and he saw a clean paw print.

He stopped.

A cougar print.

He took a breath. Cougars generally didn't bother people. Oh, they could be curious when they wandered from their mountain den, perhaps following a bighorn sheep. They could get distracted by humans camping near the timberline.

They weren't considered dangerous.

Until lately.

The well-heeled jogger who had been attacked probably thought there was nothing to be afraid of, jogging on a mountain road.

It must have been like that scene in *Jaws*. Only instead of teeth, there were claws digging into him, like a cat's claws, but so much stronger, ripping, tearing at your insides.

Jesse stood there.

The cougar prints were in front of him.

And my gun is back at the Rover.

He thought of going back for it. But he only had a short ways to go—around the curve of a rocky outcrop—and then he could head back. The rest of the trail was clear of any cliffs and falling snow.

Maybe not clear of cougars, though.

I don't have a warning sign for that, he thought. But he was nearly done, so he kept on walking....

SEE HOW SHE RUNS

• • •

John Morningsun had prepared dinner for them, refried beans and crunchy tortillas filled with chewy pieces of beef.

It's as if he adopted us, Kate thought.

The Indian had noticed that Brian was sitting quietly, watching TV. He looked at Kate, understanding.

"Not such a good day, eh?"

Kate smiled at John. "I don't know. He won't talk."

John walked over to Brian, who sat on the floor, cross-legged, watching *Beetlejuice*. The cartoon character kept changing, now a toaster, now a striped hammer pounding a skeleton to bits. It wasn't much like the movie. Kate found it jarring.

John sat down next to Brian, on the floor.

"It can be hard in a new school, eh?" he said. The boy didn't take his eyes off the screen. "You know, my people have always had to move. Someone always came and *told* us where we could live. It was hard—and it made us angry."

A commercial came on. Still, Brian kept his eyes on the TV.

"But my people, the Pueblo tribe of San Pijoaque *used* that anger. It made us grow closer. We worked together." John touched Brian's back.

Kate expected her son to shrug off the Indian's wrinkled hand. Instead Brian turned to him.

"Why don't you tell me what happened today?" John said.

Kate was about to ask John to leave Brian alone, that sooner or later the boy would snap out of it . . . when Brian spoke.

"The other kids . . . made fun of me. They said I talked funny. That my clothes were all wrong. None of the other kids look like me. And then—"

Brian craned around and looked at his mother. "And this kid started a fight during recess. He punched me—and I punched him back, and the teacher saw me. She said she'd call you."

Kate nodded. It's going to be hard to call me when I don't have a phone, she thought. And I won't be getting one.

It was one of the rules. . . .

John patted Brian's back. "The first day is always hard. But the other children will get to know you, and they will like you. I like you." John laughed. "And I'm a very good judge of people."

Brian smiled at him.

"Come. Dinner's ready."

And—as if by magic—Brian stood up.

28

Suzy Tyler sat in front of her small color TV, dressed for work as a barmaid—her mini-dress up the yin-yang and the spandex top way too tight.

On the small TV, Oprah made a face at one of the women sitting up in front. It was the fat Oprah, her bouffant hairdo looking like the dark cap on a plump mushroom stalk.

Oprah wrinkled her nose. She took a breath as if thinking about a question, trying to find just the right way to put it, so delicately. . . .

Suzy Tyler looked at a clock above the small sink of the trailer. She was late.

Oprah tilted her head. "When did you decide to tell someone that you were raped?"

Suzy's hands came together. She glanced at the clock.

The woman facing Oprah looked around, looking to escape. Her face reddened as if she was about to start crying.

Suzy Tyler licked her lips.

"I—I didn't want to. But then I started to think. . . ."

The woman's voice started to break. A camera from behind Oprah caught her butt walking to the front to be close to the woman, to comfort her.

"I thought about all those other women he might rape, maybe hurt, maybe—"

She was crying, and on cue Oprah was right there, sitting beside the woman, holding her hand. Even Oprah's eyes were watering and—

A wet drop fell to the small table of the trailer's dinette. Suzy Tyler rubbed at her eyes.

The camera was close on the woman.

"I didn't want this to happen to anyone else."

Oprah patted her hand, comforting her. Suzy shook her head. Then Oprah looked out at the camera. Gasping. "We have to

SEE HOW SHE RUNS

break," she said, her voice clogged with emotion. "But when we come back, we'll hear of her heroic battle in court to put her rapist behind bars."

Though she was late, Suzy Tyler didn't move.

There was blood on the trail.

Jesse stopped. He stopped, and listened. The blood looked fresh, glistening brown red on the snow. It was fresh, and the cougar could be ahead, guarding its kill, and—

I don't have my gun.

He thought again of walking back to the Rover.

He listened. But outside of the wind whistling through the bare aspens, a shrill noise as it slammed against the tight branches and needles of the blue spruce, there was nothing. . . .

All quiet on the western front.

Jesse took a step, taking care to step over the bloody streaks. There was more blood, and a hole in the snow. Something happened here, thought Jesse.

He bent down and touched the snow. This should have been where the cougar made its kill. It wasn't a large elk.

There should be a steaming dead body here.

Instead—he looked ahead—and he saw the signs of the elk galloping away, the hoofprints spaced far apart.

It got away. After the cougar had its claws into it, after it had drawn blood, *the elk got away.* . . .

Jesse quickly looked up from the snow. There was still only the sound of the wind. No crunch, no sound of something moving up on him, looking for easier prey.

He stood up.

Something's wrong here.

The cougar's wrong, that's what. Something is wrong with the cougar and he missed dinner. And now . . . now he's hungry.

He thought of Annie.

She liked to walk the trails around the cabin, trails that ran up and down the slope.

He thought of Annie and he turned around and started back to his Land Rover.

"Thank you," Kate said.

John Morningsun was cleaning up in the kitchen while Brian did homework and Emma played out in the living room.

John smiled. "For what, feeding new guests? You don't do that in New York?" He rinsed the last plate and stuck it in the dish drainer.

She touched his arm. "You've made this a lot easier. You're so good with Brian."

John's eyes narrowed. "He's a good boy. I get mad when children are cruel to each other." The Indian nodded. "But Brian will be fine."

Kate peered out at Emma. The girl was coloring, a Pretty Pony coloring book. She was talking to herself, talking to her ponies. Kate turned back to John.

"I thought that we'd be on our own. That we'd just get here . . . and be on our own."

"This is just a stop for you. A place to catch your breath. Out here . . . this place, it's no place to bring up children. But I've helped others before you, and I hope to help more."

He started to walk out of the kitchen.

She grabbed his arm. "Why?" she asked quietly.

He stopped. She saw him look at Emma siting on the floor. She saw the tremendous pain and sadness in John's eyes. She wished she hadn't asked the question. She wished she could call it back.

"You don't have to—"

John backed into the kitchen.

His voice was low. A sad smile bloomed on his dark, wrinkled face. "I had a daughter. She was beautiful. . . ."

Russ went to the side door of the service area, and Gary Moll, dressed in a sleek, expensive suit, stood there. He had a big smile on his face. A big, shit-eating grin, Russ thought. Russ smiled back.

"Good first day, Tom?" Moll said.

He said "Tom" kind of funny, thought Russ. As though he knows, shit . . . he *knows* the name is bullshit. But wait a minute. . . . It's probably only my paranoia.

"Everything was fine, Mr. Moll."

Most of the other mechanics had left already. Moll looked over his shoulder, checking the showroom, to see if any customers were walking around, looking over the BMWs . . . the Mercedes. . . .

Moll looked back. "Glad to hear it. If you have any problems, let me know."

Russ rubbed his beard. "Sure will."

SEE HOW SHE RUNS

Moll nodded. Russ wished he'd step aside. *Let me through, let me get the hell out of here.*

I want to wash up. Put on some clean clothes. There was a bar he heard some of the other guys talking about, a titty bar where the dancers stripped down to nothing, *nada*, zilch, they said.

"Watch out, man," a Mexican with a thick accent said to him. "They'll suck up your pay with their pussy."

I'm a free man, thought Russ. I can do this now—now that I don't have a family anymore. Now that my responsibilities are taken care of.

It was all for the best.

Moll looked over his shoulder. "Oops," he said, "a potential customer. I better go."

Russ saw someone standing in the showroom idly moving from one car to another.

Moll turned and walked back to the showroom.

Russ let his smile fade from his face.

Ready to go to the bar where the girls could suck your wallet dry . . .

Suzy Tyler held the handset up, listening to the phone ring once, then again, and she thought of hanging up. She started to remove the handset from her ear.

Then someone picked up. It was a woman.

The voice said, quietly, simply, "Hot line . . . can I help you?"

Suzy said nothing.

"Can I help—?"

"I—I was raped." It was a whisper. Suzy mumbled the words.

It was dark in her trailer now. Dark and cold, and she was very late for work.

"Ma'am, I can't hear you."

"I was raped." Suzy said it louder, and now she was crying. Somehow she had started crying, her throat closing, her chest heaving.

"Please, just stay on the phone. We're here to help you. I need your name, address. We can have people to you in minutes. Please . . ."

Suzy looked up at the clock.

She started to pull the phone away from her ear.

"Please," the woman's voice pleaded. "Please tell me your name, your address."

Suzy stopped. She nodded. "I'm Suzanne Tyler," she began. She began, and she wouldn't stop now, not until it was over.

The kitchen was eerie, quiet.

John Morningsun turned on the tap and poured himself a glass of water.

"Our young people . . . they are different today. Many of them have been ruined by the money. The reservations start bingo, casino gambling." He shook his head. "It's all legal." He smiled. "No taxes. Some of my people call it our 'revenge.' Others try to keep to the old ways. We work our silver and turquoise, we try to practice our art, or some of us farm. We send our children to college. . . ."

He took a breath.

Kate still wished she could call back the question, to take a breath and pull her words back. *Why?* It was such a powerful question.

"I had one child, a daughter, Natanni. My wife—something went wrong and she died giving birth. And I gave all my love to my daughter. I worked hard at my jewelry." He raised a finger. "It was beautiful and I charged a lot. My daughter went to college, and came back to teach at the Indian school."

John put down his empty glass. He looked away. The light had left the windows, and the fluorescent light in the kitchen was ugly and bright.

"She came back changed. She was more Anglo than Indian. But at least—I thought—she came back. She would be with me, with her people."

The Indian rubbed at something in one eye. "She met a man. A white man. She told me how much she loved him. She begged for my blessing. 'Look,' I said. 'There are so many of your people here, fine young men. Some have gone to college like yourself. Why do you need to love *this* man?'"

Kate heard a sound and she turned. Emma touched her back.

"Mommy, what color do I make the clouds?"

Kate looked at the page, at the purple pony with rainbow hair, leaping into the sky, and the clouds.

She ran her fingers through Emma's hair. "White, honey. Puffy white clouds."

Emma nodded and then said, "But I don't have any white."

John rubbed his hands together. "But I do. Wait."

He went back to his own apartment and then returned with

SEE HOW SHE RUNS

what looked like an expensive set of pastel crayons. "Here," he said, smiling at Emma.

"I don't think—"

He looked up at Kate. "No, it's okay. It gives me joy," he said, and she believed him. He stood there and watched Emma run back to the living room.

John looked at Kate. "But perhaps you've heard enough?"

Kate had to shake her head.

John rubbed his chin, as if still wondering about it all, still thinking how it might have happened. "I begged. I pleaded. But she was in love and she married the man." He shook his head. "And she never told me."

"Never told you?"

"That he hit her. He was a bad man. A bad husband. But my daughter kept it hidden from me. I saw sadness in her eyes, but I didn't know where it came from. She told me she was going to have a baby, but there was no joy."

John stopped, and he stood there. Kate saw that he was shaking. His strong hands had grabbed the counter behind him; he was shaking, and quietly he was crying.

"One night I got a call. It was the police in Taos. That's where they lived. There had been screams. Terrible screams and neighbors called the police. They called me. She had my name in her wallet. As if she knew something might happen." John looked up, his eyes watery pools.

Why... I had to ask him why.

John put his hands up, craftsman's hands, strong fingers that worked silver, that twisted the metal into beautiful shapes. His hands reached out—

"My Natanni was dead. She was on the floor. Her husband had beat her. He had kicked her. He didn't stop. He had been drunk, the police said. There was bleeding inside her body. I looked at the phone. 'This can't be,' I said. The phone can't take my daughter away. It can't do *that*."

He stopped. There was silence.

Emma was talking, lost in her playworld.

Kate reached out and touched John's hand, now a fist, grabbing, trying to hold on. "It can't be." He rubbed his eyes. "But it was. I was going to kill myself. There was no life for me now. Nothing mattered. But then I thought, Is that how I remember my little girl? Is that how I honor her memory. And I knew that there had to be something else I could do."

He took a breath.
For the first time he noticed Kate's hand on his.
He smiled.
No. The clouds had been dark, black.
He smiled, and there was light in the small kitchen again, light and air, and his voice was no longer a whisper. "That was a long time ago." He nodded. "There have been many before you. And as long as I can, I'll be here for others."
He covered her hand with his and squeezed it tight.
"Now, it is getting late. I have work to do."
He moved past her.
"Good night," she said.
She saw him lean down and caress Emma as he walked to the door, and out of the small apartment.

Russ stood at the bar of Ends Up, and the music, crazy music with everyone screaming, pounded out of the speakers.
Not even seven o'clock, and the place was packed. He stood shoulder to shoulder with Indians, Mexicans, cowboys with hat brims folded to the sharpness of a knife edge.
Got to get me one of those hats, thought Russ. And some good boots. Try to fit in here . . .
He sucked on a long-necked Coors. His second, and he watched a dancer, a cute blonde, lean against a pole and turn herself upside down. Naked as a jaybird except for a ruffled garter holding a bunch of bills tight to her thigh.
All the good seats were taken.
There was a ring of stools surrounding the stage, and nobody was moving, not when the blonde was turning cartwheels and giving everyone a real good look at her pussy.
Russ took another slug of beer.
Freedom. It's a wonderful thing, he thought. I can come here every fucking night, if I want. Sure I could. Of course, the beers are expensive—four goddamn bucks for a beer, and there was a ten-buck door charge. Could get pricey . . .
A short squat guy, maybe an Indian, maybe a wetback working the Taco Bell circuit, bumped into him holding two beers. The man looked up, his dark eyes expressionless, staring at Russ.
Got a problem, fella? Russ thought. You got some kind of fucking problem?
The Indian moved on, to a table near the back.
Russ looked back at the dancer.

SEE HOW SHE RUNS

Wish I could get closer, he thought. The blonde's body was tight, nice little buns, little tits that pointed straight up, and a cute little mouth.

Russ gulped his beer.

He thought of the waitress he met at Manuela's. She was cute too. She looked kind of lost, flustered. Like she needed somebody.

I'd like to see her again. Make it my regular place to have lunch, get to know her.

The blonde did a split and kissed the shiny platform floor with her cunt. Russ grinned. Sure is agile. He drained his beer.

"Another," he said, turning to the bartender, a big guy who looked as if he could handle his own bouncing. With a new beer, Russ turned back to the stage.

He saw someone start to move off one of the stools. The guy was getting up. Great, thought Russ. He started to push through the crowd of men, their eyes locked on the dancer.

An older guy with a cowboy hat, a blue work shirt, and jeans got off the stool.

"Excuse me," Russ said, pushing in between people. "Excuse me."

The guy was off the stool and it was empty. Just a few feet away, and Russ started to reach out with his full beer, ready to lay claim to the stool, to a primo location—

Russ slid onto the stool. He looked up at the blonde, waiting for the dancer to come closer.

When someone tapped him on the shoulder.

Russ ignored the tap.

The guy tapped him again.

"Hey, man," Russ said.

"You're in my seat, son."

The guy looked at Russ as if he was a bug, something disgusting crawling across his hamburger bun. Like a fucking bug.

Russ shook his head and turned back to the blonde.

"I said that you're in *my* seat."

The music was yammering at Russ's ears, all those black voices wailing, laughing. I hate that shit, Russ thought. And this fuck who thinks that he's gonna—

Russ kept looking ahead.

"You're *in* my seat."

Russ shook his head and took a slug of his beer. "You got off the stool—and I don't see your name on it," Russ said, looking straight ahead.

Russ could feel the cowboy at his back, staring at him. Russ didn't bother looking at him.

The blonde was right in front of him now, maybe sensing trouble. She looked at Russ and smiled. He smiled back.

Then his stool tipped backward, and Russ went flying with it. He hit the floor hard, his head smacking noisily against the sticky wood. His hand had been locked on his beer and now the bottle tumbled over, dribbling beer onto the floor, onto him.

Over the music, the crazy music, he heard laughing. They were laughing at him. The beer wet his pants leg.

The cowboy picked up the stool and squatted down, as if Russ wasn't even there.

Russ got up. He started to take a step toward the cowboy when he felt two hands lock on his arms.

"Better head home, boy. Cool off."

Russ tried to squirm away; people were looking at him, little Mexican guys, the dancer, everyone grinning at him.

The bartender held him tight and growled in his ear, "Take a hike." Then he turned Russ around and guided him to the door.

The guy pushed him through the door, out into the cold. Russ fell onto the ice and heard the bar door slam shut behind him.

They all think that this is over.

That's what Russ thought.

But they're all wrong about that.

29

The smell of the service station—the oil, the ripe tobacco smell of Bob O's chew—seemed stuck to Mari. God, she thought, I need a shower.

"Mom," Jake said. "I forgot to tell you. Dan called."

"Uh-huh," she said. He probably wants to finalize plans for the ski trip, she thought. "Should I call him back?"

Jake shook his head and Mari realized that she hadn't really looked at her son since she came home. *Such a good kid, and sometimes I'm too busy to notice.*

Take time, Mari, she told herself.

"No. He said he'd be out. He'd get back to you." Jake turned to go away.

"Hey, how was school today?"

"Okay. I got a science test tomorrow. Got to study."

Mari nodded to herself. Right, and I've got to shower. . . .

"Need a hand?" Jesse said. Annie was lifting a heavy pot off the stove. He worried about her, using her one hand to hold such heavy things.

"Nope, I'm okay."

"Smells good."

He watched her dump the boiling water and the spaghetti into the colander. A steamy cloud instantly fogged the window over the sink.

"It's just spaghetti and meatballs."

Jesse came behind her. He let a hand trail down her back until he could cup one of her ass cheeks through her jeans. "Let's stay in tonight."

Annie turned and blew a strand of hair away from her eyes. She reached down and gave his privates a playful squeeze. "Is that a cucumber in your pocket or are you just glad to get out of the snow?"

Jesse leaned forward and kissed her. He looked in her eyes. He could see the hole there, that there was something missing.

Someone this good deserves children.

He thought of the tracks. And the weather, getting worse every day. He held her tight.

She smiled and pulled away. "The pasta's getting cold."

Jesse stood there. "Annie—I wanted to talk with you about something. . . ."

Russ waited in his car, off to one side of the Ends Up parking lot. He watched guys drift out, some wavering slightly while others staggered to their cars, ready to risk their lives on the mountain roads.

He *waited*.

I'm trying so hard to make a clean start, he thought. And all those assholes laughed at me.

Russ looked at the rearview mirror. He saw his eyes, catching the light. He made his lips curl back from his teeth. He whispered to the mirror, *I'm going to chew him up. I'm going to chew the bastard right up.*

Maybe the cowboy's car will be over here, Russ hoped, all the way over here. In that case, Russ was ready. He had a knife under his seat.

But what if the asshole's car was near the entrance, right under the big white lights?

Then—

Then I'll have to do something else.

Russ waited. He thought of the blonde inside, and maybe now, other dancers, winking their cunts at their customers, sucking up the dollar bills. Dancing to whacked-out rappers, their noses all runny, bleeding from too much high-priced coke.

Russ licked his lips. He pounded the steering wheel. He whispered, "C'mon." The pressure was on, always coming on him like a fever, making the blood in his veins boil.

He had thought that he made the edge go away. Alex Russ is gone. And his family . . . now you see 'em, now you—

The door to Ends Up opened.

The big white lights above the entrance were nasty, electric white. Alex licked his lips.

Why the fuck does everything still have that *fucking* edge?

He didn't have an explanation.

He saw someone come out alone. A big guy. Alex sat up straight in his seat . . . watching the cowboy come out.

Dan called back while Mari was in the shower, and she threw a big towel on and took the cordless phone from Jake, who handed it through the half-closed door.

"Yes," she said.

She felt chilled, standing in the bathroom, her long black hair sending streams running down her body.

"Mari, something happened. I thought I'd let you know."

Mari listened as she grabbed another towel to soak up the moisture on her body. She saw herself in the mirror, saw a little puffiness around her middle. Letting myself go, she thought. I should join a club, work out. Otherwise—

The world was filled with single mothers who couldn't find another husband. Or—Christ—even get laid.

"What happened?"

Dan's voice was quiet, gentle. "Mari—a woman called the Rape and Domestic Violence number. She lives way past Coldwater

Springs. She says she was raped."

Mari toweled her hair. "And she let some time go by?"

"Yeah. She saw something on TV . . . it made her want to call."

Jake peered around the bathroom door. Mari made her eyes go wide in an expression that she hoped said, *Do you mind?*

Her son whispered. "Is the ski trip still on?"

Mari nodded and then waved him away.

"She said . . . that she was raped by a guy she met in a bar. She gave the locals a description . . . then some state detectives showed her some pictures. One of my friends with state police talked to her. She wasn't sure. . . ."

Mari took a breath. "But he looked like Alex Russ?"

"They're not sure, Mari. And this is all off the record. But he was a guy with a beard. Young, good-looking. It could be him. Could be. I thought you'd want to know."

Mari took a breath. If it was Russ, what madness was going on inside him? What kind of nasty trapdoors had been opened in his head? What kind of person are you after you kill your family . . . ?

"Did she say anything about where he might have gone?"

"I don't know. I don't think so."

Mari took a breath. She wiped at her legs, two wet stalks. "I want to talk with her."

"I don't think so, Mari. You have nothing to do with this. I'm just telling you what's happening and—"

"Dan, don't tell me that I have nothing do with this. Christ, please don't tell me that. Those children are dead because I screwed up—"

"I don't think—"

"I screwed up, and they're dead. You don't have a good photo of Russ. Even your sketch is lousy. But I saw him. I could help."

Mari took a breath. She knew Dan was going to say *no way*. "I want to talk with her."

There was a pause.

"Dan, I could find out something." She bit her lip. She heard car sounds coming through the phone. Dan was on the road somewhere, prowling the streets of Denver.

She whispered, "Please."

She heard his radio, perhaps his car radio, a distorted squawk in the background.

"Okay. I'll tell you. I'll see if you can meet her. But here's the deal—"

He was interrupted. Someone came over and spoke to him. Mari waited.

"You find out anything, you let me know . . . and I'll get the word to the detectives working the case."

"Okay."

"She's—"

"Wait. I need—" Mari hurried out of the bath and into her cluttered bedroom. The bed was unmade, clean clothes lay strewn on the floor. God, I need a housekeeper, she thought.

She found a stub of a pencil and a green Post-It, her shopping list, which was, fortunately, blank on one side.

"Go ahead," she said.

By the time Mari hung up, she was dry.

Russ waited. The big cowboy got into his car. Russ had a full-blown headache now, and he couldn't wait to get out of the parking lot and away from the light.

Where you goin', big guy? he thought.

And what am I going to do to you?

Now, that was good question. Because Russ didn't know. He remembered flying back, tumbling ass over end, and everyone laughing. Their laughter mechanical, as if they were funhouse people, laughing their stupid heads off, jerking up and down, laughing their silly fucking mechanical heads off at him.

The cowboy pulled out. He had a big pickup. Of course, a sleek black Ford pickup. Uses it to haul his pork bellies to market. Or maybe bring his wife down to the state fair. Keeps her happy by throwing her some cornhusks to chew on.

What am I going to do to him?

Russ didn't know.

But as the cowboy pulled away, spitting gravel into the air, Russ followed. He felt the throbbing, the pain leaving. It always felt better when he was doing something . . . always.

He went slowly until the cowboy was well ahead on the country road.

Russ followed.

"Annie, I think you should spend some time in the city. Stay with Terry, and—"

SEE HOW SHE RUNS

She looked up. "That's stupid," she said. "I don't want to leave you here."

She followed the weather reports as well as he did. Already more snow had fallen on the mountains than during any other winter in the past twenty years. And every day that it snowed, things got more dangerous up here. Jesse was worried.

"Roads can get closed, Annie. We could get bottled up here for weeks."

Annie twirled some spaghetti and then broke off a piece of meatball. "Sounds like fun. Nice and romantic."

"I might have to leave. If some stupid cross-country skiers get themselves stranded, I may have to hit the trails."

"And I'll be here to make sure that you check in."

"Look. The Ski Basin Station can keep track of me. You're too isolated up here."

She smiled. "We've got plenty of food, cans of stuff I haven't even looked at, and enough frozen food to last until next winter. Stop worrying."

Annie reached to the wine bottle and refilled her glass.

There was a small light over the table, but her face caught the warm glow from the fireplace across the living room. Even Jesse could feel its heat.

"There's something else," he said.

She licked a drip of the wine off her lips. So far he was unable to make her budge. She opened her eyes in an exaggerated expression of mock fear.

"What could that be?"

A log popped and crackled in the fireplace. Jesse spun around to look at it.

My fear is real, he thought. I have to let her know that.

"What?" she said, waiting.

"I saw some tracks today," he said.

Lonely roads, twisting roads. Inside his head, he felt his thoughts traveling around, picking up speed, as he imagined hurting the cowboy, doing bad things to the cowboy.

Once, Russ felt his car slip on the ice, and he jostled close to a blackish hummock of old snow. I should have ripped off some better tires for this car, he thought.

But then the road, leading away from Galisteo, even farther away from Interstate 85, was lined with walls of snow. Russ jacked up the heater and it made a groaning noise. He turned on the radio, and there was country music.

I'm drunk and busted and my wife just left me.

"Count your blessings," Russ said.

The cowboy's pickup disappeared and then reappeared, and Russ had to slow down as the truck in front of him climbed. He's got to see me, Russ thought. God, He's *got* to know there's a car behind him.

Russ grinned at that.

Could get pretty annoying... you're a little tanked up, and these damn headlights keep popping up in your fucking mirrors.

Annoying, and then maybe—

If we're real lucky, thought Russ.

A tad worried.

Now, just where is this cowboy going? Where is he leading me?

Russ took it slow, feeling the icy patches appear on the road, sending a nervous jiggle right to his bowels.

What am I going to do here?

Maybe I should stop. Go home. I don't need any trouble. I need to blend in.

He thought of the blonde, thought of her moving in slow motion, doing a slow-motion cartwheel, flashing her cunt, staring at him, then laughing with the rest of them, laughing at him.

He thought of that waitress. He gripped the steering wheel. She needs someone, Russ thought. The images flipped back and forth in his mind, the blonde, the waitress, the blonde, the—

The throbbing in his head was back. The pickup disappeared, taking another curve, climbing, higher, higher, and—

Russ knew what he was going to do.

Annie laughed.

"Cougars? C'mon, Jess. You know that mountain lions mind their own business. You yourself told me—"

"I *know*. I told you. But this is different, Annie. Something's wrong with this one. Maybe it's sick, maybe it's hurt. I should have found a body of an elk. There was nothing. That means that there's a hungry cougar out there."

She shook her head. "And you're not hungry, I guess?"

Jesse hadn't touched his plate. He looked up. "Why not spend a week or two down in Santa Fe. It will be fun."

Annie stood up, picking up her half-finished plate. "This is stupid." She looked right at him. "Are you trying to get rid of

SEE HOW SHE RUNS

me? Got a girlfriend hidden in the caves around here?"

She walked to the sink.

The fire crackled, grumbling.

Annie turned on the water, spritzing the plates.

They made love later. Annie had turned away, sulking, but Jesse reached out and pulled her close.

Then she laughed, feeling his erection. She turned to him and brushed his face with the two small fingers of her stunted arm. He kissed them.

Annie reached down and fondled him.

Jesse turned her and nuzzled at her neck, and then lower, pulling aside her loose granny nightgown—and he nibbled the nipple of one breast.

"Hmmm," she said.

She smelled of a shower and wood smoke, soap and wood. He slid lower, pushing up her nightgown with his hands, wanting to say . . . to tell her that he loved her.

But thinking that it would sound too corny.

30

The fucking car heater was doing *nothing*.

Russ blew at the windshield, and damn if he didn't see a little cloud.

It's like driving a meat truck, he thought. Driving it from *inside* the refrigerator.

The road, it dipped, and then climbed, then dipped again—but there was one thing Russ knew.

We're going *up*. The cowboy was heading up to the mountains.

First, Russ thought that he'd just follow him, right to his house, and then he'd run out. He'd have a little *chat* with him. The cowboy was a big bastard, but that didn't matter. Russ had his knife, he had his gun. That would take care of him.

Except—and here he slammed the steering wheel—damn, he

was letting himself act stupid. The whole point was to disappear, to come down here and *disappear*.

He breathed heavily, shivering. He reached out and touched one of the heater vents. It felt barely warm.

That was the idea. The cop—that had been necessary. But what was this?

He considered stopping, turning around, and heading back to his small rented room off Canyon Road. Go home and think about that blonde. Shaking her boobies. Think about her, or maybe that waitress.

Kate . . . Kate was her name. She didn't seem like a waitress.

The road dipped down and Russ felt his car wobble, another icy patch jiggling the car, jiggling Russ's insides.

But then, inside his head, he was there, back at Ends Up, on the floor, on his ass while everyone laughed, and laughed, and—

Damn!

He hit the wheel again.

He saw the damn cowboy laughing at him. Russ took a breath. And he kept following the cowboy.

He nodded to himself.

He hit the steering wheel, banged it. He shook his head.

I haven't been caught yet.

And I won't be this time.

The cougar saw the lights. He stopped and stared at them, so bright they made the snow glisten. The cougar stood there, and he breathed in, strongly, smelling the air, tasting it.

The pain never stopped now.

The cat looked around. The smells were strange. His den was somewhere up high, somewhere too difficult to climb.

The cougar looked back at the lights.

He had a new pain in his stomach. He licked at his whiskers. When he licked his paws, he tasted the blood of the animal he nearly caught today. That only made his stomach rumble some more.

He looked at the lights, the strange smells.

The cougar took a step closer to the house.

In high school there had been a punk. A big punk, a tackle on the football team. He started it, calling him Crazy Alex. Watch out, Crazy Alex is here. Don't get *Crazy Alex* upset.

SEE HOW SHE RUNS

Over and over until everyone was saying it, or looking at him. Crazy Alex. Crazy fucking Alex.

Until he knew he had to do something bad to the football player. Not just slashing tires, though Russ had done that before. Not just fucking with a locker.

Something real bad.

Russ knew cars. The football player had a new Mustang. His father owned a real-estate company.

The Mustang had power brakes and it was easy to rig them so the cables would come loose. The brakes would fail. Maybe I'll get lucky, Russ had thought.

He did. The brakes failed on Grantham Avenue, and the Mustang plowed into a bus. The accident didn't kill the football player, but it put him into the hospital with smashed legs, a fractured skull, and enough bone damage so that he'd never play football again.

Alex Russ felt better after that.

He needed to feel better now.

The cougar circled the house, looking up at the lights. The snow was harder here, there was no crunch with each step. He heard sounds from inside, and—

Around one side of the house he smelled food. It was just *there*, so close, but he didn't see anything to eat. The cougar butted his head against something—the smell was right there!

He scratched at the side of the wood, but it didn't open.

He banged his head against it.

He opened his mouth and made a noise.

"What the—" Jesse said. He got up from the bed and walked out to the living room.

Annie heard the sound of an animal nosing about the garbage too. They couldn't get at the two garbage cans inside the small shed. Even raccoons had a hard time with the clasps.

But the noise scared her.

Annie heard Jesse open the front door. "Jesse," she said. "Jess, what is it?"

Usually when he went to the door, it made the animals scatter. She waited.

"Jess?"

He didn't hear me, she thought. I'm speaking too quietly. He'll be right back.

She pulled the covers tight around her.

• • •

There was something else he could do, Russ thought.

Following this guy to his house was a stupid idea. Could be people there, his wife, kids, looking out, seeing my car, seeing me cut the shit out of him.

Russ had his knife on the seat next to him.

Laughing his ass off at me . . . I'll cut the cowboy a new asshole. That's what I'll do.

But maybe there was another way, a better way.

I'm thinking now, Russ thought. That's good . . . I'm thinking. . . .

The cowboy had to see me by now. Another lonely traveler on a lonely mountain road. But it was getting damn icy and I don't have four-wheel drive. I'm going to have to stop soon.

The cowboy's pickup turned one loop of the mountain road. Russ looked past the loop, at the dark mountains, the trees, the tremendous drop to the side. You could have a nasty accident here, he thought. Have a few too many and you could have a real nasty accident.

Russ licked his lips. I can't do that. My car's a piece of shit and—

He slowed, touching the brake very gently, just a tap. He felt one tire spin on the ground, losing traction to the ice. He licked his lips again.

He took the curve. He saw the cowboy ahead . . . he had also slowed.

Russ's heart was beating fast.

But it is a good idea, he thought. Clean. Nothing here to fuck up my fresh start. My new life. Nothing here to mess me up.

Nice and clean.

The road dipped down, a small piece of straightaway before the next curve. The cowboy's pickup was slowing down. The road was bad. It curved right. But at the outside of that curve it looked like there was nothing. Only a rock barrier, a foot or so high.

And what's on the other side . . . ?

The pickup was only a few car lengths ahead.

Russ licked his lips, he took a breath. "Okay," he said to himself. He laughed, a nervous laugh. "Okay," he said again. Then again, and again, and again as his foot touched the accelerator, tapping it, edging closer, ready to hammer down, hammer down with the V-8, a mighty fine engine.

"Okay . . ."

SEE HOW SHE RUNS

• • •

Jesse stood at the open door. That's one good thing, he thought. It's too cold to snow tonight. He looked to the side and listened. If it was raccoons, they'd scatter as soon as they heard him come out.

He shook his head.

They could keep at it all night.

Jesse stopped and listened. If they kept it up, he'd have to put on shoes and his coat. He'd have to run out and yell at the critters.

Garbage was a pain in the ass in winter. It drew the animals like flies.

Jesse heard a sound.

Shit, he thought. They'll keep playing with the latch, trying to get at the chicken bones, some nice cold string beans.

There was another bang.

Damn, Jesse thought. He went back inside and put some clothes on.

Okay...

The pickup was nearing the curve, slowing.

Which was when Russ hit the pedal. He expected his gray Camaro to shoot like a bullet, straight at the pickup. He'd ram it on the side and send it flying off the mountain.

Yeah. Like that cat... That was so funny. That cat on Saturday Night Live, the cat who could drive a car. Except not too fucking well.

But Russ's car started skidding to the left. He heard something, his fender scraping against the icy embankment to the right. *Shit!*

Russ turned the wheel, trying to straighten out. The pickup truck was well into the curve.

My headlights have to be annoying the hell out of him, Russ thought. Glaring in his rearview mirror, his two side mirrors. And then he hears me fucking gunning my engine.

The Camaro straightened out. Now it moved like a rocket.

For a second Russ thought he'd miss the truck. It was hard to hit a moving target. *I'll miss it and, shit, go flying right over the edge.*

Russ's hands were locked on the steering wheel.

But he was moving fast, and he aimed his car and smashed into the side of the pickup. The collision sent Russ flying back in his seat. His hand sprang off the wheel.

He thought he was going to die.

There was a scrunching noise, the Camaro rubbing against something. It was still in gear, still in fucking gear....

"Shit."

Russ popped the car into neutral and then he looked straight ahead. The pickup was there, hanging off the edge of the road. Dangling . . . nothing had happened.

Russ watched. He could see the cowboy. He's in my headlights, thought Russ. Like it's a movie, he's in my headlights.

The cowboy looked at him. Russ wanted to grin back. But there was no time. No time at all, because the cowboy's pickup tilted up, like a ship starting to sink.

And disappeared.

Russ didn't see it, but he heard a crash, and then another crash, and then another, and then nothing.

Russ sat there, breathing in and out, like a bellows, in and out, his hands back on the wheel.

He happened to look out his window, just to his right.

He saw something that took all the joy out of the moment.

"Jess, what's wrong?"

Jesse pulled on his coat. "Whoever's looking for dinner isn't going away. I got to go scare them off."

Jesse pulled on his boots. He had his parka on over his nightshirt. It would only take a few seconds.

"What is it?" Annie said.

Jesse stood up, both boots on. "Raccoons, maybe a fox, maybe—"

"Jesse, you told me—"

He pulled up the zipper.

"That there was cougar around. Maybe a hurt cougar."

Jesse nodded, and then, in the darkness, he turned away, toward the front door. "I never heard of a cougar going after garbage."

No, Jesse thought. Cougars prefer fresh meat.

There was no way that a cougar could be screwing around with their garbage bins. He walked out of the house, grabbing a shovel to bang and rattle at the animal.

Looking down, Russ saw that the front end of his Camaro hung over the edge of the road. Except for his engine, it was quiet now. No more crashing noises . . .

SEE HOW SHE RUNS   215

He had expected the pickup to explode, the gasoline tank turning the cowboy's pickup into a giant Molotov cocktail. But it didn't.

Maybe the cowboy isn't dead, Russ thought. That wouldn't be good. Because if he isn't dead, then maybe I should walk down there—

(How far? How fucking far?)

And make sure he's dead.

(Right, and leave my tracks all over the mountain. That would be *just great*.)

But he had more pressing concerns.

I'm hanging over the edge here, he thought. Hanging over the edge, and maybe a little tilt, maybe just me leaning forward will send my car tumbling down there too.

He laughed.

But then he stopped. Nothing funny about this. He tried to think. What do I do? What the hell do I do?

He looked at the Camaro's stick.

I take it out of neutral ... very slowly. That's what I do.

He reached down and put his hand on the stick. His hand was shaking. He locked his hand on the knob.

Then—then I put my foot near the accelerator.

Russ was aware that he was shifting his weight, putting more weight in the front of the car.

He waited.

Okay. Now, I move the car into reverse.

The stick didn't move easily. He had to pop it up and to the right for reverse. He heard the car groan. Something moved, sending a sick ripple though his body. There was another groan, another sound, and Russ felt like throwing up.

But it stopped.

The car was in reverse. Russ pressed down on the pedal, very gently.

He pressed down as if he was driving a needle into a cavity, right inside his tooth.

The car didn't move, there was just the noise.

Please, he begged. Please. He pressed down some more, the car shook, and then, amazingly, it backed up away from the precipice.

There was the sound of crunching metal.

Russ forced himself to wait, to creep back some more before

he risked looking out his window, and then he saw only the shiny, icy road.

He kept backing up before he finally cut his car hard to the left, ready to turn around and head on home.

There's no way the cowboy could be alive, he told himself.

Tried to convince himself.

No way.

He cautiously—oh, so slowly—started down the slope, away from the terrible accident.

The cougar backed away from the bin and then scratched at it.

He heard noises, sounds.

Something was coming toward him.

Carrying different smells.

The cougar turned his head. There was opportunity here, he felt. A chance for something to eat. But this was also *new*, new and dangerous. So he slunk back, under the trees, away from the brilliant white light.

Jesse came to the bin. There were no raccoons scattering, running away from him and his shovel, held out to bang at the animal bandits.

"Fast little suckers," he said.

He fingered the latch and then looked around. He looked down at the snow, but here it was patted firm from him and Annie walking back and forth with the trash. There were no prints.

He didn't lean down. He didn't get down, low, and look at the side of the bin. He didn't see the scratches, ripping through the green paint, exposing raw wood.

Jesse waited, looking around.

Then he turned and went inside.

The cougar drifted away. He was interested in the smells, the noise. But it was still too new. When he backed into the woods, he came to the half-eaten carcass of a rabbit. Its insides were cold, nearly frozen solid. Some other animal had killed it and eaten its fill.

The cougar licked at it. It had been dead for a while. But the cougar was so hungry it didn't matter. He licked at the frozen red carcass, the scratchy fur. The cougar chewed at it, stomach grumbling, eating it all up quickly.

• • •

When Russ was down from the mountains, there was no snow. It was like a dream. In fact, the air inside his car was colder than the air outside.

Russ looked at his gas gauge.

Just enough to get back.

The front end of the Camaro was pushed in. The car was drivable—after all, the pickup had been moving in the same direction.

Still, Russ knew he'd have to get another car . . . in case there were any questions.

(He imagined the cowboy, staggering around in the mountain, trudging through the snow, climbing up to the road.)

No. He's *dead*. No way he could have fucking lived.

I need a new car. That's my real concern.

No problem, thought Russ. Gary Moll might have something I could borrow, some heap from his back lot.

Nobody's going to worry about a little fender bender.

Nobody would connect me with a nasty mountain accident so far away.

Russ turned on the radio.

More country-and-western music. But now Russ didn't mind. The pain in his head was gone.

31

Mari knocked on the thin metal door of the mobile home. The wind whipped against the side and she saw the trailer rock—slightly—with each gust.

That's probably the extent of its *mobility,* she thought.

She had called the woman, the rape victim, and had asked if she could come talk with her. Suzy Tyler's voice had been quiet. Mari heard the emptiness there and could guess what Tyler had gone through, talking to police, describing the rape.

He did what? Yes, and then—

Every detail, dredging it up, *reliving* it.

Mari raised her hand to knock again, her fingers stinging from the cold. The door opened, and she smelled cigarette smoke.

Suzy Tyler stood in the doorway.

He was there again the next day. And though Kate still felt flustered, wondering—

What the hell am I doing—God—waitressing?

—things were getting more manageable. The cooks didn't laugh at her every single time she came in for an order. And she didn't feel like crying every few minutes.

The guy was back . . . and Kate found herself smiling at him. Tom Abbott had told her that he was going to be her regular.

"Things getting better?" he said.

She nodded. "Much. Nothing could be as bad as yesterday."

He rubbed his beard. It felt good talking to him—she had been alone for so long, alone, trapped with David. David wasn't anything like this. Nice, and easy . . .

Kate remembered Jayne's rules. Watch who you talk to . . . watch what you say.

"What would you like?" she said.

He looked up and fixed her with his eyes and—he spoke softly. "How about a date?"

She smiled, and laughed nervously. "I don't think so. No—"

The light went out of his eyes, and Kate felt as if she had lost something.

"I mean, I can't—"

He smiled again. "Someone else?"

She shook her head. "I just—"

"That's okay." He raised a finger. "But I have to warn you. I'm persistent." He picked up the menu. "I'm afraid I'll just have to keep asking you."

Kate stood there, not bothered by his words.

He stared at her. "You look like you need a friend, Kate," he said. For a second she wondered how he knew her name, then she remembered her name badge. HELLO, I'M KATE.

He held her there a second, then nodded and looked back at his menu. "And I think I'll have—"

She wrote down what he said. There was a time, she thought, that I liked men wanting to be with me. I can't be so different now.

There was a time.

Even with David.
There was Block Island. . . .

"Would you like—"
Suzy Tyler turned in her tiny kitchen area. She could stand still and reach everything. Her entire pathetic larder was at arm's length.
"Some tea? Or I could heat some instant coffee."
Mari didn't want anything, but it might be better, she thought, to say yes. Give Suzy Tyler something to do while she spoke.
"Fine, tea would be great."
Suzy nodded. She put a kettle on the tiny two-burner stove.
"I hope there's still propane. I'm due for a delivery." She turned to Mari. "It didn't come yet." She laughed. "Sometimes they forget me."
Mari saw a blue flame under the small kettle.
"Why do you live way up here?"
The woman grabbed the back of one of the benches attached to the kitchenette table. Suzy looked around at the tiny windows of the mobile home, windows that let in scant light. "It's pretty up here. I like being away from the city." She pushed her blond hair off her forehead. "I didn't like living in the city." She looked right at Mari. "I had too many problems in the city."
Problems . . . what kind of problems? thought Mari. What can you do to make yourself want to live up here, bouncing around the gin mills that dot the Front Range, the valley roads to Vail, all the way to Steamboat Springs.
She sat down. "I wanted to thank you for seeing me," Mari said.
Suzy nodded, and Mari felt as if she should reach out and take the woman's hand. It was quiet for a minute, just the hiss of the gas stove as they waited for the whistle of the kettle.
"Can you tell me about him?" Mari said softly.
Suzy looked away, to the window covered with a woven curtain, something you'd make or buy—cheap—at a craft fair.
She nodded. She told her story. Another recitation. Not the first, and certainly not the last.

Block Island . . .
She and David had fought. Their plans for a weekend at Block Island fell apart. He had stormed out of Kate's apartment, yelling at her, telling her she could go herself.

Have a great fucking time, go to fucking Block Island and have a fucking ball.

Kate stood there after the door slammed.

Like a gunshot that morning, the door slammed. She stood there. For a moment the idea of going to Block Island seemed absurd.

But then he'd win, she knew. She'd sit in her apartment and wait for his call. Then he'd come over and make up.

He'd win.

She stood there, imagining him going down the elevator, then out to the street, to his car, and she wondered: Is he walking out of my life?

She turned away from the door.

I'm still going to go, she told herself. I can still go. Sure . . .

Going was better than staying and waiting.

She didn't know—not then—how much of her life, her identity, her soul was tied to David's approval. She didn't realize how sick it all was, how sick it would become. . . .

She waited until she was sure that David was well away from her apartment building. Then she grabbed her bag, her leather coat and purse, and hurried downstairs to her car.

She wasn't sure how to get there. She knew she'd have to head up the New England Thruway, up to Westerly, Rhode Island, to get the ferry. David had written down the directions, so nice and organized. But she didn't have them.

I don't need directions, Kate thought. I can do it.

Halfway there, she thought about stopping, pulling to the side of the road and calling David. They had talked about marriage. She wanted it, to be protected and watched by this man.

She imagined her dreams vanishing, disappearing . . . a ghost image of a life, a home, a family, fading.

But no, she felt that this was important. Even then, she knew that she was too eager to give up her whole life to him.

She missed one ferry and then had to wait on the dock smelling of lobster pots and the tarlike caulk that filled the cracks of the fishing boats. The sky had been bright blue, but now the water mirrored back a nasty gray, the ocean was dotted with frothy white hooks, curved spits of foamy white.

She had no interest in going to Block Island.

But she went anyway.

• • •

SEE HOW SHE RUNS

Suzy lit another cigarette from a small nub, passing the torch, keeping the chain alive. She had been crying, but now her eyes were dry. Mari didn't interrupt her while she spoke, letting it come out.

If it was Alex Russ, Mari thought, what kind of switch has been thrown in him? And is that switch still thrown?

"That's all there is," Suzy said.

Mari nodded. I shouldn't be doing this, she thought. This woman has enough pain without me forcing her to open the wound up again. It's almost another kind of rape. . . .

Mari looked down at her empty teacup.

"What some more?" Suzy said. The hostess, holding a little tea party in her mobile home, a chunk of tin on wheels stuck on a hill.

Mari shook her head. "No. No, thanks. But there's something else I want to ask . . . do you have any idea where he might have gone? You never saw him before."

Suzy nodded.

"Did he give you *any* idea where he was going?"

Suzy sucked on her cigarette. "No."

She didn't even take the time to think about it, Mari saw. She was closing down, pushing everything away, stuffing it all back into some dark closet.

Mari nodded.

It was over.

She reached out and covered Suzy's hand that didn't hold a cigarette. "Thank you." Mari dug out a card. "If you remember anything, anything at all, will you call?"

Suzy took the card, and she stared at it as if it couldn't possibly mean anything to her. "Sure," she said.

Mari got up and carried her empty cup to the small aluminum sink.

The hotel on Block Island was called the Breakers and it sat across from where the ferry docked. The beautiful blue sky had completely deteriorated, and the rain was splattering against the window of Kate's room.

It was a miserable place to be, alone, stuck on a rock in the ocean.

But Kate decided to keep to David's plan, staying at the hotel, listening to the sound of the choppy sea smashing into the stone breakwater, the rain against the windows.

It was still raining when it grew dark. She ate dinner—late—

in the dining room, and the salmon tasted dry, frozen.

Kate went straight back to her room, resisting the allure of the bar and the people wandering around the lobby, all of them looking terminally bored.

She lay on the bed and started to read a book. The ferry headed off for its last round-trip run to Westerly. She fell asleep.

Minutes later—or maybe it was the middle of the night—she woke up.

The doorknob to her room rattled, and then it opened. Kate yelped, scared. She looked around, taking in her surroundings, wondering, Where am I? What the hell am I doing here?

Then she remembered.

Someone must have the wrong room.

The wrong room . . . but I locked the door.

David walked in, soaking wet, smelling of the rain and the sea. His face was grim, dark, and Kate felt scared.

Kate said his name, and she was scared.

"David."

He tossed off his London Fog, his hat, and shut the door behind him.

She sat up in bed, waiting for him to say something, an explanation of why he was here. It gave her an odd thrill to think that David followed her, *chased* her to this small rock in the Atlantic.

He smiled, kicking his wet coat to the corner. "I missed you," he said. He walked to her, the wet smell stronger, intoxicating, making her suddenly very awake, aware. "I couldn't let you go."

His words thrilled her.

He sat on the bed. He touched her face. His hand felt cold as it caressed her cheek, as a fingertip touched her lips.

With that hand he reached behind her and pulled her close. "I'll *never* let you go," he said.

He kissed her, and she threw her arms around him, pulling him close, tighter.

His lovemaking was rough. He yanked up her sweater, tugging her jeans off, and entered her quickly, fucking fast, faster until her moans mixed with the crackling sound of the rain, the wind.

He whispered into her ear. Words of love, she thought.

I'll never let you go. . . .

• • •

SEE HOW SHE RUNS   223

Emma stood by the phone. She was so happy. Her new friend Lela wanted her to come to the birthday party.

My *first* birthday party at my new school, thought Emma. I love birthday parties, the hats, the presents, all that cake. And I'll make even more friends, more new friends. . . .

I can tell Daddy all about this.

She reached up on her tiptoes and grabbed the phone. She heard a hum, the sound that Daddy told her to listen for. She opened the small piece of paper.

But she didn't really need it. She knew the number now, she knew all the buttons to push. Emma started hitting the buttons, playing a crazy tune in her ear, the song of Daddy's phone number.

"This game ain't for dweebs," the boy yelled at Brian.

Brian stood at the edge of the box-ball court. He had played box ball at his old school, but they seemed to have strange rules here. You could catch the ball and then throw it into someone else's box and get them out.

A big kid, Mark—his friends called him Marky Mark, like the rapper—was looking at Brian, ignoring the game.

He's got his eyes on me, Brian knew. For some reason, he's decided he's going to make my life miserable.

"I'm just watching," Brian spoke up.

Marky Mark shook his head. "You don't *get* it, do you, 'new kid.' I don't want your face watching me play."

Marky Mark had the ball, and without warning he threw it at Brian, catching him by surprise. It hit Brian in the stomach—and all the air was knocked out of him.

The ball bounced and rolled back to the court.

"C'mon, Mark, take your stupid turn."

Brian looked at the other kid who spoke. I may have a friend there, he thought. Somebody who might at least tolerate me.

Brian should have walked away then. He knew that. But seeing this kid grinning at him was too much.

"Yeah," Brian said. "Why don't you get off my case." Then, muttering under his breath: "You fat—"

He might as well have waved a red flag at Marky Mark. The kid dropped the ball, and turning to see that the teacher was not looking, he ran right up to Brian.

He butted Brian with his belly, plastering his face right up to Brian's. Brian could smell what the kid had for lunch . . . peanut butter, Doritos, the sweet smell of Hi-C.

He bumped Brian.

"What did you call me, dickhead? What did you say?"

Brian backed up. None of the other kids were trying to get Mark away from him. He was ready to knock Brian over and plant his big butt on him.

Brian looked around. Maybe the teacher would see, maybe the teacher would come and rescue him. But the teacher wasn't anywhere.

He looked back at Mark. The kid probably works on a ranch with his father, feeding pigs, lifting bags of animal food, throwing pitchforks at chickens.

I'm over my head, and—

Marky Mark gave Brian a quick push with two meaty hands, and Brian nearly went over. He kept looking around. He felt his eyes watering. Shit, he thought, don't cry. Don't cry here, let everyone see, and—

Marky Mark looked at his friends and then he gave Brian a big shove, laughing, grinning, and Brian went down. He tumbled to the cement, his back slapping against the stone—

Something fell out of his pocket, clattered to the side.

Brian turned and saw his pocketknife. I could get into big trouble if I'm caught with a knife, he thought. He quickly reached for it. But then the kids started yelling. "He's got a knife. Look!"

Brian quickly snatched his small knife.

Tom Abbott was still there, nursing a cup of coffee even as the lunch crowd disappeared.

"Won't you be late for work?" Kate said. She had already refilled his coffee cup a couple of times.

He shook his head and smiled. "No. I have an understanding boss. The work will still be there whenever I get back."

She nodded, straightening some menus at another table. "We're going to close soon and get ready for dinner."

"Okay. I get the message. But, y'know . . ."

She stopped and looked at him.

"If you need a friend, I'd like to be one." He stuck out his hand. She laughed and then came close to shake it.

"Great," he said. Then she watched this man, watched Tom get up and leave.

The teacher was there, magically appearing after she had been nowhere in sight. She looked at Brian lying on the ground.

SEE HOW SHE RUNS

One of the kids, a scrawny girl with nasty-looking bug eyes, said, "He's got a *knife,* Mrs. Lopez."

Mark had backed away, melting into the crowd of kids gathered around to gawk at Brian sitting on the ground.

"Do you have a knife, Brian?" the teacher asked.

Brian stood up. "It's just a penknife. It's something I got for a gift, Mrs. Lopez, it's—"

The teacher took a step close to him. "We don't allow knives here, Brian. We don't allow fighting." Another step, and her hand was out, flat, waiting for Brian to put the knife into it. "You're not doing a very good job of adjusting to St. Theresa's."

Brian looked around, hoping that someone would speak up, that someone would explain how Mark had started the fight, that the knife just fell out of his pocket—

"Give me the knife," Mrs. Lopez said.

Brian got up. Shrugging, he put the knife into the teacher's hand.

"Now come with me to the principal's office."

Brian looked at the teacher. He thought it was all going to be over, that it had ended. But there were more bad things to come.

Mrs. Lopez started off for one of the backdoors of the red-stone building. Brian followed, and he heard the kids laughing at him.

The phone rang . . . like the last time. Once, then again, and Emma looked down the hall.

I'm not supposed to do this, she knew. My teacher would be mad at me if she knew I wasn't in the bathroom. I don't want to be in trouble. I like this new school. The kids are nice—

She looked down the other way. There was no one there.

Another ring. She should hang up. The stupid machine would come on again.

I don't want to talk to the machine, she thought.

There was a click. Then a voice, someone said, "Hello."

Emma didn't expect to hear anyone.

The voice—was it Daddy?—said hello again.

And Emma, so excited, so much to tell him, said, "Hello? Daddy? It's Emma!"

"Will you accept charges?" the operator said.

And Daddy said, "Yes."

● ● ●

David sat on the cushion of his Nautilus machine. It was slippery with sweat. Sweat dripped off his face, a gentle rain. He had pushed the StairMaster to the highest speed, climbing imaginary floors, making his legs burn, his thighs, his calf muscles.

Then—pausing only to dab at his head with a towel and gulp some water—he had returned to the Nautilus machine, adding weight, making the stacked weights clang as each muscle worked harder, and harder—

"Hello." It was her voice, her sweet voice. She had called again, and now he heard her so clearly. "Hello, Daddy!"

"Emma," he said.

"Daddy. I'm in a new school. And I'm going to a birthday party. I have—"

How much time is there? he thought, how much time will he get to talk before someone stops her. How much could he learn?

"Emma—listen, ba-baby." He stumbled on the word. He sneered, angry that he was getting excited, losing control. "Listen. . . ."

Daddy sounded so *close*. He sounded as if he were right there. Emma looked down the hall, the empty hall. She couldn't stay here long.

'Cause I don't want to get in trouble.

"Daddy," she said. "My new friend's name is Lela. She's a real Indian, and there's this nice man—"

Emma stopped. She shouldn't tell him about that. Daddy shouldn't know about that or—

"Where are you, honey?" His voice sounded nice, and she'd like to talk to him, tell him. But he's not supposed to know where we are. She knew that. Mommy had told her. No one should know where we are.

"Daddy, I can't tell you. Mommy said—"

She looked down the hall. She should get off the phone. I don't want to get in trouble. . . .

David stood up. "Listen, Emmie. I have some new dolls. I think that you'll l-love them."

"Uh-huh."

She was distracted. David could feel the line being cut, Emma pulling away. Where is she calling from, Christ, where is she? David wondered.

"Emmie . . . I don't want to know where you are. I know that's a

SEE HOW SHE RUNS

secret. I can keep secrets. But if you tell me the phone number there, maybe sometime I could ca-call you. Wouldn't that be fun?"

The sweat was cooling on him. He felt the beads on his forehead turning icy.

Emma didn't say anything. Was she gone already?

No, David thought. Let her still be there. . . .

Let her be—

That would be okay. Wouldn't it? Just a number, Emma thought. Then Daddy could call me. Maybe that would be okay.

"What's the number there, sweetheart?"

Emma looked up. It was hard to see. There were small numbers at the top of the phone.

"It's hard to see."

"Try, honey. Try."

She could see the numbers. "Five . . . oh . . . five, and two. I think a six. Then . . ."

David wrote the number down.

"Are you s-sure that's right, Emmie? Is this the—"

But then there was click—and the line went dead.

Emma heard steps, voices. The snapping sound of a woman's shoes.

She quickly reached up to hang up the phone. She missed the hook, but then, with a small leap, she did it.

She turned and hurried back to the class.

I don't want to get in trouble. . . .

Brian looked down the hall and saw Emma walking away, turning to a door, opening it.

Mrs. Lopez looked back at him. "Come on, Brian. Recess is nearly over. I have a class."

Emma disappeared into a room.

Brian caught up with the teacher. He felt icy, chilled by the doom that lay ahead.

Mom's going to be so pissed. She doesn't need this, Brian thought. This isn't helping her. This doesn't help any of us.

That was weird, though, he thought, seeing Emma in the hall, hurrying away, as if—

"Here we are," Mrs. Lopez said.

She escorted Brian into the principal's office.

Kate took the call at Manuela's, standing outside the kitchen while dishes clattered and Spanish words echoed high and shrill.

The principal told her what Brian had done, how it was completely unacceptable, how they simply *couldn't* have this going on at St. Theresa's.

Kate apologized to the woman. She said that it wouldn't happen again. She said that Brian was a good boy, that we . . . we've been through a lot.

The principal listened, but then gave her a warning.

"Things like this can't happen at St. Theresa's. We're not a public school, you know."

Kate looked up. She saw one of the kitchen crew staring at her as he stuck greasy dishes into the rack for the giant dishwasher. Staring at her, leering . . .

She turned away.

She thought of what Tom Abbott had said.

You look like you need a friend.

"I'll talk to my son," she said. "Please . . . don't worry."

When she hung up, she stood by the phone, prisoner on a strange planet. Alone, alien.

Alone.

32

David Cowell walked out of his gym. He had a large towel wrapped around him. He was cold and excited. He picked up the cordless phone, pressed Wharton's number, and then held the phone up to his mouth.

"Yes," a sleepy voice said on the line.

He's supposed to be working for me, David thought. How? By sleeping all morning? He's supposed to be the best. The best what?

David continued walking to his bedroom. "Wharton," he said.

SEE HOW SHE RUNS

"Oh, Mr. Cowell. Nothing to report. I have, er, people looking at charge records, gas charges, and—"

"Mr. Wh—" David stumbled over the name. "Mr. Wharton, I have a phone number. My little g-girl called."

"Fantastic. Praise God, Mr. Cowell. Fantastic news. A number. I can trace it. What is it?"

David told him.

"Hold on. Let me check." David waited while he heard the sound of a drawer opening, pages flipping. "Okay, okay—got it. It's—oh, dear. Oh, Mr. Cowell—it's in New Mexico."

"What's wrong with New Mexico?"

"If you use the courts there, Mr. Cowell, there may be problems. Yessir . . . They won't automatically force your wife to come back with the kids."

David looked at himself in the full-length mirror. He looked and he thought, My body has been hurt. I lost something, but now *look* what I've done to—to . . .

He couldn't remember the word. There were black holes, spaces, memories, feelings. . . .

All lost, misplaced.

Then it was there. Look how I've *compensated*.

No. More than compensated.

"So, wh-what do we do?"

Wharton's voice became low, conspiratorial. Like a funeral director talking about the loved one, the type of service you'd like, the fees. "We'd better arrange a snatch, Mr. Cowell. It will be much safer that way. I'll have to fly out there, locate them, do some surveillance, but that's the best way to go."

David clenched his fists. His left hand still acted slow, a reluctant claw. He looked at it, disgusted. "Yes," he said dully.

He unclenched his fist and then clenched it again. His biceps had been pumped, but now they looked smooth again, calm.

I've more than compensated.

He thought of Kate. He thought of what he'd do to her.

She tried to take my life.

"Go ahead," David said. "Go out there. Do what has to be done."

"Er, we'll be talking about the more expensive figure I quoted you, Mr. Cowell. All my expenses, and—"

David cut Wharton off, stuttering, angry with the stupid man. "D-do it. Just do it."

David Cowell pressed disconnect. He let the fluffy towel slide off his shoulders and went back into his gym, ready to begin again.

PART FOUR

SANGRE DE CHRISTO

33

Thursday

"What's this for?" Brian asked John Morningsun, holding up a tiny silver hammer.

Not too much time in the workshop with Dad, John thought. Too much TV, too many of those dumb video games. The boy didn't know that there was more you could do with your hands than eat and push buttons.

John was also helping the little girl mold a piece of silver, bending and twisting it into a shape. She said she was trying to make a butterfly.

"It's a hammer," John said to Brian. "A very delicate little hammer for my silverwork." The boy nodded.

Kate had told John what had happened at school. He wanted time to talk with the boy.

John brought the children to his apartment, letting them play with his bits of turquoise, the solder, thin strips of silver, watching them play with his small hammers and jewelry picks.

While the mother went out . . . someplace.

She seemed nervous, embarrassed to be asking. He thought—at first—that she might have wanted to do some shopping. The stores were open late. But he saw something in her eyes.

He stood there. Waiting for her to say something.

"I'm meeting someone," she said.

He nodded. He didn't say all those things he wanted to say . . . that she shouldn't see anybody. That maybe she should stay home and wait until it was time to leave here, for their next home, their real home.

He didn't say that it was dangerous.

Because he saw in her eyes that she needed someone.

Not just an old man.

So John had smiled and said, "Certainly. We'll be fine." He

nodded, forcing his wrinkled face to smile. "Go," he said. "Don't worry about anything."

After she was gone, he thought that he should have said something. But that would have been so hard.

She reminds me so much of my Natanni. I could never say no to her either . . . even when she brought that man home.

He was a bad man. I could see that, and I tried to tell her.

John looked away from the children, gazing at his small kitchen, the open door to the bedroom, the photographs on the wall there.

Some things we get only one chance to protect.

One chance . . .

He moved closer to the boy and put a hand on his shoulder. "So," he said, "a new school is rough, eh?"

Brian looked up and John thought that he might not say anything, that he would stay quiet. The boy nodded. Then he spoke. . . .

The waitress at the Route 66 Diner was a college kid, probably living down Central Avenue at the University of New Mexico.

Patrick Wharton smiled at her. He saw a simple cross hanging form her neck. A nice Christian girl working hard . . . it made Wharton feel good to see that.

He still felt achy from his late-night flight.

The waitress looked so fresh and wholesome, a sweet kid with her hair in a ponytail and a little peaked cap—gosh, right out of a time machine.

She was even chewing gum. Part of the uniform?

"Yeah—I'll have the cheeseburger special," he said.

She popped her gum, writing down his order. "And a cup of coffee."

She looked up at him. So cute, with her hair and red lipstick, a living artifact out of the fifties. The old Rockola jukebox was also spinning tunes from the time vault. Roy Orbison wailing "Crying," then Perry Como singing "Dance, Pretty Ballerina, Dance."

Oh, this was a nice place he had stumbled into. There were old Highway 66 signs, and a map of old Route 66 on the wall, and a glossy photograph of George Maharis behind the wheel of a classic red-and-white Corvette hung behind the soda fountain.

Wharton looked at the pay phone. Then up to the big clock

circled by a magenta band of neon, then back to the pay phone on the wall.

In ten minutes I'll get the call.

The waitress put down a dark black cup of coffee in a heavy green china cup.

This will keep me up, alert, thought Wharton. Which is what I have to be . . . up. Alert. He thought of the children, how they'd be scared, how he'd tell them that he was their friend, that God was watching over them, and they had nothing to worry about.

A song ended, and another fifties ballad started.

Wharton shook his head. Such a nice place . . .

John Morningsun turned away so the boy wouldn't see him crying. The boy's voice had gone quiet, with a coldness, a wind blowing off the mountains, cold and dry.

"I didn't want to tell Mom," the boy said.

John nodded. No, how could the boy tell his mother about his father coming into the shower, how he touched himself, looking at Brian, laughing.

As if to say, "Look . . . I am a man. Look at me, *I'm still a man.*"

"I want you to have something." John stood up. "I want you to learn it."

John found a piece paper and wrote down his phone number.

"Your mother can't have a phone. You know that. But this—" He handed the paper to Brian. "This is *my* number. And I want you to *memorize* it." John rubbed his eyes. I can never hide anything, he thought. Like an old woman . . .

"Learn it. If you ever need it, if you ever need help, you can always call."

Brian looked down at the piece of paper as though it were magic.

The boy smiled.

The man patted his shoulder again, happy to see that smile. "Anytime, eh? Now, let's make some real Pueblo jewelry."

Kate looked up and Tom Abbott smiled.

They were at Café Argent. The café was small, and it looked cozy from the street. Opera music was playing on speakers.

Kate hadn't heard much opera since college. A girl in her sorority used to play it all the time, she wanted to be a singer.

But all she had going for her was weight, as if she ate enough junk, got enough bulk, she'd be a great singer.

Tom smiled. Kate had said no to him, every day. *No, I really can't date*. But then she thought, How could it hurt?

"Have a cup of coffee with me," he said. "We can talk."

She tried to guess his age. He had to be near her age, she thought, despite the peppery beard. And he wasn't educated. She doubted that he had ever gone to college.

He said things that made her laugh. For a while she didn't feel alone.

But every now and then she saw him do something funny. He looked out the window, at the cars moving up Hyde Street, watching each car, then slowly bringing his eyes back to her.

What is he watching for? she wondered.

A police car went by. She heard someone say that the New Mexico Legislature was in session and there would be more traffic, some real traffic jams coming.

She watched the cop car, and her stomach went slippery and loose, as if it might fall to the floor.

When Kate took her eyes off the patrol car, Tom was looking right at her, through her.

She flushed.

I feel so exposed, she thought. Maybe this isn't a good idea.

She asked about him, where he was from, but somehow Tom kept bringing the conversation back to her. She said she didn't want to talk about herself.

Then she felt as if it was time to go.

She looked at her watch. He touched her arm. He let his hand rest there.

"I got an idea," he said. "This Saturday, how about I take you and your kids someplace? To one of the pueblos. They can see real Indian dances."

Cars kept crawling past the small café.

"I don't know."

He smiled. "Think about it. No pressure. If you have nothing to do—"

She thought about the apartment, so small, sitting in a barren piece of land, with nothing around. It would be good to get the kids away.

She nodded. "I'll think about it," she said.

• • •

The phone rang, and Wharton—seeing the waitress looking at him—ran to the pay phone and picked it up.

"Okay, I'm here," he said. He nodded to the waitress. *It's okay . . . this is where I get all my calls.*

The man on the line was an ex–FBI agent who was now spending his golden years working for a variety of security services.

There had been no problem getting the location of the phone from which the child had called. The man had it. A pay phone in Santa Fe, a school. Wharton wrote down the name—St. Theresa's—then the street address.

"Right," Wharton said, sticking the piece of paper in his shirt pocket. "Great. I'll call you if there's anything else for you."

This man wouldn't do for the snatch, Wharton thought. No, he needed people he knew really well, experienced people who wouldn't frighten the kids. That was important to Wharton.

The kids have been through enough.

"Thanks," Wharton said, looking at his half-eaten cheeseburger special. "Thanks a lot."

"Your mother told me about the knife," John said. "She was very upset."

Brian looked up from his silver piece and John saw that the boy's eyes were lined in red.

That's the last thing the boy wants to do, John thought. He'd never want to hurt his mother.

"It was only the penknife. It fell out of my pocket."

The man patted the boy's shoulder. "They don't like knives at school."

Brian turned and looked up at him. "I was keeping it with me."

The man nodded.

"I wanted it."

The words weren't coming easy. John looked over at Emma, playing with tiny bits of turquoise, arranging them in patterns.

John looked back to Brian. "I wanted to keep the knife." Brian looked away.

John squeezed the boy's shoulder.

At the Royal Jack Motel, Wharton sat on the saggy bed, with the map of Santa Fe open. The orange-colored carpet was dotted with dirty-brown cigarette burns and the pathetic heater wasn't doing much to get the room warm.

Wharton used the Sharpie marker to circle the street the school was on, Alameda Street. I'll have to get an early start tomorrow, he knew. See the kids come to school, and then leave, follow them to their home.

Watch them on Saturday, then—maybe—set the thing up for Sunday.

You can't wait on these things, Wharton knew. Sometimes they run again. And you're back where you started.

34

"There. All set?" Mari said to Jake. He had his large Denver Broncos duffel bag packed with his stuff for the ski weekend with Dan. There was a clunky hard-shell case for his ski boots. Dan held the skis.

Jake nodded. "Sure, Mom." His eyebrows suddenly went up. "Oh, I want to bring some money."

"Good idea, guy," Dan said, grinning. "My budget's kinda limited."

For a few moments Mari and Dan stood alone in her kitchen. "What's the weather?" she said, worrying.

Dan shrugged. "I think they're expecting some snow. Could be good skiing . . ."

And the roads could get bad, Mari thought. Each year people got stranded on mountain roads, and helicopters had to get them out. People got trapped, buried, their frozen bodies found weeks later.

"Just keep a watch on things."

Dan nodded, and Mari knew he wanted to say something. Something about us, she thought. Maybe he'd ask her to dinner next week. Maybe—God, she didn't know—but maybe she'd say yes. And—

Dan looked to see if Jake was hurrying back. Then, seeing that they were alone, he said, "Mari . . . the DA's office has come up with some stuff about Russ." She nodded. "No clues." Dan smiled. "But his school records are filled with creepy stuff. He graduated from seeing school psychologists to a major shrink from Denver Human Resources. The shrink's report called Alex Russ 'psychotic, with unpredictible violent tendencies.' "

Mari nodded. *Tell me something I don't know.*

"He was violent, crazy. Russ could be fine one day and then he'd start getting into trouble, and one thing led to another, usually bigger, nastier. His senior year a kid disappeared. They thought that it was a guy picking up kids hitchhiking on the highway. But now, well, maybe Russ has snapped before."

Jake came running back, breathless. "I had to dig up my loot from under the bed," he said, grinning.

Mari had her eyes locked on Dan. He made a face, a shrug that said, *who knows?* Could just be a coincidence. Could all be bullshit...

She turned to Jake, wearing his electric-blue parka and a crimson headband, ready for the slopes.

"Have a great time, Jake." Then, to Dan, a warning: "And be careful." She touched his arm. She felt his eyes linger on hers. He opened his mouth, ready to say something....

"Sure, Mom," Jake said, moving past her to stand by Dan. A good man, like his father. The boy needs a father, she thought. Mari watched them standing together, looking so perfect, and she felt cut out, not part of the picture.

"Have fun," she said quietly.

"Let's go, guy," Dan said, walking to the door with the skis.

Mari followed them, and then she shut the door, standing there, her only companion the hum of the refrigerator.

She stood there for a good five minutes before the phone rang.

They had a TV, but Annie knew that each of them was reluctant to be the first one to turn it on. It was an act of weakness, to admit that it was damned lonely up here, that the crackling fire and a glass of Chardonnay and a good murder mystery—*G is for Gumshoe,* or the new John Sandford—somehow wasn't enough.

Annie heard a noise above the cracking of the fire, a spitting noise. She got up and went to the window. It was wet. Tiny bits of frozen rain, sleet, hit the window and slid down to the sill.

"God," she said, "it's turning warm out there."

Jesse looked up. "That's not what NOAA's been giving out."

Annie put her hand against the window and it was wet to the touch.

She looked back and saw Jesse walking to the two-way radio. It had shortwave and commercial bands hooked up to the powerful Rastar antenna on top of the station.

He turned it on.

Annie heard the latest temperatures in Albuquerque, Taos, Galisteo, Santa Fe. Then the woman on the radio said that the mountain reports would be coming up next.

"Weather's going to turn nasty," Jesse said.

She turned to him. Feeling as if it was simply the two of them on the mountain, on this planet.

The mountain report, covering the southern Rockies, began. *A weather advisory has been issued for all travel in the Sangre de Christo range, from the Colorado border to the North Truchas Peaks.*

"That's us," Jesse whispered.

By Saturday, unusually mild moist air will hit an extremely strong front of arctic air.

"Brrrr," Jesse said, smiling.

Snowfall is expected along the southern end of the range, where the moist low air will meet the front. At upper elevations, there will be heavy snow and hazardous travel on all the mountain roads.

Annie walked to the radio. Jesse would go out, she knew, when it all started. Sure. He'd go out and check the roads and the spots where the snow built up. It would get bad, and—damn—then he'd go out.

She brought her good hand up to her lips, rubbing them, tasting the dampness from the window.

"Strange winter," Jesse said. "As if we need more snow . . ."

Annie walked to him. "It will still be mild tomorrow morning."

He smiled at her. "Yeah—maybe we can go swimming."

He put his arms around her and pulled her close. "Got any hot movies for the VCR?"

The radio was still on.

NOAA is monitoring the system and regular updates will be made to the severe storm warning—

Click. Jesse reached out and shut off the radio.

On this planet there was just the two of them. And he pulled her close. . . .

"Yes?" Mari expected it to be someone trying to sell daily delivery of the *Denver Register*. *Good evening, Mrs. Comas. And how are you tonight?*

Not too damn good.

Or a wrong number, always good for brightening up my quiet life. Don't go, stranger. Since we're both on the line, we may as well chat. *Seen any good movies?*

"Ms. Comas . . ."

It was a woman's voice, and for a moment Mari couldn't identify it. There was an accent, the words slurred, someone who had been drinking, and—

"Suzy . . ." Mari flashed on who it was.

"Yes. I—I didn't know whether it was too late. If it is—"

"No, it's okay. Really."

Mari tried to think why she would have called. Maybe she needed to reach out to someone and all she had was my card. Got myself a friend. Maybe I've been selected to hold her hand while the legal system abuses her.

There was a pause. The sound of ice rattling, Suzy Tyler drinking.

"You said to call, y'know, if I remembered anything."

Mari looked around the kitchen for a piece of paper. She found an envelope, an unopened gas bill. Then she searched for a pen, a pencil, anything.

"It's probably nothing. You asked me, did he say where he was going?"

Damn, where was something to write with? Mari wanted to get this down, to transcribe what Suzy Tyler remembered, to study it.

She opened a drawer and found a thin sea-green marker. She took a breath and removed the cap. Testing it, she found that it was nearly dry. It would be like carving letters on a stone.

"He said something?"

"No. He didn't say, like, I'm going *here,* or I'm from there. He didn't do anything like that." More ice rattling. Another gulping noise. "He was all hyper, though, like he had been drinking—or something."

"What did he say?"

Mari saw that she had smeared those words on the envelope, big fat green letters, as if painted by a too-dry brush. *What did he say?*

"He was nice at first. I told you that. He was good-looking. He had great eyes. But he talked about lots of things. I guess I didn't remember it. It didn't seem important. But he said—"

Mari write those words down. *He said . . .*

"Have I ever been to Santa Fe? And what was it like? He just asked that. I don't know—and I guess we talked about other stuff. It didn't seem like anything."

The letters were big, the last two letters more streaked with the white of the envelope than the green. *Santa Fe.*

"Did he say anything else? Is there anything else you can remember?" Think, Suzy, think. . . .

For a moment Mari felt angry at this woman. How could she forget this? It could be important.

And it could mean nothing.

"Should I tell the detectives?"

"Yes." Mari wanted to call Dan's apartment. He was leaving, but she knew he checked in with his machine, he always checked in. Couldn't leave work alone. Good cops can't do that.

"I wanted to tell you," Suzy Tyler said.

Mari thanked her and told her she could call anytime, anytime at all. She hung up and looked at the envelope that said *Santa Fe.*

She picked up the phone.

35

Friday

Wharton lit a cigarette. His Budget rental car, a not-too-discreet-looking cherry-red Buick Skylark, was illegally parked across from the school. He didn't like the color, but he'd be switching vehicles before Sunday.

He thought: I haven't seen a cop since I pulled into town.

He got lost trying to find the school, getting stuck on Paseo de Perlata and looping around the town twice until he was again heading back toward the interstate.

By the time he finally got to the school, most of the children must have arrived. He checked the late-arriving car for Cowell's wife and the two kids.

Either I missed them, he thought. *Missed them . . .*

Or they're not coming today.

Lord be with me, Wharton prayed.

SEE HOW SHE RUNS

Have they moved on? They couldn't be planning to stay here. No, this had to be a stop, a place to mix in with the tourists, the skiers, the people buying Indian jewelry. A place to get lost for a while.

Wharton had passed the garish signs advertising the Pueblo reservations on the way from Albuquerque. One pueblo offered bingo. BIG-TIME BINGO an enormous sign said. Another pueblo offered Genuine Indian Pottery. That might be worth a visit.

Pick up a clay pot for the missus . . .

Wharton stubbed out his cigarette in the ashtray. He looked out the window. Santa Fe's streets and sidewalks were pristine. No trash, no cigarette butts. This isn't New York.

Kind of nice, Wharton thought. If you like orange. All these orange adobe buildings. It would drive me crazy.

I'll have to scout out a good place for lunch.

His stomach rumbled in anticipation.

Then he saw someone open the front door of the school, a gray-haired woman. She looked left and right, maybe checking that she wasn't about to lock out any lost sheep. She looked across the street, to the narrow street where Wharton had his car parked. She stared at him.

Oh, no . . . can't stay here now.

Schools tend to frown on strange men lurking outside their buildings.

Besides, I'm hungry.

He started the car. A stream of cool air blew at him. Not enough time for the heater to work its magic. Wharton released the brake.

Can't do the snatch here anyway, he thought. School's not the place to do it. But he had a plan. Satisfied with that plan, he pulled away in search of a Denny's, a Big Boy, someplace that could put a plate of runny eggs and pancakes in front of him *prontissimo*.

Now the big cat circled the house. His normal patterns were barely remembered, there was so much pain, and now—so much hunger.

All he knew was that there was food here. He had smelled it.

The pain was constant, made much worse by the hunger.

He circled the house, still well away, but with each circle, the cat came closer.

• • •

Mari listened for the beep at the end of Dan's message. "Dan, I'm guessing that you'll check in. That woman, the one Russ raped, she said that—"

Mari didn't question that it was Russ.

"—Russ asked her about Santa Fe." She paused. "If you check in, can you call down there, to Santa Fe. Let them know."

Let them know what? she thought. That maybe Alex Russ went to Santa Fe. And just as likely moved on, maybe to Mexico, losing himself in the land of frozen burritos.

Maybe. Or maybe he went to Santa Fe and stayed.

"I'm going to go there," she said. The decision sudden. Talking to the machine.

The Santa Fe police have the same crummy photos, the same sketches the Colorado State Police had.

"I'm going to go there," she repeated. She paused, thinking of what else to say. There was a clicking sound, and she hung up.

Russ looked at Gary Moll's door, out in the showroom. A guy in a suit, one of the salesmen, sidled up to him.

"Hey, pal, can I help you?"

Hey, pal. I'll *hey pal* you, Russ thought. Russ felt the encrusted grease on his hands, the leaden weight in his head from two many beers.

Hey fucking pal.

The suit looked at Russ as if he was a roach who had scurried into the room, threatening to give birth to billions of baby roaches in the front seat of these fine new cars.

Russ licked his lips. His face felt tight, the wires of his muscles taut.

Russ looked at Moll's door.

Russ wanted to ask Moll for a loaner, maybe a Jeep. Having some car trouble. Just need a car while I work on my wheels . . . on my own time.

Russ looked at the door.

"Don't you have something to do back there?" The man in the suit gestured in the direction of the service station. Back there, in your hole, animal, in your fucking cave.

The morning news had the story about the accident on Old Mountain Highway. Police were investigating it, the honey-sweet woman reporter said. Russ kept looking at her lips. How could someone look so succulent so goddamned early in the morning?

SEE HOW SHE RUNS 245

There was footage. The place where the car went over the rocks, the rocks all scraped up.

Russ could see, in the light, how bad a drop it was.

Whoo-eee. Nasty, nasty.

Then the camera closed in tight on two people in trench coats. Detectives, crouched down, looking at—

Yes. *Another* set of tires.

That kick-started Russ's heart.

Why the fuck did I do that? he thought. I could have just let the prick go, didn't have to—

The laughter, though, filled his ears. Clown laughter from the ghosts of the people at Ends Up, screaming inside his head. Ha-ha-ha-ha . . .

And he knew that if he was there—right now—he'd do it again. Butt the guy's 4×4 right over the edge.

The red-lipped anchor had said something about the weather. Bad weather was heading to the Santa Fe/Albuquerque region. . . .

"Mr. Moll's obviously busy, pal. So why don't you come back later?"

Russ looked at the salesman. There was a ringing in his head. His eyes narrowed. But he smiled. The salesman wore a worried expression. *Wake up and smell the coffee.* "Sure. Thanks . . . thanks, pal."

The guy relaxed. It was eerie, Russ thought. The way I can get people to relax. I can tighten their screws, and then loosen them. It's a special gift.

"Thanks," Russ said.

Picturing the salesman with a bullet hole blooming in his forehead.

Russ walked back to the service area. My fresh start . . . it just isn't working out.

No fucking way.

He thought of something more pleasant. He thought of lunch.

Kate was disappointed when she looked at the table, the one he usually took, and it was empty. Guess he's not coming today, she thought. She had decided that she'd go with him tomorrow. It would be interesting to see one of the pueblos, the Indian dances, the artisans. It might be fun. *We sure could use some fun. . . .*

But Tom Abbott wasn't there.

Kate picked up two plates of chalupas. She was getting sick of looking at guacamole, slimy green snot on top of the lettuce and refried beans.

How appetizing . . .

I'll never be able to eat Mexican again, she thought.

John had said to her that she'd stay here a month, maybe a bit longer. Things were being set up for her, somewhere in Oregon. *I wonder what Oregon's like?*

Will I have to be a waitress there? she thought. Will my kids have to lie about their names?

Has this all been wrong?

She walked out the swinging kitchen doors, and then—he was *there* . . . and she knew she'd see him Saturday.

Wharton felt an acid belch coming on. His stomach had trouble handling the hash browns. Too many onions.

He said a little prayer, a prayer he always said after a meal. Dear Lord Jesus . . . guide me in my day's work.

Wharton believed that bringing children back home was, in fact, the Lord's work.

He stood at a pay phone on a corner of the Plaza of the Governors facing an old Spanish-style church with a bell tower. It looked like the tallest thing in town, and a steady stream of tourists fought their way past cutesy shops to get to it.

Most of them, Wharton noted, didn't get there before being sucked into one of the open doorways.

Wharton finished pushing in Cowell's phone number and then the dozen digits of his calling card.

"Hello," a voice said dully on the other end. Wharton wondered if he had awakened Mr. Cowell.

"Pat Wharton, Mr. Cowell. Yeah, I got here fine. I'm in Santa Fe."

Looking the other way, he saw Indians sitting glumly under a building that looked like the Alamo. Some of the Indians sat on stools, others sat on blankets, with their jewelry and pottery spread out in front of them.

"I saw the school, but I haven't seen them yet, Mr. Cowell."

David Cowell asked, "Why? Why haven't you seen them?"

He didn't sound happy. Wharton cleared his throat. At a price tag of twenty thousand bucks and up, Wharton didn't want to tell the client that he had gotten lost.

"I had to get a good spot to watch the school. I'll be watching for them at dismissal. I'll follow them, and—"

SEE HOW SHE RUNS

Cowell interrupted. "Call me," he demanded. "As soon as you have the address."

"No problem, Mr. Cowell." Wharton's stomach bravely dealt with another fiery belch. "I'll call the moment I know where they are."

Cowell grunted. Strange guy, Wharton thought. Pretty intense . . . and he felt a twinge of concern about delivering this guy's kids to him. But no, they were his kids, his family. . . .

"I'll speak to you," Wharton said. He hung up the phone, shaking from another surprise burp. Next objective would be a pharmacy to score some extra-strength, lemon-flavored, double-powered Mylanta. And some handy chewable Tums.

A breeze blew up from the church. Even the church was *orange*.

A twinge of concern. Yeah, he definitely felt something.

But he took a deep breath—and it passed.

Kate hurried to clean up and leave Manuela's. Emma had a birthday party to go to and Kate still needed to get a present and then race to school to pick the children up.

She was running late—the result of a last-minute crowd streaming down from the Santa Fe ski area, all rosy cheeks, laughing.

One man—trim, good-looking, but easily fiftyish—kept watching her, with hungry eyes. When Kate stared back, he kept his eyes on her, boldly.

I guess you can do that with a waitress, she thought. Low rung on the sexual-harassment ladder. There were no harassment cases involving waitresses pending before the Supreme Court.

She hurried out of the restaurant and drove to a trendy toy store on DeVargas, something called the Weasel Goes Pop.

Oh, yes it does. . . .

A line of yellow buses pulled in front of the school.

Oh, Wharton thought, if Cowell's kids get on a bus, I'll never be able to see them. They'll be shielded by the other buses. That won't work. . . .

Wharton glanced at the parking lot. There were lots of cars pulling in, nice fat cars, lots of Benzes and Volvos and a sprinkling of Japanese luxury cars.

Wharton couldn't figure why someone would want to get a luxury car from Japan.

Didn't make any sense. Not when you could have a good

American Cadillac. No sense at all . . .

I can't stay here, he thought. He looked at his watch. It was nearly three o'clock, and sitting here, he wasn't able to see the front of the school.

It would be hard to see the parking lot.

Got to get out, he thought.

Mingle . . .

He got out of rental car, leaving the lights on, hoping it would deter any cop. Just picking up my kid, that's all. Don't need to ticket me, Officer.

He looked across the big avenue, then ran over to the buses. The drivers, short guys with copper skin, looked at him. Wharton smiled.

Okay, he thought, I can see the buses fine here, and still get to my car, in time. No problem.

He looked down to the parking lot. He couldn't see a thing, it was masked by the corner of the squat adobe-style school building.

Can't see both, he thought.

That's a problem. Can't be two places at once.

Got to play the percentages, the odds. Are the kids taking the bus . . . or is Mom picking them up?

He looked at the buses, then back to the lot. Maybe there'd be time to run down and check if she was there.

You see—Wharton thought—*I* have the advantage, I know what she looks like, and she doesn't know *anything* about me. Though her antennae have to be just there, at the surface. He knew what it was like when the people he followed felt his eyes. It was physical.

One of the shrimpy drivers looked over at Wharton while he made his way down to the parking lot.

"You'd like it wrapped?"

Kate nodded, thinking that this was all going *soooo* slowly. In New York, everyone moved in triple time—here, it was all in slow motion.

The woman took forever to wrap the giant bubble set, cutting the paper with clean, *slow* snips of the shears, folding the paper over, carefully pulling down a piece of tape.

Come on, Kate thought, Come on, I'm late and—

Finally it was done and Kate ran out of the store, looking at her watch. It was three o'clock.

SEE HOW SHE RUNS

• • •

Wharton stood in the parking lot. He looked over the cars, women in sunglasses waiting inside most of them, a gray-haired man in one.

Nobody took notice of him. Nobody looked over, locking their eyes on him, sending out powerful vibrations of paranoia.

So physical...

He didn't see anyone who looked like Cowell's wife. Wharton checked his watch. It was after three. Children came to the side door of the school escorted by a spindly-looking woman.

In my day, a school like this would have been all penguins, Wharton thought. Filled with nuns, bless their cold hearts, with their festive black-and-white plumage and claw hands that liked nothing better than grabbing a boy by his hair and rattling his head as if it was the clapper of a reluctant bell.

Left Wharton with a bad taste for religion. But then he met his wife, who showed him the true nature of Jesus, and faith—and his life changed.

Children streamed out and the doors to the fancy cars popped open with random clicks. The kids moved away from the teacher, moving to the cars. The teacher stood by the door. Cars started pulling out.

But Wharton looked back at the door, and two kids stood there.

Looking around...

His heart started beating fast. It was easy to recognize them, easy when you've studied tons of pictures, when you've made it your life's work to memorize faces.

They stood there, searching the parking lot.

Wharton saw the little girl's eyes land on him and he felt uncomfortable. Though there was no way she could suspect anything. Still, the girl looked at him—so Wharton walked away. As if he had just been taking a stroll and happened to casually wander into the parking lot.

Where's Mommy, kids? What happened to your mommy who stole you?

Wharton started to walk away, slowly, looking back at the kids. The little girl—she's Emma—turned to the teacher. Probably asking what they should do. Wharton looked at the boy, a good-looking kid.

He thought of Cowell's dull voice. *Call me....*

This was never easy.

Then a car appeared, a heap, something out of place in this upscale parking lot.

Wharton kept walking. Have to get to my car, he thought. Oh, yeah. Don't want to blow this. Still, he wanted to see her. The car stopped, and Wharton risked a look over his shoulder.

First, he thought that there had been a terrible mistake. The woman's hair was short, close to the scalp. And darker. Kate Cowell had long, sandy-blond hair.

More steps, and he risked another glance, catching the kids hurrying into the car. It was Cowell's kids, no doubt. The woman, the driver, looked over at him.

For a second—their eyes met—Wharton felt an electric charge run through him.

She had cut her hair and dyed it dark brown.

But I'm good at faces. Real good.

Wharton walked faster, coming to the corner of the building, then faster, to get to his car and follow Kate Cowell and her kids to their hideaway.

36

Kate wasn't sure which one of the homes on the hilltop belonged to Lela, Emma's new friend. All the sleek homes were perched precariously on hills dotted with scrubby, stunted pine trees. And all the houses looked gorgeous. Lela's father was an art dealer, her mother a sculptor.

Then she saw a dozen balloons streaming up from the open gate of an entranceway.

"Here we are," Kate said. She slowed and started to turn. She checked the rearview mirror and saw a red car there.

The red car slowed too.

She pulled into the circular driveway.

"What a house," Brian said.

Kate nodded, stopping the car. We used to have money, she thought, before we ran away. Nice cars, nice home.

SEE HOW SHE RUNS 251

Kate opened her door. "C'mon, Emmie."

Emma got out of the car and carried the present, with difficulty, tightly under her arm. She ran up to the front door, which opened magically. A maid was there, dressed in a regulation gray dress and white apron. Kate heard children's voices. She bent down and kissed Emma's cheek.

"Have fun, honey," she said.

Emma nodded and walked into the home.

Wharton had to pass the house.

They can't be living here, he thought. Oh, this could be a major problem. They'll have a security system, and whoever's helping them obviously has major money. *Major bucks . . .*

He stopped the car and did a three-point turn to head back to the entrance gate.

Just as he finished his turn he saw Kate Cowell's car come out of the driveway. There was one head missing. The little girl was not in the car. Okay, I get it, Wharton thought. Sure. It's a play date. No—there are balloons. It's a party.

They don't live here.

Good . . .

He slowed down, already too close to the other car.

Now they'll head home, he thought. He slowed to a stop. He dug out a Vantage cigarette and lit it from the car's lighter. He watched Kate Cowell's car sail down, off the hill.

When she was well ahead, he followed her.

If I lose her, he thought, I can come back here and wait until she has to pick up her daughter.

Emma looked around at all the other little girls.

Do they have secrets too? she wondered. They were laughing, playing in their pretty dresses. Emma stood to the side, looking around.

Lela came up to her and pulled her close to the other girls.

She's my new friend, thought Emma.

She felt better.

Wharton followed Kate Cowell's car as it left Santa Fe on a stretch of road that looked like Route 46 in New Jersey. Gas stations, warehouses, sleepy-eyed Indians standing around, looking at the cars, maybe waiting for a work truck to pull up, loaded with day jobs.

He let her get a few lights ahead, and once he thought he lost her when a truck pulled out, blocking the car.

But Wharton drifted to the side, over the yellow line, and he glimpsed Kate's car way ahead.

The truck turned down a street.

Wharton saw brake lights come on, Kate's car slowing, turning.

Wharton kept on driving, smoothly, passing the place where she turned. He looked back at the squat building, the apartments in a place that was once a motel.

He smiled. It was perfect.

He spoke aloud, jubilant. "Praise Jesus."

When the truck disappeared from the rearview mirror, Kate saw the red car again. It was back there, the same red car she saw when she dropped Emma off.

She gripped the steering wheel tightly. She had been warned about this, the fear, the paranoia. But she had also been told that things *could* happen. She could be found, spied on . . . the children could be stolen.

The red car had hung back, even when Kate slowed.

I'll see if it stops when I stop, thought Kate. Then I'll know.

The apartment was just ahead. She slowed, and then turned into the parking lot, hitting a nasty pothole because she wasn't watching in front.

"Hey, Mom, *careful!*" Brian said.

Her eyes locked on the mirror.

She saw the red car sail by. . . .

It didn't even slow. She turned around and watched the car keep on going, down Cerillos Road, out toward the desert.

She turned back and drove the car into a space below their second-story apartment.

It was nothing, she thought. Nothing at all.

Bad weather is coming.

Mari looked at the map and wondered: What if this is all wrong? What if the guy who raped Suzy Tyler isn't Alex Russ? What if his questions about Santa Fe meant nothing . . . ever been here, ever been there?

She had picked a route that would keep her well away from the hills, but still it would be night by the time she got to Santa Fe.

She traced the route on the map with her finger. There had been no call from Dan. Maybe he hadn't checked his machine.

SEE HOW SHE RUNS 253

Maybe he was trying to forget work. Maybe pigs could fly.

She had also called the Denver State Police and left a complicated message that—she realized—didn't say much of anything. *Somebody who might be Alex Russ might have gone to Santa Fe.*

And then again—*he might not have.*

A detective assured her that they'd let New Mexico CID know. She didn't ask what CID was. They have the photographs, the detective said.

Right, thought Mari, great . . . but the photographs are no damn good. What you need . . .

Her finger trailed past Los Alamos, down to the city, down to Santa Fe.

What you need is someone—

Crack! Something from upstairs, a can hitting the floor. Then—*crack,* another, maybe groceries being unpacked, canned goods rolling off the table, falling to the floor. Sounding so much—

Like gunshots.

She took a breath. She had spent the day debating, and now she just had to leave, drive to Santa Fe in the dark. There was no backing away.

There was an obligation here.

The sounds upstairs . . . sounding like gunshots.

Bang. Bang. Mari could smell the smoke, the blood, and she was in the house again. Only now she felt as if she was heading toward something far worse, and she shivered.

Far worse . . .

Lela's mother was pretty, with long straight hair, and she wore a beautiful colorful dress that went right to the floor.

"We're going to play a game now," Lela's mom said.

She explained the rules. Lela sat right next to Emma, and Emma felt so happy now, happy and proud with her new friend.

All the children were sitting in the big living room, on the shiny wood floor under a white ceiling that was so high.

"Lela, the birthday girl, will pick one of you to stand up and start spelling their name. You stand up and walk around the circle. You tap each child as you walk around until you reach the last letter of your name."

Lela's Mom paused, as if she had a very funny secret. "And *then* you have to run around the circle one time without being caught by the last child you tapped!"

Emma nodded. Yes, this is like Duck, Duck, Goose. It was fun. She looked at Lela, sitting next to her, who gave her hand a squeeze. Later there would be cake and opening the presents.

I like it here, Emma thought.

"All right, Lela, pick one of your friends to start."

Lela looked at Emma and said, "I want Emma to go first."

Emma stood up and smiled. She turned to the girl to her right, and she put out her hand—and started spelling her name.

"E . . . M . . . M . . ."

Wharton stopped and pulled off the road. He reached in the back and picked up his binoculars.

No trees here, he saw. Nothing to cut off his view. He brought the binoculars up and focused.

He couldn't make out their faces, but he saw two figures walking along a balcony to an apartment door, one door in from the left.

"Well, there we are," he said. "There we are. . . ."

Wharton wondered whether Kate Cowell had any friends who might help her . . . that could make things difficult. It might be worth following her for a day, checking that out. He brought the binoculars down.

Which means I got to get another car today. She may have spotted this one. I have to get something else, something black, brown . . . and I can hang way back.

Sunday. That seems like the day for a snatch. The Lord's day. And this is the Lord's work, bringing children back to their father. Stealing children is . . . wrong. Sunday would be the day.

I'd have to move fast or they may leave.

There were two people that could help him, both ex-FBI, both eager for a quick grand or two.

I could bring the children to the airport, Wharton thought, have Cowell meet them there, and let him take them home.

Or I could even drive them all the way to New York. If he wanted to pay for that . . .

Wharton shivered. The wind at his back cut through his jacket.

Wish I brought something warmer, he thought. It's getting so cold out here. He looked up at the sky, and it was a mosaic of grays and blacks.

Nasty, he thought. And cold.

SEE HOW SHE RUNS

• • •

"A..."

Emma was strolling around the outside of the circle, all the girls watching her tap a child on the head.

"C...O...W...E...L...L..."

She finished her name, tapping the last girl, and dashed away. The children were laughing, and Emma ran super fast, hurrying back to her spot, hurrying, until, she fell to the floor, breathless, giggling, falling next to Lela.

I did it! she thought. I made it back. She didn't catch me and—

She looked up. Lela's mother was looking at her. She wasn't smiling. No, her face looked worried. Was something wrong? The way Lela's mother kept looking at her, what could be—

Emma froze, hearing Lela's giggles, feeling her friend squeeze her hand.

My name! Emma thought. I spelled my *real* name. And Lela's mother, she knows that I'm not Emma Martin, she heard me spell—

Lela's mother kept looking at her, and as she looked Emma started crying quiet tears. She felt the wetness on her cheeks, the drops rolling down, falling on her party dress.

Emma shook her head.

I forgot. I *forgot*.

Lela looked at her and asked, "What's wrong, Emma ... what's wrong?"

But Emma couldn't talk.

Wharton stood by the phone at the Exxon station while his car was being filled with unleaded regular. Budget Rent-A-Car had already told him that he'd need to return the car to the airport ... they couldn't do a swap in Santa Fe.

A little inconvenient. But that was okay. I've got time. No problem ... the drive will give me time to plan what I'm going to do, he thought.

He waited for David Cowell to pick up the phone.

Instead he heard the dull, mechanical voice of Cowell on the answering machine, then the beep.

"Mr. Cowell—I got her address, 1295 Cerillos, a ratty two-story apartment, an ugly place. She's on the second floor, one in from the left. I'm going to swap cars—"

A gust of wind made his suit coat flap in the air. "And watch her tomorrow. See if she has anyone who could stop me. I'll call you at six P.M. tomorrow, sharp, and give you the details, Mr. Cowell. Then you can come and get them or—"

The machine made a noise. No more message time, thought Wharton. He debated calling again. But no. Cowell will be sitting by his phone tomorrow at six. I can lay the whole plan out to him then. And how much it will cost.

Cowell will have no trouble getting a plane out of Kennedy Saturday night if he wants to pick the children up himself.

The gas jockey pulled out the nozzle and jiggled it back onto the pump.

Wharton took out his wallet and walked over to him, shivering as a freezing gust cut through his jacket.

Kate stood inside the hall of this house, an open foyer stretching two stories, with a balcony above and giant abstract paintings in desert purples and orange filling the left and right walls.

She expected to see a smile on Emma's face, and they'd go pick up Brian and John Morningsun and hit McDonald's for dinner.

But she could see that Emma had been crying, eyes red, puffy.

Kate looked up. Lela's mom stood there. Kate's face asked the question *What happened?* Did something happen to my daughter?

Lela's mom's face looked serious. She came close to Kate. She gently guided Kate to the side, away from the other children. Emma followed, as if pulled by the tidal motion.

"They were playing a game. . . ."

Kate nodded, trying to follow what happened.

"A *name* game. And Emma went around the circle—"

Kate chewed her lip. Right, a name game, and Emma went around the circle—

"Spelling her name. And—none of the children noticed, I mean, they didn't notice *anything*. Some of the girls can barely spell their names. But—"

Kate reached down. She touched Emma's shoulder and her girl's hand trailed up. Emma whispered,

"I didn't mean to, Mommy. I just forgot, and then—"

"She spelled a *different* name. Then she started crying. She seems very scared. Very scared."

Kate nodded. What do I do now? What can I do now? Just back out, say thank you? Thanks for inviting us to the party. But we have to go now. We have to leave.

Kate nodded. "I'll talk to her."

SEE HOW SHE RUNS

As if Emma had knocked over a glass of milk, teased another child. *I'll talk to her.*

But the woman's hand went out and touched Kate.

"Is there something I can do?" she said quietly. The doorbell rang, someone else picking up their children, people who didn't have two names, who didn't have to hide and watch for red cars in the rearview mirror.

Kate shook her head. "No. We—we'd better go."

Lela's mother pulled back her hand, scrutinizing Kate.

What is this woman going to do? thought Kate. Forget this? Call the police? What the hell is she going to think?

This is just a stop, she told herself. A stop. And maybe it's time to move on.

Kate turned and walked to the door. Other women were there, one hidden by bushy furs, another in a tight, sleek leather jacket.

Kate didn't look at them. She imagined the phone calls, the women talking, telling their husbands, people asking questions. . . .

She guided Emma to the door and then outside.

Emma said, "Mommy, will we still go see the Indian 'vations tomorrow?" She sniffed once . . . for effect.

Kate kept walking. She nodded. "Sure, honey. Sure we will."

Russ lay on his bed, the lights off. Occasionally, the glow of car headlights moving up narrow Canyon Road sneakily cut into the room.

Russ had his shirt off, wearing only his jeans. He idly felt the outline of his cock through the jeans.

He was thinking about things.

He had gotten home in time to see another TV news story about the pickup truck that was butted off the road. A reporter said that now the police knew the color of the vehicle that had done it, and the type of tires.

Russ was sweating in the room. Maybe the heat was too high.

This isn't working. He clenched his fists. Every time I try to clear things up, every damn time I try to take care of things, it only gets—

His cock strained against the crotch of his jeans.

—more complicated.

Until he felt that there could be no fresh start, no escape.

Russ thought of prison. He'd met a guy once who had done some time. He used to laugh at Russ and say, "Boy, would they have fun with you there. Boy, would they *love* having your ass around."

He told him about the monsters, human monsters who worked on their bodies, lifting weights all day and night, until they were all muscle.

"Split you open like an orange," the ex-con had said.

Then Russ thought of the waitress.

She's running too. He knew that. That's why she met me, he knew. We're two runaways. Kind of ties us together.

But what's she running from? What secrets does she have?

Ties us together... and he wondered: maybe she could be another chance for him, another way out. I'd be okay with the right person.

I could be okay....

Someone who understood what it is to hurt, to feel like you were going to scream, to lose your mind...

He pulled down his zipper.

Did she leave a husband someplace, chopped into pieces like a Purdue chicken? Is that her secret.

More headlights cut into the room.

She was pretty, sweet, and with eyes that begged to be saved.

Can't save myself, thought Russ. Could I save her? Could she save me?

She was like one of those animals in a zoo, a gazelle, an antelope, all *big* eyes, so nervous, so fucking scared....

Russ touched his cock, thinking about her.

Maybe I can save her.

He didn't think of her children then. He didn't think that they had anything to do with him, anything to do with his future at all....

37

Russ dreamed.

Not a nightmare, not at first, even though he was back in the house. He had just shot his little boy, Bobby, right in the head.

It was like the boy was still sleeping.

Silently. No waking tonight and wanting a drink of water.

In the dream, the sounds came slowly, echoing weirdly through the hall. His older boy, Tom, waking up, stirring.

Another shot, and then he was sleeping too.

It still wasn't a nightmare. It's what Russ wanted to do.

Even when Elaine staggered toward him, screaming, finally aware, eyes glowing, the bitch finally fucking aware how bad things had gotten.

Her screams were bad.

But then Elaine took her bullet in the head, then another in the chest. Another . . . the blood was syrup, spilled on the floor.

Then the nightmare began.

He saw someone. . . .

There was a message here, in the nightmare.

There's no getting—

Russ was talking to the cop who stopped him on the highway. The cop spoke, spurting blood, talking to him—*registration, please, and your license*—while a geyser shot from his throat.

"Could I see your license and registration?"

Gurgle, gurgle . . .

Then he was at the front door of his house, empty now, and he was opening the door to get the hell out.

But the house was hanging off the side of the mountain road. He looked left, and then right. And the cowboy, the fucking laughing cowboy from the bar, was a skeleton gripping the wheel of his pickup, laughing, screaming, then falling, looking over at Russ. . . .

Screaming, wearing a cowboy hat.

The skeleton that could drive a car.

Screaming, falling, and Russ's house started to move, to slide down the slope, and—and—

The nightmare wasn't over, not nearly, Russ flailed at the bed to hold on, sinking, sinking. . . .

Getting the message in his sleep.

Getting the message *good*.

38

Saturday

Kate watched for him, waiting, and then she saw Tom Abbott's Jeep pull up. "C'mon," she said to Brian and Emma. "Let's go." She led the kids out.

John met her on the walkway outside the apartment. He looked down to the Jeep, then at the children.

He doesn't think I should go, Kate thought.

John looked at Kate. "You'll be gone all day?"

Kate smiled, wishing she had a justification for her need to get away, to do something, to talk with someone. To explain whatever was pulling her away.

"I imagine so. I guess, er, we'll be back before dark."

John nodded, not smiling. Then Kate saw him force his wrinkled face into a smile. He looked at Brian and Emma. "You'll like the San Fiero Pueblo. Their dances are wonderful." John pulled his sheepskin coat tight. "Though it may be too cold today, too cold for dances."

He nodded. "And their pottery is very good. Not as good as my people's work, but still"—he grinned, smoothing Emma's hair with a hand—"very nice."

The Jeep stopped below. Kate looked down. She watched Tom Abbott get out. He waved.

"Guess we should go," Kate said.

"Yes. And I think I'll go visit some friends today." He looked

SEE HOW SHE RUNS

at Kate, and she thought she saw a deep sadness there. "Every year there are fewer of them."

Kate ushered the children by John, down to the Jeep.

She felt John watching her.

She didn't look back.

Wharton studied the movement through his binoculars, the woman, the children walking down the steps, meeting someone.

Oh... it could happen anytime, he thought. They could bolt anytime, and I'd be left here holding the bag.

Wharton stood beside his rented Cutlass, a light tan color. It looked like what it was, a tourist's rented car. But it had a nice big backseat, good and roomy to hold the children.

He looked through the binoculars again.

Yes. They could be splitting.

You never know.

He wondered whether they noticed his car yesterday, whether Kate Cowell got spooked.

Got to stay way back today, he thought. *Way back.*

He watched them get into the Jeep. Who's the guy? Wharton wondered. Who's that?

Is he a fly in the ointment? The old Indian—the landlord, whoever he was—didn't look like any problem.

But who was this guy? Wharton licked his lips, studying the lanky man with a beard. I'll have to check on him, he thought.

He put down his binoculars and started the car.

Mari woke up after only a five-hour sleep in her room. The Desert Inn was only blocks from the Plaza of the Governors.

She woke up, and the sheets, the blankets felt cold against her skin. She got up and jacked the heat way up, but flicking the switch didn't bring any reassuring noise, no clicks or rumbles indicating that more heat was coming.

She looked at her watch.

Well, here I am, she thought. I'm here, and maybe Alex Russ is here, in Santa Fe.

Or maybe not.

And if he is here, how the hell will I find him? Do I wander the streets, hit the bars, the little Tex-Mex places, the shopping malls? Last night she had passed a mall done in a pseudo-adobe style. A big sign announced that *lots* of space was available for lease.

The recession is everywhere.

She got out of bed, went to the window, and opened the vertical blinds, letting a dull gray light into the room.

This may be a pretty stupid idea, she thought.

She turned on the TV. Cartoons were on. A gap-toothed monster changed into an alarm clock, trying to wake up a sleeping skeleton.

Mari watched the dumb cartoon, but she wasn't paying attention.

She had an idea . . . and she knew where she'd go first.

Tom Abbott drove out of Santa Fe, chatting to the kids, and Kate felt as if she had to explain why they were so quiet. "It's been hard," she said. "Moving to a new place. They're still settling in."

Tom nodded and smiled. But then he did an odd thing. He looked back and said to the kids, casually, "How do you like school?"

Kate looked at him. It was as if he hadn't heard her explanation, that he was going to ignore it. As if he was going to *make* them talk.

Kate turned and looked out the window, at the open desert, the scrubby bushes, the sand laced with pink, and then, to the east, the black-and-gray mountains, jagged points reaching to dark clouds.

It didn't feel like such a great day to be going someplace.

Kate kept looking out the window.

Wharton thought, There's no way to disappear on the damned open road. For miles ahead there was only the Jeep, heading south.

And if he looks in his mirror, he'll see me.

Well, maybe that's not such a big problem, Wharton thought. I'm not in the same car as yesterday, and I can just cruise behind them.

He turned on the radio.

Some CD cowboy was singing about how "My ex and me are lovers . . . *again.*"

Wharton fiddled with the radio dial, looking for a Good News station, a Christian radio station. Has to be one somewhere, he thought.

Russ checked the mirror.

There were a couple of things wrong. No, more than a couple.

There were those news programs, saying that everyone was looking for the gray car—they knew it was gray—that pushed the poor bastard cowboy off the road.

And this trip—maybe this wasn't such a good idea. He looked over at Kate, sitting beside him. She looked cold, though the Cherokee's heater was turned up full blast. She looked cold, and far away. And her kids were sitting in the back so damn quiet. What's the hell's wrong with those kids? How come they don't say anything?

Then there was the car sitting in the rearview mirror.

Just hanging back.

Russ tried an experiment. He eased up on the gas, slipping below sixty, then fifty-five, creeping toward fifty. He kept looking up to the mirror. No one was saying anything, no one making conversation.

What's wrong? Someone die here, *someone fucking die here*?

Kate turned to him as if feeling his eyes on her. He smiled at her and she smiled back.

She turned away.

The car in the mirror slowed. Monkey see, monkey do. A cream-colored car, hanging back there.

This could be bad, Russ thought, real bad. If they've found me, if they've tracked me here—

How the *hell* could they have tracked me here?

He pressed a bit more on the accelerator, his eyes locked on the mirror. Sure enough the car was there, hanging on, an invisible string holding us together, thought Russ.

Russ looked at Kate, his heart beating fast, and he tried to figure things out, growing more confused with every mile he traveled.

Mari was ushered into the chief of detectives' office, inside the Santa Fe Municipal Building. The chief, Walter White, was an Anglo, tall, with a sun-hardened face. He stood up as she entered.

"Miss Comas, you picked a mighty cold day to visit Santa Fe."

Mari nodded, feeling embarrassed about what she was going to say. She looked around the wall of the man's office, at his citations, the pictures of White on a pinto horse, a family photo— a wife and two smiling children with close-cropped hair.

She explained who she was. She told White about Elaine Russ, about the children. She told him how she was too late to help them. She told him about Alex Russ. "A psychotic," she said. The chief nodded as if the word didn't mean anything to him. There are no psychotics here. . . .

She told him how Alex Russ got away.

White nodded. He had the files. Sure, and the picture was on their board, all the information was in the computer.

"We're all set here," was how he put it.

She shook her head. Not to disagree. She smiled.

"No."

Mari told him about Suzy Tyler, how Alex Russ might have been the one who raped her, that it might be the same man. White squinted, dubious.

"Your photos, they're out-of-date," Mari said. "I've *seen* Russ, I was trying to help. I know what he looks like. If he's here—"

Now White smiled, indulging her. "You'll what—find him? We're a close community here in Santa Fe, Miss Comas. But Santa Fe is still a city. We get a lot of visitors." He nodded. "A *lot* of transients. This isn't New York, but we get our share of problems."

Right, thought Mari. What did I think? That I could walk around the block and bump into Russ? That I could grab him as if we were playing ring-a-levio—

Cor, cor, one-two-three.

I've got you.

"If he's here, we'll find him. Don't worry. He'll turn up."

No, thought Mari. Maybe he won't. He might just move on.

And I couldn't live with that.

"I thought I'd spend a few days. I might—"

White laughed. "Spot him? Go ahead. It's a nice city to visit. But you'll be disappointed. You should leave the police work to—"

The chief's phone rang. A real call? Mari wondered. Or was it the secretary bringing the conference to an end?

Mari took out a small spiral notepad and a pen. She wrote—

"One second," White said into his phone. "I'm afraid that I'll have to—"

Mari stood up and came close to White. "A family died because I didn't see the danger. I want to help . . . I *need* to help. If you pick up anyone—even close to matching the description—please call me. I'll be staying here until Monday."

The chief took the slip of paper.

"Please," Mari said. White looked up at her, his call on hold. He nodded. "Okay," he said. Then again: "Okay. You got a deal."

SEE HOW SHE RUNS

Mari smiled, believing the man.

Sometimes you just know when someone was telling the truth. She walked out of the office.

Dan Stein stood just inside the lodge, holding the phone, punching in Mari's number. He watched Jake scooting down a slope, cutting back and forth.

He heard the phone ring. Then again, a third ring, and Mari's machine answered.

Dan just wanted to check on her, she was so upset. He was going to tell her that he'd call into his office later and see if there was anything new.

"Hi, Mari, it's Dan."

Jake got on the line for the ski lift again, tireless, waving at Dan.

"We're having a great time." He paused. His face looked concerned. "I'll call later."

He hung up. The wall phone sat there, holding its secrets. He considered checking his machine at home. Probably messages from work on it, annoying things . . .

But Dan was cold—so he walked over to the snack bar to get a cup of coffee.

"Let the light . . . let the light of Jesus shine on!"

Wharton sang along with the New Word Singers.

"Let the light!" he sang, answering their chorus. "Let—"

Wharton stopped singing.

The Jeep he was following slowed. Probably looking for an exit. Where are they going? thought Wharton. Heading to Albuquerque? Hitting some stores? Hopping a plane to Canada?

Oh, that wouldn't be good.

Then the Jeep seemed to glide away, speeding up, and as the road curved Wharton lost it behind a hummock of stone and pink sand.

But when Wharton took the same hummock, he had drifted too close to the Jeep . . . as if it was a trap. He eased off the accelerator, blowing air through his pursed lips.

Ooooh.

Maybe the guy didn't see me. What's he got to be worried about? Wharton nodded.

Kate looked over at the speedometer. The Jeep was doing well over eighty miles an hour. She said, "Going a bit fast—"

She saw Tom looking at the mirror. *At the mirror—*

Kate turned around. There was a car behind them. She turned forward. Yesterday she had thought there was a red car acting strange, up in the hills. Now there was this tan car back there.

Tom was looking in the mirror as if he was concerned, as if wondering why anyone would be following them.

This is a bad idea, she thought. A real bad—

But then Tom said, his voice sounding tight, pinched, "There it is. Okay. There's the exit for San Fiero."

He looked at Kate, and he wasn't smiling. "We're almost there." Then, with Kate watching, his eyes flew back up to the mirror. Kate turned around, pretending she was looking at the kids.

"We're almost there, guys. We'll get some food—"

She looked out the rear window. Tom had his blinker on. The other car didn't.

So maybe it's not following us. Kate turned back. Make it go away, she thought. *Please. Make it go away.*

Tom slowed, and took the exit to the San Fiero Indian Reservation. . . .

39

They had to pay to enter the pueblo, a collection of squat buildings covered by the gritty mist of dust devils dancing around.

The Indian woman in the entrance booth took the money from Tom and handed him a map and a sheet of paper. Then she shut the sliding glass door to her booth, sealing in the heat made by a space heater.

There were only a few cars in the parking lot.

Kate looked at the sheet of paper.

"This is it?" Brian asked. "This is the pueblo?"

Kate looked up. It didn't look like much. Some adobe buildings, a small church, a well.

"No problem parking," Tom said.

Kate smiled at the joke. She glanced behind her. The tan car was gone. A phantom, just another nightmare.

"It says here that we can't take any photographs without paying a fee in the visitors' center."

Tom laughed. "Pay to get in, pay to take photographs. What the he—"

He caught himself.

Then she saw some Indians stirring from the buildings, as if cued by their arrival. An old man with a floppy hat shuffled out of one building to another.

"Gee, this is pretty exciting—not!"

Emma laughed at Brian's crack.

Kate opened her door. "Well, let's get out and take a look around. It says that there's a craft shop, and museum, and a picnic area by a waterfall."

"I'll pass on that," Tom said. He opened his door.

Kate turned to Brian and Emma. "We'll get some food. What do you say?"

Together, the kids opened their doors.

Wharton had to slow down and pull over to the side of the road. Then he backed up, slowly, while an eighteen-wheeler roared past him, followed by some rusty pickups.

Wharton backed up to the exit.

At the off ramp he drove slowly down. He could see small canyons ahead as the ramp cut between two hills. A sign announced that YOU ARE NOW ENTERING THE SAN FIERO RECREATION SITE— OWNED AND MANAGED BY THE SAN FIERO PUEBLO INDIANS. FEES REQUIRED.

Wharton went around one hill and saw the buildings and cars. He quickly stopped. That's about far enough, he thought. Good enough to stop here, keep a watch on things right *here*.

He was hungry. Could do with some burritos, and a cup of hot coffee. He held the binoculars up, and he saw the Jeep.

A truck rumbled by, an ancient green monster leaving a trail of black smoke. Indians stood in the back of the truck, holding on, looking at Wharton.

Wharton glanced up and smiled.

Only doing some bird-watching, friends. Got any birds in this desert?

Wharton got back into his car, keeping the engine running, radio on. Making sure no one flies away . . .

Matthew J. Costello

* * *

The Plaza of the Governors was deserted except for the line of squatting, stoic-looking Indians, wares displayed in front of them, waiting for tourists to come.

I doubt very much they'll be much business today, Mari thought.

She turned around. The few trees in the green at the center were stunted, shriveled against the cold. Mari walked down the line of craftspeople.

No one tried to call her attention to their jewelry, the pottery, the wood dolls, but she saw some beautiful work. Glittering teardrop-shaped earings dotted with turquoise. Intricate rings and pots, smooth, seamless, perfect . . .

The Indians, from various Pueblo reservations, were all ages . . . an old man puffing on a pipe, a young man with shoulder-length hair and a Metallica T-shirt talking excitedly with a friend, a moon-faced woman with a small boy sitting next to her, whittling a piece of wood.

As Mari walked along she saw one Indian stand up from his crouch and pack up his silver pieces, carefully rolling them in a black velvet cloth. The first to give up . . .

She looked around at the plaza, the fancy clothing shops across the way, right next to a five-and-ten. What was I thinking? she wondered. That I could come here, walk around, and stumble into Alex Russ? Grab him, hold on, and scream. Help me. . . . *You all have to help me hold this man!*

The idea now seemed comical.

She was halfway down the line of native artists, at the entrance to the Palace of the Governors. A damp, icy wind blew, and Mari thought she might go in there for a few minutes.

She walked into the entrance to the palace, but there was no one at the desk selling tickets. A tall guard, the size of a basketball player, took a step toward her and said, "She's gone, but she'll be right back." The guard, an Indian, spoke in slow, measured tones. He smiled. "She went to the rest room."

Mari nodded and waited. She looked to her left and saw an exposed section of the wall. The placard to the right said that this was one of the original beams from the palace, constructed in 1609. The Spanish governor used this building as his personal residence.

The museum attendant came back, her face looking sullen and uncomfortable. Mari bought a ticket. The young dark-eyed woman didn't look at her.

SEE HOW SHE RUNS

Mari walked into the palace. She looked one way and the other, and then—for no particular reason—she went right.

Kate picked up a slice of the bread offered by the Indian woman. It was covered with a thick dab of homemade honey butter melting on the still warm bread. Kate bit into it.

"Um," she said. "This is excellent." The Indian woman smiled, pleased. "I'll take a loaf." Kate watched the woman select a loaf of brown bread from the row of twenty or more, all waiting for Anglo customers.

Kate turned to find her kids. Brian had picked up a toy tomahawk with a rainbow shaft and a rubber head. Emma held a small wooden doll with feathers at the top.

Tom was talking to an old man. He came over to her.

"He says that there's something at the community house, something called the buffalo dance, that we can see."

Kate nodded. She had hoped to relax. But Tom felt like a stranger, and this place took her even farther away from her world. I want to go home, she thought. But I have no home.

"Fine," she said. "The kids will like that."

Tom kept looking at her, as if he could read her mind. Then he smiled. "Great," he said.

Oh, I'm so hungry, Wharton thought. When are they going to leave this dreary place?

Every few minutes he brought his binoculars up and checked the parking lot. He didn't want to be caught sitting here as they flew by.

But all he could think of was food, a fat cheeseburger, a BLT, and maybe a slice of apple pie. Then getting a good night's sleep before the snatch.

Oh, yeah. And calling Cowell. Letting him know that everything's all set . . . Mustn't forget that.

The first exhibit gave the history of the palace, how the Spanish lost the building to the Indians and how the Spanish took it back again . . . only to lose it to the Indians again. Then the pioneers came from the East and started New Mexico on the road to war and statehood.

There were coins, plates, and Bibles centuries old. There were framed line drawings of the elegant Spanish governors.

Mari moved into the next room, through a maze of walls and freestanding exhibits. This room was filled with primitive phonographs, some that played Edison cylinders, others that played large metal records with holes, more like player pianos. She saw a Victrola with a megaphone as big as a giant pizza.

Music was important to the pioneers, a placard said. A few minutes of a Verdi opera thumped out on one of these machines could be their only touch of civilization.

She walked around one freestanding wall.

She heard a step.

The palace had seemed empty. No one here except me, Mari had thought, me and the guard and the ticket woman in distress.

Mari took another step, but she wasn't looking at the rows of cylinders on display. She felt goose bumps rise on her skin, her heart picking up a faster rhythm.

I'm all alone.

She took another step.

A handful of cold-looking tourists stood in the ceremony room. A dozen Indians trudged around in a circle, bending up and down while chanting, muttering to the earth floor. They were all draped in rainbow shawls, except for one dancer who wore a buffalo headdress. Some Indians to the side beat drums.

Do they do this every day? Kate wondered. Is this the big attraction for the tourists?

An Indian came close to Emma and Brian. He looked at Kate, nodding. Then he spoke to the children. "This dance was done by our young hunters to tell the buffalo that we will kill them with *honor*. The drums are the hoofbeats of the animals, and the hunters look up."

"C'mon," Tom said. "We've seen enough of this."

Tom spoke loud enough so that the Indian heard him. Kate turned to him. "The kids are enjoying it—"

She felt embarrassed. That was a stupid thing for him to do, she thought. What am I doing here with him? Am I that desperate?

"I've had enough. Let's go." It was a voice, ordering her. Like her father used to order her mother, the same sound David made when he told her what they were going to do. A voice, ordering her, taking away any need for a decision.

Kate felt cold. She touched her lips. *I'm here. I'm doing this, letting someone tell me what to do. Again* . . . There was a terrible awareness, a dull recognition. She looked at Tom. . . .

He grabbed Kate's arm.

She felt his fingers lock on her arm, pinching it.

SEE HOW SHE RUNS

"Hey," she said. She saw Brian looking at her, his face concerned.

"You should stay for the whole ceremony," the Indian said. "It is a sign of disrespect to—"

"Right. But I need some air, Cochise. Let's—"

Kate pulled her arm free. She turned to the Indian. "I'm sorry." Then, to Brian and Emma: "Kids, we'd better go."

She followed out the door, letting dust whirl into the room as she followed Tom to his car.

Wharton sat up, spotting them getting into their Jeep.

Good thing, he thought. It will be dark soon and I've had enough of this. He started up the Cutlass.

The engine made a sick noise.

A noise as if the battery was dead.

"Oh, no—Lord, no," he said. He turned the key again.

Mari took another step away.

She heard another shuffling step in answer, then another, and God, she felt trapped here, with nowhere to go.

She told herself that there was nothing to be scared of. She pressed her back to the side of an exhibit.

Then the guard was there, lanky, a thin, reedy, giant Indian, smiling, talking in clear tones that sounded ancient.

"Oh—I was looking for you. If you go the *other* way, the exhibit is chronological." He grinned. "'Course, you can go whichever way you want. There's a display of period firearms ahead."

Mari nodded, her heart quickening. "Thank you," she said. "Thanks."

No point in staying here, she thought. She walked past the guard.

No point at all.

All of a sudden Tom was quiet. As if a switch had been thrown. Kate made a point of looking back at the children, reassuring them that everything was *okay*. This was supposed to be fun for them, but now there was this tension in the air.

He pulled out of the driveway fast. The dusty sand flew into the air behind them. He said nothing.

Kate opened her mouth to say something, to make the tension go away. But she said nothing.

• • •

Russ pulled away from the exit fast, catching the Indian in the booth staring at him, looking at the nasty trail of dust that the speeding Jeep was leaving.

Fuck you, Russ thought.

He had spotted the goddamned car when he was standing by the pueblo community center. The same damn tan car that had followed him on the road leading to the pueblo.

The same damn car!

There was no doubt about it now. No way I'm not being watched. No fucking way. They're only waiting for a good time to pick me up. They know about this woman, and her kids. Maybe they even know where I live.

They won't let me find a way out.

Gotta think. This is bad. Got to think and do something.

They'd love your ass in jail. Yessir!

He roared up the hill.

Wharton killed the radio, then the dash lights. They couldn't have sent the car out with a bad battery. That wasn't possible. Still, he heard the sick chugging noise. This can't happen to rental cars! He heard a noise—the fan blowing cool air now.

Wharton shut it off.

He tried the ignition again. There was another chug, a cough, and then the engine started.

Praise the Lord!

Wharton did a fast three-point turn, whipping around. The tires screeched as if he was in a movie. But this wasn't good. Whoever that guy is with Mrs. Cowell, he's probably helping them and he could help them get clean away.

Wharton saw his money, his mission getting clean away too. He gunned the car, racing toward the Jeep that was a good five minutes ahead of him. He came to the highway and now the sky was darker, and the mountains in the distance were lost to the black clouds.

A fog rolled toward him, pouring off the mountains. Wharton paused at the highway crossing for only a moment.

I'll head north, he thought. Wait until they're well ahead of me, gone back to Santa Fe, and then I'll follow them.

Again the car screeched as Wharton pulled away. Thinking that he still hadn't been seen.

• • •

SEE HOW SHE RUNS

"Could you take it a bit slower," Kate said. "It—it's frightening the children."

He looked at her—just as the Jeep took a curve fast—and Kate thought that they'd slide into one of the dunes that seemed like barriers.

"Sure," he said.

But he went just as fast. He kept looking at the mirror, then craning around to look out the rear window.

What's he looking for? she thought. What did he see?

Kate saw a car in the distance, heading in the direction of Albuquerque. The car was just a dot on the horizon.

She looked at Tom, studying the car, watching it in the mirror.

40

Wharton went only a few miles in the wrong direction, then he turned around, hurrying to get the Jeep back in sight.

I have to find out who that guy is, he thought. One thing you learned in the FBI, a free agent could screw things up in a big way. I may have to do something to make sure he doesn't mess things up.

This was getting complicated.

He stayed back, just barely able to see the Jeep.

Mom's scared, Brian thought. He held the toy tomahawk tight. She's scared again. She hasn't felt like this . . . not since . . .

She asked the man to slow down again. He was driving so fast. Brian was angry. Why did we have to meet him? Why did we have to come here?

It got dark, and Emma snuggled close to him, playing with the feathers on top of her doll. Closer, and she put her head down on Brian's shoulder. He didn't shrug her off.

She fell asleep while Brian stared ahead.

Kate saw the lights back there. The car hanging back, and now she knew someone was following them.

She looked at Tom. Maybe I should tell him? Tell him why we're being followed. He must have seen, must have noticed the car.

She saw the way he gripped the steering wheel, the way he kept looking up to the mirror, and—

Something cold ran through her, a sudden jolt of electricity. She sat up. There was an awareness. . . .

I thought it was me.

It . . . it still could be. Sure, that car could still be following *me*.

But—

She looked at Tom, holding the wheel, going so fast down the highway. He gripped the wheel so tightly, his knuckles picking up the light from the dashboard.

More awareness, like light bulbs coming to life in a dark, dead house. Yes, now we can see. Now it's clear.

God. No.

He has a secret too. He's running from something, and—

She turned to the back. She saw Emma asleep against her brother. Checking out. All systems down. Brian sat there, the tomahawk in his lap, looking at his mother. They didn't say anything to each other. They didn't have to, Kate knew.

She turned forward again.

While, as if in a dream, they roared through the dark desert.

They know. Yes, thought Wharton. Oh, Lord, they *know* they're being followed.

Well, I'll have to see how we'll play this game.

He banged the steering wheel. This is exactly the mess that he didn't want. He looked at his watch.

I told Cowell I'd call in . . . Now, it's ten minutes to six. But I can't stop. I have to find out who the guy in the Jeep is. Can't have any wild cards . . .

He's doing seventy-five, and my rental car is barely keeping up.

Things were not going smoothly.

Russ nearly missed the turnoff for Santa Fe, the spur that led to Cerillos Road. He slowed as he entered the city limits.

SEE HOW SHE RUNS

I don't want any cops, he thought.

He was making plans. You always have to have plans, something for every—

What was the word?

Something for every contingency.

No one said anything, until they were in the city, and then Kate said, "Could you just take us back? The kids are tired."

He heard the fear in her voice. Yes, he could do that, that was part of his plan, his way out of this.

He nodded.

He thought of the reporter on TV, bending over the tire tracks, looking out of the screen, looking at him.

They're closing in. Yessir, that's what's happening here. It's gonna take some drastic fucking measures to make sure that doesn't happen.

You don't get a chance to start all over.

They'll love your ass in jail, boy. Oh yeah . . .

I'll take them back. The bitch, her kids. I'll take them back. That would work . . . fine.

Wharton lost the Jeep at the intersection near the DeVargas Mall. He got caught at a red light and considered running it.

Maybe I'm getting too old for this, because it's getting all messed up now.

He saw a red light ahead, and the Jeep was stopped.

He's probably taking them back to their apartment, Wharton thought. That's fine. That's real good. Because then I can follow *him.*

Mari picked up another slice of the small pan pizza she had picked up at the place next to the motel. It was cold, the crust hard, the cheese like dry plaster.

I may as well be on the moon for all the good I'm doing here.

The Channel 10 Action News was on. The weekend team, a young black woman and a silver-haired guy with a telltale red nose, were doing an adequate job of reading the news.

The man looked up and said, "Still no more information on the strange hit-and-run accident on Old Mountain Road."

There was a snippet of video, a twisting road, the black smears of tire tracks, the open space where a car went flying off.

Somebody did that? she thought. Butted someone right off the highway?

What kind of a crazy would do that?

Later she checked her machine. She heard the message from Dan—and she wished that he was here. It was strange, a yearning she hadn't felt in so long. She pulled away from it.

She called Dan's number and left a message.

"Dan," she said when the machine beeped. "I'm in Santa Fe." She told him where. She gave him the phone number. She waited, as if it might answer. Then she hung up.

Kate turned and told Brian, "Wake her up gently, Bri."

Kate didn't pop open the door and hop out of the Jeep, as much as she wanted to. . . .

She didn't look at Tom.

"Thanks," she said. She looked at the apartment building. The two apartments—hers, John's—were dark.

Emma groaned, slowly coming awake.

"C'mon, honey," Kate said. "We're home." Then: "Go ahead, Bri."

She heard Brian open the door. Emma groaned. "Mommy."

Kate got out of Tom Abbott's car. He hadn't said anything. It was so creepy. The air was chill and damp on her face. I just want to get into our apartment, she thought. Just get in, lock the door, and forget all about Tom Abbott.

She reached down and picked up Emma, no light load. Brian held on to Kate's skirt—just like he did when he was a kid.

Emma was so heavy. "Mommy, I'm tired."

Kate started up the stairs. She was tempted to look back. Thinking that he was watching, that he'd get out of the car.

What is he running from? she wondered. She felt sick. She struggled up the steps, holding a whining Emma. Brian trailed behind. She looked behind her, and just as she looked the Jeep pulled away.

Kate breathed hard, with every step. "Almost there, babe. Almost home."

The wind was fierce here, twice as strong as she got higher.

Home, Kate thought. That's a laugh. When she was beside the apartment door, she let Emma slide to the ground so she could dig out the key.

41

Night

Now where is the guy going?

Wharton rubbed his chin, leaning forward to look at the Jeep taking crazy turns up small roads, past boxy adobe homes, some missing great chunks of orange stone.

There were no streetlights here, no sidewalk, and the squat houses pressed close against the edge of the road.

Got to do this, Wharton knew. The guy's a wild card. That's what we called them in the Bureau. Don't want any wild cards showing up in the deal, the regional director would say.

You knew it was your neck if something unexpected happened.

Just like it's my neck now. Or my thirty grand . . .

He has to see me, Wharton thought. But that was okay, the woman was gone. Let the punk feel some paranoia. If he's not involved, then he won't have a clue what's going on here.

And if he is helping Kate Cowell—then that's a real problem.

The Jeep took another turn down a small canyon. There were two blackish hummocks on either side of the car.

It was snowing. Big saucer-shaped flakes cartwheeled through the air. They hit the windshield and melted. Just a few flakes, but then, as if they were calling up reinforcements, there were more and more, and they didn't melt so easy.

Wharton turned the wipers on low.

Where the heck does this guy live? In a cave . . . ?

"How about a pizza?" Kate said. "I'll call Domino's."

Brian sat in front of the tube. He looked at Kate after they came home as if she had betrayed them.

"Sure," he said. "Okay. Get extra cheese."

"You got it." She turned to Emma, sitting at the kitchen table. Emma had all her dolls out to greet the new arrival, the colorful wooden Indian doll.

"Pizza, Emmie?"

Emma nodded, and Kate picked up the phone.

Jesse started his snow watch. Annie saw him throw two more chunks of dry wood on the fire and then walk to the window. There was nothing in the manual that said that he *had* to check the road during a big snowfall, that he *had* to make sure that no one had their ass hanging off the mountain buried by a mountain blizzard.

But to Jesse, this was his mountain, his responsibility.

He grew quiet. He went to the window, pulling aside the curtain.

Annie knew better than to try to talk to him.

This was it, then. Maybe there is no getting away. Maybe there is no fucking way out. No salvation, no exit.

Russ had his knife and his gun sitting beside him. He glanced at them. I didn't want it to be like this. Why couldn't they leave me alone. Why couldn't they—

And who else knows? Who else is after me?

Have they spoken to Gary Moll? Maybe they know all about the gray car. Oh, Christ, maybe they've seen the gray car and they're matching up the paint, the goddamn tires.

He started breathing in quickly.

The pressure inside his head grew immense, throbbing. The snow looked like lights dancing in front of him, mocking him.

Have they spoken to Kate?

Maybe she was part of it all along. Go with him, talk to him. *Help us out*. Keep an eye on him. He nodded. It was possible. Sure it was.

He shook his head.

No. Maybe they haven't talked to her. Not yet. Not fucking yet . . .

He was alone. Unprotected. Wasn't that always the way it was? No one to watch out for him, and all this fucking pressure.

The Jeep bounced down the twisting road, down a narrow canyon . . . until he stopped.

The road seemed to end. There was one last hairpin turn, and then a twisty path continued up another hummock.

Wharton saw that the Jeep had suddenly stopped in front of him. There was nothing he could do except hit his brakes. The

Cutlass slid on the mud, gliding on the covering of slushy snow.

He looked up, his eyes pleading. "Do you need to do this now, Lord?" Wharton said, waiting for the tires to grip.

But there was no traction.

After fishtailing and scraping the bushes on the right, the car finally stopped . . . and the Jeep was just ahead, also stopped, waiting.

Okay, pal, you know I'm here. So what are you going to do about it?

Wharton waited for the Jeep to get moving again. Instead he saw the door open, and the guy got out.

Wharton shook his head. *Now what is he doing?*

The guy walked back through the snow. Wharton saw him, the beard, a young guy. Maybe I should be a bit careful here. Wharton reached out for the gear shift. There was no way to get past the car, so—

Wharton looked behind. Oh, if I back up I might hit one of those hills.

He pulled the stick down to reverse.

The guy was beside the car.

Wharton froze. Talk to him. Yeah. Tell him he has nothing to be concerned about. Talk my way out of it. Maybe level with him. Not a great idea—but it was a possibility.

Wharton looked back to the mirror. Maybe a better possibility was trying to maneuver the car backward, up the slippery road.

The guy smiled and tapped on the window.

Wharton turned to him. The car was in reverse. Can always gun it, he thought.

Jesse turned from the cabin window.

Annie was wiping the kitchen table. Jesse usually helped with the work, cleaning the table, washing dishes. There wasn't much with only the two of them. He even had a basic repertoire of three meals he could cook.

Tonight, though—he was a sentry.

"Annie, could you turn on NOAA." He smiled. "I think they're right on the money this time." He took a breath. "It looks very bad out there."

Annie turned on the radio, just catching the beginning of the winter-storm-warning update.

She puttered in the kitchen, as if looking for something to do.

• • •

The guy signaled Wharton to roll down the window. He's smiling, Wharton thought. Maybe he's lost. Maybe he hasn't even flashed on the fact that I'm following him.

Wharton checked the clock in the dash. I'm way overdue calling Cowell. *Way* overdue.

He started to crank the window down.

"Problem, pal?" Wharton said. He was a small man, nothing that Wharton couldn't handle if the situation turned nasty. He looked up the hill and then back to his Jeep. He leaned close to Wharton.

He almost stuck his head in the car. Wharton didn't like that. Then the guy spoke quietly, in a tone that sent an alarm running through him.

Because the sound, the voice, the volume was all wrong. *All wrong,* while he smiled and Wharton smelled his breath, flakes sneaking in sideways, landing on Wharton's face.

"Why are you following me?"

Wharton's hand was still on the shift. Could gun it, he thought. Get away from here.

Instead—a thought—maybe there was an ally here. At least I could neutralize him. Let him know that he should keep his nose out of this.

Wharton shook his head. "I'm not following you, pal. Not at all. You see—"

The man had pulled his head out of the window a bit. Now there was a knife there. Wharton had time to see the blade.

"Oh, Lord—"

That was all he got to say. Because the knife jabbed in, puncturing Wharton's throat. He felt all this warmth, and then stinging. His hand came off the shift to grab at the knife, the hole. He pressed down on the accelerator.

Tires screamed, slipping on the snow, the mud. But his foot slipped off the accelerator, the contact too difficult to maintain.

Then, with his hand still trying to find his throat—it was so difficult—

The knife danced back and forth, making the hole wider, and wider, back and forth. Wharton's head started bobbing. Trying to pull away, trying to get away. But can't get away, can't because—

He felt the seat belts. The warm wetness falling in his lap.

SEE HOW SHE RUNS

His hands found the hole, so damned large now. Such a *giant* hole. His fingers went inside the hole.

Then his head keeled forward and hit the steering wheel.

But he didn't feel *that*.

Kate opened her door and went to John's apartment. It was still dark. I'd like to talk to him, she thought.

As she stood on the balcony she saw a car pull up with a small Domino's sign spinning in the snow, hanging lopsided from the antenna.

The driver was running late. If he misses his thirty-minute mark, it's three bucks off the price of the pizza. So pimply-faced teenagers risk people's lives so we can eat mediocre pizza on time.

The pizza kid looked up at the apartment, searching for numbers. Kate stood on the balcony, in the snow, and she waved. Yoo-hoo, we're up here. The kid nodded and ran up the steps holding his special red thermal pizza carrier out in front of him.

Kate saw the snow starting to stick to the parking lot. Even as she stood there the snowfall got heavier.

She went inside the doorway to wait for the Domino's boy.

42

The pizza was nearly all gone—everyone was hungry—when there was a knock at the door.

Kate ran to it, expecting John. There were still one slice left, cold now, but she could heat it up for him.

Kate ran to the door.

She opened it.

Tom Abbott was there.

Brian stood up and came beside her. There was a commercial on the TV. It sounded like a cartoon; there was Bugs Bunny, and a basketball player.

"Tom," Kate said.

Brian stood beside her. Good boy, she thought. You're a good boy. . . .

Tom stepped into the apartment. There was a white curtain behind him. He shut the door.

"We've just eaten. I—I was putting the kids to bed."

She checked Emma, but Emma didn't look up. She sat at the table, lost to her dolls.

"We're kinda tired," Kate said. "What's wrong?"

He's not saying anything, she thought. Why isn't he saying anything? There was only the click of the door being shut behind him.

Here on the moon. Here in this abandoned motel.

"Bri, take Emma . . . wait in your room."

The boy didn't move.

Tom took a step closer to her. She gulped, as if the pizza, the chewy crust was coming up. What is this? she wondered. What's happening here?

And worse: *What have I done?*

He took another step. She saw his eyes, narrowed, tiny blue lights, staring at her. She looked to his hands . . . stained with something. They have sauce on them. He's been eating pizza too. He's been—

She moaned. Oh, God. No. Not—

"Brian," she whispered.

He was close enough now—and Tom pulled back and smashed her with the back of his hand.

Annie came and stood next to Jesse. He put an arm around her, pulling her close as they looked out the window.

Annie saw the tire tracks disappearing as the snow got heavier, deeper, burying everything. NOAA used all the right buzzwords. Extreme caution. Hazardous travel. Dangerous conditions.

She knew Jesse took it all in.

He gave the small fingers of her left hand a squeeze, reassuring her.

"It's Saturday," he said. "So what do you think the odds are that there are some assholes out there, coming back from skiing, or hunting, or whatever? Guys who don't give a shit what the radio says. What do you think?"

Annie said the words quietly, not scolding him. "That's not your responsibility."

Jesse turned and looked at her. "Then whose responsibility is

SEE HOW SHE RUNS   283

it? Who else will save the lone idiot who decides that his Japanese four-by-four is a match for anything the Rocky Mountains throw at him?"

"I don't like you going out there," she said.

Jesse laughed.

"Neither do I."

Kate stumbled backward, but Brian stayed beside her, grabbing her hand.

No. What is this? she thought. Her cheek stung.

"Don't you think I knew?" he said. "Don't you think that I *saw* what was happening today, how I was being *watched* by that fat creep in the car."

The car. The tan car. The one that I thought was following me. Kate smiled.

No. This is all a misunderstanding.

"No, you're wrong. I mean, I thought that—"

"Did they come to you? Did they tell you to watch me? To help them?"

"I don't know what you're talking about."

Her eyes trailed down to his hands. Stained. Not with grease . . . "No. Tom, I thought the car was following me. I've run away. I've brought the kids here, to get—"

"Mommy. Mommy, what's wrong?"

Emma was there on the other side, her children like bookends. And haven't I done well by them? she thought. *Look what I've done*.

He raised his hand.

"Tom, please—"

"Don't you hurt my mom!" Brian's voice rang out, loud, clear, so brave.

The man grinned. Kate knew then that his name wasn't Tom. It never was Tom. He was someone *else*. He had secrets. He was hiding too.

Hiding from what?

He said quietly, "You've spoken to no one?"

She shook her head. "N-no. No one's asked about you. I told you that I thought that the car was following me."

He turned away. He looked around the room. "I've tried to get away. Damn, I've tried to start over, but—" He raised his hands. "I can't. They won't let me." He turned to her. "But I'm not going to prison." He laughed. "No way I'm going to prison."

Brian spoke, his voice small and hard. He squeezed Kate's hand. "You leave my mom alone."

The man looked at Brian.

Kate saw his stare. I'm going to be sick, she thought. She started to shake her head. No. Whatever it is you're thinking, whatever, you can't—

He looked up. "He's dead. That cop's dead."

Emma started crying. Kate pulled her close. She said, her voice rising, "You're scaring my children."

"He's dead, and you know they'll come here now."

She shook her head. "No. How could they?"

He nodded. "Sure, they followed me here, and they know about you. They'll come here. But you could help me."

Kate nodded. Yes. Anything to get him to leave. Anything at all. Anything so he doesn't do something bad to my children.

"I'll help. I'll do anything. I—"

"They'll come here." He took a step closer. "And they'll talk to *you*. And you'll say that I've run away. But you don't know where. You won't know *anything*."

Closer. He reached out. Not for Kate, for Brian.

"Don't touch *him*. Don't you goddamn touch him!"

"I'll go to Mexico. But you won't tell them that. And if you don't—if I'm not followed—"

He reached into his back pocket. He pulled out a knife. So fast, he must have done this before. It was so smooth. Kate moaned, crying. She covered Emma's eyes, Emma sobbed against her.

He grabbed Brian's arm and pulled him close.

"Don't move," he said to the boy. "If you move, Brian, I will cut you."

Kate forced herself to look. He had the knife against her son's neck. The knife's blade wasn't silvery. It was stained, and—

"Please," she begged. "Please, don't. I won't say anything."

"They'll be so careful if they know I have your son. Somewhere on the way south, I'll let him go."

Brian struggled and Kate yelled, "No. Brian, stop." The blade was against the boy's neck. "Stop!" she said. "Do what he says."

Do what the crazy man says.

And baby—I'm sorry I've done this to you. I'm sorry....

The man backed up. He reached for the doorknob.

She heard the knob turning. She hoped someone would be there. That John would be standing there. That he'd pull Brian away from the man, and then, then—

Kill him, she thought. She'd watch him die.

The door opened. Eddies of snow billowed into the room.

"Please," she begged.

They stepped out, her son and this man, and—in answer—the door slammed shut.

43

Kate sat there, crying, and Emma stood by her, weaving her little-girl hand into Kate's, leaning into her.

"Mommy," Emma said. "What's going to happen to Brian? What will the man do?"

Kate brought a finger quickly up to Emma's lips. No, hush. Please, baby. *Please...*

I can't think about that.

She looked at the door. She told herself: I have to tell the police. That's what I should do. She sat there, wiping away her tears. She thought of a novel she read in college.

She tried to remember the name.

(*Appointment in Samarra*... Yes, and a man sees death in the marketplace. And death raises his arm and gestures at the man, as if saying, *Yes, I'm here for you.* So the man runs away, miles away to Samarra. And that night, thinking he is safe, walking the streets, he meets death *again.*)

Emma snuggled on top of her lap. Kate looked at the girl, then out the window, filled with white flecks, dancing. Thinking, my boy is out there....

(And the man says to death, "I ran away. How did you find me?" But death replies, *I wasn't looking for you today. I reacted with a start when I saw you in the marketplace. Because ... our appointment was here, tonight.*)

Emma said, "Mommy," wanting reassurance. Needing her. Kate squeezed her tight.

• • •

Brian didn't move. He looked out the window and didn't move, thinking that if he sat perfectly still, the man would stop the car somewhere and let him go.

He looked straight ahead.

The man said nothing. The only sound was the wipers pushing the snow away. They were going back and forth fast, back and forth so fast. And the heater made a whispering noise.

Brian watched where they were going.

Straight ahead, he saw the road, climbing up.

They were passing houses.

The man spoke.

"If you touch the window, if you try to open it, try to open the door, I'll hurt you." He paused and Brian nodded, as if to say, *Yes, I know that. I understand that.* "Do you like being hurt?" the man asked.

Brian answered, and his voice seemed to come from so far away. "No."

"Good. Then you just sit tight, and somewhere I'll let you go."

The Jeep was climbing. There was nobody on the road. They passed a stoplight and the red, then the green went all blurry as the big flakes hit the windshield.

Higher. We're climbing high, Brian thought. He looked left and saw a gas station. No, not just a gas station. There was a store there, too, selling milk, beer. Alvidsen's was the name.

Brian remembered it. He said the name in his mind. *Alvidsen's...*

He moved a bit in his seat. He reached down to his pocket. Slowly. He didn't want the man to notice. So very slowly he reached down to his pocket, to feel what he had hidden there.

Kate looked up. Emma was sitting beside her, in the quiet. I should be talking to her, Kate knew, I should be trying to tell her that everything is *okay,* and—

I'm all alone. We could disappear, melt away, and nobody would know.

She shook her head. *I should never have left.*

There was noise from the apartment next door, John's apartment.

"Honey," Kate said, getting up. "Excuse me."

Kate stood up. I don't know, she thought. Maybe I shouldn't—

But her thoughts didn't keep her from walking to the door,

opening it, seeing the blizzard outside, the parking lot blanketed in white, and the snow so heavy, falling straight down.

"Mommy!" Emma said.

"Just a minute, Emmie," Kate said.

She walked the few steps to John's door, and she knocked.

Brian felt the outline of the penknife. His mom had kept it after the principal gave it to her. She hid it from him—but Brian had found it again.

There were no more streetlights, no more stoplights. He saw houses, high up, stuck on the hillside as if floating in the sky, in the snow. Houses with warm, yellow lights, all looking so safe.

The Jeep's wheels whined, and the car skidded, struggling up the hill.

"Damn!" the man said. "Fucking snow!"

The snow might stop him, Brian thought. But then—what would he do to me? What would happen to me?

We're going high. We're climbing up. This isn't where he told Mom he was going. I don't think that there are any towns up here, no places to drop me, no street corners.

He saw another house, glowing, glistening on the hill, and then there was nothing but clouds, closer now, and dark blotches on either side—trees—and the white snow sticking to the road, leading higher and higher.

Jesse turned from the window, holding a cup of tea in his hand. It was not decaf tea, and that told Annie what lay ahead tonight. . . .

He looked right at her. "Well, they nailed this one right, babe. And it came on a Saturday no less."

Annie walked to the window reluctantly. She didn't like acknowledging what was happening. Saturday was bad because there could be skiers on the road, cross-country skiers who waited too long to get off the North Truchas Range and now were about to be trapped in the snowbanks.

"You're going to go out?"

He nodded. "But not yet. I'll give it a bit more time."

She squeezed his hand. "Who will pull you out if you get stuck?"

He laughed. "In the Rover? Not likely. And anyway, I'll be back safe and warm before this storm really hits its stride. We may get snowed in." He reached down and pulled her close. "That wouldn't be so bad, now would it?"

She leaned up and kissed him. I love him too much, she thought. So much that it's scary.

She kissed him and saw the snow outside, piling up on the tiny sill, dotting the window, eager to get in.

John made Kate sit down, and then he brought Emma into his apartment. The apartment was ice-cold, but he had his oven on and the door open.

He walked Emma into the kitchen near the stove, and he put a pile of chocolate-chip cookies in front of her.

Kate told John what happened while he took off his hat, a funny hat with a round top and big brim, shaking off the snow. He listened. His face said nothing.

But his eyes had narrowed, looking at Kate.

Judging me, she thought.

Of course. I deserve to be judged.

She repeated the words, as if they were a chant, as if saying them would make them true.

"He said he'd let Brian go. If I kept quiet. If I said nothing when they came to see me."

"Came to see you? Who was he talking about?"

"I—I don't know. That's just it. I thought someone was following *me*." She laughed. "That's who I thought was in that car."

"A car?"

Kate explained about the tan car following them.

"But he was hiding something. He's running too."

The teakettle started whistling. It was a sound Kate remembered from her childhood. A warm, reassuring sound. Her mother in the kitchen on winter afternoons . . . before her father came home. Nobody has teakettles anymore. Everybody uses a microwave, the soothing whistle replaced by the shrill beeping.

John poured a cup of tea for Kate and then some cocoa for Emma. He brought the cocoa over to Emma, who sat at the kitchen table playing with the different odd shapes of turquoise. Kate watched him, thinking: I'm not alone. I can trust this man.

"Here you go, Miss Emma," he said. "Some nice hot cocoa." Emma smiled.

Then he brought Kate her tea. He pointed to the phone. "Kate, you *have* to call the police."

She shook her head. "No. He said—"

John covered one of her hands with his, encircling it. She felt

SEE HOW SHE RUNS

his warmth, the texture of his wrinkled skin, the history, the art in the hands.

"You must call the police. Every minute takes your boy"— he looked over to Emma, but she was playing, losing herself in the sliver scraps, the blue stones— "farther away. You *must* call."

Kate shook her head. "I don't—"

He picked up the phone. He dialed the number.

She shook her head again. No, she tried to say. Because, if she told the police, well, what would happen to Brian, my little boy?

She heard the phone ring once. Then a voice. Saying, "Santa Fe police."

She froze. John nodded.

"I—" He squeezed her hand, giving her strength. "My son has been taken away. . . ."

Mari looked at the map of Santa Fe. It was a giant photograph of the city. It didn't cover the outlying areas, she saw. And that's probably where Russ would be living, holed up in some boardinghouse.

If he's here.

Still, she looked for places where someone might go on a Sunday. Tomorrow she could walk around the plaza again—that was a good idea. And there was the DeVargas Mall, and a strip of bars along Hyde Avenue, heading west.

She looked at the map.

What were the odds she'd spot him? she thought. Even if he's here, what are the odds?

She pushed her hair off her forehead. At least I tried. Yes, I could say that. At least I tried to do something.

She shook her head.

The things guilt makes us do.

She thought of going out now. Into the blizzard.

Yeah, right . . . That's a real stupid idea. Check out the nightlife in Santa Fe when there's a couple of inches of snow on the ground, and more due.

I may be stuck here for a while, she thought.

The phone rang.

Russ slowed down. The Jeep was fishtailing all over the fucking place.

Even the weather is screwing me up, he thought. His headlights—on bright—could only pick up a few yards of road. He barely saw the sides of the twisting highway.

Russ shook his head. He banged the steering wheel.

Maybe I should go the fuck back down.

But that wasn't his plan. The idea was to go over the mountains, back to the empty desert highways on the other side. Head over to Texas or up to Oklahoma.

Lose the boy in the desert.

Russ looked at him. The kid was sitting so quietly. Nice kid, well behaved.

Lose him. Waste him.

But this was no fucking good. I didn't know this snow was coming, he thought.

The Jeep slid a few feet to the left. The boy reached out to the dashboard. Russ cut the wheel to the right, realizing that the move was all fucking wrong, and now the Jeep began to slide badly, right to the edge.

He remembered the cowboy.

The goddamned skeleton cowboy, wearing his ten-gallon hat as he went flying right off the mountain.

But the snow was thick, and the Jeep slid only a few feet. It hit the fieldstone barrier to the left and then stopped.

Russ sat there.

The engine running, the wipers scooping off great handfuls of snow.

His headlights picked up a sign.

SANTA FE NATIONAL FOREST—TRUCHAS REGION.

The letters of the sign were each outlined by white, the snow building up around each letter, higher and higher like little peaked hats.

Russ took a breath.

I've got to be near the top, he thought. It's got be close, and then I can find a road down, and I'll be okay.

Sure . . .

He started the car forward again. The wheels spun, the Jeep slid a few inches more, and then it went forward.

Russ looked at the boy, his hands still locked on the dash. "Okay, kid?" Russ nodded. "Everything's fine. It won't be long."

He straightened the Jeep out.

"Won't be long before I find someplace to let you out." Russ grinned. "You don't want to be let out here, do you?" He laughed. "This doesn't look like a good fucking place, now does it?"

He kept laughing as the Jeep crawled up the mountain highway.

44

The police acted as if they knew what they were doing, as if this happened all the time, that every Saturday night a boy was taken by a psychotic. Kate tried to talk calmly to them.

Every Saturday night a blizzard swallows up someone's son.

They asked questions, two men in electric-blue parkas. They were detectives. They gave their names, but Kate couldn't remember them.

They asked her to tell them everything. She repeated the description that she gave over the phone.

One of the detectives nodded and then pulled his partner aside. They made phone calls, talking quietly into the receiver.

"We're covering the roads now," a detective said. The man had blond eyebrows and a tan face. He didn't look like a detective from the movies, all seedy, a cigarette hanging out of his mouth. He looked like a skier.

He said that it was good that they knew what the man was driving, that it was *real* good. And they knew what he looked like. That might help.

But then the other detective, a thin man with dark eyes, dark skin, said, "The weather's bad. The weather isn't helping."

His partner looked at him and shook his head. That was a dumb thing to say.

Kate told them: "He said he was going south, to Mexico. He told me not to tell anyone and my son wouldn't be hurt. You won't—"

"No. We will be very careful. We won't let anything happen to your boy."

Kate nodded. Sure. They won't let anything happen to Brian.

Then another thought, running through her mind like a mad roller coaster, up and down, all around, again, and again—

How the hell can they know that? How can they stop him from being hurt. He's, he's a—

(*Hostage*.)
And sometimes . . .
Sometimes, hostages are killed.

"Okay. I'm going to do a run."

Annie got up from her seat by the fireplace. She had been sitting there, waiting for these words.

"C'mon, Jesse. It's too bad out. At least wait until the snow is over."

He shook his head.

"What if some poor bastard is off the road, getting buried?"

Jesse didn't have to tell her the story. No, he had talked about it with her too many times to need to bring it up now.

How a station wagon full of cross-country skiers got trapped in the mountains, just near the Colorado border. It wasn't part of the National Forest, so when their car went off the road, into a snowbank, they were stuck.

They must have figured that their best bet was to stay with the car. They kept the heater on . . . until the gas started to give out.

The car was buried under a foot or more of snow. And by the time they realized that no one was coming for them, it was too late.

They were found days later, frozen.

All the papers had the grisly photo, the door opened, and the four skiers sitting there, eyes shut, sleeping forever.

"I'll do one run up and down the road." Jesse smiled. "Better now than after another few hours of this."

Annie came to him. "Check in . . . on the radio."

He smiled. "Sure. I always do."

He turned and left.

"Jesus fucking Christ! What is this shit?"

The man kept going. Brian looked at him, at the man's face picking up the reflection of the light on the dash. The man licked his lips, the tongue sticking out of the beard like a pink snake.

Brian was scared. He was conscious of every breath. He sucked in air, let it out. Then again, another breath.

Even with four-wheel drive, the wheels of the Jeep kept spinning, the Jeep kept sloshing this way and that.

"Fucking snow."

Brian turned away.

He saw another sign in the headlights.

SEE HOW SHE RUNS

RANGER STATION AHEAD. 1/2 MILE.

They passed the sign.

But Brian knew that the man had seen it.

The detectives left to organize the search. It made sense, they said, that he'd head south.

Kate called him Tom, Tom Abbott. But that wasn't his name. They were pretty sure of that.

"Will you be okay?" the blond detective said. "We should have everyone out on the highways so that we can . . ."

Kate nodded, looking at John.

Then the detective said, "I've asked someone to come here."

Kate felt confused and—for a second—there was the paranoia. *They've figured out who I am. They know that I've stolen my own children . . . and now I've lost one.*

She looked at Emma, still sitting quietly, lost to her play. Kate turned to John. She saw the alarm on his face.

"There's a woman who, we think, might know who this guy really is. We spoke to her, and she wants to talk with you. She can stay with you while we look. She works with families."

Kate nodded. "She knows who he is?"

The detective looked uncomfortable, as if that wasn't a good question to ask. As if that wasn't a good thing to know.

"Maybe. Maybe not. You'll see her?"

Kate nodded.

The police left.

Now Russ saw that his plan wasn't so good. No, the snow was piling up, and the sides of the road were disappearing.

Russ stopped the Jeep.

I'll kill myself up here, he thought. It was a good idea. Cross the mountains, get down to the other side, hit the desert, and sail away. A good idea—if there hadn't been a blizzard.

The kid moved in his seat.

For a second Russ couldn't remember why he brought the boy.

But then he remembered. They know about me, they could find me. And if they did, I could show them this boy. And I could say:

Do you want to watch?

Do you want to watch what I do to him?

Or do you want to fucking leave me alone?

Russ licked his lips. *Got to think . . .*

The windshield wipers struggled with the snow. Russ checked his gas gauge. Still half a tank. Plenty of gas. No problem there, no, just—ha-ha—nowhere to go.

There was a station ahead. The sign had said RANGER STATION AHEAD.

Someplace to stop, Russ thought. Stop and wait till this shit ends.

He put the Jeep into first. He eased down on the gas pedal. The wheels spun. Oh, no, maybe I'm not going anywhere. The damn Jeep ain't moving. He eased off the pedal. Took a breath.

He turned. The boy, Brian, was looking at him.

"It's okay. No problem," Russ said. No problem at all . . .

They left one cop with her, standing in John's kitchen. Kate wanted to stay here—there was a phone and the police had the number. The cop fixed himself some coffee.

When John was sure that Emma was playing, somehow amazingly shutting all this out, he came and sat next to Kate and held her hand. She looked at him. She expected him to say that she had made this happen.

But he didn't say anything.

It got very quiet, only the sound of Emma clicking the stones together, talking to one of her dolls.

So quiet . . .

There was a knock on the door.

Even with chains the Land Rover had a tough time getting up the road. So far Jesse hadn't seen any marks in the snow. So, he thought, nobody's been up here.

And maybe nobody's come down.

It was doubtful anyone could still be up there, stranded.

"Not too likely," Jesse said.

"What's that? Over."

He smiled. Annie must be sitting on the radio.

"Just talking to myself, babe. Why don't you get some sleep? Over."

Annie laughed. "Right. As if I could actually sleep while you're out." She paused. "Is it bad? Over."

"Oh. I don't know. On a badness scale of one to ten, I'd say it's about a nine . . . maybe nine-point-five. Over."

He saw a shape up ahead. A couple of shapes, standing by the road.

SEE HOW SHE RUNS

"Nobody here but some frigid-looking bighorns. Looks like they were expecting spring. They look kind of befuddled. Over."

"Jess. Leave your button on transmit. Over."

"Sure enough. You can listen to me ramble, if that's what you want. Over."

"I want. Over."

Jesse pressed the transmit button down into the lock hold. Now Annie will hear me talk to myself. I have to take care not to scare her. Because it's bad up here. Crawling at five miles an hour, and even with heavy chains the Rover was having a bitch of time.

Jesse was quiet. . . .

There were lights, a house off the road, a log cabin. Brian watched the man turn the Jeep into the driveway.

"Why—why are we going here?"

The man said nothing.

The house looked pretty, covered with snow, with warm yellow lights in the windows. There was a big metal thing—an antenna— on top. That's important, Brian thought. That does something.

Then he knew what it was.

It's the ranger station.

The Jeep's tires started spinning, caught in a rut.

The man banged the steering wheel. He made the Jeep rock back and forth. It moved a few inches inches and then was stuck again, caught in another rut.

He stopped the car.

The door to the cabin was close now. Brian looked at the man. The man turned to him and spoke quietly, just above the sound of the snow falling.

"You do exactly what I say. You don't move unless I say so. You see the knife. . . ."

He held a big knife up to Brian, the blade in front of his face. "I've killed people with this knife. If you say or do anything I *don't* tell you to, I'll kill you." The man paused. "Do you understand?"

Brian nodded. The man is crazy. Brian knew that.

Then the man said, "Good." He leaned under his seat and Brian saw a dark object. It was a gun.

Brian felt his cheeks go funny. They were quivering. It was strange; Brian couldn't figure out what was wrong, why his cheeks were quivering like that, shaking. Strange . . .

I'm going to cry, he thought. I'm going to cry. . . .

Because—the man is going to kill me. Eventually he's going to kill me.

"Get out," the man said.

Brian nodded, and he pushed open the door.

The young cop went to the door. Kate watched him open it, expecting more police, or maybe the detectives. There was a sick flicker of hope. They had found him. God yes, and Brian is okay. *He's all right!*

Maybe they won't ask any questions. Maybe we'll still be able to keep going, to Oregon, to have a new life.

John patted her hand.

But there was a woman at the door. She had dark hair dotted with snow and dark eyes. She spoke to the cop, but Kate couldn't hear what she said. The cop moved to the side and the woman came in.

Kate got up. The woman stuck out her hand.

"Kate—I'm Mari Comas."

She said something about Denver, that she worked with families in trouble. Yes, Kate thought. That's us, all right. Yes, we're a family in trouble.

Kate stood there, feeling like a dopey store mannequin. What do I say? Who is this person . . . why is she here . . . ?

"I think I know who has your son."

Kate nodded. She didn't say anything, she simply listened as Mari described the man. There came a moment when she paused.

Kate asked, "What has he done? What did this man do?"

Mari said, "Can we sit down?"

Kate nodded and looked around for a place to sit. John moved to one end of his small couch. Kate sat down and then Mari sat beside her.

The woman spoke softly. "His real name is Alex Russ."

Yes. Kate nodded. *Go on. His name is Alex Russ. And what has he done?*

Mari looked away. "They're going to find him," she said. "He can't have gotten far."

Kate nodded. "Tell me," she said, her voice hoarse, as if she could barely speak. "Who is he?"

Mari Comas told her.

Later—after the crying was over—Mari had her arm around the woman. The police already knew that the woman's name, Kate

SEE HOW SHE RUNS

Martin, wasn't real. It wouldn't be long, Mari knew, before they learned where this woman had run from . . . and why.

Mari held her close until Kate finally stopped sobbing, imagining the worst. Mari promised herself that she wouldn't abandon this woman. Not this time.

The cop left. They wanted everyone on the roads, hunting for Alex Russ. Mari said she'd stay. The Indian, Kate's friend, fixed them some tea. The little girl fell asleep, so tired, and John carried her into the bedroom.

Mari said, "Will you tell me who you are?"

The woman looked up at the Indian. Mari saw him nod. And then Mari heard Kate's story. . . .

"Stay beside me. Stay right *here*."

Russ turned from the boy and knocked on the front door. He knocked, but he didn't hear anything.

That's okay. If there's no one here, we'll just break in and make ourselves at home till this shit ends.

Like Goldilocks and the Three Bears. Get us some nice warm porridge . . .

Russ knocked again.

He heard the door being opened. No dead bolt on, no heavy latches. Sure, what's there to be afraid of here? Bears . . . raccoons.

A woman opened the door. Pretty, small.

Russ thought he recognized her, had seen her before. . . .

"Hi—miss. Hey, sorry to bother you. But the road is impossible. Me and my boy here—well, I don't know if we can keep going."

She stood there, holding the door. Her eyes looked confused. Did she recognize him? There was something wrong. She wasn't used to late callers and—

He looked at her left arm. It wasn't an arm, but a spindly twig, and there was no hand there, only a ball with two small fingers. Russ stared at it.

We have met before, at that store.

She pulled her arm away, behind her back.

"What are you doing here? Where are you coming from?"

Russ smiled. "Er, mind if we step in? The snow's kind of covering us here."

There was a moment's hesitation. Russ felt the boy move beside him. Russ turned and glared at him. The boy stopped.

She looked at the boy. "Well, I mean—sure—"

The door opened. Russ felt the warmth, smelled the food. This was ideal, he thought, up here, all alone. Just great.

When he entered the room, he heard a voice coming from a speaker. "Nearly to the top, babe. I'll be coming down soon."

The woman shut the door behind him. Russ saw a giant radio. He remembered the antenna.

Russ smiled. "Who's that?" he said.

45

Annie went to the radio. God, I had to let them in, she thought. So bad outside, I couldn't let them sit out there. The boy looked so cold. The man was someone she had seen, in town, somewhere. . . .

She wished Jesse was back.

She went to the radio.

"My husband's the ranger. He's checking the road." She nodded. "He'll be back soon. He leaves his radio on."

The man nodded. Annie watched him look around the room, slowly, as if searching for something.

"We have a phone. But there's no point calling for help. No one will come up here till the plows come."

Russ turned to her. "Can't even order a pizza?"

She smiled back. She guessed she should ask for their coats. They looked cold, the snow on their hair, on their coats, was melting. She looked at the boy, a good-looking boy. Annie took a step closer to him. He looked cold, nervous—

"Want some cocoa?"

The boy looked at her, then at her arm. It didn't bother her when children did that. Children were curious. And they soon put it past them.

Adults should know better, she thought.

"Would you like some nice warm cocoa?"

The man answered for him. "Sure, he'd love some."

SEE HOW SHE RUNS

"Annie, I'm getting mighty cold out here." It was Jesse again, on the radio. "I hope you'll make me nice and warm when I come back."

Annie felt herself redden. I should tell him, she thought. I should tell Jesse we have people here. God knows what he'll say, using the radio to have phone sex with me.

She walked to the radio.

"I'd like some too," the man said.

Annie nodded. "Sure. I just want to let Jesse know—"

Her hand closed on the microphone. But no, Jesse had his radio locked in the talk position. I won't be able to—

The man was there. His hand covered hers. Cold, wet from the snow. He spoke quietly.

After Kate finished telling her story, Mari got up and walked to John.

"You've been helping them?"

He nodded. "I help . . . when I can."

Mari turned and looked at Kate, sitting on the edge of the couch. "There will be problems," Mari said quietly. "When this is over."

John nodded. "I know."

"But I'll do what I can. I can help her."

He smiled. "Good. Now, if they can only find the boy."

Mari walked back to Kate, prepared to sit with her as long as possible, ready to stay with her during her vigil.

"Put it down."

Annie didn't move.

"About a quarter mile, and then I'm heading down." Jesse's voice . . .

"Put the fucking microphone *down*."

Annie wanted to say, *I can't talk with him anyway. There's no way I can break in.*

The man pried the microphone from her hand.

"You—you'd better leave," she said. She saw the boy hanging back. That's not his son, she knew then. And if he's not his son, then who is he?

"When will he be coming back?"

"Soon," she said. "*Real* soon. So you better go."

Annie thought that was the thing to say. She thought that as soon as the man heard that Jesse was coming back, he'd leave. He'd want to avoid trouble.

That's what she thought.
But she had it all wrong.
The man pulled out a knife.

That arm of hers, that's weird, Russ thought. But other than that, Annie was very cute. Her husband, Jesse, was coming ... from someplace. Who knew how long he'd be?

He grabbed Annie's wrist and pulled her close. He brought the knife up so that she could see it catching the light from the fireplace. The red stain on it was clearly visible. He felt the woman shaking.

"Okay, let me explain what's going to happen here."

He saw the boy watching. "Go in the back," he said to the boy.

He turned to the woman. "You have a room back there?"

She nodded.

"Annie." Jesse again. "I'm going to click off. Need to hear your voice, babe. . . . if you're still with me. Here's goes. Over."

"Move, you little fuck!" Russ screamed at the boy.

"No," Annie said. "Please. Just go."

He brought the knife close, just under her chin. Her skin was creamy white, and she had such a cute mouth.

The boy moved toward the back.

"Move."

Russ looked at the woman.

Brian walked into a dark bedroom. The bed was unmade and there were books on it. It was cold here. The heat from the fireplace couldn't reach here.

He heard the man's voice, and then the woman, Annie, crying. Brian stood still.

I have to do something, he thought.

I have to do something.

He heard his own breathing, in and out, heavy breathing.

I'm so scared. I've never been this scared.

His hand dug into his pocket. He felt the penknife. He looked at the door, the light from the other room. He kept breathing heavily, faster. He slipped the knife out. He looked at the door, then down to the knife, feeling for the small indentation in the blade to dig his thumbnail in.

He felt it, but it was hard to pry the blade out. He always chewed his nails, and now his thumb kept slipping, and—

SEE HOW SHE RUNS

Then it was open.

Okay. It's open, he thought. He quickly slipped the small knife behind his back.

Then he shook his head. This is stupid. The man will kill me.

He heard steps.

Brian kept the knife behind him.

The man was at the doorway, kicking the door shut.

Brian stood in the darkness.

The sounds from outside were muffled. But he had an idea . . . and he started to look around the room, in the darkness, the knife held out in front of him.

"Annie . . . hey, you there, babe. Anne . . . Over?"

That was funny. If anything, Jesse expected Annie to be hanging on the radio, ready to pipe in.

She sure hasn't gone to bed. Not while I'm still on the road, he thought.

He crept down the road. If I lose traction going downhill, it's good-bye Charlie.

Maybe she was in the shower.

That's what I'll need when I get back, he thought. Nice shower, and we can get under the down quilt, and let it snow, let it snow, let it snow. . . .

"What happened to your arm?"

Annie stood there. Jesse had stopped talking on the radio. Doesn't think I'm listening, she thought. How close is he, how soon before he gets back?

The man pointed at her arm with his knife. "How'd that happen?"

It was a stupid question. It was a question stupid people asked. It was the dumb question little kids asked.

I got it caught in the food processor.

My father stuck my arm in a meat grinder because he was mad at me.

A witch put a curse on me.

"I—I was born with it."

"What? Speak up. I can't hear you."

Annie cleared her throat. "I said, I was born with the arm. It's a birth defect. I—"

But when she looked at the man, he wasn't looking at her arm.

He was looking at her face. Annie took a step back, toward the kitchen.

And everything became . . . what?
Outlined by colors, filled with light, from the fireplace, from the air.
Life became more intense, more real. For a few moments everything became electric for Russ. It felt *good*.
Like this.
The woman backed away, looking so sweet and scared. Russ smiled at her. He said: "We have some time here, don't we?"
Yes, of course we do. Her husband's out there in the snow, bouncing around the mountain. Ranger Rick. I'll have to do something about him, I know that. So many problems . . .
But it's just the two of us now.
She bumped into the kitchen table. She shook her head.
Russ laughed and stepped closer.

Brian felt by the bed, feeling a book, knocking over a glass. It slowly rolled off the end table and his breath caught in his throat.
But he got his hands under the glass, breaking its fall before it smashed to the wood floor. He moved to the other side of the bed, banging his legs against the frame, moving around. There was another table, a lamp, and then—a phone.
He hated the noises outside. The woman was crying. He heard the man laugh.
Brian felt the buttons of the phone. He put down his knife. He picked up the phone.
He thought:
What's the number? What's John's number?
820-76 . . .
No. Not 76. 67 . . . 6 . . . 7. 8.
And 9. Yes, that's it, but—he couldn't see the numbers. His fingers touched the lamp. He could turn it on—for just a minute.
But what if the man saw the light? Brian shook his head. There was a voice in his ear.
"Please hang up and try your call—"
He pushed the phone down, cutting the voice off. Then he picked it up again.
The numbers go in order, Brian thought. One, two, three, right

SEE HOW SHE RUNS

across the top, and the next row, starting with four....

He pictured the numbers in his mind. He pressed the buttons slowly, listening to each beep, as if he were unlocking a safe.

He pressed the last button. He heard ringing. For a moment he thought he had pressed the wrong number. No one was answering....

Then he heard a woman's voice.

It wasn't his mother.

Russ was right next to her. Annie had her arms up in front of her, pushing him away.

Kind of halfheartedly, Russ thought. Of course, he did have the knife right there, in front of her face.

"Do you know what I like?" he said, leaning close, close enough so that his whiskers were scratching her cheek.

"What I like . . . is when a woman kneels down."

His eyes met hers.

There was a rush here, a thrill.

"Very slowly. She kneels down and then she grabs my fly, all the time looking right at me, and—"

Russ stopped. He thought he heard something coming from the bedroom. A voice, the kid . . . He stopped and listened.

"Hello," Mari said. "Hello . . ."

Mari took the call. She told the detectives that she'd screen calls. Reporters might get the story and start calling.

"Yes," Mari said. There was no one there. She was going to hang up. Kate was looking at her, her poor eyes filled with hope. Mari shook her head. Is this more my fault? Mari wondered. Am I to blame for this?

She went to hang up.

"Mom," Brian said. He whispered. Then, just a tad louder: "Is my mom there?"

Brian thought: I must have gotten the number wrong. I should call the operator, get the police.

Then, the woman said: *"Brian?"*

"Brian?"

Kate jumped up and stood next to her.

She grabbed the phone away from Mari. "Brian, honey. Brian,

where are you? Where did he let you go?"

Mari looked at John. "Is there another phone?"

He shook his head. She leaned to Kate. "Let John get on, Kate, maybe he can—"

But Kate was shaking her head. "He hasn't let you go? Brian, oh God, oh Brian, I'm sorry."

Mari grabbed her elbow tightly. "Kate—*let* John get on. He can find out—"

Mari pried the phone out of Kate's hand.

Then John was there, his voice steady, calm. "Brian, can you remember how you went, did you come to a city, did you see any signs?"

Mari watched the Indian nod, listening.

"I want *you* to do that."

Annie shook her head. Russ made his knife dance close to her face.

"You wouldn't want a fucked-up face to go with your fucked-up arm, would you?"

She shook her head. No. Of course not.

She started to kneel. But as she knelt, Russ heard the boy's voice again, low, steady, as if—

Russ looked around the room. He saw a phone sitting by the couch. The boy was in the bedroom. Russ shook his head.

"Aw, fuck!"

He ran toward the bedroom.

"We went up the mountain, John. We passed a sign, and it said 'Ranger Station.' The snow was bad. And—and—I'm really scared here, real scared."

John nodded. The boy's mother watched him. "Go on," he said calmly. "What else did you see?"

"The road was bad, so he stopped at the house, right after the sign."

John covered the mouthpiece. "I know where he is," he said quietly.

"Thank God," Kate said.

He turned back to the phone. "Now, Brian—"

But John heard a man's voice, yelling, screaming. Then the boy's scream, the phone falling to the floor, and then—

Nothing.

SEE HOW SHE RUNS

• • •

Russ kicked the boy. "You little bastard. You *fucking* little bastard. I'll kill you." He kicked the boy.

Then the woman jumped on his back, trying to pull him away. Russ lashed back with his knife, missing her. But he threw her off.

The boy was writhing on the floor, groaning. "You little prick . . . Who were you talking to?"

Brian coughed. Russ saw something dribble out of the boy's mouth, black in the dark room. "My mom," the boy groaned.

Russ crouched down. Annie was getting back up. Russ turned to her. "Don't you fucking *move*." Then back to Brian: "What did you say? What the fuck did you say?"

The boy looked up. Russ didn't like the eyes on the boy, filled with hate, and pain. The rush, the thrill was gone. This was getting all screwed up. *It always gets all screwed up.* . . .

"I said I was—scared. I said—"

"Did you tell them where you were?"

The boy was crying. "I don't *know* where I am. I'm not from here."

Russ nodded. That made sense. Right, the kid's not from here, and—

All screwed up.

46

"I'm going," Kate said when John told her where the place was.

She went to Mari. "Will you stay with Emma?"

Mari said, "You should let the police—"

"The police are looking on the *highways*!" Kate said. "The highways heading south! Call them, get them up there. But I'm going now."

She put on her coat.

"You won't get anywhere," John said. "The snow—"

She started for the door.
Then: "Wait. I'll take you. In my truck. I'll go with you."
But Kate was already out the door, out to the snow.

The Rover hit a patch of ice and, even with the chains, Jesse felt himself sliding out of control.
The vehicle bounced against the side of the road, and then slid a few more feet before he felt the tires locking on icy snow.
He stopped for a moment, breathing heavily.
When he looked up, he saw the warm lights of the station, his house, just ahead. And he saw a Jeep parked in front.
So, somebody *did* get stuck up here, he thought.
Annie's probably fixing him a nice cup of Lemon Zinger.
Even more slowly Jesse turned the Rover away from the road's edge and pulled closer to home.

"J-just sit there."
The crazy man—that's how Annie thought of him. I'm trapped with a crazy man. He pointed at the small sofa. She sat down with her back to the door.
The boy was still lying on the floor in the bedroom. The crazy man had told him that if he made another sound, he'd put a bullet in his head.
Annie believed that he would.
She sat there, thinking of how she could warn Jesse.
But she couldn't see where the crazy man was now.
Annie played with her fingers, a nervous habit, played with them—such small fingers—thinking: What am I going to do?
The crazy man paced back and forth.

"The police will beat us there," John said.
"Good," Kate said. "I'd like that. But can't you go any faster?"
John gestured at the road. "Look. Look how deep the snow is."
She turned to him. They had started to climb above Santa Fe. The snow kept coming down. "Please." John shook his head. And pressed down on the accelerator . . . just a bit more.

Annie sat, waiting. I have to do something. She risked turning around and she saw him standing there. The crazy man had his gun out now. It isn't real, she thought. This is a dream.

SEE HOW SHE RUNS

He promised that he wouldn't hurt Jesse.

She wanted to believe him.

She heard the door being opened.

Jesse...

"Whoa—it's nasty out."

His voice. Everything is still okay in his world. Everything is fine. His voice is so normal. For another few seconds—

"Jesse!" she yelled, turning. The crazy man looked at her. Jesse was in the doorway.

She saw his face. "Jesse, there's—"

The man pulled the door open wide. Jesse turned. Annie stood up.

He wasn't going to hurt Jesse. He said that he'd only get him to sit down and they'd all wait out the storm, wait until the man could go....

(And would he take the boy? She didn't want him to take the boy, she didn't want him to hurt the boy any more.)

She looked as Jesse turned to the man, and then there was a gunshot, so loud in the room. Jesse reached for his midsection and crumpled to the floor.

"No," Annie screamed, yelling at the crazy man. "You said, you said that you wouldn't hurt him. You said—"

She ran to Jesse and knelt beside him. Her husband looked at her as if she had betrayed him. She was crying, cradling his head. "Jesse, I'm sorry."

Jesse looked up at the man. Annie thought that the crazy man was going to shoot them both. Why not? There were no rules here.

"Help me," she whispered. "He's bleeding." Annie put her hand on Jesse's bullet wound, but the blood kept oozing out. "Please, help me...."

Annie looked at Jesse's face. His eyes rolled back in his head, and for a flash she saw only white. She shook her head. He can't die, she thought. Please, don't let him—

The man kicked the door shut.

He stood just outside the light. Hearing the noise. The pain in his stomach was constant now, that and the ache in his leg.

The cougar saw the light of the open door. For a brief second, his nostrils twitched, smelling the heat, and then—smelling blood. He made a mewling sound.

He came closer to the house.

"This is not good," John said. "I—I can't even see where the road is."

Kate nodded. But they had already passed a sign that announced that they were entering the North Truchas National Forest.

We're going up. We're making progress, she thought. John shook his head. Kate said nothing.

Annie stood up. "He's dying," she said. "Bleeding to death. Please, help me carry him onto the couch. Please don't let my husband die. He hasn't done anything to you."

The crazy man's eyes narrowed. Then he smiled.

What he said made Annie feel sick, as if she might vomit.

The man smiled. "Okay. If we can get back to what was interrupted."

Annie froze. For only a second. Then she nodded. "Yes. Anything."

She went to Jesse's feet and grabbed them with one arm, wrapping her stunted arm underneath for support. It was surprisingly strong. Jesse used to joke that she could easily win an arm-wrestling contest with it. Nobody could believe how strong it was. . . .

"Could you get his head?" she said.

The man nodded. He stuck his gun in his pocket.

He grabbed Jesse's shoulders and Jesse moaned. "No," Annie cried. "No. Be careful, you're tearing his wound." Then: "Ready," Annie said. "Now lift." They picked up Jesse's body.

Brian stood up. He felt all the bruises on his body, the places where he had been kicked. He felt the dry tears on his cheek.

He thought: There can be no more crying.

The phone had been ripped out of the wall.

I'm all alone here, he thought.

He walked back to the table, to the useless phone, to the place he had put his knife.

But it wasn't there. . . .

Annie grunted. Jesse wasn't a big man, but his legs kept slipping out of her grasp. The couch was still several feet away. Jesse wasn't making any noises.

A few more feet. One leg slipped away and crashed to the floor.

She reached down and then locked her arms more tightly around the ankles. A few more feet—

"There!" Kate yelled. "There's the sign. We're almost there, oh God."

John nodded.

Did she have any idea what they were going to do then?

John felt scared for her, for what she might find.

Brian was on his knees, feeling around, his hands gliding over the wood floor. Where is it? he thought. Where could the knife be? Did the guy find it? Maybe it's not even here and—

His hands touched something, the knife handle. He pulled it up. It felt so small in the dark.

Brian stood up and walked to the pencil-thin outline of light, to the door, the knife held tight in his hand, as tight as he ever held anything. . . .

47

Brian opened the door. He walked out to the living room. He had heard the gun blast and now he saw someone lying on the couch. He saw the streaks of blood on the floor.

The woman was kneeling by a man on the couch, pressing a cloth at the spot where the blood came from.

Brian kept walking.

The man with the gun stood there, looking down at them.

Brian squeezed tight, tighter on the knife. He watched the man turn, seeing him.

"Get the—" he started to say, and now Brian kept moving, faster, running. And though he promised himself that he wouldn't cry, that the time for crying was all over, he sobbed when he raised his arm.

• • •

"Stop here!" Kate said. And then, before John could do anything, she had the truck door open, and she was running out, stumbling in the heavy snow.

John reached behind him for his rifle. He unsnapped it from its rack, hurrying. The gun stock was caught. My old-man fingers are cold and stupid, he thought.

He saw Kate hurrying ahead to the cabin door.

Then the gun stock popped free, and John opened his door.

Of course, they all have to die. There was no getting around that. The man on the couch was nearly dead, and his pretty wife had to die, and then the boy, and—

Russ shook his head.

Accepting the inevitable.

He turned, to yell at the boy to get back, to get the hell out of here. The boy was crying. Russ hated that noise. His own boys would cry and he had to hit them until they stopped. He couldn't take all that crying.

Then he saw it. Brian had a knife.

That was funny, the boy had a knife. He watched Brian bring it down.

So funny. Imagine that—

Russ didn't have time to move away. He heard the little knife— a scout knife, a toy knife—dig into his chest, hitting something hard, some bone, or—

Russ groaned, and stumbled backward.

"Kate!" John yelled. "Kate, stop. Wait!"

John landed off balance in the deep snow with his gun. He saw Kate look through the window to the side, and then she opened the door.

"No," he said. The door opened, and John could only watch what happened.

Kate opened the door to the house, rushing in—a late party guest. She saw Alex Russ standing with his back to the door, next to a woman. She looked down and saw the red smears on the wood floor.

"No," she said. "No . . ."

Then she saw Brian, God, sweet Brian standing to the side.

"Bri," she said. "Brian, honey—"

But Russ was turning, seeing her, feeling the cold. He had a knife in his hand, a long knife, already wet with blood. Kate saw the man on the couch. It wasn't Brian who was hurt. . . .

Brian started to run to her.

Russ snarled. He opened his mouth, and he looked like a dog snapping at the air. He reached out to stop Brian. Brian didn't see the man's arm. Kate came closer, into the warmth, closer to the snarling dog.

Russ looked at her, his arm positioned to stop Brian, to grab him.

He smiled. This was fun for him. So much fun.

He stopped Brian, grabbing his shirt.

"No," Kate said. She saw that Brian had something in his hand. What was it? Something small—small, and—

Brian stuck his penknife into Russ's chest. The boy did that and Russ's arm recoiled.

"Come on, Bri. Come on!" she yelled. Her boy ran to her. Russ reached down and Kate watched him yank the knife out and then there was blood everyplace.

Kate's hand closed over Brian's hand, pulling him, tugging him out the front door, into the heavy snow.

It had taken only seconds. The truck was only yards away. John stood there with the gun, yelling something. Waving at them, yelling something, his mouth open.

Kate looked at him. She was confused. So confused.

Hearing John say: "Stop. Stop. . . ."

Kate kept running, dragging Brian through the snow, falling, getting up again. Wondering, Why? Why is John yelling stop. Why on earth does he want us to stop?

Falling in the snow. Looking up.

Seeing it . . .

48

Kate didn't know what it was. It's a dog, she thought. No, it's not a dog. It's a cat. She stood up. A big cat, and it was between the truck and the house.

Kate stopped. Brian huddled close, not seeing.

"What is it, Mom? What's wrong?"

Kate thought of saying, *Shoo. Go away.* Like making the raccoons scurry away from the trash. *Get out of here....*

But this was so much bigger, and it was close. Kate saw the cat's eyes, all filmy, dull.

It took only seconds for Kate to look around. There was a song she thought of. I've got nowhere to run . . .

The cat leaped at her, so tall, now towering above her, landing, swatting them both down in the snow.

John held the gun. When they came out, the mountain lion was there, waiting. There's something wrong with it, he thought. Mountain lions don't come around people.

Kate and Brian were startled, and before he could shoot, the cat pounced on them.

John once saw a big elk killed by a cougar, watched how the cat neatly opened up the elk's throat and then sliced its belly open— so quickly, so perfectly—the trapped animal was still bellowing and snorting to the sky even as its entrails oozed onto the icy ground.

John held the gun. He saw Kate, the boy, the lion, rolling around the snow, and there was screaming. John held the gun.

But there was no way he could shoot.

Kate felt something dig into her leg, through her jeans, and then she felt the sting of her skin being ripped.

She had only one thought.

SEE HOW SHE RUNS

God, I'm glad it's hurting me and not Brian.

She remembered saying to Brian, whispering, whispering, "Run, honey. Go, get away. Run."

But she felt his body so close to hers. She heard him cry, too, and she knew that the animal was digging into her boy, her son. The icy snow worked its way down her neck. She turned her head, and she tasted the short, brittle fur of the animal. There was more pulling, more ripping, the pain of her skin tearing.

Brian yelled. He called her name. *Mom. Mommy.*

Her lips brushed the fur of the animal again, a thick, mucky odor filling her nostrils, competing with the sensation of cutting. It was all going so slowly. She didn't think about what she was going to do.

She opened her mouth.

Wide, wider, as wide as she could. Then she pressed her face close to the animal's skin.

And she bit down.

The cat suddenly spun away from them as if stung.

There was a moment and John took it.

He got off one shot, but the cougar rolled around in the snow and John didn't know whether he had hit it. There was no chance for another shot as the cat rolled behind Kate and Brian.

A man came out of the doorway, staggering into the snow. Chasing after Kate and Brian.

He hurried, and even from across the driveway, John saw the man's wound—he wondered how he got that wound—open and red, leaving a trail on the snow.

Alex Russ walked into the cat.

He stopped, looked down. The cat looked up.

Two paws came flying up. The light from the doorway, the yellow, warm light, caught the dull glint of the claws.

Instinctively Russ's hand went to his stomach to protect it. Because that's where the claws were headed. No doubt.

But the cat was too fast.

Russ had one thought. I will feel pain. Intense pain. Pain as I've never felt it.

He had only one question.

For how long?

• • •

Kate searched for Brian's hand, heard him crying, wailing. She found his hand. With the taste of fur and gristly skin still fresh in her mouth, she pulled the boy up.

She nearly tumbled down again. One leg didn't work so well, it kept slipping away.

"Come on," she begged, hoping that Brian would be able to get up. "I can't carry you. I can't pull you up!"

Brian struggled to his feet, no longer a deadweight. Kate felt a hand grab her. John held her now, and she held Brian, and they ran to the truck.

She turned to look over her shoulder, expecting the animal to jump on all three of them, toying with them.

She heard a terrible yell, an inhuman squeal. Then a scream. She wished she could cover Brian's ears. The sound was the worst thing she had ever heard.

She turned.

The cat was on him, on Russ, and—as she kept hobbling, John holding her under her arm, while she held Brian tight—

She looked.

She watched Russ, his legs kicking at the air, his arms reaching up, grasping as he howled at the air.

John opened the door to the truck. He eased Brian up. She nearly yanked him back. No, you can't have him, she thought. *No* . . .

Then John was there, helping Kate up. It was hard to move her leg.

As John shut the door—he was staying out there—Kate watched the cat, digging at Russ's midsection, pulling things out, until the howling stopped.

John waited, watching the cougar eat noisily, looking over its shoulder. Better this, John thought.

Better this than a trial, and court and lawyers.

This was justice.

He raised his rifle and took aim at the globe-shaped head of the mountain lion. He pulled the trigger.

The front of the cat's head exploded, spraying the snow.

It was over.

49

Kate watched the woman, Annie, expertly bandage Brian's cut leg. She had cleaned the wound and then covered it with a topical anesthetic and Mercurochrome.

Then, holding the tape with the two fingers of her left hand, she worked on Kate.

John was outside talking to the police. An ambulance was right behind them, struggling up the snowy road. The plows were out now, and the heaviest snow seemed behind them.

"You really should go to the hospital too," Annie said.

Kate shook her head. She noticed how this woman pushed Brian's hair off his forehead, how she looked at his face, smiling at him.

"No," Kate said. "This will hold me. I want to get back, to tell Emma that everything is okay." Kate smiled. "Besides, the ambulance has only room for two—your husband and Brian."

Annie's husband was sleeping. He was in serious condition, having lost a lot of blood. Kate watched Annie look at him watching his chest rise and fall, the breathing steady.

"I'm sorry," Kate said, when Annie saw her looking at her husband.

Annie shook her head. "It's not your fault."

Kate nodded. Then she said, "But what am I doing here? I—I wanted to—protect my children. And I made all this happen."

Annie touched her shoulder. "No. That's not true, not true at all."

There was a siren in the distance. Coming close, closer . . .

The ambulance.

The front door opened.

"It's here," John said. A state trooper stood next to him, still looking wide-eyed at the strange scene.

Kate held Brian's hand tight.

• • •

They wheeled Jesse out and then Brian, both of them hooked up to IVs. Kate walked behind the gurney, still holding Brian's hand. "I'll come to the hospital soon . . . just as soon as I check on Emma," she whispered to him.

Brian craned his head around and nodded. His wound went deep, down to the bone, and he'd lost a lot of blood. Still, he smiled at her and squeezed her hand hard.

The ambulance had snow chains on. The sky was taking on a purple color in the east. Two men in white coats eased Jesse and then Brian up into the ambulance. Then they shut the backdoor.

John came and stood beside Kate, and they watched the ambulance pull away, the chains sending up a snow-cone spray.

Kate took a breath. A trooper was talking to Annie, writing things down, then he came to Kate. "People will need to talk with you," he said.

Kate said, "In the morning. Tomorrow . . ."

The policeman nodded.

Kate turned to John. "I want to see Emma."

John led her, hobbling, over to the truck.

Sometime in the night Mari had fallen asleep, and then there was a knock. She went to the door and opened it. A young police officer was there. She saw that the snow was still swirling around, but it wasn't coming down heavily.

"Any word?" she said.

The cop shook his head. "No. There were patrol cars following them, only minutes behind them. But there's no word yet."

Mari nodded. The cold made her want to recoil from the open door. "Want to come in, have some hot tea?"

The officer shook his head. "No, ma'am. I was just checking on you. And if you're okay—"

Mari smiled. "I'm fine," she said.

The cop touched the brim of his hat, iced with white, then turned and walked away.

Mari shut the door. She went back to her chair. She thought of turning on the TV. But she sat there, waiting, thinking, until she fell asleep again.

In her dream she was with Jake, and it was summer, at the lake, and Jake was swimming. And Dan was there, and they were happy. Happy . . . like they were a family. They had a life. It was a beautiful dream.

But through that dream she heard noises, sounds, close by. Odd sounds that didn't fit with the splashing, the children diving off rafts, and the wind rustling the aspens.

But the real sounds didn't wake her.

Kate fell asleep on the way back, and only when John's truck stopped did her eyes pop open. It wasn't snowing. The sky had lightened, but she saw that dark clouds were still stuck overhead.

She saw the squat apartment complex, the second-floor railing. She tried to straighten up in the seat and was rewarded with a sharp pain in her legs.

John turned to her. "Are you okay?"

She nodded. "Sure." She opened the door. And ever so slowly lowered one leg, and then the other, to the metal step of the truck, then down to the snow-covered parking lot.

Without waiting for John, she limped toward the stairs leading to the second floor of the apartment complex.

She walked over a rut made by a car, the deep impression made by the tires. Someone else had been out tonight. . . .

John came beside her, slipping his arm under her, supporting her.

She was able to take some of the weight off the bad leg. Then, when they reached the stairs, every step was agony, making her leg bend, pulling it up, feeling all those tears, cuts opening, bleeding again.

I should go to the hospital, she thought. No question about it.

Climbing, until they were on the walkway that ran alongside the apartments. It was only a few feet to John's apartment. . . .

He had his key out. He stuck it into the cheap lock.

Kate saw Mari, this stranger sitting in a chair, rubbing her eyes. She watched the woman's glance as it trailed down to her leg.

"Is everything—"

"Everything's fine," John said. "It's all over."

"And Russ?"

Kate answered. Her voice was cold, flat, coming from miles away, she thought. "He's dead." Kate looked at Mari. "He's dead." She took a step, terrible pain. "I want to see Emma. . . ."

Kate limped into John's bedroom.

Emma was asleep in John's bed, curled up with her special doll, Patty. Hugging her close, so warm and protected.

"She's fine," Mari whispered, behind her.

Kate nodded. She rubbed at her eyes. No reason to cry now. None at all . . .

She touched Emma's brow, savoring the wonderful feel of the little girl's skin under her fingertips. She sniffed the air. *I'm not crying, I'm not*—and she turned and walked out of the room.

John shut the door quietly behind him. "I'm going to the hospital," he said.

Kate turned to him. "I'm coming."

He grabbed her arm. "No. No, get some rest. I'll come back for you in a few hours."

Mari stood close.

Yes, Kate thought, and then what? Won't the police have a lot of questions? When they find out that I'm not who I say I am . . . that I kidnapped my children. There was no getting away.

She was about to argue some more, but John raised a hand.

"Let me go. I'll be back. You lie down."

That sounded wonderful to her. Just a few hours. Kate nodded. John said something to Mari; he turned and left.

Mari sat beside Kate and listened.

Alex Russ was gone. Now there was this family who needed help. Maybe, Mari thought, this is another way to pay back Elaine Russ and her children. . . .

Kate took a breath. "I'm scared. I'm scared I'll lose the kids when they find out who I am. My ex-husband has so much money."

Mari told her, "Don't worry about that now. I'll help you. But you should rest."

Kate nodded. "Yes. I'll go to my apartment, I'll lie down. You'll wake me when Emma gets up?"

Mari nodded. She helped Kate up and walked with her to the door, and then out to the landing, over to her apartment.

Mari had Kate's key. She opened the door. The apartment was dark and Mari threw on the light. Kate walked in. She stopped and turned to Mari.

"I'll be fine now," she said. "Stay with my Emma."

"You sure?"

Kate said, "Yes, I'm sure. And thank you for staying."

Mari nodded and walked out of the small apartment.

Kate looked around at the apartment. She heard the door click behind her. She needed to be alone, to think, The police will have questions, maybe they'll let New York courts know, and—

SEE HOW SHE RUNS

She had to think. She took a step. The apartment smelled musty. It was cold, the heat set so low. Kate walked to the thermostat.

She looked down at the rug.

She saw a wet spot. And there, just ahead, another wet spot.

She kept walking. Someone must have tracked snow in here, someone must have come in, and—

Another spot, dotting the faded brown rug.

Why would someone come in here?

The police? Why would they—

She heard a step.

Kate looked up. Another step.

A voice . . .

50

"Kate."

She looked up, and there was David. In slow motion she shook her head. No, this can't be. *No.*

"Kate." He took a step closer to her and smashed her face with an unexpected fist. Kate went flying to the floor. It's so hard to stay standing, her leg was so weak. . . .

She looked up.

David's face was red, the muscles of his neck pulled tight.

He spoke to her, whispering, hissing. "Y-you took my life. You took my life away."

She shook her head. "No. I—"

She tried to crawl backward. This can't be happening. Then she thought of the man, following them, the man Russ kept looking at.

Realizing . . .

I never got away at all.

She grabbed at her cheap sofa and pulled herself up. "No, David. No. I had to get away. You were—"

He hit her again, this time smashing her head into the arm of the sofa with a closed fist.

"You t-took them from me. And n-now you'll lose them for—"

He kicked her midsection. Kate heard something crack She groaned. She tried to scream now, but she could barely gulp air in.

He's going to kill me, she thought. Oh, God, he's going to kill me.

She clawed at the sofa again, digging her hands in.

When she looked at David, he was smiling, he had all the power now, all the money. In some sick way he'd been reborn.

She got to her knees. "No," she begged.

"Emmie's next door," he said. "I know that." Spit flew out of his mouth with the words. "I can t-take her. She's my daughter."

He went to kick at her again. But Kate was able to slide away. His foot went past her and he stumbled. Kate forced her arms to pull herself up, her legs kicked against the floor. She saw the rug stained with red, her wounds open.

She was standing. Then she staggered backward, to the door, and grabbed the door handle. She pulled it open.

She screamed.

Mari heard the sound, the scream.

Then she knew what the noise had been, in her dream.

A car had been outside, in the heavy snow, and there was the sound of someone walking outside, forcing open the apartment next door. Steps, fading, leaving only the wind and the water at the lake.

Mari got up. She heard the screams again, screams that were cut off.

Kate backed out of the door, slipping on the snow. But David was on her so fast. He locked his hand around her throat and pushed against the railing.

He's going to push me over, she thought.

He could even say I attacked him. Sure he could.

His hand closed her windpipe. He started to lift her. He brought his face close. "You destroyed my—"

Higher, his fingers digging into her throat. She gagged, trying to get air.

"—*life!*"

Mari ran out and saw Kate, sliding up, over the railing, and a man holding her there.

She ran to him, locked her arms around his chest, and yanked him away.

Kate fell to the walkway, but the man pried Mari's arms off, and she felt how strong he was. He reached out and grabbed her throat.

For a moment he was off balance.

Mari took a step to the side and locked her hands on his jacket. The railing came up to just below his waist.

Mari yanked him back toward the railing. He was completely off balance, hands flailing, reaching out.

She pushed then, grunting, and then watched him slowly pivot, tilting backward, miraculously tipping over.

He fell off the balcony, flailing. Mari leaned over the railing, and saw him land on the snow-covered parking lot.

It was silent. Then a sound . . .

Mari looked up.

In the distance she saw a police car pulling into the lot, a Colorado police car. She looked down to the man, lying in the snow. She heard him moaning, but he didn't move.

The police car pulled up and the door opened. She saw Dan. Then another man got out, his partner.

"Mari," he called up to her. He walked past the man and then hurried to the stairs.

"Dan," Mari whispered. She watched him hurry up the stairs.

Mari turned to Kate and helped her up. "It's over," she said to her. "It's all over."

Then Dan was there. He quickly went to the other side of Kate. "I got your message," he said. Mari smiled at him grimly. She felt him helping hold Kate up.

Together they walked back into Kate's apartment.

EPILOGUE

Over Denver, a few clouds dotted the sky. There was a chance for some rain tonight, Mari thought.

She glanced at the clouds and then looked back to the baseball field. Jake was up, holding the bat, gritty with determination.

"Hey, he looks like he's ready to smash it out of the park," Dan said.

The first pitch went over, watched by Jake, and the umpire called a strike.

"C'mon, champ. Take your swing," Dan said.

At times like this, we're like a family, Mari thought. The two of us, here, watching Jake play baseball, watching him grow up.

Almost a family.

"C'mon," Dan said.

The pitch came. A curveball; it looped over the plate and again Jake watched it fly by.

"Uh-oh, he isn't to going to get much now."

It's possible, Mari thought. Isn't it? Doors don't have to stay closed forever.

Another pitch, a bad one this time, but Jake went fishing. He caught a piece of it and sent the ball hooking foul off first base.

Mari saw her son adjust his batting helmet. He touched the brim and then, choking up on the metal bat, he looked over at Mari, at Dan.

Dan smiled at her. Then, shyly, he covered her hand with his. For a moment she didn't respond—but then she made her fingers close around his hand, squeezing it, holding on.

It's possible . . . isn't it?

Then they both turned to the ballgame. Jake smiled at them.

It was another bad pitch, way outside, but Jake took his swing. He leaned into the pitch and Mari heard the clang of the metal bat catching the ball.

She went to her feet. The ball looped to center field, just behind second base. Jake ran past them, running full out, getting to first well ahead of the ball.

While she was standing Mari realized that Dan still held her hand, both of them standing, cheering.

She looked at him and smiled.

Jake waved at them from first base.

And the sun slid away from the lone cloud covering it.

Above the mountains, the sun shone brightly.

Jesse was outside, under the Rover, changing the oil, the brake fluid, something. He hadn't spent much time resting as he had been ordered to do . . . not really.

He came right out of the hospital and in days was back on the roads.

Because this is his place, she knew. *His* park.

She stood beside his feet, sticking out from under the Rover.

"Are you surfacing for lunch . . . or should I lower down another quart of ten-W-thirty?"

He laughed and then his feet wriggled as he started to scrunch out from under the Rover. He looked up, his face all smudged. "Lunchtime already? Time flies."

Annie crouched down. He looked cute, small black smudges on each cheek. A boy and his car . . . and his park.

I'm happy, she thought.

Except . . .

His brows furrowed. "What's wrong, babe?"

She reached out and rubbed his cheek. She had tuna salad inside and some apple pie left over from last night. Soon the summer season would begin and she'd see less and less of Jesse.

She rubbed the other cheek. "You need a shower," she said, smiling.

"Is that an offer?" he said, grinning.

She thought of that night, of the fear . . . her own, and the boy's fear—the terrible fear he must have had, that beautiful boy. And how brave he was, using the phone, then taking out his penknife.

What a wonderful boy. . . .

How brave.

Jesse sat up, wiping his hands on his greasy jeans. "Annie, what's wrong?"

She had been thinking about it for a long time. How sometimes you had to be brave, how you had to take a chance. There were

SEE HOW SHE RUNS

odds, she knew, not great odds, but still there was a good chance that everything would be okay. If she got pregnant...

And if not, I could be brave, I could do whatever had to be done.

Jesse reached out and touched her.

"I—"

"Babe? Annie—you're scaring me. Is something wrong?"

She looked at him. He knew how important this was to her. He had to know....

"Jesse, I want—I want us to have a child."

His mouth opened. They had talked about it so many times. The chances of something being wrong. Chances were all they were, and she and Jesse would know so very early. *I just can't be a coward about it. Not anymore.*

She touched his lips with her fingertips. "It's what I want—for us—more than anything in the world."

And then—wondrous thing—he smiled. As if he had been waiting for her to say it.

"It sounds like a shower for two is exactly what's required."

He grabbed her shoulders. She thought she'd cry. So stupid, she didn't know what he'd say. He grabbed her shoulders, pulled her close, and kissed her hard.

Then he pulled her away.

"There, you're all dirty anyway."

And she laughed.

The great blue sky was dotted with tear-shaped hot-air balloons of every color. A few were still tethered to the ground, but most of them were already rising high above the open scrubby brush, high as the mountains, drifting away....

Kate walked over to a vendor selling burritos, hot from a griddle, the refried beans steamy, and the fresh guacamole cold.

She checked on Emma playing inside a castle made of air. Emma bounced on the floor of the air-filled castle, bouncing with other children, some Anglos, some Indians. She was laughing, and for a moment Kate wanted to stare at her.

My beautiful little girl, she thought, *looking so happy.*

Then she turned to search for Brian. The Santa Fe Air Fair had a number of rides—kid stuff, Brian announced—but still, he was having fun on a mini–roller coaster. This was his third trip, at least. Later they were scheduled for a small adventure in a balloon.

She felt a tap on her shoulder, and spun around. Too fast, she thought. It's always going to be there, she thought. The fear, making me act strange....

"Everything okay?"

It was John Morningsun. My friend, Kate knew. No matter where I go . . . what happens to me. This man will always be my friend. She smiled at him. She reached out and squeezed his hand.

"Yes. They're having lots of fun."

John smiled, and his eyes narrowed, and he looked impish. "I've planned something special later. There's a ceremony, very exciting. We'll be able to go."

Kate nodded. She thought that after it was all over, she might lose the children. What's the penalty for kidnapping?

But there were laws to protect the children, especially in New Mexico. After the first hearing—with Mari and John testifying—she received a court order of protection from David and his lawyers.

She had hoped David would die.

She had hoped that in the fall, he'd landed on his back and smashed his head.

Die, she prayed, just *die*.

His family flew out with the expensive lawyer, with his papers and threats.

But Mari stood by her. Another new friend, and all of a sudden there were these people to help Kate, lawyers who worked for nothing. When David was charged with violent assault, his family started to back off.

"You'll have to stay here," Mari told her. Until the court process went through. Just for a while.

But now, as the days ran into each other, she began to think that maybe this wouldn't be a bad place to live. The air, so thin that it could give you a nosebleed, was clear and crisp. She had a good shot at a job doing research for the state legislature—thanks to Mari's help.

School was going well for the kids.

Kate looked at the bright, giant hot-air balloons, making the deep blue sky look like it was hung with Christmas ornaments.

Brian came running up, breathless. "That—that's a baby ride."

She looked at him. He still winced when he ran. The leg had healed, but the scar tissue was pulled tight. The mountain lion had ripped his leg open to the bone.

"When are we going up?" he asked, pointing to the balloons.

"Soon," she said. "Ten minutes. And we'll get your sister out of her castle."

She watched Brian walk close to the air castle, close to the little children, shoeless, bouncing up and down, rolling into each other. She watched Brian walk close, waiting for Emma to look up, a goofy smile on her face.

When Emma did look up, Brian waved at her.

And she—just before rolling down like a wobbly bowling pin—waved back.

We're going to make it, Kate thought.

We're going to make it. . . .

"A tightly wound psycho-thriller...riveting and menacing to the last page..."–*Newsweek*

"Tantalizes and terrifies...A one-sitting book defying the reader to budge until the end."–*Los Angeles Times*

"A fast-paced thriller...so stunning that it's hard to put the book down."–*Library Journal*

GONE

Three kids alone. A psychopath is watching.
Where is their mother?

KIT CRAIG

Single mother Clary Hale manages to keep life pretty normal for her three children. But Clary's hiding a terrifying secret from her past–a teenage boy's twisted obsession that led to her parents' deaths. Now, twenty years later, he reappears at her door, determined to finish what he began. And the next morning, the Hale children wake up to find their mother gone...

__0-425-13944-1/$5.99

Payable in U.S. funds. No cash orders accepted. Postage & handling: $1.75 for one book, 75¢ for each additional. Maximum postage $5.50. Prices, postage and handling charges may change without notice. Visa, Amex, MasterCard call 1-800-788-6262, ext. 1, refer to ad # 467

Or, check above books and send this order form to: The Berkley Publishing Group 390 Murray Hill Pkwy., Dept. B East Rutherford, NJ 07073	Bill my: ☐ Visa ☐ MasterCard ☐ Amex _____(expires) Card#_____ ($15 minimum) Signature_____
Please allow 6 weeks for delivery.	Or enclosed is my: ☐ check ☐ money order
Name_____	Book Total $_____
Address_____	Postage & Handling $_____
City_____	Applicable Sales Tax $_____ (NY, NJ, PA, CA, GST Can.)
State/ZIP_____	Total Amount Due $_____

"MARTINI WRITES WITH THE AGILE,
EPISODIC STYLE OF A LAWYER QUICK
ON HIS FEET..."—*John Grisham*

Steve Martini

THE NATIONWIDE BESTSELLER
COMPELLING EVIDENCE

An electrifying courtroom drama
of murder, betrayal, and deceit.

"RICH, CUNNINGLY PLOTTED...REMARKABLE."
—*Los Angeles Times*
"CONSIDERABLE STYLE, GRACE, AND INTELLIGENCE."
—*Chicago Tribune*
"COMMANDING." —*The New York Times Book Review*
__0-515-11039-6/$5.99

PRIME WITNESS

"PACKS A SATISFYING PUNCH."—*Kirkus Reviews*
"PRIME IS INDEED THE WORD FOR THIS INVOLVING READ."
—*Publishers Weekly*
__0-515-11264-X/$5.99

Look for **THE SIMEON CHAMBER**
Steve Martini's newest Jove novel coming in May

Payable in U.S. funds. No cash orders accepted. Postage & handling: $1.75 for one book, 75¢ for each additional. Maximum postage $5.50. Prices, postage and handling charges may change without notice. Visa, Amex, MasterCard call 1-800-788-6262, ext. 1, refer to ad # 432

Or, check above books Bill my: ☐ Visa ☐ MasterCard ☐ Amex	(expires)
and send this order form to: The Berkley Publishing Group Card#___	
390 Murray Hill Pkwy., Dept. B	($15 minimum)
East Rutherford, NJ 07073 Signature___	
Please allow 6 weeks for delivery. Or enclosed is my: ☐ check ☐ money order	
Name___	Book Total $___
Address___	Postage & Handling $___
City___	Applicable Sales Tax $___ (NY, NJ, PA, CA, GST Can.)
State/ZIP___	Total Amount Due $___

Chilling National Bestsellers by
New York Times Bestselling Author

ROBIN COOK

__TERMINAL 0-425-14094-6/$5.99

Miami's Forbes Cancer Center is renowned for its high success rate in treating brain cancer. Then visiting Harvard med student Sean Murphy discovers the shocking secret behind the Center's "success": a conspiracy that puts a price tag on life to meet the staggering cost of medical research.

__HARMFUL INTENT 0-425-12546-7/$5.99

When an innocent doctor is charged with malpractice and harmful intent, he follows the deadly trail of the real murderer in a desperate attempt to prove his innocence.

__VITAL SIGNS 0-425-13176-9/$5.99

Dr. Marissa Blumenthal's dream of becoming pregnant has turned into an obsession. A successful pediatrician, she will try any scientific method available to conceive. Until the horrible secrets of an urban clinic erupt in a nightmare of staggering proportions.

__BLINDSIGHT 0-425-13619-1/$5.99

Under a haunting aura of suspense, forensic pathologist Dr. Laurie Montgomery discovers a darkly corrupt scheme of murder, high-level cover-ups, and inescapable fear.

Payable in U.S. funds. No cash orders accepted. Postage & handling: $1.75 for one book, 75¢ for each additional. Maximum postage $5.50. Prices, postage and handling charges may change without notice. Visa, Amex, MasterCard call 1-800-788-6262, ext. 1, refer to ad # 433

Or, check above books Bill my: ☐ Visa ☐ MasterCard ☐ Amex	
and send this order form to:	(expires)
The Berkley Publishing Group Card#_____	
390 Murray Hill Pkwy., Dept. B	($15 minimum)
East Rutherford, NJ 07073 Signature_____	
Please allow 6 weeks for delivery. Or enclosed is my: ☐ check ☐ money order	
Name_____	Book Total $_____
Address_____	Postage & Handling $_____
City_____	Applicable Sales Tax $_____ (NY, NJ, PA,CA, GST Can.)
State/ZIP_____	Total Amount Due $_____